Edward Emmerson Oliver

Across the Border

Or Pathân and Biloch

Edward Emmerson Oliver

Across the Border
Or Pathân and Biloch

ISBN/EAN: 9783337252427

Printed in Europe, USA, Canada, Australia, Japan

Cover: Foto ©Andreas Hilbeck / pixelio.de

More available books at **www.hansebooks.com**

ACROSS THE BORDER

OR

PATHÂN AND BILOCH

BY

EDWARD E. OLIVER, M.Inst.C.E., M.R.A.S., &c.

ILLUSTRATED BY
J. L. KIPLING, C.I.E., &c., &c.

WITH A MAP SHOWING THE LOCATION OF ALL THE TRIBES
AND THE SURROUNDING COUNTRIES

LONDON: CHAPMAN AND HALL, LIMITED
1890

RICHARD CLAY AND SONS, LIMITED,
LONDON AND BUNGAY.

CONTENTS.

CONTENTS.

LIST OF ILLUSTRATIONS.

> Saqia bar khez o dar deh jam râ
> Khak bar sar kun gham-i-ayam râ
> Sâghar-i-mai bar kafum nah ta-z-sar
> Bar kasham yen dalq-i-arzaq farn râ.

> Get up, O Saki (wine-cup bearer), and give (me) the cup ;
> Never mind for the cares of the world.
> (Literally, throw dust on the head of the days of grief.)
> Hand me the wine flask in order
> That I may remove the blue heavens from my head.
> (Viz. That there may be nothing between me and God.)

MAPS.

ERRATA.

Page   5, liue 24, *insert* " after Afridis."

,,   15, ,, 18, *for* son *read* soon.

,,   58, last line but one, *for* Monroe *read* Monro.

,,   85, line 5, *for* serials *read* cereals.

,, 168, ,,   2, *for* raidera *read* raiders.

,, 181, note, *dele* " to which seven guns are to be added."

,, 285, line 3, *for* incredulous *read* incredible.

,, 310, ,,   2, *for* Abner *read* Abana.

ACROSS THE BORDER.

RETROSPECT AND PROSPECT.

OUR past and present relations with the North-West frontier of India are not inaptly typified by Mr. Kipling's two sketches. The magnificent "leader" of the caravan slowly threading its way through passes and across deserts, from the distant cities of Central Asia to the marts of Ind, is being fast displaced by the less picturesque but more potent locomotive, and the iron road for which Mr. O'Callaghan's men are tearing a hole through the last range separating us from Kandahár—a road that before many years are over may possibly see through booking to Europe *viâ* Samrkand and Bukhâra.

Up to a few years ago, the English action that prevailed in regard to this frontier was fairly summed up in the expression "masterly inactivity." Less than a decade ago, not only were the Afghâns to be left to "stew in their own juice," a scientific frontier ridiculed, the Gandamak treaty abrogated, Kandahár abandoned, the Quetta railway stopped, but, it was "hoped that Peshin and Sibi might at no distant date be evacuated." Along the whole of the trans-Indus districts from Peshawur to Sind, a length of 400 or 500 miles, including all the most important passes, there was not, after some thirty-five years of occupation, a single road worthy of the name. The Indus was unbridged, a railway had certainly crept up towards Peshawur, but under protest, and after a warm discussion as to whether a narrow gauge along the edge of the trunk road should not suffice. There were not wanting advocates of a more forward policy,

" From Kandahár"—The Leading Camel of the Káfila.

both in India and in England, but the general tendency was to let matters slide; the place of action taken by polemical discussion, the only expenditure, an expenditure of magazine articles.

The Border itself was managed on a strictly close system. Negotiations with the Kâbul Court were practically conducted by the Commissioner of Peshawur, its military arrangements were under the immediate orders of the Lieut.-Governor of the

Punjáb. All dealings with the tribes beyond were settled by the adjoining district officers, whose hands were tied with every possible restriction. While the Russians from their side were exploring and exploiting—often to our considerable annoyance— our officers were forbidden in any way to lift the *purdah* that was metaphorically hung along the whole, as carefully as if behind it was concealed the most sacred harem. Instead of our officers being encouraged to obtain information regarding the neighbouring people and territories, they were discouraged, prohibited, liable to be punished for any endeavour of the kind. Within a few miles of this arbitrary barrier there were—and there are still— important passes and valleys of considerable fertility and extent indicated on our maps by blanks, their resources and capacities so many sealed books. It used to be said, somewhat flippantly perhaps, that so solid was our ignorance, if a hostile army had been brought up to within striking distance of the Border, we could not have been certain of its precise whereabouts. So far the gods were on our side, however, that neither men nor horses could have been fed, but the assertion indicated the policy of shutting our eyes to all possible contingencies. Much of the information acquired was often in spite of orders, and almost by stealth. Even now, such as exists is too often elaborately and carefully locked up, in a form so confidential, as to be known to all anxious to obtain it, with the exception of the officers who are likely to most need it. "Strictly confidential" frontier maps and publications are probably more easily obtainable in Petersburg than in Peshawur.

To remedy what was not less a discredit to our administration than a source of the greatest danger to India, and contingently of misfortune to England, very much has undoubtedly been accomplished during the last ten years. And if there is any truth in the dictum that obvious preparedness for war is the best security for peace, another ten years of similar progress should render the contingency still more remote. In this connection ought never to be forgotten the debt of gratitude owed to the persistent placing of the facts before the country, the merciless exposure of ridiculous theories about impassable deserts, and the constant hammering away with unanswerable arguments, of the late Sir Charles Macgregor, and others, at the time called "alarmists." Combined, it may be added, with the hearty co-operation and wise forethought of men like Lord Dufferin and Sir Frederick Roberts.

Within the Border at least, communications are rapidly being made good, if not perfected. The railway has been carried through from Karâchi to Peshawur without a break, crossing the Indus by splendid bridges at Sukkur and Attock. From either extreme of the line there is through communication by the Hurnai and Bolân railways to the Khwâjah Amrân. A few months more will see this range tunnelled for a double line to our outpost at Chaman, capable of extension to Kandahâr on the shortest notice. The opening of the bridge over the Chenâb at Sher-Shâh, completes a line from Multân, linking in the frontier cantonments of Dera Ghâzi and Dera Ismail, with the great garrison of Rawal Pindi and the base at Lahore. An extension is under construction to Marri, opposite Kâlabâgh, and a survey in progress will connect this again with the branch to Khushalgarh, and with the main line at Attock, and so provide a line along the Indus from the Kâbul river to the sea. It is only necessary to connect this at one end with the Bombay, Baroda and Central India system, and extend it at the other by Hazâra to the Jhelum Valley and Kashmir, to enable the resources of India to be promptly concentrated at any point along the entire frontier referred to in the following chapters, from Karâchi to Kashmir. The projected and already surveyed line to Bannu will bring into touch with the railway system the last, but by no means the least, important frontier garrison ; while the survey commencing at Dhaka by the Kâbul River route, looks as if the other arm was fairly on the way to be stretched out towards the Koh-i-Bâba; an extension badly wanted to balance our advanced position near Kandahâr.

We have got a broad road, that not even misgovernment can efface, from the Punjâb to Srinagar in the heart of Kashmir, and Colonel Nisbet as Resident may be trusted to see that no time is lost in pushing on the extension to Gilgit. Roads, metalled, bridged, and complete for every arm of the service, have been finished from Khushalgarh, by Kohât to Bannu; from Dera Ismail to the same objective; from Dera Ghâzi to Peshin; and Colonel Sandeman's recent successful negotiations with the Mahsud Waziris will probably be followed, at no distant date, by one *viâ* the Gumal and Zhob.

Tact and firmness have established a position in Bilochistân, as profitable and popular with the tribes, as it is strategically and administratively valuable to us. Without bloodshed, without heart-burnings, without a sign of ill-feeling, a large portion of the Biloch country has quietly passed under settled government: has become an integral part of the Indian Empire, with no more loyal servants of the crown, than the men who but a few short years ago, were distracted by constant intertribal warfare. Similar faculty for dealing with the most desperate and reckless of wild clansmen has in the Khaiber raised among the Afridis levies second to no irregular troops in the world; and who under their commandant, Major Aslam Khân, showed in the recent Black Mountain expedition what an immensely valuable additional store of force is waiting—anxiously waiting—to be utilized, should the necessity arise.

The Frontier Force has been brought directly under the orders of the Commander-in-Chief, and an end has been put to the anomaly that retained a brigade command under the orders of a civilian governor, and an organization alongside, but perfectly distinct from, the military organization of the country. As a part of the army that garrisons alike Peshawur in one direction, and Quetta in another, the field for distinction should be greater, the experience and interests broader, and the organization in every way more complete. And last, though dying hard, the "close system" stands condemned. The orders prohibiting officers from crossing the Border, or obtaining information regarding it, have been relaxed. They have still to obtain permission, which will only be granted under certain conditions, and will be refused when appearances indicate any danger of tribal disturbance, but the concession marks a return to a more rational view of Border policy. For there can hardly be two questions as to the extreme desirability of knowing all about the people and the country beyond that border, their temper and characteristics, its bearings and capabilities. Whether we hold that our line of defence should be drawn on the Oxus, at Herât, or on that shorter, stronger, and more natural position between Kâbul and Kandahâr, with a railway on either flank; if we fix it in front of the passes or behind them, the steel heads of the Border freelances pointed to the foe or against ourselves; or whether, like the apocryphal story of Dalhousie's movable red line, we hold the more convenient method is to draw it, in strictly Muscovite fashion, with a pencil that has a bit of indiarubber on the other end, there can be no valid excuse for remaining ignorant in matters of this kind. The state of things which excludes our officers from territories almost within rifle-shot of their lines, would not be tolerated by any other great power. If the petty Khâns and village headmen are not hostile to us, there can be no objection to free communication. If they are, the sooner this hostility is known the better, and the more the necessity for teaching them nicer manners is obvious.

The want of the most ordinary topographical knowledge

has been brought home to us over and over again. In the Afghan War of 1878, our troops had to blunder along, finding roads, halting-places, and water for themselves, exposed to needless delays and inconveniences at every stage. The flank march on 'Ali Musjid lost half its value for want of a good map, and the direct attack might have been thoroughly accomplished in a few hours, had it been known how easily the position could be turned from the left. In the Kurram Valley expedition, nothing was known of the Peiwar Kotal before the storming, which had to be delayed in consequence. The first experience of the Black Mountain Expedition, was to find our maps showing the Indus miles out of position, and the insignificance of the foe alone saved a disaster. Almost, all the minor expeditions across the frontier have been handicapped by similar ignorance, involving frequent mistakes, costing needless lives. While officers would often have gladly filled up idle hours at a frontier outpost by informing themselves more fully, or have occasionally exchanged leave to Kashmir, for liberty to combine sport and reconnaissance in an unexplored valley, had more facilities been afforded them.

It was good a system like this should be modified; it would be better if the change introduced last year could be made even more radical. The origin of the present sketch was in a suggestion, that such information as was available, put into a compact and intelligible form, would be appreciated by many Indian readers, which led to the publication in the Lahore paper of a series of twenty-four articles, dealing with the leading Border tribes. The first of these urged the desirability of a change, and that the acquisition of the fullest information in no sense involved any aggression. The substance of the remaining chapters, have from time to time, in one form or other, been contributed to the *Civil and Military Gazette* and the *Pioneer*. That the policy advocated has to some extent been accepted would perhaps be hardly sufficient excuse for reproducing them; but it seemed to the writer, considering the constantly increasing attention given to Indian affairs, some handy account of its most important frontier people, however imperfect, might be acceptable to a wider public.

Along and across such a length of Border, with a series of tribes and clans, of passes and peaks, of valleys and streams, whose topography, ethnography, statistics, and history fill eight or nine volumes of special, and "confidential" gazetteers, not to speak of papers, reports, and monographs, it is obviously impossible to deal more than generally. And in cases where to many readers the differences are not of more consequence than between tweedledum and tweedledee, and where the people are subdivided into nearly as many clans and septs as there are valleys and glens, it would be wearisome to differentiate too closely. Such divisions as present some marked peculiarity only have been dealt with, and for these endeavour has been made to notice the more general, rather than the especially particular, characteristics. Readers who are sufficiently interested, or curious, to require information more precise, will find they can fall back on a field of study of the most extensive character, one in fact, more resembling the vast, and too frequently dry-as-dusty plains of India, than the circumscribed but fresher green with which the less aspiring are content.[1]

These hills and highlanders are, however, very full of interest, although the interest be of a different kind to that inspired

---

[1] The works mainly used in the following pages, and from which I have often quoted are: The Official Gazetteers of Afghánistán, Bilochistán, and the North-West Frontier, so far as the matter is not confidential; the *Settlement Reports* of Dera Gházi, Dera Ismail, Bannu, Kohát, Peshawur, and Hazára; Paget and Mason's *Expeditions against the N.-W. Frontier Tribes*; Niámat Ullah's *History of the Afgháns*; Priestley's *Haiyát-i-Afghání*; Plowden's *Kalid-i-Afghání*; Elphinstone's *Kábul*; Bellew's *Yusafzai* and *Races of Afghánistán*; Raverty's *Gulshan i-Roh* and *Selections*; Hughes's *Bilochistán*; Hetu Ram's *Bilochnáma*; Burton's *Sind*; Biddulph's *Tribes of the Hindu Kush*, &c., &c., &c.

by some modern productions of British rule in India, by the congress agitator, or the aspirant for senatorial fame. Neither Pathán nor Biloch can be said to be in the forefront of this advanced party. They probably do not muster a single B.A. or eloquent talker, demanding education in every direction—save, perhaps, of good manners. Their ideas on the subject of Representative Councils are probably limited to the tribal *jirghas*, or the regimental durbar. Like a famous borderer of Scott's, though "good are they deemed at trumpet sound," "gentle" is not an epithet that fits them well. Nevertheless, they probably have the touch of nature that makes them kin to the sympathies of Englishmen in a greater degree than certain others in Hindustan, who are at present making themselves more heard. It is impossible to associate with them, even in a casual way, without feeling they, at least, are men.

Possibly it may be thought too much has been made of their romantic side, their alternating pillage, murder, and sudden death with softer sentiments, and, as Elphinstone somewhere says, desperate forays with strains that might have tuned a shepherd's pipe. But besides being splendid fighting animals, both have undoubtedly qualities taking and excellent, and the supposition that every Biloch is a thief, and every Pathán a murderer in his heart—in the sense those terms are understood by us—is altogether wide of the mark. Both have held their own as freemen through centuries of disturbance ; both echo the Briton's sentiment that anything is preferable to slavery. That if " never united they should always be free," is a familiar saying of their own. Both have the warlike instincts and enterprise which brought the Briton to India, and have kept him there, that whilom established the Pathán soldier of fortune, or his descendants, from the Punjáb to the Deccan, and that if the British power were withdrawn, would not improbably find him so establishing himself again. To look at a gathering of Biloch chiefs or Pathán soldiers in one of our regiments, compels a tribute of admiration. "By Jove, sir," was the remark of an essentially British officer at a recent camp, "if I could not command a British regiment, I would ask for nothing better than to lead a Punjâb one." The regiment probably contained more Sikhs than Pathâns, but the sentiment applies to both, and represents fairly enough the feeling that would inspire a soldier.

Perhaps it may also be argued, that to advocate the bringing of these independent tribes more directly under our rule, is illogical, and sounds very like an attempt to take away their liberties. This is only true in the narrowest sense. The Biloch, the Khattak, or the Yusafzai, has lost none of his manly characteristics, because he has exchanged anarchy for civilized government. He is just as free as he was before, he is certainly more prosperous; further, he is contented, and even proud of having become a British subject. Granting he has been deprived of the excitement of turning his knife or his rifle against his neighbours, he still looks forward to the chance of using them against an enemy. Moreover, it is a necessity of the situation. Sooner or later, and much better sooner than later, this great fringe of Borderland must come more immediately under British influence. The theory that we should sit down on the left bank of the Indus, and wait until an invading host has formed up on the other side, has been, for better or worse, permanently abandoned. In its place, we have accepted the more reasonable one, that it is better to deal with an enemy outside the gate of the fort, than to let him in, and fight him afterwards inside. There can be no middle course ; no meeting him halfway, or fighting with the river at our immediate back, except under the direst necessity. The passes along the border are the gates of India on the north ; to hold them properly, we must be perfectly free to come and go on both sides, and having admitted so much, the only logical continuation of the argument, necessitates the tribes who now occupy the passes becoming our certain allies, or our loyal subjects, and the latter appears the safer.

The idea that the difficulty can be got over, if the passes are covered by dotting down a fort here and a fort there, garrisoned by our troops, is a hopelessly impracticable one. It is hardly credible

" To Kandahár "—Tunnelling for the Railway through the Khojak.

that its advocates have carefully examined a map, allowed their imagination to dwell on the gigantic network of hills and valleys to be defended, or considered the enormous garrisons to be permanently withdrawn from our modest available army. If forts and garrisons are required, their place is surely in front, and not behind the passes, just as the position of the bastion is in front and not behind the ramparts. And of these natural ramparts and fortifications, the Border tribes should essentially be made a part of the garrison; they may in the future be found a most valuable part.

Lahore, *February*, 1890.

CHAPTER I.

Of the 1,000 miles of this North-West frontier, extending from Karáchi to Kashmir, from the Arabian Sea to the glaciers of Nanga Parbat, the first 300 border the province of Sind. A length of which it may be said that though the physical conditions do not differ materially—except perhaps occasionally for the worse—from those prevailing in the Derajât division of the Punjâb : the Border tribes, our intercourse with them, our familiarity with their country, and the strategical conditions affecting it, belong to an entirely distinct category. Roughly speaking, along the whole of this, and about 100 miles of the Dera Ghâzi Khân district, our neighbours are all Biloches of various tribes, beyond again all Afghâns or their connections. Besides the difference in race between these two, their natural and political organizations have little in common, and our relations with them are managed on two different systems. In the Biloch, we have to deal with a strong tendency to the aristocratic and monarchical form of government under acknowledged chiefs ; in the Afghâns, with decided republicans, recognizing little more than the petty head-men of petty clans.

Through Persia and Khelât, which Biloch capital is within fifty miles of the Sind plains, is perhaps our most vulnerable point, for an invading army could by this route, reach India with infinitely less difficulty than by any through Afghânistân or the Hindu Kush. But on the other hand, we are most advantageously situated to defend it. From Karâchi as a base, unassailable so long as England is mistress of the seas, we have, in addition to the great highway of the Indus, railway communication running from all parts of India to the front beyond the passes, to an almost impregnable position on the Khwâja Amrân range, and within easy striking distance of Kandahâr. By our friendly arrangements with the Khân of Khelât, and the occupation of Quetta, commanding on the north and west all the direct routes from Kandahâr to the Punjâb, and on the south the passes leading into Sind, a position has been established that would render aggression from that direction practically impossible. The Peshin plateau, moreover, is of considerable extent; and our cantonments there, capable of extension at any time. The climate is well suited to Europeans, and with easy railway communication to India, will soon become more popular with the native army. The Khân of Khelât was perhaps not more anxious for us to go there, than the Bukhâra and Khivan Amirs to welcome the Russian; but he has now thoroughly allied himself with us, and he is undoubtedly far more firmly established as the acknowledged head of the Biloch State than he could ever have been without us, if indeed he had been able to hold his own at all. For constant feuds and complete anarchy, has been substituted peace and tranquillity. Except a few insignificant raids by Marris and Bughtis on the Upper Sind frontier, the people have settled down to accept our presence, and as their prosperity increases—for our advent has brought substantial benefits in the shape of hard cash—to look on our coming as the best fortune that could have befallen them. From Karâchi to Quetta is only 600 miles, or by the Bolân 550, the tunnel through the Kojak will shortly be finished, the materials are ready to carry the line on from the other side of the range to Kandahâr, and it only remains to insist on the construction of this bit of railway, some seventy miles, to measure the distance from Karâchi to Kandahâr, or a suitable position on the Helmund by hours, and those hours might be made as few as from Bombay to Delhi.

The whole of Bilochistân has been thoroughly explored, and to some extent surveyed, up to the Persian frontier. Much information about the tribes and the less known routes was acquired by Sir Robt. Sandeman's mission to Southern Bilochistân. The Persian survey of Sir Oliver St. John, has been connected with the Indian system, though something may still be desirable in the way of maps. Our surveyors have advanced much beyond this; even the wild Marri and Bughti hills, in fact, pretty well the whole of what is shown on modern maps as Sewestân, is being gradually brought under systematic survey. The districts of Harnai, Thal Chotiali, and Vitakri, have been examined in almost every direction, and the "Route Book" of the Sewestân country will son be as complete as of any other part of India.

Before crossing the rugged hills that separate the almost more rugged Biloch from the Delta and lower valley of the Indus, it is but fair to halt and take in a general view of this, the most westerly and probably the warmest little bit of our Indian Border. A hotter sort of Egypt, but physically and politically suggesting many resemblances in common; a country literally made by another, and a greater, Nile. So much of it as is not a delta, at one time or other formed a channel, a bank or an island, of the Indus, whose waters, according to history and tradition, seem to have travelled over the whole of it, backwards and forwards from Kachh to Karâchi; its very name a Sanskrit term signifying water. Even now a vast waste of silt, sand, or arid rock, with occasional intervals of rich cultivation, due to a net-work of canals, water-courses, and old creeks; its towns and villages mainly houses of sun-dried bricks, or huts of wattle; its only mountains, a succession of bare, comparatively low ridges locally known as the Kirthar—which rise occasionally to 7,000 feet—and Hâla ranges, and the Pabb hills, separating it on the West from Balochistân. For the rest, 150 feet is a lofty hill to break the universal flatness. On the east, sand; plains of sand, deserts of sand, hills of sand, rolling waves of them. And through the whole length the mighty Indus, the leading feature of the picture; that collecting together the five rivers of the Punjab, all the hill streams of the Sulaimâns, the Sufed Koh, and a great length of the Himalaya, rolls down a turbid stream, at once the great fertilizer of the country, the highway for the transit of its merchandize, and for long, the only means of communication for its inhabitants.

A land of dust-storms, of extremes of heat and cold; a summer where for weeks together the thermometer never falls below 100°, and a winter where it often sinks below freezing point. That enjoys the minimum of rain and the maximum of heat. With little of grandeur and not much variety of scenery; even the great "sweet-water sea" being essentially a monotonous river. From the low, flat, and often insalubrious mud banks of the coast, to the dusty plains of Shikârpur, "the gate of Khorasân," there is little in the way of woodland, groves, or gardens, while of forests there are none. There are creeks, that perhaps occasionally rise to the dignity of lakelets, but these exceptions savour more of the waters of the Styx, than of the abode of naiads or of nymphs, and what there is of the picturesque depends mainly on bold outline, and the scenic effects of changing light. Except the camels on its salt plains, the buffaloes in its marshes, and venomous snakes everywhere, it has few animals of any consequence, though it is naturally stronger in birds and fishes. And though a classic ground by association with almost every invader of Hindustân—Greeks, Arabs, Mughals, Persians, Afghâns, and Biloches—

they seem to have left behind them no monuments or records of their presence. Perhaps there was no bit of it lasting enough to make such records possible in a country like this Sind.

Of living records however, in the shape of naturalized tribes, there are many—Arabs, Afghâns, Biloches, and even Africans, who together make up a considerable proportion of the population. The Sindi proper, a somewhat mongrel Hindu, converted under the Khalifs to Islâm, does not occupy a very high place in the scale of oriental peoples. If his detractors give him a worse name than he deserves; even his admirers put his merits as a somewhat negative quantity. Inoffensive, kindly if not cleanly, and indifferent honest; what between a long succession of invasions, the Border people who constantly harried him, and the Hindu dealers and go-betweens who impoverished him, he probably had but a poor chance of exhibiting much of sweetness or of light, and the prosperity of both the people and the country dates from the time of British occupation.

It has not been possible for this occupation to change the climate, or to alter the natural features of the country, but it has done almost everything else for Sind. The development of a system of irrigation, by canals drawn from the Indus and its tributaries, has served to make that river do almost what the Nile does for Egypt. A flotilla of steamships, and subsequently a railway through the centre of the country, which by the completion of the Sukker Bridge now provides uninterrupted communication with the entire Indian railway system, has gone far to make it the highway for the bulk of the trade of the Punjâb and North-Western frontier. While the small fishing village, wrested by the Taipur Amirs from Mekân half a century ago, has become one of the first of the great seaports of our Indian Empire, and with its extensive conveniences, its excellent harbour, and its flourishing institutions, it is hard to say what possibilities the future may not have in store for Karâchi.

CHAPTER II.

BILOCHISTÂN AND THE BILOCHES.

BILOCHISTÂN, in the ordinary acceptation of the term, includes all the country between the Arabian sea and Afghânistân ; Sind and Persia. The Persian frontier, once a subject of constant dispute, was settled by a mixed commission under Sir F. Goldsmid in 1870. On the north is the Biloch desert, blending with the Afghân districts formerly dependent on Kandahâr, but both this and the north-eastern boundary is, to say the least, ill-defined. It is perhaps more correct to say the country is here bounded by the assigned districts, or British Bilochistân, the northern boundary of which is at present under consideration in the Foreign Office of the Indian Government. Within these limits is included, the mountainous province of Sarâwan, with its capital Khelât. West of the Hâla range, the equally mountainous province of Jalâwan, its chief the second noble of Bilochistân. Between the Hâla mountains and Sind, is the proverbially sultry Kachhi Gundâva, the country of the *bad-i-simum*, or "blast of death"; the flattest and hottest province of all, but as including the two great thoroughfares from Sind, commercially the most valuable. South again, between the final spurs of the Hâla range and the sea, is the little triangle of Lus, with its capital Beyla, under its hereditary chief called the Jam. And last, the less known,

the most barren, though by far the most extensive region of
Makrân, the ancient Gredosia, extending from Lus to the boundary
of Persia, and including the *Kohistán,* or land of mountains, on
the west, and the bulk of the Bilochistân seaboard.

The most striking characteristics of almost the whole of this

The Best Trade on the Stony Hills of Bilochistân.

extensive country, are a succession of rugged mountains and narrow
valleys, for the most part barren or uncultivated, conditions due to a
great extent, to the want of water. Of rivers, there can hardly be
said to be any ; what streams there are, have more of the nature
of torrents, filled only at rare intervals, and which frequently

disappear in the ground at no great distance from their source. In the north, a large part of districts like Nushki, Chagai or Sistân deserve no better appellation than desert, and the very names of plains like the *Dasht-i-be-daulat*, " the plain without wealth," *Dasht i bedar*, " the uninhabitable waste," *Dast i Goran*, " the desert of wild asses," or the *Registân*, " the country of sand," are sufficiently expressive. There is a saying that the most useful knowledge for a traveller to possess is a knowledge of the watering places, which the Biloch classifies as " sweet," " good," " drinkable," and " bitter."

Really or nominally, all these provinces are under the Brahui Khân of Khelât, and the chiefs acknowledge him as their suzerain. Albeit this suzerainty has always been more nominal than real, and it may be doubted if it was ever complete. At no time can it be said the turbulent Biloch chiefs were kept in order save when the Khân received, not merely recognition, but assistance from the British Government. When that assistance was withdrawn, chronic anarchy resulted; and even now, anarchy would follow almost immediately if British control were withdrawn again. The history of the dynasty for a century back, is mainly the story of successful robbers on a large scale, a succession of deeds of lawlessness, rapine, bloodshed; for though the average Biloch would deem private theft disgraceful in the extreme, plunder and devastation of a country have always been held as honourable deeds deserving the highest commendation. The hereditary chiefs of Sarawân and Jalawân with their hereditary standard bearers bearing banners of red and yellow, had always the privilege to sit on the Khân's right and left, their place in battle right and left of the centre, and the national flag tri-colour with the red, yellow and royal green. No measure of importance could be passed without their consent, nor the two large provinces they represent taxed, save by a Vazir chosen from among the Tajiks, the principal revenue payers, who had almost equal hereditary financial powers. The revenue varied with the ability of the Khân to enforce the payment of so-called state dues. The claim for military service—based on a description of feudal tenure, but differing from that of the ancient Normans, or equally ancient Rajputs, in that the troops, once on active service, were at the charges of the state—was generally acknowledged, but the number of troops that could be assembled depended on the popularity of the Khân, or the cause for which they were required to fight. Several of the chiefs, like the Jam of Beyla recognised no claim, beyond rendering to the head of the confederacy this feudatory service in case of need.

The Brahui Khân, Nasr, is practically the first man of any rank who stands out of the historic fog enveloping the more modern Brahui and Biloch genealogical story. He seems to have united a formidable confederacy of chiefs, maintained a sort of supremacy, and established something like a decent government. But he was first a nominee of the great Persian conqueror, Nadir Shah, and subsequently a fief of Ahmad Shah of Kâbul, a position from which even his declaration of independence in 1758 did not entirely relieve him. His forty years of rule—from 1755 to 1795—is what a distinguished authority calls the Augustan age in Bilochistân ; but even then it would have been difficult to define the various rights of the ruler, his Sardars, and his subjects. On all hands he is admitted the most distinguished Biloch as a soldier, statesman, and ruler, and to have combined the most exceptional virtues with the most vigorous government. He put down rebellion and encouraged trade, made triumphant war and established successful gardens. His justice and equity are still household words among the people, and he had discretion enough to interfere as little as possible with his feudal chiefs. But when he died, full of years and honours, the whole country almost immediately fell back into anarchy. The governors of provinces, and the chiefs of districts withdrew their allegiance, the country was distracted with broils, and the power of the ruler of Khelât diminished even more rapidly than Nasr had augmented it. When the British moved through the Bolân to Afghânistân in 1839, the Khân though said to be dangerous, was comparatively insignificant. General Wiltshire, with about 1000 men, is reported as taking Khelât in "a few minutes." When a second Nasr was recognized by the Outram treaty of 1841, he described himself as a vassal of Kâbul. From the conquest of Sind by Sir Charles Napier in 1843, to the revised treaty with Khelât drawn up by Major Jacob in 1854, the Khân was little better than a puppet in the hands of an intriguing minister, while the tribes, each on its own account, plundered unrestrained in all directions. Raids on the Border were constant, life and property everywhere unsafe. With Jacob's treaty and his powerful control, came a brief period of wonderful prosperity, to be succeeded again by a broken treaty and a renewal of disorder. Nasr the Second it is said was poisoned, the present Khân, Mir Khudadâd, who as a boy succeeded, was driven out and another set up only to be murdered. The chiefs of Lus, and of Wadd in Jalawân were in chronic rebellion, the people of Kej in Makrân threw off all pretence of allegiance. The Marris and Bughtis were constantly on the war-path. Anarchy became so hopeless, the British Government had again to interfere, not less at the request of the Khân than of his subjects, and to restrain the tribes from tearing themselves and their country to pieces.

The treaty of 1854, with certain additions, was renewed in 1876, on the basis of the Khân's receiving substantial aid from the British Government, including a subsidy of an annual lakh of rupees. He to have no relations with any other foreign state, and to permit the occupation of such positions in his territory by British troops as the Government of India may consider advisable. Since then, the relations have been drawn closer, our Government has accepted the situation of the paramount power, the old disputes between the various chiefs have been happily settled, and the position of the Khân as head of a powerful confederacy, and ruler of all Bilochistân, established. Certain districts, including the valley of Quetta have been made over for permanent occupation by our troops; while by the treaty of Gundamak, all Afghân rights, real or pretended, in the districts of Thal Chutiâli, Sibi, and Peshin, up to the mountain barrier that separates that valley from the plain of Kandahâr, were assigned to us, and have now been regularly incorporated with the British administration. The Border line has, in fact, been moved up to the Khawâja Amrân range.

The tribes which give the name to the country are, as will be subsequently noticed, neither the most numerous nor the most powerful. The race from which the present rulers are drawn, call themselves Brâhuis, and assert, on somewhat doubtful authority, a prior occupation and a distinct origin. Bilochistân however, and not Brâhuistân, has universally come, even by the Brâhuis themselves, to be the accepted name of the country, and its people to be spoken of as Biloches. They or their various divisions, are the dominant race all along the Border, practically as far north as the commencement of the Dera Ismail Khân district, and in them we have by far the pleasantest of our neighbours.

Essentially a nomad—good-looking, frank, with well-cut features, black and well-oiled flowing hair and beard, attired in a smock frock, that is theoretically white, but never is washed save on the rare occasions when he goes to durbar—the Bilochi is a general favourite. He is a bit of a buck, and when he finds himself passing into the sere and yellow, dyes his hair. It is not uncommon to find an old gentleman with eyebrows of deep black, and the tip of his beard gradually shading off *through* purple to red, to the roots of pure white. His wife makes quite a toilet and arranges her hair in many effective plaits, but any connection with soap and water would be voted by either as a mark of the worst effeminacy.

He shares with the Pathán many of the virtues and vices peculiar to a wild and semi-civilized people; but in most respects he presents the most agreeable contrast. Both are given to hospitality, both ready to exact an eye for an eye, and a life for a life; but the Biloch prefers to kill his enemy from the front, the Pathán from behind. To both, "Allah is Great and Muhammad is his Prophet;" though the Pathán is often a dangerous fanatic, while the Biloch is perfectly willing to have his prayers said for him. As Ibbetson pithily puts it, he "has less of God in his head, and less of the devil in his nature." There is a story of one who, asked why he did not keep the fast of Ramzán, replied that he was excused, as his chief was keeping it for him. "What are you doing?" said another to a pious Muhammadan saying his evening prayers in the plains. "Praying in the fear of God," said the plainsman. "Come along to my hills," rejoined the Biloch, "where we don't fear anybody." Both have but dim perceptions of the difference between *meum et tuum*, preferring "the good old rule, the simple plan, that he shall take who has the power, and he shall keep who can."

There is a Biloch proverb that "God will not favour a man who does not steal and rob;" and there is no doubt that, though he does not much like work, he is extremely partial to rupees. Whatever he does, he first inquires what his *hakk*, or "share in rupees," is to be. Both are English in their love for horses and everything connected with them. Like the Dean's sister in *Dandy Dick*, a Biloch who cannot afford a whole mare, will own as many legs as he can manage, keeping her a quarter of a year for each leg of which he is owner. The political organization of both is tribal: but the Pathán is essentially a Radical—every man as good as his neighbour, and better—and will obey no one but the *Jirgah* or democratic council, and not always that; while the Biloch is as loyal to his chief as a Highland clansman to a McIvor. Consequently, Government can deal as safely with a

Biloch *tumandar*, as with any other limited monarch; and this fact alone has materially simplified all the frontier arrangements on the borders of Bilochistân.

To attempt any detailed notice of the subdivision of the many tribes and clans would be wearisome; but most of them have similar characteristics, which go to make them good subjects and valuable feudatories. They are physically powerful, hardy, bold, and manly, naturally warlike, open in manner, as a rule truthful and faithful to trust. They have been so often and so fully described, ethnologically and otherwise, by many writers, it is perhaps unnecessary to enter into much detail about them. Of their use as auxiliary troops there are probably not two opinions. The late Sir Charles Macgregor, who knew them very well, entertained a high estimate of their value. He speaks of them as " a hardy, warlike race; their style of fighting peculiar and much more deadly than that of their neighbours, the Pathâns. The Biloch dismounts and pickets his mare, and then enters the *mêlée*, sword and shield in hand, while the Pathân engages with his matchlock from a distance, if possible under cover, and seldom closes with his adversary. Their courage is of a sterner kind, and this is shown not so much in their encounters with us—though, all things considered, they have fought better against us than the Afghâns ever did—as in their tribal feuds, and in the infinitely bolder manner in which they carry out their raids in our territory. An Afghân at feud with his neighbour gets into a tower or behind a rock, and waits till he can murder him in cold blood; a Biloch collects all the wild spirits of his clan, and attacks his enemy in force, sword in hand, generally losing very heavily. The determined gallantry of the 700 Bughtis, who refused to surrender to Merewether's horsemen, though escape was hopeless, but allowed themselves to be shot down till more than two-thirds had fallen, is worthy of a page in history. Although as a race they are poor, living from hand to mouth, they will not be induced to take regular service, as they will not wear uniform or undergo discipline, and are impatient of control. Their objections to our service are mainly as follows :—They are afraid of their hair being cut; they object to any but white, or dirty-white clothes; and they do not wish to leave their homes. It is, in fact—with the Biloches as with all wild races at first—they require careful handling, and they will wear anything, go anywhere, and do anything they are asked." The most ordinary tact would suffice to ensure a large supply of particularly excellent material, pre-eminently suited for irregular cavalry. Born horsemen, the breeders of a particularly hardy and enduring race of horses; and equally hardy and enduring themselves, they have further the spirit engendered by generations of freedom.

CHAPTER III.

OF anything approaching to authentic history, the Biloches have less than most Border people. From whence they came, the route they travelled, who were their progenitors, are still very much matters of conjecture. They have no written character, and consequently no literature. War is looked upon as the first business of a gentleman, and every Biloch is a gentleman. Even agriculture is despised, and the arts viewed with contempt; the art of writing would fall actually beneath contempt. The Douglas, in *Marmion*, thanks his saint " that son of mine, save Gawin, ne'er could pen a line ; " and this is very much the attitude of the Biloch. Whatever there is of tribal or national tradition has been handed down in the poems and ballads of which they are exceedingly fond, and many of which are probably of considerable age.

> " Sweet, singing minstrel, bring your guitar ;
> Bind a large turban on your head.
> Let the good man receive gifts from the generous.

> " Sweet, singing Relân, bring hither the guitar of rejoicings ;
> Bring unto my life the fresh breeze of the morning—
> Strike powerfully with your fingers,
> Drive out grief from the bright body,"

and others of the invocations collected, and admirably translated by

Dames,[1] might, with little alteration, pass muster among Sir Walter
Scott's collection.

Like most Muhammadan tribes, Biloch tradition uniformly points

Laghári Biloches.

to Arabia as their original home. One popular story derives the
word Biloch, from *Bachh*, a son, and *Luch*, a slave girl in the harem
of Muhammad bin Harun. According to Rawlinson, it is derived
from Belus, who is identified with the Nimrod of Scripture, the son
of Cush. The Persians write the word Bilush, and "*Kush wa
Bilush*," is a term employed in that country to indicate certain
nomadic tribes. Personally they consider a derivation from *Bad*

[1] *Sketch of the Biloch Language* by Dames.

Log, "lawless" folk, as more in keeping with their universal reputation for rapine and murder; and a favourite couplet is to the effect that the Biloch who steals and murders, secures heaven to seven generations of ancestors. Though if half the stories of their former habits be true, both the moss-trooping ancestors and their descendants would probably find a heaven, without forays and with no neighbours' cattle to lift, an insufferably dull place. They existed, says the *Biloch Nâmah* of Hetu Ram,[1] before the days of the Prophet. The famous old Persian King, Naushirwan, is in the *Shâh Nâmah* made to complain that "the ground had become black with Biloches." In these far-off times they claim to have dwelt in the low hills of *Halab*—Aleppo. The Aleppo people called them Biloches, and more than one Muhammadan author explains this to mean "barbarous tribes, inhabiting the mountains of Garmsir, Sistân and Makrân." When Yaziz, the second Ummiyah Khalif, fought with Hazrat Imâm Hasan, and the latter was killed, the Biloches who, according to their story, sided with him, had to fly to Kirmân and Sistân in Persia, from whence again they moved to Makrân, the present Bilochistân, and the Sulaimâns. Their wanderings form the subject of many poems.

> " We are the servants of Hazrat 'Ali,
> The true Imâm of the Faith.
> From Aleppo we came,
> On account of the struggle with Yazid."

"There are four and forty tribes; the foremost is Mir Jalâl Khân"—or the poet's tribal chief for the time being.

> "By stages we march. From Kurbala and the cities of Sistân.
> The Hots[2] settle in Makrân. The Khosas in Kach. Dividing out
>   water and dry land.
> In Nali the Nohs.[3] The Jatoes [and others] in Sibi and Dadur.
> The Rinds settle in Sarâwan. The Lashâris in Gandâva.
> This is our footprint and track. This the Biloch record."

---

[1] Douie's translation of the *Biloch nâmah.*

[2] Mazaris and Dreshaks.   [3] A branch of the Rinds.

Another story tells of friendship between the Kirmân ruler and the Biloch Chief, Ilmash Rumi, who had become vastly powerful— forty-four *tumans* of 10,000 each, says an old Persian chronicle. A *tumandar* being the head of 10,000 men, as he is now the tribal chief. By and by the successor of the Kirmân ruler picked a quarrel with the successor of the chief, demanding a girl for his harem from each *tumân*. The Biloches dressed up and sent boys in girls' disguise ; but, as the legend goes, fearing the ruler's dis- appointment, quitted Kirmân, and took refuge in Makrân, " a somewhat waste country," but which they " devoted themselves for 500 years to cultivate."

Ballads and traditions testify to a common origin of tribes now widely separated, and differing greatly ; so much so that it is doubt- ful if a northern Balochi could make himself intelligible to a Makrâni of the south. And though a Brahui of Khelât might understand a Bughti, some philologists would classify their respective languages as belonging to entirely different stocks. Four sons and one daughter of the chief under whom they made the Makrân migrations, gave their names to as many famous tribes, of which two stand out as markedly prominent—the Rinds and the Lashâris. Of the former there is now no representative clan bearing the name, though almost all the leading frontier Biloches claim to be of Rind extraction. All true Border Biloches, in fact, are either Rinds or Lashâris, and it is these sections that furnish the two great legendary heroes—Mir Châkar the Rind, Mir Gwaharâm the Lashâri ; the Percy and the Douglas of Border ballad.

> 'Originally they were both brothers,
> God knows both of the same family."

But Rihand Rind and Rawân Lashâri were in love with the same woman. " A fair one of a thousand wiles and sweet sugared speech. A bane of many lovers." They staked their fortunes in love on a

horse race, the loser to abandon his suit. Some Rind meanly
loosened Rawân's saddle-girth, and he lost the race.

> " The Rinds practised a great deceit,
> The hero Rawân was displeased.
> In the gloaming he sped away,"

and ill blood ensued. Mir Châkar, the " ever victorious " Rind
had a mistress exceeding fair and wealthy withal ; possessing flocks
and herds, especially of camels. A Lashâri chief, also an unsuccessful rival for the lady's favour, was so ungallant as to steal some
of her camels in revenge.

Thereupon the Rind chief—

> " Fell into a great rage ;
> In exchange for fair Gohârs young camels,
> We will take a seven fold revenge with our swords,
> We will gamble with heads and hair and turbans.' "

Said he—

> " On both sides damage was done,
> On this side was Gwaharám with his sword ;
> On that side Mir Châkar.   For thirty full years
> War continued about these young camels of Gohâr's."

This finally seems to have developed into a great struggle.   The
Lashâris won a victory, killed a Rind chief and 800 of his followers.
Mir Châkar is then described as obtaining assistance from the
ruler of Khurasân, possibly Sultân Hussain Baikâra, and with his
aid beating the Lashâris so completely, they were driven out of
Gundâva (Kachi) to Tatta and Hyderabad in Sind, where many
reside to this day.   A few settling under Rind protection in
Khelât.

Mir Châkar is the national Rind hero, the Grettir, the Sigurd, the
King Arthur, of the Biloches.   The subject of innumerable stories,
stories romantic, historical and legendary.   He is able at will to
change the tribal buffaloes into stones, and so blockade the defiles

against his enemies. His name still survives in the *Chákar ke Marri*, his "upper story," the *Chákar-ke-Tang*, his "defile" and many a peak and pass scattered throughout Sewestân.   He is described as forming an alliance with the Khurasân ruler in the fifteenth century, and both with fighting and assisting the Mughal Humayun in the sixteenth.   With leading the Rinds into Makrân, with founding the old fort of Sibi, the centre of a kingdom ; and, still more improbably, with emigrating in disgust to the Punjâb and dying at Lahore.

> " Forty thousand men came at his call
>   All with shields upon their forearms ; all with bows and quivers,
>   With silk scarves and overcoats ; and red boots on their feet.
>   With silver knives and daggers ; and golden rings on their hands."

And they are " all kinsmen to the bold Mir," waiting the signal to let loose the furies of Border war.   The Mir is not contented with " man-devouring Sibi," or " dusty Gundâva," while though they " eat fat-tailed sheep and brew strong liquor in their stills," they " rub no scent in their moustaches and have only children's sticks in their hands."   Let us, he says to the Rinds, forward—

> " To conquer streams and dry lands,
>   And deal them out among ourselves.
>   Let us take no count of rule or ruler."

The Rinds are in fact described as the lords and masters of the rest.   Compared to them, all other sects are of small account. Quite a long list of clans are described as

> " All nought but slaves to Châkar,
>   He gave them to his sister Banâdi
>   As her dowry, when she married Hadiya
>   But Hadiya scorned to take them."

They evidently acted on their hero's advice, and the period of their obtaining supremacy probably marks the time when they began, under various petty leaders, to settle in their present holdings along the Derajât frontier, and the various divisions to be known by their existing tribal names.

Such is the story as told in the songs by the tribal bards, the *davtars*, or professional reciters of genealogies. Leaving out of the question any attempt to fix a date for so ubiquitous a hero as Mir Châkar, there is sufficient solid historical ground to prove that Biloch adventurers had extended as far as the Multân district towards the end of the fifteenth century; while others had got as far north as the Jhelum by the beginning of the sixteenth. They might, therefore, have well been strong on the Sulaimân by the middle of the fifteenth.

Another influence, besides the Rind hero's desire for fresh fields and pastures new, was moreover at work, which made a forward movement more necessary. The Biloches were themselves being driven out of the fertile valley of Khelât, by what is generally thought to be the kindred tribe of Brahuis who, probably some time in the fifteenth century, became strong enough to establish themselves there. Similar legends credit the Brahuis as being equally Biloch, and equally hailing from Aleppo; and the *Biloch-náma* ingeniously suggest that settling in the hills, they were originally called Rohis from *Roh*, a mountain, which gradually passed into the term Brahuis. When Mir Châkar took Khelât, they had only got as far east as Makrân and Sistân, but while the Rinds were pressing back the Pathâns from the lower Sulaimâns, and ousting the Jât from what is still called the Derajât border, while the Ismail Khâns, Fatteh Khâns, and Ghâzi Khâns were founding the Derahs [1] named after them, the Brahuis were wresting Khelât from Mandi Khân, whose tomb is there still, and establishing the dynasty of the Khân of Khelât, a chief who previous to this had been an ordinary *tumandar*, with nothing of an army to speak of. To Khelât, the Brahuis added Mastang, Quetta, the Bolân, and part of Kuch Gandâva. Ultimately they

[1] Or encampments.

became the dominant people, and their chief was accepted as supreme by all the modern trans-border Biloches. The social distinction is still marked by their right to draw rations of wheat flour when on service with the Khân, while the Bilochi has to content himself with the coarse millets. The supremacy of the Brahui Khâns would, however, no doubt have entirely passed away, but that it has been our Border policy to support it.

Within our Border the chief of the Dumki, a Rind people, is the nominal head, but the tribes are perfectly independent of one another, and are only restrained from their old intertribal wars, their old plan of harrying their neighbours' home and driving off everything possessing four legs, by the presence of English rule, and for some time they were not even restrained by that. But the provision of many and expensive law courts, and more expensive lawyers, nevertheless provides in a great measure a sufficiently exciting substitute, and it is now possible for two chiefs to ruin themselves, and impoverish their clans more quickly by a suit than by a whole series of fights; and the Border Bilochi is fast becoming civilized enough to adopt the process.

CHAPTER IV.

WHAT the story of the unfortunate star-crossed Pathân lovers, Adam Khân and Durkhâni, is to the Yusafzai, the pathetic tragedy of Sassui and Panhu is to the romantic Biloch on the Sind border. The latter, however, purports to be much older, and the lovers are described as living about the time of the introduction of Islâm, some 900 years ago. Besides the Biloch version, the story is told in Persian,[1] Bilochki and Punjabi. In the latter the heroine is known as *Rul Mui*, "she who died wandering," to distinguish her from *Dub Mui*, "she who died drowning." The story is familiar among all the wild tribes on the Sind and Biloch borders, and, says Sir Richard Burton, who gives an epitome of the legend in his work on Sind, "the camel-man on his journey, the herdsman tending his cattle, and the peasant toiling at his solitary labours, all while away the time chaunting it in rude and homely verse."

Panhu is a desperately good-looking Biloch, the Benjamin of his family, the idol of his parents, a terrible Don Juan among the ladies. Ari, his father, is the Jam, or Prince of Kej in Makrân. The heroine was a daughter of a Brahman of Bhambuna,

---

[1] Mir M'asum of Bakkar tells it, under the title of *Husn O Naz*—Beauty and Blandishment.

"

of whom it was predicted she would become a Moslem, and so
bring disgrace on her family. Her father was for killing her, but,
at her mother's request, put her in a box and let her float down
the Indus, from which she was rescued by one of the 500 appren-
tices of a well-to-do washerman, named Mahmud, at Bambhora,
who, being childless, adopted her. She was christened Sassui—
" A piece of the moon "—grew up all virtue and accomplishments,
and was beautiful enough to cause the most disastrous conse-
quences—" Every one who saw her wished she was his own, and
wherever she seated herself men crowded round her like the
cluster of the Pleiades."

To Bambhora[1] comes Babiho, with a string of camels and merchandise, trading on account of the Kej Jam, whose servant he
is. There he falls in with Sassui in the midst of her companions, with whom he exchanges a little chaff as to the prices of
his wares. The ladies appeal to his gallantry, and demand the
present of a trifle of musk, to which, as a Hindu, he naturally
demurs. Sassui encourages him, and promises ready money if
he will only freely display what he has to sell. While he is
doing this she is struck with his good looks : " See his beauty,
O my friends ; how handsome he is." But Babiho disclaims any
pretension to good looks, passing on the compliment in favour
of Panhal Khân, his master's son " the beautiful Biloch, with
long flowing locks ; of beauty like his I have not the fortieth
part." To such good purpose does he praise Panhu that the
lady's ears become enamoured—" ofttimes the ear loveth before
the eye "—and she solicits Babiho to act as Mercury and bring
that Biloch to her, for which he shall receive great reward. Babiho
raises all sorts of difficulties : " Panhu cannot get leave from his
mother even for the chase ; how is it possible for me to bring
that well-guarded Biloch ? Worse than this, the beautiful Panhu
has two wives already, whose voices are as sweet as the Kokilas "

---

[1] Then the most famous port of Sind, now a ruin between Karáchi and Ghâra.

(cuckoos). The lively young lady, however, laughs at difficulties, and will take no denial. "I, too, am a maiden, the pride of Bhambora, and surely my accents are not less dulcet than the Kokila's song." Finally, the trader is started off to Kej with all sorts of tender messages to Panhu, and rich offerings for his papa the Jam.

Babiho returns to his master, renders an account of his merchandise, and takes the first opportunity to give Panhu the lady's message and presents, painting her loveliness in the most glowing colours. The description is more than sufficient for the inflammable Panhu, who fired with such sympathetic ardour, is for starting at once, with or without the parental consent. As a matter of fact, he has a good deal of trouble in getting away. His father is for sending any of his sons, save the Benjamin. His mother is all anxiety, and charges all the men of the caravan to "guard her little Panhu with every care." His eldest wife takes matters coolly, though the younger one rushes out, seizes the camel's nose-string: "Husband,' says she, "for Allah's sake leave me not thus. Either pass this night with me or send me home to my father's house again." But Don Juan, got up in his best, armed to the teeth, mounted on his favourite camel, will not be stayed, and rides away in great glee, delighting the whole *káfila* by the spirit and smartness of his conversation.

Temptation awaits him before he has gone very far. At a town *en route*, named Lohee, lives Sehjan, a lady more noted for her good looks than her good morals, who is so struck by a sight of Panhu that she disguises herself like a man, follows the camp, and makes love to him while he and Babiho are playing chess. The former, whose eye is not deceived by the disguise, does not require much encouragement to put away the chessboard, and is soon so charmed by the frail one, that he not only accepts her invitation to a feast, but halts the whole caravan.

Sassui meanwhile, all impatient to see her young Biloch, sets to work to write him a letter, or rather gets Akhund Lal, a silent admirer of hers, to write one for her. Now Akhund Lall had gone blind from weeping over his hopeless affection for Sassui, but he wrote so moving an epistle for the lady that he instantly recovered his own sight by virtue of hearing it, and it was therefore well calculated to hasten Panhu. This "moving epistle" she sends by a messenger to him, while he is still dallying with Sehjan at Lohee, from whence the lady will not hear of his departing. Panhu is finally reduced to the expedient of dropping opium into the syren's cups and leaving Babiho behind to pacify her when sober, with a story of a messenger from Kej, and news of his mother's death. This fiction saves Babiho, who leaves the outwitted Sehjan calling upon her companions to "come and kiss with their eyes the place where my beloved Panhu abode," and joins the caravan in time to make a state entrance into Bambhora, where all the people turn out to see so fine a show.

They pitch their camp in Sassui's garden, but that young lady, having got her adorable Biloch so far, now turns coy, and requires a good deal of wooing. Panhu only obtains a meeting by shooting a pet pigeon so skilfully that it falls into her aunt's lap, and while the old lady upbraids him, Sassui gives him his arrow back and a chance to explain himself. As a test, she demands that he become a washerman, which affords an opportunity for many love passages, and he soon washes himself deep into the lady's affections, to whom he is married, after a serious quarrel with Babiho, who goes off back to Makrân in high dudgeon.

Their matrimonial happiness did not last long. The wife begs as a favour of her fickle spouse, he will avoid passing out by a certain gate of the town, which of course he immediately seeks, and falls in with a very fair, but also frail goldsmith's wife, one Bhagula, who makes no secret of her admiration for the Balochi's handsome person. "May God cause us to meet," she remarks aloud, and Panhu at once finds that the scabbard of his sword is broken, and he must take it to be mended. Bhagula, not contented with seducing Panhu's affections from his bride, tries to persuade him that the latter is unfaithful. Sassui takes in the situation quickly enough; she tries her best "to extract the poisoned arrow from her truant husband's breast," and indignant at her rival's accusations demands that the quarrel be decided by fire. An enormous fire is consequently prepared for the ladies' benefit, at the very sight of which Bhagula turns pale, and would have fled, but Sassui seizes her by the ears and forces her to enter. Needless to say, the false dame is burnt to ashes, all save her two ears, held by the hands of the virtuous Sassui. Panhu is convinced of his wife's chastity and love, and the two, for a brief season, are happy once more.

The final catastrophe, however, approaches. The old Jam in Makrân is being frightfully scandalised at the stories carried home by the irate Babiho, and sends off six of his stalwart sons to bring the Benjamin home. They arrive at Bambhora, and shortly after to avoid fuss, cause an intoxicating potion to be given to Panhu and his wife, and at midnight carry off the former tied on the back of a camel. Sassui awakes to the consciousness of her misfortune. When at dawn she looks round, her lover is not on the couch beside her, nor are the camels of her brothers-in-law to be found. She recognizes that Panhu has been carried off, and "weeps tears of blood as if sprinkling the hill over which her husband was travelling."

"Alas, alas, how shall my wounded heart survive the loss of him thus torn away?"

She will not be consoled:

"My spinning wheel gives me no pleasure now that my husband is gone,
Nor feel I joy from the conversation of any companions.
My soul is among the hills where the Baloches urge their camels."

She declares her determination to follow her loved one's footsteps,
nor will she be deterred by all the dangers, real or imaginary,
which her friends conjure up in the most direful form, for her
benefit, as lying between Bambhora and the wretched huts that
compose the Biloch village. She even dissuades her friends from
accompanying her. "I will not return without my husband; but

Sassui and Panhu.
(*Facsimile of a Punjáb lithograph.*)

you, when you come to die of thirst, might curse him." Alone
she starts upon her journey, apostrophising the hills

"Why point ye not out the direction of my lover;
  It was but yesterday the string of camels passed over you,
  Was not my husband in that *kifila*?"

And in spite of all the dangers of the road, on which the author
enlarges at length, in spite of the sun, the simoom, heat, fatigue
and bruised feet, perseveres in her quest. At last, in one solitary
jungle she meets a goatherd, a perfect "Demon of the Waste" in
ugliness and wildness, from whom she demands, in the Lord's
name, to know the path taken by her brothers-in-law.

This wretch, who had been told by the old witch, his dam, that on this day he should meet a beautiful bride decked in jewels and rich attire, considers Sassui to be the very person, and begins the most abrupt and unceremonious gallantry. To gain time she complains of thirst, and begs her horrid admirer to milk one of his goats. When he replies that he has no pot, she draws out a brass pipkin, and while he fetches the goat, knocks a whole in the bottom. Caliban's eyes are so much charmed by the beauty of his prize that he does not notice the time it requires to draw a draught of milk. Sassui, in despair, meanwhile prays to Heaven to preserve her honour, and begs, if no other means of escape be possible, that she may be allowed to sink into the earth. Her supplications are heard, and suddenly she sinks into a yawning gulf which closes over her, and the wretched goatherd perceives his mistake too late. Unable to cancel the past, he occupies himself in raising a tomb and platform in her honour.

A few hours after, Panhu, who has escaped from his brothers with Lallu, a slave, comes in hot haste *en route* for Bambhora. Attracted by the appearance of the platform, which the goatherd must have been very quick about, he proposes to rest awhile, when he hears the voice of his bride calling him from the tomb :

> "Enter boldly, my Panhu, nor think to find too narrow a bed,
> Here gardens bloom and shed sweet savour round.
> Here are fruits and shades and cooling streams,
> While Islám's light pours through our abode,
> Banishing death and decay."

Panhu hands over his camel to his slave, and giving him a parting injunction to carry tidings of his fate to his father and his friends, calls upon heaven to allow him to join his Sassui. The ground opens and swallows him in the same way as for his lost wife, and the story finishes by Lallu informing the old Jam that the lovers have met to part no more. As he says :

> "The souls of those two lovers are steeped in bliss ;
> The rose is at last restored to the rose-bed."

Their tombs are in the Pubb Hills, between Karáchi and Lus-Bela where they are visited with great advantage by many pilgrims. A believer, who is sufficiently devout, will be fed on bread and milk by a hand stretched out from one of the tombs; while to many of the Faithful, St. Sassui or St. Panhu appears in person; the beautiful lady to the male pilgrims, the handsome Biloch to the female. But no camel must approach Sassui's tomb: she has never forgiven that animal for carrying away her husband.

"The Drowned Beauty," is another popular heroine of the Lower

Sohni swimming the Indus.
(Facsimile of a Punjáb lithograph.)

Indus Valley. Sohni, the *Dub Mai*, she who died drowning, is usually described as the daughter of a Ját cultivator, who gave her in marriage to one Dam, an individual of the same clan. Dam was not musical, probably not attractive, and as the nuptial procession went to the banks of the Indus to perform certain rites and consult the omens, Sohni was sent by her husband to fetch some milk from the forest, where she saw an omen for herself, in the shape of a buffalo-keeper, a most skilful player upon the *bansli* or reed-pipe, and instantaneously fell in love with him. Her head, like the buffaloes in the Punjábi sketch, was turned, and reversing the practice in the story of Hero and Leander, she, guided by the sound of the *bansli*, used nightly to swim the Indus, supported upon one of the large earthen pots which the fishermen commonly use on that river for the same purpose, and spend the hours of darkness listening to the sound of her lover's pipes; returning home before dawn.

A malignant mother-in-law discovered the assignation, and substituted a jar exactly similar to the one used, except that it was unbaked. One night, as Sohni sat in the moonlight with her lover, she drew his attention to a little spot she noticed in his eye. He replied that it had been there for many months, and her not having remarked it before portended some immediate misfortune for both. The lover's portent proved too true; the next time she tried to swim the stream, the jar so treacherously substituted burst, and the fair Sohni, literally, "the beautiful," was drowned. Sympathy is still with her, and the couplets sung in her praise evidently consider that her beauty fully condoned any trifling errors of judgment on her part.

> "Sohni was fair in body and mind,
> Nor had she one defect you could remark.
> She husband left and home in search of happiness,
> In quest of love ; but found a grave."

One more legend relates to the course of the river itself. There is some, if not very good, authority for supposing that the Eastern Nára, or Snake river, marks an old course of the Indus, and down this very channel Alexander sailed with his fleet ; that he halted his boats at Aror, not very far from Bakkar, while he made a little expedition against a place General Cunningham thinks might be Larkána. The ancient hydrography of the Punjáb and Sind, moreover, still forms the subject of many learned disquisitions. Whether the "lost river," that used to empty itself into the Rann of Kachh, started entirely on its own account with the Sutlej, or the holy

Saraswati, or whether, getting tired of wandering about the sands around Khairpur, it suddenly found a gap and turned sharp west, may be still an interesting problem ; but the popular legend affords a solution much more simple.

Between Bakkar and Khairpur was a city called Aror, or Al-Ror, a name which clearly survives in Rori, the modern town hard by ; a city " adorned with palaces and villas, gardens and groves, reservoirs and streams, parterres and flowers." It and Multân— " the boundary of the house of gold "—were then the "main pillars of the country, the two finest capitals and royal residences." "If you stop anywhere," writes one very early Sind historian to his nephew, "you should choose the most delightful place." Multân and Aror were both so charming, it was difficult to choose between them. For a long time the extensive dominions of which Aror was the capital, was ruled " in ease and prosperity " by a dynasty of kings who " possessed great wealth and treasure, diffused justice over the earth, and whose generosity was renowned in the world," from Kashmir to Kaikânân. The people all lived happily, as many of them at least as got their share of the Indus water. But Larkâna, Mehar and Schwân were a " mere waste," because " the water which is the fountain of all prosperity," flowed by Aror through the country south to Muhammad Tur, a famous town where resided many great men, disciples of the Shaikh of Shaikhs, Bahâwal Hak, and which was probably not very far from the present Shakarpur on the Gungru. " After fertilising all these lands, the river poured its water into the ocean at the port of Dewal," which Sir H. Elliott places at or near Karâchi.

All this flourishing country was, however, after a while, unlucky enough to come under a proverbial wicked king, Dalu Rai, a tyrant and adulterer, who taxed traders without mercy, levied a toll of fifty per cent. on all goods that came by the river to Aror, and every night possessed himself of a maiden. At length came a merchant, one Shâh Husain of Delhi, with an exceptional amount of goods, great wealth, and a handmaiden "young and beautiful as the full moon," descending on his way to Mecca. The tyrant not only increased his usual demand, but insisted on the transfer of the lady. The traveller determined on a bold effort, which with the help of Allah, and of Allah's special representative, Khwâjah Khiza, "should stand recorded on the page of destiny until the day of judgment." He obtained three days' grace before forwarding the duties and the damsel, and having collected "a vast number of skilful and expert artizans, men who excelled Farhâd in piercing mountains, and who could close a breech with a rampart like Alexander's," he set them to dig a new channel and erect a strong embankment above Aror, apparently taking good care to keep his own boats above it. So well did they labour, and so great was Allah's mercy, that before the three days expired, the Indus was turned from its course, and was flowing towards Siwân and the Lakki Hills, taking the merchant and all his craft with it. Dalu Rai woke one morning, and instead of the fathoms of water passing his capital, found nothing but mud and a dribble of muddy water, the merchant and the moon-faced maiden escaped, and his country ruined. Every effort to turn the river back into the old channel failed ; it would not be induced to return. The Rajah's regret and repentance came too late. " When the evil is done—O fool"—remarks the chronicler, "what avails your regret ? " The tyrant paused not in his evil courses, until his crimes destroyed both himself and his people. And, though there is much mud round the ruins of Aror, the Indus still holds to its channel among the rocks of Bakkar, where it has just been bridged, and into which Gazetteers persist in saying it was "diverted by some great natural convulsion." But the Gazetteer makers do not make sufficient allowance for the "skilful and expert artizans," of the Sind historians, or for the "great mercy of Allah."

CHAPTER V.

TWO SIDES OF THE SULAIMÁNS.

The long narrow strip of country, which, extending northward from Sind, is shut in between the dreary monotonous succession of knife-like ridges, forming the Sulaimán range, and the river Indus, with its still more monotonous and constantly shifting banks and islands of sand, corresponds very nearly with the civil district of Dera Ghâzi Khân, and for nearly 250 miles is seldom much more than twenty-five in width. Like Sind below, and a good deal of the remainder of the Derajât Division above, it is practically a rainless tract. The torrents that pour down the bare hill-sides furnish at times a certain amount of irrigation, which the cultivators husband to the last drop; and by a complicated system of artificial embankments, turn a strip of arid and naturally unproductive clay into a fertile fringe, locally known as the *pachád*. Where the lands come within the influence of the Indus, the country is also fairly cultivated and green, canals or shallow wells become gradually more frequent, trees appear on the scene, and villages are more numerous the nearer the river is approached. More than half the cultivated area of the district, and by far the larger proportion of the population is to be found within this "*Sindh*" tract—Sindh or Sindhu being the old name for the Indus. Between the "*Sindh*" and the *pachád* intervenes a barren belt of desert, a succession of rolling sandy undulations, varied

occasionally by stretches of low hills, that look as if some malicious
spirit had carefully sown them with assorted boulders of every size
Almost without water, inhabitants, or vegetation, it is about as un-
inviting a strip of country as the most grasping earth-hungerer
could wish to annex. Looking at the map and at the number of
little hill-streams that appear on paper,—numbering, in the Dera
Gházi Khán district alone, over 200,—it might be thought that
the *pacháï* must be a land flowing with milk and honey. But,
save in exceptional seasons, not a drop from any one reaches the
Indus; some only collect such rain as falls in the low hills, in
others the supply is most precarious. Only two are perennial, and
it is rare that water from one of these raises a flood sufficient to
break through the embankments that lie between it and the river.
In the hot months, with these exceptions, all fail; the shallow
wells dug in the dry beds do not last much longer, the few ordinary
wells are often 300ft. deep, and then yield but a brackish and
intermittent supply. The country ceases to be habitable, the
tribes who inhabit it either drive off their cattle to the Indus bank,
or more usually betake themselves further into the hills; and
during May, June, and July the *pacháï* is practically deserted.

Nor are the characteristics of the mountains, that form the
historical western boundary, such as would at first sight appear to
offer much inducement to an advance beyond them. The outer
hills consist of several parallel ranges, the principle ones occasionally rising to a considerable height. The Gandhári peak
opposite Rojhán is over 4,000 feet; the Diagul opposite Harrand
over 5,000 feet, Ek-Bhai opposite Sakhi Sarwar 7,500 feet, and
the Takht-i-Sulaimán, nearly west of Dera Ismail Khán, has two
summits, both over 11,000 feet. The eastern slopes are rocky and
precipitous, with little or no vegetation, and, with the exception
of a few stunted wild olives, bare of trees. The openings, narrow
gorges, almost destitute of water, tend to increase the forbidding
aspect. Nevertheless, the whole frontier is here a net work of

passes and lateral communications, laid out by nature with a regularity that might have formed part of a scientific system of parallels and approaches. As a natural barrier, the whole line is pronounced by experts to be a complete fraud. It has, says Major Holdich of the Survey, "generally a double line of main watershed, the commonest geographical feature throughout Afghânistân, with a series of broken, but approximately parallel minor ridges, forming narrow lateral valleys, running about north and south, all parallel to the main formation, and to the line of the frontier, and combined into a general system, which is broken through by the main drainage lines in innumerable places. Thus, roads to the plateau are opened, more or less difficult according to the nature of the gorges and drifts formed by the direction of the drainage across the lines of the watershed." The number of these may be judged from the fact, that there are upwards of ninety leading from the Dera Ghâzi Khân district; and Dr. Duke gives an itinerary of no less than fifty-three routes through the Sewestân country beyond. All are held by Biloches nominally independent, but subordinate to our Government; who, in consideration of certain allowances, are made responsible for their safety, for the return of all stolen property, and for the police duties through the respective tribal lands. Commencing from the south, the most important are the Suri, which, starting from the edge of the Mazâri country passes through the territories of the Bughti and Mârri tribes; the Zangi, leading past the Gandhâri mountain into the same country; the Câchar and the Kahâ, both into the country of the Khatrâns and the Luni Pathâns, the former of which was once extensively used, and was the one by which the Emperor Jehangir returned from Kandahâr to Delhi in 1601; the one by the Rakhi Nullah, which was selected for the new military road from Dera Ghâzi Khân to Peshin, passing over the Khar plain by Fort Monroe, and is now a splendid highway adapted for all arms of the service. This last is merely a branch of the better known one by the shrine of Sakh

Sarwar, a route affected in former days by Bárber, when he went up to Ghazni after his campaign in 1505. In more modern times, this was the route by which the Kábul rulers got their mangoes sent to Kandahár, and it has been made still more famous by the shrine at the foot of the hill. It was here that, 650 years ago, Saidi Ahmad mended the legs of the camels going from Khorasán to Delhi. One merchant, whose camel's leg had been broken, found, when he got back to Delhi, that the leg had been mended with rivets, and the then Emperor was so much taken with the miracle that he sent four mule loads of coin to the ingenious Saidi, who built the shrine with it. It has been endowed by many people since then. Hindu merchants from Lahore built the steps. Nadir Shah and the Duráni Shah Zamán presented jewels, and some Sikhs added a shrine to Baba Nának. The *majáwars* or keepers, who always number neither more nor less than 1,650 — including women and children, all entitled to equal shares, when the proceeds of the shrine treasure chest is annually divided—have hit on a simpler method of raising money, more suited to the times, which is, to send out their pilgrim hunters furnished with bills drawn, payable at sight, on wealthy believers likely to be substantial and obliging enough to take them up. Curiously the shrine is affected equally by Hindu and Muhammadans, and it certainly involved considerable pilgrimage to get there. Whether, now that the new road will make the journey so much easier, the income of the shrine will increase, remains to be seen. Further up, the Vidore pass, opposite Dera Gházi Khán, offers a still more direct, but also a more thirsty route, past Ek-Bhai into the Rakhni Valley. The Sowári, the Shori, the Mahoi, the Sangarh, and Kawan, lead through the territories of the Bozdárs, the Luni Patháns, the Musa Khels, and the Kakars into the Zhob Valley; the most important of these being the Sangarh opposite Mangrotha, which was the one taken by General Chamberlain in the expedition against the Bozdars in 1857.

E

Through these, in times gone by, the hill men swept down for many a foray, " riding," as they describe themselves " like ravening wolves towards the sheep-house, the Low country." Wild-looking men, with thick flowing beards and long curly black ringlets coming down to their shoulders, surmounted by huge turbans twisted rope-like rather than folded. In voluminous smock frocks and expansive trousers, so begrimed as to show little of the original white. Their shields secured to their backs by a plaid of the same tint, and their belts set off by a perfect armoury of weapons. Perhaps more ferocious in appearance than in fact, but each with swagger enough for a host. The whole party mounted on small thin, lank, but wiry and enduring mares, a quality most necessary and often surely tried; for, riding all through the night to some flourishing village, their masters would before dawn be pushing home again with all the cattle and plunder they had been able to collect. Nor was the vendetta always unassociated with romance, for Sassui was by no means the only young lady who exchanged love-tokens across the Border, and whose fancy turned towards the stalwart young Biloch ; nor was Panhâl Khân, the only " thief of renown " whose heart burned with secret longing for the Peri of the Plains, or the objective of whose raid was not merely all the camels, goats, and village gear, but " the fairest of maidens in the reed huts by the Saints' Canal." " How," says one young lady, whose capture is related in a popular ballad, which describes her as a dove, a very pea-hen in gait, a mist cloud in lightness, with locks like the tendrils of the creeper, but whose will was hard as the hills, when it came to a question of flight. " How can I part from my mother, for my father to heap curses on her head?" But the freebooting lover has no time to stop and argue.

> " Then I seized her pliant form in my arms,
>   And with the end of my turban I stopped her mouth :
> She struggled like the kid in the tiger's jaw,
>   But soon she rested her head on my shoulder."

And having got back safe through the stony paths of the passe
and divided the plunder, declares—

> " My bride was pleased with none but me,
>   Forgotten her mother, her playmates, her companions,
> For she walks with a dainty boy on her hip."

Like a good deal more of the unexplored, moral and physical,
the difficulties of most of these passes to a great extent disappear
when they come to be examined. The narrow gorges through
which the drainage forces its way to the plains, and the ruggedness
of the defiles naturally leads to the idea of still greater difficulties
beyond, while the character of the wild tribes has always been an
element calculated to exaggerate the dangers. By a curious process, there seems a belief in some minds that the more bare, rocky
and impassable the mountains, the worse and more barren the
country, the more numerous and warlike the inhabitants. Either
is possible, but not both, and experience has proved both to have
been greatly overrated. As a rule, the passes are only difficult in
proportion as they are unknown. By far the worst features of
them are turned towards India. The first difficult range surmounted, comparatively fertile valleys appear—" *Shams*," as they
are locally called—and often comparatively open lines of communication. Even the slopes of the rugged Sulaimans ease off
considerably towards the west. By far the most formidable difficulties in making the Peshin road just referred to have been met
with in the approaches by the Rakhi torrent up to the sanitarium
of Fort Munroe. The descent on the west is by easy slopes over
what by comparison may be called grassy downs. The Rakhni
Valley, immediately below, offers finer grass and better sport
than can be got almost anywhere in the Dera Ghâzi Khân district,
and for a considerable distance the construction of a good
cart road was comparatively easy. Like so much of Bilochistân
and Afghânistân, there is a deficiency of water; but this will

in a great measure be remedied by a system of storage, and the country only needs irrigation to turn it into a garden. As it is, many of these "*Shams*" are fairly well off. Many tracts are rich in grass. The Khetrân Valley along its

One of the Donkeys that made the Peshin Road.

whole length is celebrated for horse-breeding. The Paniali Valley is reported admirably suited for a similar purpose. Near Gumbaz are wood and grass for three or four regiments of cavalry, with splendid manœuvring ground. The Smalan Valley is both productive and beautiful, its elevation about 5,000 feet, and its water

and supplies certain. The Bori valley has been selected for the
new cantonment of Loralai. The hills between this and the Zhob
are penetrable in all directions, and the latter valley is for some
distance fourteen miles wide, The further explorations of these
valleys are carried northward, the more favourable the country is
reported. The fertility of Quetta and the valleys adjoining have
long been famous: so have the melons and grapes of Mastung
The characteristics of some of the hillsides are not unlike certain
in South Italy, or only need vineyards to be so ; and there is no
reason why the vineyards should not follow.

CHAPTER VI.

THE "FHAIRSHON" AND "MCTAVISH."

WHETHER the Biloch stock originally came from Aleppo, *viâ* Bághdâd and Makrân ; whether, as some assert, he had whilom an intimate relationship with the Jews, or was of Turkman origin— with which people he has certainly many points in common—or if, still more probably, he is a result of the admixture of the original inhabitants, reinforced by Jew-Arab-Turkman immigration, and assisted by hosts of conquerors from Alexander downwards; his tribal divisions are numerous enough to include the whole. He has certainly this in common with the Jews, that, in respect to these divisions, probably not all the children of Israel scattered over the wilderness of Sinai, would have offered such a complicated family problem; and he has divided his inheritance almost more minutely than they did the land of Canaan.

To attempt a systematic numbering of the tribes would, in the first place, require the mantle of Moses, and in the next, it may be reasonably doubted whether ordinary readers have patience to follow a stringing together of names, compared to which the First Book of Chronicles would be light reading. The tribes, or *tumans*, numerous as they are, moreover represent only the beginning.

For these *tumans* are again divided into clans (*paras*), the clans into sections called *palli*, and sometimes these again into sub-sections, each with a head-man, whose local following is often a mere handful. The Gurchânis, for instance, run to eleven clans and eighty-one sections; the Bughtis, six clans and forty-four sections; the Mazâris, four clans and fifty-seven sections : while probably none of the three can muster more than 2,000 or 2,500 fighting men, even counting all from fourteen, instead of the Israelitish twenty years of age, as able to go forth to war. To add to this there is an aggravating habit which the Biloch has of ringing the changes on a single name. Thus the town of Dera Ghâzi Khân was founded some 400 years ago by one Hâji Khân, who begat Ghâzi Khân and called the town after him. Ghâzi Khân then begat a son, and thought it only right to call him Hâji Khân, and for fifteen generations from father to son, without any variation of patronymic, this was continued, until the people got sick, and christened the whole place Hâjighâzi, an expression suggestive enough. Like the Highlands of Scotland in former days, almost every valley and hill-side boasts a clan of its own, under a petty leader, independent but still acknowledging allegiance to some more powerful tribal lords. The principal occupation of the local " Fhairshon," and "McTavish " is, or was before our advent, small feuds against their neighbour and raids on his cattle. In fact, the best understanding of the average Biloch clan can probably be obtained from a study of Bon Gaultier's Gaelic ballad. It is only necessary to alter slightly the names, and the story of the invasion by the Macpherson, with his four-and-twenty men and five-and-thirty pipers, adapts itself very closely to the politics of the Mârri and Bughti hills. In most affairs, of the small fighting tail, the largest number would be employed in driving " ta`cattle," and the few casualties be due to the sudden appearance on the scene of the aggrieved party in force; the McMarri—

> "Coming wi' his fassals,
> Gillies seventy-three, and sixty Dhuine wassails."

Bearing northwards from the Jacobabad and Sibi railway, the

more important of these clansmen, along what can now only be described as our old Biloch frontier—for our occupation of Peshin has now placed them behind us—to a greater or less extent also hold lands within purely British districts. Such are the Mazâris, Dreshaks, Bughtis, Gurchânis, Laghâris, Khosas, Lunds, Bozdârs, and Kasrânis. In the hills just beyond, are the Mârris, Khetrâns, Luni Pathâns, and Musâ Khels. Further still in the Hurnai, Thal Chotiali, and Peshin districts, the Tarins, Dumars, and a somewhat too extensive sprinkling of the various divisions of Kâkars. With a few exceptions all are Biloch, or closely allied and differing only in minor points. The Mazâris—whose name is variously said to be derived from the Mazâr—a stream in Sistân—or the same word meaning a tiger—hold the country from the Sind border to near Mithankote, and are perhaps the most important and flourishing. They can muster probably 4,000 fighting men, mostly living within British territory, where they own many villages. In former days they were referred to by Elphinstone as famous for piracies on the Indus, and accomplished as highway robbers. They were at almost perpetual war with their neighbours in every direction, and had the reputation of being the most adroit cattle-thieves along the line. Since annexation in 1849 they have given no trouble. They are perhaps not now good agriculturists, preferring to graze their flocks along the river banks in the hot weather and in the low hills in the cold; but they have settled gradually down into becoming peaceful and loyal subjects, and their chief was not long ago made a Nawâb for " distinguished loyalty and good service." Their neighbours and former enemies, the Dreshaks, though probably deriving their name from the Drekhan, a stream in the hills, have now no possessions there at all. The Gurchânis—or as they would call themselves, Gorishânis—somewhat mongrel Biloches, who traditionally trace their descent to a converted Hindu Rajah of Sind, own the bulk of the Mârri and Drâgul hills, though they cannot, or very recently could not, be said to hold them. Constant

feuds with the Mârri rendered their lands beyond the border somewhat less profitable than an Irish estate. One of their chiefs
joined Humayun in his march to Delhi in 1556. Others maintained a state of constant war with the Sikhs; systematically
harried the plains east of the Indus; and at the time of the
Punjab annexation had the reputation of being "the worst-behaved
of the Biloch tribes." They are probably now only restrained
from falling on the adjoining Laghâris by our presence; yet they
have in various ways been brought under complete control, and
their conduct reputed as "uniformly good." The Laghâris, a
powerful tribe, located around the Sakhi Sarwar pass, as well as
the Khosas, Lunds and Kasrânis, originally all more or less given
to the trade of Turpin and Macheath, have developed comparatively industrious habits. Several of their head men have turned
their energies to canal-making; have acquired extensive estates;
become honorary magistrates; and are now among the staunchest
supporters of social order. The Bughtis of the rocky and barren
country on the Râjanpur border, and the Bozdârs of the hills
opposite Mangrotha, have at times given a little more trouble; and
the former are credited with at least one famous raid into Sind,
when they succeeded in lifting some 15,000 cattle. Both have
had to receive lessons more or less severe, but have profited
greatly by the teaching, and with the Mârris, in many respects
the most important of all, whose raids in former times were
constant and indiscriminate, are now exceedingly friendly.

The reputation of the Mârri is sufficient to ruin a far better
man. He is charged not merely with devotion to theft and
robbery of every kind, but with being always ready to welcome
the seven other spirits more lawless than himself. His character
may be estimated from his own maxim, quoted by Duke in his
interesting history of the tribe:—"We are," says the Mârri, "the
enemies of all our neighbours: we do no good to any one: nobody
wishes us well. Let us then afford every encouragement to strife

around us: let us give passage through our country to any neighbour who seeks to injure another. Whichever side is injured or destroyed matters not to us; in any case we shall be gainers." Though he occasionally acts up to this policy, even he has his redeeming side; for, though he has small scruple in making the traveller or trader pay, he holds stringently to the laws of honour; a ring or token given as a receipt for black mail is a sufficient guarantee for further safety; and he would take the most ample vengeance upon any one else failing to recognise the pledge. Though generally regarded as Brahui Biloch, the tribe is occasionally spoken of as Pathán, and some clans talk more readily a Semitic Pushtu than a Márri Bilochi; but they are really a confederation drawn from several races and peoples, grafted on to a Biloch stock. They profess a nominal allegiance to the Khán of Khelát, but they pay him no revenue, act independently of him, and have no more scruple in raiding his territories than our own. The three main divisions comprise no fewer than eighteen clans, and are supposed to number 4,000 or 5,000 fighting men, who carried fear into all the surrounding tribes; but, according to Duke, excluding those in Sind and Khelát, they number little over 2,500 males. Raiding as a profession, though it certainly offers plenty of excitement, is neither lucrative nor safe. The Márris have made too many enemies, have fallen on bad times, and constant reprisals have gone near to wearing them out. On the whole, their recent relations with us have been fairly satisfactory. The prospect of plunder being too strong, they took advantage of the Maiwand disaster to attack our workpeople on the Sibi line, and cut up some of our clerks and coolies, which drew on them an expedition under the late Sir Charles Macgregor; but care, firmness, and tact on the part of our Political Officers has now brought about a result sufficient to justify a use of the past tense in regard to their misdeeds.

The Khetráns immediately below Fort Monroe, the Lunis in the next valley, and the Musa Khels a little further again, are all

Pathâns. The first of the three, whose name signifies "cultivator," was probably a Pathân graft on a Jât stock. They speak a dialect between Sindi and Punjabi, still retain some Hindu customs, and are fairly industrious and agricultural. More notorious as receivers than thieves, they are peaceful and unaggressive, but they have had the Mârris for next neighbours. Similarly the Lunis, whose country extended from the Râkhni to the Bori Valley, have been so weakened by feuds, mainly with the Mârris, that five of their fine valleys through which the new road to Peshin passes, have been deserted, rendered "*bar*" or desolate, and their flocks and herds restricted to a little more than a fifth of the area they once possessed. Little was known about them till a few years ago; but they are fine men, somewhat fond of showy armour and tasselled spears; good raw material for excellent soldiers. The Musa Khels are traditionally Kâkars, who left their old haunts somewhere between Kandahâr and Herat, to seek fresh fields and pastures new under Musa, settled down on the further slopes of the Takht, from whence they were ousted about eighty years ago, and have since taken up an extensive and prosperous position on the Toi stream. They too are mostly shepherds, disposed to be friendly with our politicals; but friendly from a respectful distance.

The time would fail to attempt to tell of the many tribes that occupy the debateable land between Bilochistân and Afghânistân, whom our new lines of railway and road are making us daily better acquainted with, like the Spin or White Tarins of Thul Chotiali, the Dumars, the Pannis of the Sangan Valley—who were celebrated free-lances in Bârber's time—and the many other petty septs of Pathân origin. By far the most important, both as regards numbers, strength, and distribution are the Kâkars, a numerous Afghân race, divided into many distinct tribes, who have very little in common save the name of Kâkar. They are scattered over a considerable area from Hurnai to the Zhob Valley, and from the Takht to the Registan, or place of sand, beyond Peshin. The

three best known of their tribes are the Panizai, Sarangzai, and
Hamzazai; but they have not even a *jirgah* or general council of
the whole, the various sections quarrelling freely among themselves.
The warlike reputation of some of their chiefs has been consider-

An Uchakzai Pathàn of the Peshin Valley.

able: and for a long period the Bilochis carried on almost a
national war with them. Elphinstone tells of an engagement in
which a large force of Brahui Bilochis were entrapped in the
Khulaz defile, and some 800 or 900 cut to pieces: very near the
spot from which the Kâkars rolled stones down on our troops

during the Southern Afghán campaign. The same tribe murdered Captain Showers in the Osdapslie pass in 1880; and the Zhob Valley sections still continue to give trouble now and then. Colonel —now Sir James—Brown was deputed by Lord Lytton, in 1877, to specially report on them; and presumably there is much information of interest concerning them locked up in the Simla archives. What has been done however in the case of the Márris can no doubt be equally well applied to the Kákars. It is only necessary to open out their country, establish communications, and adopt a friendly but firm policy. The marching of our troops by way of the Zhob Valley and the Gumal pass to and from Dera Ismail Khân to Peshin—a proposal our Government, after many years of debating, is now insisting on carrying out—will probably be the best possible beginning.

Meanwhile, there can perhaps be no better illustration of the advantages to everybody concerned of opening such countries out to the civilising influence afforded by free communications, good roads, and the presence of British officers of tact and judgment, than the contrast between the Biloch who has come within our influence, and the independent tribesman. It is almost startling. The one is so obviously sleek and comfortable, has generally a decent suit, a good mare—all the four legs,—is well to do, and can afford to appear prosperous. His villages are thriving and populous. The other is lean, hungry, living from hand to mouth; his dress a few dirty rags or tattered sheepskin; in constant anxiety for his life, his crops, and his cattle, which he can seldom call his own. His house is often a round tower in the field entered by a ladder, which he draws up after him. Occasionally even this has to be abandoned, as being too far from his village. When not raiding himself or being raided upon, he is wearied out by constant watching for surprise from raiding parties, and " *chapáos*," which carry off the whole of his cattle and occasionally kill off the attendants. A *chapáo* is simply the Biloch expression for an organized raid, and at one time probably formed the best part of a chief's income, a fifth of the whole spoil—which often amounted to a large sum in property of all sorts—falling to him. The footman had one share, the horseman another for his horse, or so many legs of it as he owned; another half share, if he possessed a gun, while if he was killed his relations got his share. The tribal headmen got a proportionately better share, and the booty was all carefully valued according to a regular scale, in terms of bullocks. A mare being equal to four cows, a gun to a bullock, a sword to half a bullock and so on.

But even successful raiding is obviously not a very lucrative business. The raiders had nearly as hard a time as the raided, they could never afford to rest, any one who by chance fell out or got left behind, was at once murdered, if not mutilated. It was literally a case of the devil taking the hindmost. "The members of a *chapáo*," as Fryer writes in one of his graphic accounts, "have to travel long distances by night, lying concealed by day, and they have no food but what flour they can carry with them, which they dare not light a fire to bake. They often end by falling into an ambuscade themselves, or by finding their intended victims too much on the alert for an attack to be ventured." He instances a party of Márris whom he met returning from a raid on the Luni Patháns. They were half-starved, and worn out with fatigue, having been out for three weeks; and after deducting the leader's share, their plunder was only sufficient to give the third of a bullock to each man. The liberty of the " Fhairshon " is clearly not worth very much to him.

CHAPTER VII

SULAIMÂN AND SIND SAINTS.

" MAY Allah not set Sayuds and Mullahs over us !" is a common local proverb trans-Indus, and yet superstition of the most degrading kind is probably greater among the Muhammadans west of that river than among the Hindus on the east. The latter holds his sacred Brahman cheap, compared to the abject deference the former pays his spiritual guide. Variation there is in degree; from the independent Bilochi—who, grossly credulous as he may be, is compared to a Pathân, almost an agnostic—to the snivelling Bannuchi, described by Edwardes as "accepting the clumsiest imposture as a miracle, and the fattest fakir as a saint." But whatever reverence enters into the composition of the Border tribesman is for saints and shrines ; his credulity in this respect has no limits, and he accepts the connected miracles as a matter of course. The whole Sulaimân range would appear to have been a favourite resort of the fraternity. Hardly a pass, a peak, or an old mound, but boasts a legend, a tomb, or a shrine, even though the visible sign may be no more than a few rags, or a heap of stones. Perhaps, as Fryer suggests, this may be ascribed to the unattractive nature of the country, which contains so many places admirably adapted for the residence of those who desire to mortify the flesh ; or more possibly to the fact that, for many centuries, the range offered a natural resting-place for the invading Musalman hosts, saints and soldiers alike. The founders of the religious orders can be more often traced to Bukhâra or Bâghdâd, than from Delhi or Patna. The "pillars of the faithful," "the guides of the devoted," or the "Pole-stars of Islâm," would often have had a short shrift at the hands of Gakkhars or of Sikhs, and the average Punjâbi Jat has an awkward habit of disliking religious advice.

Just as Border history is mainly made up of mythical genealogies, its traditions relate almost exclusively to the sayings and doings of saints, sayuds, or priests. They are the chief figures in most relations of life, and take the place of precedence as regards the wants of the people. Among the most formidable, in that bare and stony country, has always been the want of water and supplies. The "pattern of the devoted, and wanderer in the field of generosity," Shaikh Ismail Sarbanni, whose tomb is upon Koh-i-Sulaimân, though an observer of rigid abstinence, is described as killing 400 sheep daily for the benefit of travellers. The heads, limbs, and skins were gathered up in the evening, and every morning the shepherd found all his flock alive again, and drove them off to pasture. So, also, fifty famishing travellers call unexpectedly upon "the asylum of mankind and magazine of wisdom," Shaikh Mulhi Kattal, and find nothing in his house. "In the name of Allah" he fills a pot with water, places it on the fire, sends to the potter for an earthen plate, and with his own blessed hands serves up to all his guests abundance of excellent stew, the dish always remaining full, "and," adds the ingenious chronicler, Niamat Ullah, "the plate is to this very day in the possession of his successor." Again, the tribes on the east of the Takht-i-Sulaimân suffered greatly for want of water, while those on the west had comparative plenty, whereupon a certain "falcon of knowledge and stage of excellence" opened a passage right through the mountain, and brought to their relief the Drâban stream. The stream is there still, though it has less water in it than formerly, because a subsequent "lion in the forest of unity," Shaikh Dana, caused some to flow to a tribe favoured by him.

Another difficulty was—as it is still—the control of the Indus river. Once it broke its banks, carried away the best part of a village, and might have done infinite damage, had not the inhabitants promptly repaired to that "mine of inspiration and flower of the pious," Yahya Bakhtiar, who at once provided an effectual embankment by laying down a single tile, which he had used to keep his illustrious foot out of the mud when bathing. This effectually controlled the stream, which would not run past it. He was a saint decorated with a particular divine glory. He had "kept the fast of the Ramazan even as an infant;" travelled to Mecca and back every Friday for prayers; and on one occasion so vigorously did he recite the praises of Allah that he threw his heart out of his mouth, his servants ever after carefully preserving it in a napkin. When he needed a sacrifice to appease the hunger of his followers, a fat antelope walked up to the fire made ready. So also did a lion, but, on seeing the saint, became quite subdued, and went off cheerfully with a bone. When the Indus boatmen demanded a fare for ferrying the Khwájah, a fish popped its head up with the money. When he and his disciples found themselves thirsty on a barren hillside, he took his tooth-brush, and, like Moses, struck the dry rock, upon which a spring of fresh water rushed out, and has run ever since. And when the great Timur, on one of his expeditions, approached the Sulaimáns, where numbers of the Afghán tribes had taken refuge, the Khwájah and his adherents remained at the foot of the mountain, and, as the hostile army approached, Yahya, reciting some verses of the Korán, threw a handful of dust against his foes. Not only did the dust act as a veil between the Mughal army and the saint, but the Mughal soldiers grew blind, and hearing as it were the noise of a vast host approaching them, became filled with consternation and fell back. Timur however was hardly the man to be stopped by a saint more or less. He

F

quickly found out the cause of the trouble, and attempted to tip
the Khwâjah with a horse and a robe; but the latter seems to
have thought the insult hardly large enough, so sent them back
with some excellent advice, and moved away.

Everybody who has been to Multân knows that its notorious

Shams-i-Tabrez of Multán.
(Facsimile of a Panjâb lithograph.)

heat was brought about by the influence of a saint, Shams-i-Tabrez
from Bâghdâd, an "abstracted and accomplished devotee," who
begged his daily bread in the city, not always in sufficient
quantities to satisfy his hunger.   One day, suffering from short
commons, he caught a fish which he held up to the sun and begged

that luminary to come down and cook. The sun at once drew nearer than to any other part of the earth—and Multán has suffered ever since. So much so, that unfortunate Multánis who have mistaken their way in the shades, have, as the legend goes, invariably had to send back for an extra blanket. The accomplished Shams performed many subsequent miracles, even to raising the dead: but it may, at least to residents in that dusty and almost rainless place, be a trifling satisfaction to know, that he was in the end flayed alive for his pretensions.

Shams, however, was quite a minor light beside the other celebrities of Multán, Rukn-ud-din and his still more famous grandfather Bahâwal Hakk, "Light of the truth." The former, who is credited with having a good deal to say to the trap by which Ghiâs-ud-din Tughlâk, the Sultán of Delhi, was done to death, they buried with his grandfather, but he subsequently moved into his present stately tomb of his own accord, and without any assistance. That Shaikh of Shaikhs, Bahâwal Hakk, who was directly descended from Hâsham, the great-grandfather of the Prophet of Islâm, travelled over all Muhammadan Asia for half a century before coming to Multán, where he settled down and became "a fountain of the most illustrious miracles" for another half century. Among other trifles, he raised a ship that had foundered with all hands, and is still the especial patron of all the Indus boatmen, who appeal to him in difficulties.

The son of Bahâwal Hakk, and father of Rukn, by name Sadr-ud-din, was hardly less distinguished, but he essayed a trial of saintly skill with a still more potent expert, a Sayud practising lower down the Indus at Tattah, one Pir Murâd. The Multán Shaikh sent the Tattah Sayud a cup of milk, to signify that the former's religious dignity filled the whole country, as the milk did the cup. It reached Tattah quite fresh, without a drop being spilt, and the Sayud, putting a handful of flowers in, returned it, implying that there was still plenty of room for the saintliness of Pir Murâd.

Not a flower was faded when it reached Multân again, so the Shaikh saw nothing for it but to go and tackle such a famous rival in person. The dispute was to be settled in the Tattah mosque. On the way thither, the Shaikh saw a dead cat, which he restored to life, saying, " Arise with the permission of God." The Pir was in no way put out by this, but calling into the mosque a most notorious old Brahmin idolater, bid him recite the prayers. The Hindu at once tore off his priestly thread, preached in elegant Arabic, became a luminous Moslem and explained the word *Bismillah* in fourteen different ways. Whereupon the son of Bahâwal Hakk allowed he was beaten.

Tattah must have literally swarmed with saints. Muhammad Aâzam, who wrote about a century ago—one of the many books on this inexhaustible subject—gives a list of one hundred buried in the city, and of eighty shrines of the first order of magnitude on the Mekli—or " Mecca-like "—hills adjoining. In fact the whole of that little range is covered with their tombs—to say they could be counted by thousands, would not be expressive enough. The Pir Murâd just referred to, might well have accounted for many, for at the age of forty he had acquired such sanctity, that he was compelled to wear a veil ; because any one who saw the light of his countenance became a saint on the spot. Not less than 2,000 of his pupils, says the learned writer, were " enlightened enough to rise to eminence."

One of these, an " exemplary of the pious, and strict-keeper of vigils," Mian Maluk Shah, lived a long life of such abstinence, that during his threescore years and ten he used but 112 lbs. of flour which he moistened with nothing but water. He seems mainly to have lived on the pleasure of listening to the dull creak of the Persian wheels raising water from the wells. This to him was so intoxicating, that on occasions he caused the wheels to revolve after the bullocks were taken out, and a luckless cultivator, in whose garden he sat under a tree, wrapt in ecstasy, listening to his favourite music, found his whole property flooded one morning; and, when he ejected the stranger, saw with dismay his garden, tree, well, and Persian wheel, follow the saint.

At Sehwân is the shrine of the Pir of the Kohistân, Usmân-i-Merwandi, a great grammarian, scholar and traveller, as well as saint, who died in 1274. His more familiar title is Lâl Shâh-Bâz, the " Red Falcon of Merwand," so called because in order to imitate a Moslem story of Abrahim, whose father tested him by throwing him into a fiery furnace, which forthwith became a bed of roses, Shâh-Bâz sat for a whole year in an iron pot placed upon a broiling fire. The Sind hero seems to have suffered no inconvenience beyond changing colour from a pious pale to a bright red. On another occasion he assumed a winged form to rescue a distressed brother from the hands of an infidel king. The title of Red Falcon is therefore particularly appropriate. Originally he was probably a respectable harmless old gentleman, but hardly so are the present representatives and guardians of the mausoleum that has grown up, who belong to the sect of Jelâli Fakirs, and enjoy a reputation more evil than most. Rumour has it that a girl of a particular caste is annually married to the tomb. It is pretty certain that the stout ruffianly mendicants, disfigured by shaving head, beard, eyebrows and moustachios, not only grant, but accept the *indulgenza plenaria,* or license to sin freely.

That portions of the earth's surface are movable at the will of the saints, is accepted in several cases. There are two holy brothers and " favourites of both worlds," Mians Mitho and Ratho, buried in one of the Sind border hills, that on the day of resurrection will not only go to Paradise but will take the whole hill with them. As may be supposed, the hill is still in great request as a burial ground.

Not a bad place to be buried is on the heights of Chehal Tân, the loftiest of the Biloch mountains overlooking the Bolân. The Brahuis say that the great apostle himself, the " praised one," came one night mounted on a dove, and left a whole colony of Pirs, or saints. for their guidance. No less than forty of these, no doubt much-needed, saints, were buried under the mountain, which thus obtained the name of Chehal Tân, "the forty bodies." Masson has, however, a more interesting legend as to the origin of the name. To the effect that a simple old couple, childless for years, besought the saint of Teree to take away their reproach. He was obdurate and refused, but the saint's son, a stalwart youth conjuring with his father's wand, promised the dame a son for each pebble she caught in her lap. She caught forty pebbles, and in due course was blessed with a family of forty sons at a birth. Overcome with so much bliss, the parents left thirty-nine of them to the chances of fate on wild slopes of the mountain and fled. Anon repenting of their crime, they returned, searched the mountain again to find the thirty nine at play, as happy as may be, leaping and dancing among the steep cliffs : but attempting to decoy them down again, by a view of the remaining brother, he too was stolen away, and the old couple were left childless once more. Consumed with grief, there was nothing for them to do but to raise a shrine, which to this day works wonders for similar disconsolate wives, who in good faith resort to the "hill of the forty bodies," and crave the boon of children.

Perhaps the most renowned saint of all, along this part of the Border, was the Saidi Ahmad, whose shrine at Sakhi Sarwar has already been referred to. He is the hero of innumerable of the most popular legends, not only on the Border, but over half the Punjáb. It is at his shrine that Daru, the Jât woman, after twelve years of childless wedded life, prays for a son, and attains her desire ; and when, in spite of the anger of her husband, a strict follower of Guru Nanak the Sikh, she goes again to return thanks, and the child dies at her breast, because in her heart she has resolved to defraud the shrine of its dues, it is the compassionate Saidi who is moved to restore him to life again. It is Saidi, who grazing his father's goats in the jungle, the while he studies the Korân, is set on by a fierce tiger, which he unaided slays with his staff. Chânnu, the Pathân ruler of Multân, gives the saint a horse, and much fine raiment. The first he kills to feed fakirs, and tears up the latter for their clothing, but when accused of doing this, he comes into Multân, riding the horse and wearing the clothes, which have come back to him from Heaven, from whence also come houris and fairies, bringing pots and pitchers to celebrate his wedding with Chânnu's daughter. The lady brings the saint much wealth and three servants, whose descendants are now the 1,650 keepers of the shrine. The ballads of Isa Baniya and Isa Bapâri collected by Captain Temple, tell of rich merchants who vowed large sums for the shrine if their adventures proved profitable, forgot them when success came, and fell into terrible distresses which only pilgrimages and a very liberal subsequent expenditure at Sakhi Sarwar sufficed to allay. Even the Saint's Biloch mare Kakki Sarwar, "broad in the back and brown as a partridge," is hardly less famous, for she is credited with the gift of speech, and with working many minor miracles.

The banks of the Indus were of course a favourite resort of the saints; its fertilizing waters and welcome freshness being a pleasant exchange for the bare and arid stones of the Sulaimâns. Quite one of the most famous and widely known is Jenda Pir or Khwâjah Khizr—the "Green King"—whose shrine is at Bakkar. He is practically the river god, the personification of the mighty stream to whom hymns and petitions are addressed, though the shrine is dedicated to a celebrated Pir who saved the honour of a Muhammadan young lady on her way to Mecca, from the lust of a Hindu king, by a sudden diversion of the course of the stream.

Only second in rank as a water saint was Shaikh Tahir, or Uddhero Lall, as the Hindus call him, whose tomb a little below Hâla, in the keeping of a chapter of Moslems, is the site of a great annual Hindu fair. A variety of his miracles are claimed to have

been wrought in the defence of both faiths. He used to float
about the river seated on a small sheet—of white, say the Hindus,
of indigo blue, say the Muhammadans. He saved a man of the
rival faith, challenged to the test by the same method of naviga-
tion, but who, sinking, had to save himself by resting his finger
tips on the edge of the sheet, which say the party of Islám, left

Khwâjah Khizr.
(Facsimile of a Punjâb lithograph.)

five white spots. And some of the river people affect a blue sheet
with white spots in its corners to this day.

Like the saint of Sakhi Sarwar, these two river saints are
equally venerated by both Hindus and Muhammadans, and both
creeds equally flock to the *ziarat* of Chehâl Tân.

Of many, their chief merits were their reputation for asceticism.
They abandoned home, children, wife—even though they might
have to take up with some one else's. Theoretically at any rate,

they spent their time in fasting and keeping vigils. One "abstracted sage and consummate enthusiast,"—the chronicler's titles generally run to a paragraph—is described as becoming so emaciated from "excessive abstinence" that his ribs projected like a staircase. They called him Shaikh Bakhtiar Dunkar, and whoever mentions his name is still secure from the evil eye, and—still more useful in a Patháu village—saved from the annoyance of the flies. Pir 'Adil, the just priest, whose shrine is a few miles from Dera Ghâzi Khân, and second in repute only to Sakhi Sarwar, gained his title from his abstract justice. His son killed a goat while out hunting, and accidentally, the goatherd boy who was defending his goats. The goatherd's mother appealed to the saint, who, to satisfy her, put his own son to death.

Nevertheless, very many of them contrived to make the best of both worlds. Numbers are represented as following the traditions of the profession, and making themselves especially agreeable to the ladies. It was not always *O Sanctissima* even in the West, and one "ecstatic saint" is described as "throwing his arms round a specially handsome woman in the marketplace," and as himself thrown into an oven by the Governor of Kandahâr, where anon he is found calmly eating the roast meat. Another "pilgrim in the desert of unity" remained "disguised under the garb of a worldly person," and greatly to his satisfaction rescues a certain "beautiful washerwoman." Even Khawjah Yahya is warned by a reverent brother about the danger of cotton and fire, and too near an intercourse with the sex. But Yahya was a wag, and replied by sending cotton and fire joined together in a letter; the former uninjured.

The danger of offending, or refusing a saint hospitality, is exemplified in innumerable stories. A "guide to the truth" in Kohistân, is, on occasion, driven by the inhabitants of his village into cursing them; and, "on the same day there occurred forty funerals." Even the Emperor Islâm Shâh, who threatens "a precious gem" with death for his conduct in regard to women, is from that very moment afflicted with a fistula and inflammation in all his limbs. While the merit of entertaining holy men meets, as history throughout the world amply proves, with its own reward here and hereafter. The shepherd boy who refreshes a party of fakirs with his one pet lamb, finds a flock of sheep start up from the stones. The man who builds a house for their shelter, has but to call on the forest in Allah's name, to find the timber ready to hand.

Nihil' scriptum miraculi causa. The age of miracles for the Pathán has by no means passed away, but a single characteristic modern instance must suffice. There is or rather was, on the roadside between Kohát and the Indus, a large stone or rock, a couple of feet high and several wide, on which, some few years ago, a well-known officer saw a holy Mullah sit, who being asked by a follower for a remedy for toothache, prescribed in the form of powder a little of the stone so honoured. Its reputation as a specific was insured, and under the continual scraping of believers, troubled with that distressing malady, the toothache-stone gradually diminished. Two years after the same officer found it still in great request, but scraped down to a couple of feet below the surface. To a generation that has taken Parr's life pills, and set its limbs with Holloway's ointment, there is perhaps nothing extraordinary in this; but considering the Mullah's few opportunities of advertising, his remedy had a fairly good run. Perhaps when Messrs. Cook have exploited the country, and personally conducted parties along the Border, greater possibilities may arise. If, for instance, Mr. Pears could only induce a few Mullahs to wash, what a stroke of business might be done in soap!

CHAPTER VIII.

THE POWINDAH AND THE PAT.[1]

A LONG dreary sketch of level plain, as flat as a billiard-table or
a barn's-floor, often without a tree, a bush, or plant bigger than
the camel-thorn, or the small, stunted, horny herbs that seem
equally caviare to the palate of that most useful, but unsavoury,
beast. Not always even so much vegetation as this, to cover the
monotony of the mud-coloured expanse, familiarly know as the
" *Pat.*" Firm, yielding, and elastic, it offers a fairly good substitute
for turf to gallop over, so long as the dry weather lasts ; but the
first few inches of continuous rain, fortunately not very frequent
and not very continuous, is sufficient to turn it into the most
tenacious and greasy mud, to render locomotion difficult, and roads
impassable. Almost impervious to water, the harder the clay
the worse the mud, and, apparently, the less the water can sink
through, the more easily the smallest running stream cuts out a
channel for itself. Consequently, when it does rain, the water
rapidly forms little ravines, and the hill torrents scour out deep
channels, with almost perpendicular sides, forming a series of deep
cracks which intersect the plain in every direction, like a piece of
curious old china. Here and there, where the bed of these has
widened out sufficiently, to admit of some little green thing

---

[1] Viz. the Ghilzai Clans and Dera Ismail Khân.

obtaining a footing, there is a fringe of tamarisk at the bottom of the crack ; but otherwise the banks are perfectly treeless, and the water too far below the surface, to do much towards helping struggling verdure without artificial assistance. Dry for a good part of the year, these ravines are occasionally roaring torrents, more or less formidable, as their sources are among the stones of the low hills or away towards Ghazni. Like the *pachád* in Dera Ghâzi Khân, the *Pat*, or the *damán*, to use the local equivalent word, is in places redeemed to some extent, by a laborious and ingenious system of artificial irrigation, with the result that little oases are created which, by comparison, may be called wooded. Up in the north-west corner, the town of Tânk was famed for its excellent fruit trees and luxuriant gardens, in the old days the resort of the choicest houris of its old Nawabs, whose history has been told by Edwardes; and marvellous legends are still current of the harem of Sarwar Khân. But the mean-looking mud-roofed houses, rather below than above the surrounding country, that make up the villages, are ordinarily far apart; and there are few or none of those detached farms and cottages, orchards or groves, that in other parts, even of India, help to give variety and interest to the scenery. The fame of Drâband, the town of the "closed pass," is of a single mangoe tree, the fruit of which was so good that Runjit Singh used to have it sent to Lahore. While of Kulachi, the saying is particularly characteristic :—" Never visit it save to find brave soldiers or delicious melons."

To the west side, bare and precipitous, are the Sulaimâns, in a long straight line, with the Takht in the middle. To the north, long stony spurs, the outworks of the Bhitanni or Shaikh Budin range, which, with another rugged group known as the Ruttah Koh and the Nila Koh—the red and the blue hills—form a complete barrier, extending to the Indus banks, and separating this plain from Bannu and the Marwat. The whole tract, from the Indus to the stony gorges, whence issue the hill torrents—and which represent the passes about which so much mystery was made—from Vahoa in the south, to Tânk in the north, is monotonously alike. Wherever these torrents are perennial, or there is water enough to turn on the fields, the general dreariness is broken, and when at certain times the rugged sides of the mountains are thrown into relief by the setting sun, the scene is not wanting in the elements of the picturesque. A fresh clear day, a good horse, and a gallop over the *pat* might possibly lead to the discovery of fresh beauties; but the substitution of the young camel, for the spring lamb, the slouching Powindah, for the proverbial harvester, or the rude camp village, for the "haunts of ancient peace," is not particularly idyllic; and the picturesqueness is one to which distance most eminently lends enchantment. The nearer the hills are approached, the less inviting they become, the more savage the bare knife-like edges, the want of trees, and the scarcity of water, while once inside the spurs, the sensation, as described by Macgregor, is not so much that of being in a valley among hills, as of being in a pit surrounded by perpendicular walls. The country Dera Ismail Khân has fairly enough earned its epithet of " Dera dismal."

From this not very inviting, but extremely important, " dismal camp," the principal passes by which the western barrier is crossed are the Vahoa, in front of the village and military post of that name; the Shaikh Haidar, or Zao, a title used for any exceptionally difficult pass, and this one in places is little better than a cleft a few feet wide, shut in by precipices of great height that nearly close overhead, though it was the route taken by the last Takht Survey party; the Gumal; the Tank *zam*, or river; and the Shuza. In addition are nearly seventy others, which cross the outer ranges, and communicate with the longitudinal valleys behind them. Some of these are well known in connection with frontier expeditions, others by the local names of the streams which issue from them, which names often vary within a few miles—even the

Gumal becomes the Luni on our maps—and also by the outposts which have been established to watch the tribes using them, and who, in the Sikh times, not only carried off cattle but many a likely Hindu, who had to pay up liberally to get out again. Edwardes tells a story of a whole marriage procession, bride, bridegroom, friends, and fiddlers, who, in his time, were seized by a soldier of the Dera Nawáb, wanting some arrears of pay, and whose relatives had eventually to find Rs.4,000 to obtain their release. Most of these passes rejoice in a legend regarding the stream, or a converted saint, some unite both. At Drâband is the tomb of a Shaikh, who, as usual with Border saints, was ' a polestar of guidance, a paragon among devotees, the examplar of mankind, the pattern of his age, the chief of true believers"; and by the side of the stream which passes it there is, or there ought to be, a jug constantly filled with water. When a quarrel arises between two persons, which is to be decided by oath, each of them sips a draught from it. He that is in the right remains unhurt, but the liar swells like a water-bag, from which state nothing can relieve him but confessing the truth.

In the range to the north are two passes, the Bain and the Peyzu, leading into the district of Bannu; the latter, Edwardes, in his time recommended no one to attempt without a guard, but it is now the one through which our main frontier road passes, and is probably rather safer than Regent Street. Of those on the west, the Gumal has been, from time immemorial, the chief trade-route, between Khurasán and India, the great central highway for the trading Afghán, of even more importance in this respect than the Khaiber to Kábul, or Bolán to Kandahár. Every cold weather, strings of camels laden with the merchandise from Bukhára and Afghánistán find their way through this pass ; and scatter through the length and breadth of India; and as summer approaches, return to the cooler highlands, carrying back in exchange either cash or goods for distribution as far as the Persian and the

Russian borders; their owners a border people of considerable importance.

Not so much by his fruits, is the Afghán merchant known in every Indian bazaar, as by his strange appearance, his great stature, physical strength, and rude independence of manner. It is not necessary to see him to be fully conscious of his presence. The " rankest compound of villainous smells " pervades the atmosphere through which he passes. " His loose untidy dress," as Bellew describes him, " generally in a state of dirt beyond the washerman's cure, and often covered with a shaggy sheepskin coat, travel-stained and sweat-begrimed to an extent that proclaims the presence of the wearer to the nostrils though he be out of sight in the crowd; his long unkempt and frayed locks, loosely held together by some careless twists of a coarse cotton turban, soiled to the last degree, if not tattered, also add to the wildness of his unwashed and weather-worn features; whilst his loud voice and rough manners complete the barbarian he is proud to pass for. Such is the common Powindah as seen in the bazaar." The term *powindah*, possibly from *parwindah*, the Persian for a bale of goods, is the collective name for all the migratory Pathâns who engage in the carrying trade, in fact monopolise all the trade between Central Asia, Afghânistân, and India; and includes a number of clans, mostly belonging to the great Ghilzai tribe, the most famous of all the Afghân tribes before the Durânis rose to power. The Ghilzai or Ghilji, are by many authorities set down as of Turkish origin, their name another form of *khilchi* or swordsman; but the very romantic story of the Persian prince who seduced the affections and honour of the Afghân young lady as his only chance of marrying her—for the Afghâns would not give their daughters to Persians, and the issue of which irregular union—subsequently duly ratified, was a son christened *Ghal-zoe*, the son of theft, furnishes a derivation much more probable. But whether they are to start in the past, as " swordsmen " or " sons of theft," they are in the present, an undoubtedly fine race; as regards stature, strength, and courage quite among the best of the Afghâns, with a spirit of commercial enterprise and readiness to fight to the death for the privilege of selling their wares at a profit, not altogether

A Powindah Fruit-seller.

without resemblance to the Briton himself. Assembling every year in the plains of Zermut or Katawâz, east of Ghazni, with their families, flocks, herds, and droves, rather than herds of camels, the clans combine and march in enormous caravans, often numbering

several thousand of fighting men, disposed in military order against
the attacks of the Waziris, Kâkars, and other Border tribes through
whose territory they have very often to literally fight their way:
the mass of them, by the Gumal pass ; though a few, mostly sheep-
owners, prefer the branch by the Zao.

The *pat* of Dera Ismail Khân is their great grazing ground, and
they, or their camp villages, and their vast flocks of camels, furnish
the most prominent addition to the scenery just noticed. Not a
little of that district, moreover, has from first to last been colonised by
offshoots from one clan or the other. Their numbers may be judged
from the fact that, according to the enumeration made at the mouths
of the passes by our militia stationed there for the purpose of dis-
arming them and collecting the trifling grazing and other dues, upwards of 76,000 entered the district in the cold season of 1877,
58,000 in 1878, and 50,000 in 1880. Of the last named over 33,000
were males, more than half being fighting men. In 1878 their parties
were accompanied by upwards of 77,000 camels and 188,000 sheep
and goats. Besides those coming with the regular caravans—
Kâfilas—many of whom, in spite of the railway, still continue to
travel down to Amritsar, Delhi, Benares, and often as far as Patna,
there are numerous others who establish themselves in fixed camp-
ing grounds called *kirris*, in the Dera Ismail district, where their
women, children, arms, and a certain portion of their cattle and
men are left for the cold season, while the rest of the clan go off to
trade, the same *kirris* being resorted to year after year, their droves
of breeding and young camels being driven off to graze, not always
with much regard to village boundaries. A third and still more
numerous class, called *charra-folk*, troubled with but few belongings
of any sort come simply as labourers, and wander about in gangs
not unlike the Irish harvesters, before the days of Home Rule, did
in England ; ready for rough work of any sort ; stone-breaking,
road-making, or jobs requiring energy and strength, living a very
hard and industrious life, often subsisting on what they can succeed

G

in begging at the close of their day's work, and saving the bulk of their earnings to go back to Afghânistân again.

Rough and stony as may be the rugged mountains of Solomon, the rocks and hills of the passes, whose heads touch heaven, they are the least formidable of the difficulties the soldier-merchant has to face. Before he can supply his customers in India with the silk of Bukhâra and the fruits of Afghânistân, or carry back the English calico and muslin for the " soft harems of Herât," he may have to fight a series of small engagements. Scarcely one of this " hard-bitten " race, but carries some record of skirmishes with the Border tribes through whose country he has to pass. Speaking generally, it may be said that south of the Gumal he has to deal with varieties of the Kâkar Pathân, who—disagreeable as he can be at times—by comparison with the Waziri on the north, carries peace in his right hand, and droppeth on the unwary traveller as the gentle rain from heaven. For generations the Waziri has carried on a war to the knife with the Powindah caravans. A day's march is seldom made without some little excitement in van or rear; the cutting off of stragglers, or the plunder of cattle. Occasionally these affrays develop into downright pitched battles, followed by additional exasperation on both sides: and more than once a compromise has been suggested, to take the form of a fixed black mail for the unmolested passage; but the Waziri seems to prefer taking it in the more sporting form of highway robbery. Before discussing his enemies, it may, however, be worth while to halt at the mouth of the pass, and finish dealing with the Powindah himself.

Many of the clans, though classed as Ghilzais, and spoken of as Powindahs, differ entirely in almost every particular. The Nasars, short sturdy men, have practically no country of their own, but pay for the right of grazing equally in the Derajât and the Ghilzai countries, living principally by their flocks and herds. Popularly they are divided into camel-folk, ox and ass-folk, and sheep-folk.

The camel-folk, the Trans-Indus carriers *par excellence*, owning between 30,000 and 40,000 camels, are probably the poorest, the roughest, and the most unkempt. They are largely engaged in carrying salt from the Kohât mines or grain from the Marwat, and are met with at every town along the frontier roads. The ox-folk and the ass-folk are to be seen everywhere, with their oxen and donkeys, carrying earth and bricks, or cutting and selling fuel in every frontier town. The sheep-folk, who are credited with owning some 100,000 sheep, arrive with their flocks about October, grazing them along the foot of the hills, and returning about the end of April. The Kharoties, who come from the hills near the source of the Gumal, are a poor tribe, mainly labourers and carriers, and have been nearly ruined by the luxury of a long-standing feud with their more powerful neighbours, the Sulaimân Khels, which feud is only suspended when they enter British territory, and resumed every year as soon as they re-enter the hills.

The Sulaimân Khels are the most numerous, the most powerful, and the most warlike. Fine, strong, well set-up men who, though they behave well in India, have the reputation of being a very rough set, out of it. They, with their allied clans, are scattered over a great extent of the hilly territory from Peshin nearly as far as Jelâlâbâd. Of those who come down into British territory and bring but little merchandise, many are brokers and merchants on some scale, travelling as far as Calcutta, buying wholesale and selling to other Powindahs, taking back a good deal of their profits in cash. Some of them figured rather prominently in the disturbance that took place near Tânk in 1879, and nearly all the men of the Kirri were wiped out by our troops in suppressing it. Probably the richest of the Powindahs are the Miân Khels, whose summer home is near Panah and Karabagh, east of Ghazni, but who are very closely allied to the tribe of the same name settled within our border at Drâban and Musâzai. In fact, many of the latter have not given up their Powindah life, and every now and then a leading zamindar takes a trip to Kâbul or Bukhâra, while his trading friend from Ghazni acquires an estate on this side the mountains, which his relations look after in his absence. Most of the Bukhâra trade—silk, sheep-skin coats, and drugs—is in their hands. They belong to the Lohâni or Rawâni—from *rawâni*, the Persian for travellers—division of the Ghilzais; they dress better, look better,—having often quite ruddy complexions—live

Mir Alam Khân—A Miân Khel Ghilzai.

better, and behave better than many of their less civilised allies. Neither are they so vulgarly desperate; they do not want for pluck, but are credited with preferring to remonstrate "with all the eloquence of avarice, and bribing with the generosity of smugglers." He may take castles who has nothing to lose, but they are not ashamed to own a preference to leading caravans rather than armies into that profitless breach where the exchange is against all parties.

The Dautanis are a small and unimportant tribe, who have a little strip of country between the Gumal and the Waziri hillmen, but they are almost the only Powindahs who manage to keep on good terms with the latter. They have a comparatively fertile valley, growing rice and serials, are well to do, and also carry on a profitable trade with Bukhâra. The Niâzais trade almost exclusively from Kandahâr in dried fruits and madder. The Tokhis, in former days the most prominent of Ghilzai clans, hold the northern part of the Argundah, with head-quarters in Khelât-i-Ghilzai. The Tarrakkis, who hail from Kandahâr, the Andars from the Shalgar district south of Ghazni, and the Daulatzais, who were the original settlers in Tânk, and founded a family there, are all distinctly *Kâfila* folk, and come only with fighting men and camels. The minor clans may be said to be both numerous and unimportant.

Within the Dera Ismail Khân border, many of the Pathân tribes are more or less closely allied to the Powindahs. In earlier times, traders and graziers came from the hills to the plains, and for one reason or another, a branch of the tribe settled permanently. The Miân Khels have been previously noticed, and a similar process of emigration has taken place all along the line. About the time of Akbar several of the Lohâni clans were driven forward by the Sulaimân Khels; the Marwats who settled in part of the Bannu district and the northern corner of Dera Ismail Khân; the Tatars and Daulat Khels in Tânk. The latter called in the Gandapurs, who are Powindahs though of a lawless and brutalised type, to assist them against the Marwats, with the result of an extensive settlement in the Kulâchi tahsil. Similarly the Bâbars, described by Edwardes as the most superior race Trans-Indus, and whose civilization and intelligence has given rise to a proverb that a Bâbar fool is equal to a Gandapur sage, were pressed out of their holdings by their next neighbours and kinsmen, the

Shirinis, and settled round Chandwân, where they are reported rich, quiet and honest traders.

Regarding the extent of the Powindah trade, no very reliable returns are available. In the Punjab Report to the Secretary of State, it was estimated at Rs. 33,00,000, in 1861, and in 1870 at fifty lakhs.[1] A careful estimate by the settlement officer put the imports as averaging twenty-two lakhs, of which the largest items were fruit, madder, silk, wool, and drugs ; and the exports at nineteen lakhs, the most important items being indigo, cotton-goods, and tea. The chief trade centres beyond our Border are Bokhâra, Kâbul, Kandahâr and Ghazni ; and within it, Dera Ismail Khân, Tânk, and Kulâchi Trans-Indus, with Leiah and Bhakkar Cis-Indus. What effect the extension of the railway to Bhakkar will have on this trade, remains to be seen, but it is probable that the trade is already in excess of the estimated value, and it is certainly capable of very considerable extension. Needless to say a more forward frontier policy, that would ensure a safe route for the caravans, would do wonders in this direction.

[1] Approximately £500,000.

The Flying Throne of Star-taught Sulaimân.
(Facsimile of a Punjâb lithograph.)

CHAPTER IX.

SOLOMON'S THRONE AND THE GUMAL.

ACCORDING to one of the many Muhammadan legends of the place, Solomon, not content with the daughters of Jerusalem, came once to Hindustân to marry a lady named Balkis, a beauty of exceptional fame. As the happy pair were starting back on their honeymoon, seated on a throne—"the flying throne of Star-taught Sulaimân"—carried through the air by genii, the lady begged for a halt to enable her to take one last look at her beloved home. Opportunely they had just arrived over the Takht,[1] and the distinguished author of the Proverbs, desirous of obliging his spouse, directed the genii to scoop out a stand on its top, upon which the throne was placed, and the fair Balkis was able to indulge her fancy for a view of the plain, recently referred to

---

[1] Throne.

as "Dera Dismal." The place is held in much respect, and is quite a fashionable resort of pilgrims, though the shrine—not of Solomon, but of one of the usual "pole stars of guidance, extract of the herbage of religion, crocodile in the ocean of unity" —is some distance north of the true Takht.

The summit of this mountain, which has only recently been mapped by our surveyors, is about the centre of the Shiráni country, a tribe who, with their affiliated clans, extend from our Border to the Zhob river in the west, and north to the Gumal, or rather up to the little bit of no man's land, "the bloody Border" that separates them from the Masaud Waziris. Their main settlements are in the low hills to the east, between which and us run long narrow valleys of the most arid and sterile character right along to the Kasráni country in the south, frequent but narrow gaps like the Gumal, the Zao, the Dráband, and the Dahri, affording egress to the plain. The crest and upper valleys of the Takht are well wooded, though the bulk of the Shiráni country is bare of trees, and exceptionally barren generally. The more settled clans who occupy fixed homesteads and pasture their flocks on the higher slopes, are the most friendly disposed to us; the clans nearest to us, fortunately not numerous, the least so; one or two sections, notoriously lawless, at times given to plundering villages and other malpractices. In the Sikh times they sacked Dráband, and a lot of land was thrown out of cultivation through fear of their attacks. In any other respect they are insignificant; an expedition sent against them in 1853, consisting of 2,500 of the Frontier Force and Military Police, went through the heart of their country, turned their defence, and returned to Dráband without losing a single man. The fighting strength of all the clans does not exceed 3,500, the bulk of whom are desirous of maintaining good relations with us. Since this lesson they have behaved well, but they are even for Patháns, exceptionally democratic, caring nothing for chiefs, and certain of the irreconcilables not even acknowledging the *Jirgah.* Petty thefts in British territory—which the elders admitted but p'eaded their inability to enforce order—necessitated a blockade in 1883, which brought about the fullest submission, and enabled us to carry out the Takht survey in 1884, with the aid of the tribesmen themselves; an event which, considering the intense dislike of all Pathâns to any survey, was considered one of the greatest triumphs of our Border policy.

Generally of middling stature, with bold features and high cheek bones, the men of the Shirâni clans are active, hardy, wild, and manly, but distinctly inferior in fighting capacity to the Waziris. For dress, the poorer tribesmen have seldom more than one coarse blanket round the waist, and another over the shoulders The chief probably adds an exceptionally dirty linen shirt, baggy Pathân trousers, and the greasy puggaree that secures his straggling black ringlets is surmounted by a dingy gold cap. His large thick canoe-shaped shoes were once decorated with red and gold; while if below the sheep-skin *posteen* that covers other things besides a multitude of sins, he can run to a garment of Multân silk, he is a buck of the most magnificent type. A curved sword, an old English double-barrelled pistol, and a powder horn complete the picture of the Shirâni on the war-path, who if he live up in the highlands calls himself a Burgas, in contradistinction to the Lurgas who lives in the valley. As a tribe, they are exceptionally poor; many are employed as servants by the Bârbars and Miân Khels in our territory. They marry late in life, and unlike other Pathâns, the father of the bride gives a dowry, instead of receiving a price for his daughter. They have also a sort of local Providence, who receives tithes in kind, is called *Nika*, or "grandfather," the chosen head of the oldest family. Money, as with many other people, is said to be scarce; perhaps, exceptionally so, as their trade is mainly carried on by barter. Their principal employment is agriculture, and this is impossible without irrigation. They have few horses, absolutely no camels, and no great wealth of cattle. Except fuel, of which the Takht supplies plenty, they do not seem to have much to keep out the cold : up on the heights they cut their houses out of the hill sides, and close the entrance at night with the branch of a thorny tree. All the trade which they have is with British territory, where many of the tribe are every year located, and they are dependent on us for many of the necessaries of life.

There can be no doubt that they would be infinitely better off if they were brought entirely under our rule, encouraged to settle in large numbers in the plains, helped a little in the matter of irrigation and capital for the purposes of trade ; and though the altitude of the Takht is probably too great to be useful as a strategic position, it would be valuable as a sanitarium. Its fine climate, magnificent pine forests, and grand scenery, would make it a much more pleasant hot weather station than the cantonment of Dera Ismail Khân. It is somewhat difficult of access, water is scarce at certain seasons of the year, at least our troops found it so, but this would be remedied by the construction of reservoirs, while the occupation of such a position would go a long way to securing a good trade-route with the valleys of the Gumal and the Zhob.

South of the Shirâni country the main watershed is held by a variety of wild tribes, of which the Usterânas, so called after a holy Sayud who married into the Shirânis, are the chief. Their lands are mainly across the Border, in villages just beyond the passes in the low outer hills, though large numbers of them are now regularly settled in the plains within it. Until about a century ago, they were entirely a pastoral or *Powindah* people, when a quarrel with the Musa Khels forced a number of them to take to agriculture. Their country is very barren and sandy, depending entirely on rain water, but they are fine well set-up men, quiet and orderly, many enlisting in our army and police.

Others are said to be venturesome traders, dealing largely in cattle, and travelling anywhere, from Bengal to Kandahâr. They are divided into two main clans, the one who wear their hair long, like a Biloch, and the other who cut it short; and, as between the Cavalier and Roundhead, a deadly and bloody feud exists.

Eastward of these two large tribes, and between them and the Zhob river, are the Isots and the Zamârais, two small tribes of nomad Pathâns of Kâkar origin : neither are of much importance and are both reported quiet and inoffensive, not extensive traders, but in the main dependent on their relations with us for the little trade they have. A handful of fakirs, called the Haripals, on the western side of the Takht, depend on the Shirânis ; and another settlement, the descendants of Shaikh Haider, are located at Zirkanni, the eastern entrance to the pass, a village which is a great burying-place of the Powindahs. Beyond the Zhob, and between the river and the Ghilzai country, are the Mandu-Khels, another off-shoot of the Kâkars, a fairly peaceful and agricultural community, but who rarely come down to trade with us. All of these are more or less favourable to British interests, and a large proportion of the people may be said to be well under British influence. The pass known as the Gumal, and for the opening of which negotiations under Sir Robert Sandeman seem progressing so successfully, takes its name from the village and the valley on the Tânk border, though the stream called the Gumal higher up, bears other names along its length, and finally becomes the Luni in Dera Ismail Khân. It is popularly associated wtih the Powindah traders just described, and regarded merely as the doorway of Ghazni. Really it is a highway of the greatest strategic as well as commercial importance, for after winding through the Sulaimân range to Kajuri-Kach—the plain of palms, though there are no palms, and no plain beyond a stony river bed—or to where the Gumal and Zhob streams join, the road bifurcates ; that along the last-named river leading by two important routes west and south-west to Peshin and Kandahár, the other continuing north-west along the Gumal proper to Ghazni. Up to the junction, the whole has been mapped a railway survey being actually commenced, and the route traversing the Zhob valley towards Peshin is also pretty well known. Leading more or less into this, are passes like the Shaikh-Haider, the Dráband, and the Dahna which again communicate with one another through the lateral valleys described by Major Holdich as a peculiarity not merely of the Takht, but of the range. The Dráband is even a more direct pass than the Gumal, but some lengths where nature has torn a passage through the terrific limestone gorges are at times all but impracticable. The Dahna is said to be now little better, though both it and the Shaikh Haider or Zao have at times been used as the main caravan routes.

The upper part of the western route is less known. For some distance it traverses the Zhob valley, whence it crosses into the Kundil, follows it to the head, and across the watershed separating the Gumal and Helmund drainages, to Maruf, an important place, forty miles from Khelát-i-Ghilzai.

The north-western branch, after getting clear of the Masaud Waziris, traverses the country of the Sulaimán Khel Ghilzais, across the Kohnak range by the Sarwandi Kotal, which has an elevation of about 7,500 feet, into Katawáz and the Shilgar country to Ghazni. The Powindah trade which follows this last route is mainly, if not almost exclusively, in the hands of Ghilzai clans like the Sulaimán Khels, Kharotes and Naisirs, who occupy the plains south and east of the Ab-i-Istáda, and the Indian side of the above-mentioned range. It may be doubted if any considerable portion of the trade comes from countries very distant beyond this range, but if it does, it is all carried by these enterprising clans, whose doings have already been described.

The more immediate want in the care of the Gumal, so soon

as the necessary tribal arrangements have been completed, is the construction of a thoroughly good military road, adapted for all arms of the service, by the Zhob valley to Peshin, one that would be even more valuable for the Kandahár position than that just opened from Dera Ghâzi Khân by Fort Monroe. The

On the Road to Quetta.

opening out of a subsidiary route to Maruf and Khelât-i-Ghilzai would necessarily follow, while the third desideratum would be a good trade route through the Sulaimân country to Ghazni. This third road, whether railway communication should hereafter be extended by the Dawar valley to Ghazni, or by the

Khaiber direct to Kábul, would be invaluable as a flank protection, but as a railway route it must take a place second to either.

North of the No-man's Land referred to as bordering the Gumal Pass, we have to deal with a much more powerful people, and the Waziris are among the most troublesome of all the border tribes. The most important of the divisions of these, are the Mahsud Waziris, whose territory only abuts on ours at the extreme end of the Gumal Valley by the Urmán Pass, though the main road to this country is through the Tánk Pass by Jandola, the remainder being shut off by the hill Bitannis. It will therefore be convenient to refer to the latter first, and reserve the Waziris and Waziristân for subsequent notice.

The Bitannis, or descendants of Bitan, the third son of Kais or Kesh—the distinguished Afghân, who is said to have gone to Medina and brought back the true faith, and to be responsible for founding all the existing Afghân tribes—are our neighbours for forty miles, or from the Gumal Valley to the Gabar mountain in the Bannu district. Till some fifty years ago, they lived wholly in the hills, but have now spread in numbers into the Tánk plain; and one of the three principal clans hold considerable lands there. The range separating Tánk from the Marwat is also called after them, as far as the sanitarium of Shaikh Budin. On the west they are hemmed in by the Waziris, who have necessarily to pass through their territory to reach our border. The two are generally more or less at feud though until recently the Bitanni was always ready to assist the Waziri when any robbery was afoot in our direction. In spite of their family pedigree, they are only just emerging from barbarism, their hill possessions are stony and uncultivated, their villages small, often hidden away in hollows, their houses mere hovels of mud and brushwood. Wiry and active, they have still a reputation for stupidity and thriftlessness. "A hundred Bitannis will eat a hundred sheep" is a country-side joke. Inveterate thieves when opportunity offers, they have been more frequently employed as spies and guides, abetting theft by their more powerful neighbours, and have earned the title of "the Jackals to the Waziris." The fighting strength of all the clans is probably not much in excess of 3,000 men, and their villages are entirely at our mercy. For a long time they were more or less ill-conditioned, but their acceptance in 1875 of the pass responsibility, has changed the character of that part of the Border, and for some years the Waziri lion has been restrained, and the Bitanni jackal has given no cause for complaint.

CHAPTER X.

ACCORDING to most Oriental historians, the Afghâns believe themselves descended from the Jews, if not actually from the lost tribes. They were carried into captivity together, shared their lot, but subsequently escaped and found refuge in Arsareth, which some would identify as the modern Hazârah. Their own traditions refer to Syria as their original home, whence they were carried away by Nebuchadnezzar, and planted in different parts of Persia and Media, from whence again they moved eastward into the mountains of Ghor, and long after to Kâbul and Kandahâr. They claim that they were in Ghor, east of Hirât, when the Prophet Muhammad arose in the seventh century. One of the most reliable of the Persian histories certainly mentions a people, called Bani Israil, as settled there when Chenghiz Khân conquered it in the thirteenth century. The weight of authority is in favour of their Semitic origin. There is a great likeness between the features of the Afghân and the Jew; in many cases it is so striking that the two could hardly be distinguished, but the same might perhaps be said of certain Kashmiris and others who are in no way connected with the Afghâns. The use of Jewish names is so common that some of their genealogies might be mistaken for chapters taken out of Genesis, but going back to the early tribal names, the comparison does not hold good. The tribes of purest blood have some peculiar customs, particularly suggestive of the old Levitical law. The Passover-like practice of sacrificing an animal, and smearing the doorway to avert calamity, the offering up of sacrifices, the stoning to death of blasphemers, the periodical distribution 'of land by lot, the rites of circumcision, purification, &c., of which the last two are no doubt common to Muhammadans generally.

On the other hand, their language, the hard northern Pukhtu or the soft southern Pushtu, is on all hands declared to have nothing in common with the Hebrew or Chaldaic, but is allied to the Aryan, and a branch of the Persian stock. Opinion is divided, all the learning is against the theory, more especially with the savants who have no acquaintance with the people; while those who know them best, appear to have a sneaking feeling, that however absurd the fictions of the Afghán genealogist and historian may be, they contain material which by patient study may hereafter assist to a sound conclusion. Their traditions, oral and written, persist in tracing their descent from Saul, or *Talút,* the King of Israel, celebrated not less for his wisdom than his mightiness in war. The "*Malik,*" who from the shoulders and upwards was higher than any of his people. The story is worth telling in their own style.

It is, says the erudite Niámat Ullah, well known to every intelligent, learned and accomplished scholar, that the reason why nothing has ever been satisfactorily recorded by those who explore notable events and elucidate novel facts in any book or history relating to the early Afghán nation, its tribes, and their conversion to Islám, is partly because, ever since the time that Musa. the interpreter of the All-Wise, vanquished Fharo, and since Bukhta-n-nasr, the great magician expelled and exterminated the Coptes, and was permitted to subjugate Sham (Palestine), to raze Jerusalem, and vanquish Bani Isrâil, they have been continually living amongst mountains and deserts, without any science gaining ground among them, except Islâmism and the five pillars of practice ; and partly because, since the time of "*Mâlik*," Sârul, surnamed Twâlut, " the prince of stature," their great ancestor, through whose tribe of Ibnyamin, their pedigree ascends by Yacoob, Isaâk, Ibrahim, to Nuh and Adam, "the chosen of God," down as late as the time of Sultan Behlol Lodi's accession to the throne of Ind, no one amongst them raised himself to sovereignty and became a monarch ; and it is only under mighty sovereigns the rose-grove of erudition, and the pearls of eloquence, which go to make up such compositions, are enabled to flourish.

But those who have preserved traditions, and committed to memory the transactions of ancient times, relate there was a descendant of Ibnyamin-bin Yacoob, called Kais or Kesh, the whole of whose inheritance from his father and his uncle consisted of four sheep. Kais had a son, a choice young man, whose name was Sârul, but by reason of tallness he was called Tawâlut, and besides looking after the four sheep he kept an ass and fetched water from the Nile. Two of the sheep once went astray, and while Tawâlut looked for them, he fell in with a young man of the tribe of Lâwi, named Ismâel, who forthwith anointed Tawâlut's head with oil from a horn, which instantly assumed the appearance of a crown ; and saluted him as *Mâlik*, and king over Bani Isrâel. Sârul married into the tribe of Lâwi, two wives, by one of whom he had a daughter, subsequently married to Daud, the youngest of a family of twelve sons, who had distinguished himself so greatly in the wars with the Amálika tribe, that he had been entrusted with the uncontrolled administration of the most important affairs of the kingdom, and ultimately succeeded Sârul on the throne. Of these two wives, were also born in the same hour, immediately after their father's death, two sons, Barakiah and Iramiah. Daud treated the two afflicted widows with great kindness, and subsequently entrusted to each of the two sons the government of a tribe; so that by the divine favour they were promoted to a high state, bore on the arena the ball of bravery and fortitude, and every army they led on, was by their able conduct, visited by the breeze of victory and triumph. Such proof of superiority and bravery induced Daud to grant to them exalted positions. Barakiah became prime minister, and Iramiah commander-in-chief, and by their prudent conduct, universal welfare reigned from tribe to tribe, and the cultivation and population of towns and villages increased ten-fold. Each of them was in his time blessed with an accomplished son, the former named his Assaf, and the latter called his Afghâna. After the death of their respective fathers, both filled the same important positions under the government of Sulaimân the son of Daud. Afghâna also superintending the building of the Bait-ul-Makaddas, or temple at Jerusalem, which Daud had commenced, and which by the care and labour of Afghâna was brought to completion.

After this, their descendants multiplied exceedingly; Assaf having eighteen sons, and Afghâna forty. And when Azrail, the angel of death, stood forth on the part of the Great Pardoner, and saluting Sulaimân, bore his soul to Heaven, before he had even time to take leave of Balkis : no tribe of Bani Israêl equalled them.

Time passed, and when the All-Powerful permitted Bukhtu-n-nasr to subjugate the territories of Sham, and required Bani Israêl to worship him as a God, the tribe of Afghâna adhered to the religion of their forefathers, on account of which, after great struggles and persecution they were vanquished, and had to seek shelter in the mountainous districts of Kohistân-i-Ghor, and Kohistân-i-Faroza; where the tribes of Assaf and Afghâna fixed their habitation, continually increasing and making war on the heathen infidels around them, most of whom they put to death; extending their borders to Kohistân-i-Kâbul Kandahâr, and Ghazni. At the same time part of them sought shelter in Arabia, remarking to each other, that, being prohibited the temple of Daud and Sulaimân, they ought not to neglect that founded by Ibrahim. With this view they took up their residence in the vicinity of Mecca, where they paid homage and obedience to the Compassionate, the Merciful.

Fifteen hundred years after Sulaimân's time, the sun of Muhammad's beauty—upon whom be peace—arose and illumined the darkness by the directing light of Islâm, and all the nobles of the Arabs resorted to the Majesty, and received the blessing, a small number only of stubborn people preferring to oppose it. Nine years after the light of Muhammad's countenance had appeared in the place of Ibrahim, a fellow Israelite, named Khalil, "the sword of God," son of Walid—who had become a firm adherent of the standard of Islâm, and whose descendants are to this day called Khalidi Afghâns (and are represented on our border by the Bangash tribe)—sent a letter to the Afghâns in the mountains of Ghor, informing them of the appearance of the last of the Prophets.

On the receipt of Khalil's letter several of the chiefs of Ghor departed for Madina, the mightiest of whom, and of the Afghân people, was one Kais, whose pedigree extends by thirty-seven degrees to Sârul, forty-five to Ibrahim, and 603 to Adam. As soon as the party arrived they were, under Khalil's guidance, enabled to become adherents of the Prophet, who lavished all sorts of blessings upon them, changed their Hebrew names for Arabic — Kais becoming Abdu-r-rashid, the "servant of the Wise;" and promised that the title of *Mâlik* bestowed on their great ancestor should never depart from them. As they were about to leave, he conferred upon Kais, the additional title of Pathân, which in the Syrian language signifies rudder, and drew a simile —revealed to him by the Angel Gabriel—comparing Kais to the pilot of his countrymen in the Faith, the rudder being the part of the ship which steers it in the way it should go. So successfully did Abdu-r rashid, the Pathân, steer the ship of faith, that within a few years from his return to Ghor, a large proportion of the nation had, by the divine pleasure, become Muhammadans [or had accelerated their descent to Hell], and amongst them rose up dervishes, devotees and saints, excelling in both deed and speech. There rose up also a great posterity to Kesh, who had married the daughter of Khalid, and by whom he was blessed with three sons, of whom he called the eldest Sarbun, the second Baitan and the third Ghurghusht; from each of whom descended sons and tribes on such a scale as to pass all conception.

The worthy Khwâjah proceeds to relate—In the name of God, the All Merciful! The Almighty of his universal sovereignty presents Sarbun, son of Pathân, with two sons. Sharkhbun and Kurshbun. * * * *

But it is necessary here to part company with Niâmat Ullah and his friends; the distinguished friends who supported him by their amiable kindness and consummate erudition, who collected and arranged the scattered and confused genealogies, and from the mines of Ahmedian records made schemes for authentic histories—repositories of unparalleled value, but also of unparalleled length

From these sons of Kais the whole of the Afghân tribes—some 400 *Zais* and *Khels*—claim to have sprung. The Afghâns proper, from Peshawur to Kandahâr, are credited to the two sons of Sarbun: from five sons of the first are said to have sprung the Abdális or Durránis, the Tarins, Shirânis, and Khetrâns. From the second, fused perhaps with the ancient Ghandâris, the Yusafzais, Muhammadzais, Mohmands, Daudzais, and many others in the plains round Peshawur. From Baitan's daughter and her Persian lover, all the Ghilzais, the Lodis, and the Suris, which two last gave dynasties to India. While from the three sons of Ghurghusht, with probably a large admixture of Turk and Sythic stock, combined with a dash of Jat and Rajput, are descended all the Pathâns proper, the Kákars, Waziris, Shitaks, Turis, Khattaks, Afridis, and others.

Some of these last have special traditions of their own, and though Pukhtuns are not included among the Afgháns, or only by adoption, they probably belonged to much the same stock, but for one reason or other remained much longer unconverted to Muhammadanism. The most numerous and powerful are generally included under the term Karrhai, or Karralâni. Divided into as many *Khels* and *Zais* as the others, they have just as many legends as to how they came by the name, but in regard to which the Afghán saying for all doubtful cases eminently applies— Wa-illáhu 'alam, "God only knows" the truth.

The terms Afghán and Pathán are however apt to be misleading. In India all Pushtu-speaking-people are called "Pathán," —though the Highlanders among them were sometimes spoken of as "Rohilla"—from *Roh* or *Koh*, a mountain. Even their country has only within comparatively modern times come to be called Afghánistán, it was originally a part of Khurasán, and there the people more generally speak of themselves by the name of their clan, as Durrâni, or Ghilzai, but all admit to being Pukhtâns, and are proud of it, and it is from this word that the Hindustâni corruption of "Pathán" is derived. By no means all the Pathâns who reside in Afghánistán are Afgháns, any more than the English or Scotch settled in Ireland are Irish, though they are generally called so. And as Scotchmen, Irishmen, and Welshmen, who— some of them—speak English, are called collectively Englishmen; so quite a number of vastly dissimilar people who speak Pukhtu, are included under the term Pukhtûn or Pathán.

In Hindustân the title is assumed by all sorts of mongrels, whose claim to it is no better founded than the Eurasian, who describes himself as European. But on the Border, a Pathán is so called by virtue of his language, and if he be a resident in the territory of the Amir, he may be called Afghán, however doubtful his descent from Afghána.

Sulaimán Khel (Ghilzai) Horse-dealers.

CHAPTER XI.

THE FRONTIER SWITZERLAND.

BETWEEN the " Bloody Border " at the base of Solomon's throne, and the snowy peaks of the Sufed Koh, or " white mountains," lies the great country of Waziristán—the Switzerland of the north-west frontier. A land of high and difficult hills, deep and rugged defiles, brave and hardy people, in their way as independent and patriotic, and in the presence of the common enemy, hardly less united, than the famous compatriots of Tell. Geographically and politically, the two have several points in common; and as regards the mass of hills that lie between the Gumal and the Tochi or Dawar valley, of which Kanigurum, the stronghold of the most powerful of the Waziri tribes, is about the centre, this is more especially true. The east front is protected by the bare hills held by the Bitannis; beyond which ravines, flanked by precipitous cliffs, which occasionally widen out to enclose small valleys fairly fertile, from one hundred to one thousand yards wide, but narrowing again as they ascend. Not unfrequently the mouth is a mere gorge or *tangi*,[1] where the water forces its way through a range crossing it at right angles, and forming a colossal natural barrier. In these valleys, and the small strips of alluvial land which border the base of the higher mountains, locally called "*kaches*"—which are quite a distinctive feature of the whole range—there is often a good deal of cultivation, the whole carefully terraced and irrigated by means of channels cut out of the hill sides, a great deal of ingenuity and skill being expended in leading the water from field to field. The edges of the fields, which correspond with the side of the watercourse, are planted with mulberry and willows, the houses of the owners being perched picturesquely on the slopes above. Lower down, where the valley narrows to the *tangi*, paved with rough boulders and stones—difficult enough in ordinary times, but probably filled by a roaring torrent in the rains—the Waziri has been provided by nature with the most magnificent defensive position, the valleys behind furnishing a camping-ground and a base of supplies. Until the Dawar Valley is reached, there are no passes leading directly through the country, though the Tank Zam from Dera Ismail Khân, and the Shakdu and Kaisor from Bannu, afford access to the heart of it. From the west it is even less accessible, and practically it has always been independent of Kábul. Secure in a long line of mountain fastnesses, possessing considerable natural resources, and with constitutions that would enable them to live where most other people would starve, the Waziris could probably not be dislodged by any force which the Amir is able to detail against them. Even in our case, advancing from our adjacent frontier-lines, it took nearly 7,000 men, and

---

[1] Literally, *waist*.

cost us over 350 lives, to get to Kanigurum in 1860, though the whole country could, if necessary, be dominated by us without much difficulty.

The inhabitants of these mountain homes are essentially a self-governed people; they are eminently a fighting people, but still more essentially and eminently are they a thieving people. From the comparatively civilised Darwesh of Bannu—who, if he cannot steal a pony, will take a bicycle—to the ruder Mahsud, described as the earliest, most inveterate, and most incorrigible robber of all, this characteristic is the most prominent; and they are proud of it. Every true man's apparel fits your Waziri. The travelling Powindah is his oyster, and he is ready on every opportunity, sword in hand, to open the latter's bales, to cut his throat, and to "convey" rather than "steal" his goods back to the passes. They are the most numerous, and in spite of intertribal feuds, probably the most united, of all our north-west tribes. Of blood feuds and family feuds they have many—these are luxuries it would be un-reasonable to expect any Pathân tribe to give up—but their very democratic arrangements, observed in the distribution of lands amongst the various sections, and the manner in which these sections and their sub-divisions are scattered over the face of the country, have contributed to make any formidable intertribal feuds more uncommon. And it is to this, added to the natural strength of its position, that Waziristân is not a little indebted for its independence. Taking into account all those who would be classed as Waziris, their united tribal strength would be in excess of 40,000 fighting men. A contingent that, when the quality is taken into consideration, would be no mean addition to the re-sources of ourselves, or—and the problem is worthy the consider-ation of the "Backward School"—of our enemies.

Tribally, the Waziri is split up into the usual complication of branches, sections, divisions, and sub-divisions, the enumeration of which would be clearly a multiplying of words without-knowledge.

Nor would it be profitable to try and work out the descent of Wazir-bin-Sulaimân from Saul or even Kais, to the various Musas, Mahmuds, and Mahsuds, whose names are still borne by the clans. By far the most important of the main branches are the Darwesh Khels and the Mahsuds. A few representatives of tribes like the Lalais extend up to the slopes of the Safed Koh, or Spinjah, as the Waziris would call what they say was the original home from whence they came, and some of the Gurbaz reside on the borders of Khost, but no great numbers are located north of the Kurram. The Darwesh Khels consist of two great sections, the Utmanzais and the Ahmadzais; again split into divisions and sub-divisions, important enough from a tribal point of view, but which there is no reason to particularise. The first sections are mainly on the right bank of the Kurram, occupying the hills between the Khost and Dawar Valleys. Some cultivate lands within our border, and others regularly come in to trade. Another division, the Kâbul Khels, are extremely wild and lawless, ready to join with any one in mischief and devilry, and have, as the Frontier Reports put it, "given a good deal of trouble;" an expression somewhat comprehensive—as for instance, it covers the fact, that in one year, they made twenty raids, finishing up with a murderous attack on some Bannuchi villages, some fourteen of which they sacked and burnt. In return for which Nicholson—whose name by the way is now as a household god among them—penetrated with 1,500 men into the heart of their country and retaliated in kind on their villages. Subsequently, in 1859, they came in for a second expedition all to themselves, under Chamberlain, the punishment for an audacious attack on Bahader Khel and the Salt-mines. The Ahmadzai branch are mainly on the left bank of the Kurram, north of Bannu, though probably there are now nearly as many residing within our border as beyond it. On the banks of the Kurram, and the Kaitu, which flows into it, both enjoy broad tracts of rich soil, and the hills which surround them, whose jagged walls conceal many a grassy slope, afford good pastures for their camels and flocks. Their proper settlements, if they can be said to have any, are up on the higher spurs; but of regular villages they have few, residing mainly in *kirris* or encampments, sometimes protected with a wall of loose stones, often merely stout woollen blankets stretched over curved sticks, which, like the Irish cabins, are shared with their cattle and the family camel, and guarded by the family dogs of a particularly large and fierce breed. The most permanent thing they ever possess are the tribal graveyards, which are scattered over most hill sides, and are perhaps the only places they hold sacred. The boldest thief among them will keep his sacrilegious hands off any property deposited among the tombs. The lands of both sections of the Darwesh Khels extend moreover all round the Tochi or Dawar valley, though not into it; the inhabitants of that valley being, curiously enough, almost a distinct race, greatly inferior in physique, in morals, and in courage; and considering the intense contempt in which a Dawari is held by the Waziris, and the small scruple the latter usually has regarding his neighbour's landmark, why they have permitted so important a highway through their country to remain in what might fairly be considered alien hands, is a somewhat curious problem.

Something will be said hereafter about the Dawaris and the Tochi, a route of the greatest importance to us, but to dispose first of our Waziri friends, and the most important and powerful branch of all, the Mahsuds, whose country around Kanigurum has already been referred to. These are sub-divided into three main sections, the Bahlolzai, the Alizai and the Shaman Khel; the first-named being probably *facile princeps* in the noble profession of robber; and as robbery is—unless it be done on a sufficiently large scale—opposed to the policy of the British Government, they are consequently our most inveterate foes. In this respect it is unnecessary to institute any comparison between the dwellers in Waziristân and those in the Swiss Alps. The boast of the former, that, while kingdoms and dynasties have passed away, they alone, of all the Afghán tribes, have remained free, and that the armies of kings have failed to penetrate their strongholds, might strike a chord of sympathy; but they continue in a strain most reprehensible, to the effect that they know no law or will but their own, and from generation to generation the plain country has provided them with a fair hunting-ground for plunder. The merry Switzer, wiser in his generation, contents himself by taking it out of the traveller in the form of hotel bills.

Even the Bahlolzais have, however, had to modify this boast. A series of raids filled up the measure of their iniquities, and in 1860, General Chamberlain forced his way into the heart of their country to Kanigurum and Makin, and burned the latter. On one or two other occasions the whole Mahsuds were blockaded, and paid down a cash indemnity, giving hostages for the observance of the terms imposed on them. Posts were established within the passes of the Bitanni country, and offences effectually checked for years. In 1879, instigated by emissaries from Kábul, or excited by our proceedings in the Kábul Valley, they became discontented again, and finally, amongst other tribes, came down in force and fired the town of Tánk. This led to an expedition under General Kennedy being sent against them in 1881, and they again found that not even their most distant glens, or wildest and pathless hills could protect them from punishment; and they ultimately accepted the greatest humiliation a Pathán clan can suffer, surrendering some half-dozen of their proscribed ringleaders, and sending eighty hostages to reside in Dera Ismail Khán. One of the ringleaders died in Lahore, and the rest were, in consideration of their furnishing an escort to our survey parties in the Gumal, and their general good behaviour, released in 1884.

Physically, they are a fine race, tall, muscular and courageous, in many respects noble savages. Desperate in their forays, never sparing an enemy of the male sex, even if he be but a Ghilzai boy

—nor does the Ghilzai ever let off a Waziri when he catches him—the Waziri is, on the other hand, so far chivalrous, he will never kill or rob women. He rather prides himself on a certain gallantry in this respect. Like other Pathâns, the whole people are given to hospitality : guests are welcomed by the men and women present in the village, with the greeting "*harkalarshee*," "may you come always" and entertained according to rank. They are generally ignorant, illiterate and superstitious, with dangerously little learning, and show great reverence for *Mullahs*, *Akhunds* and holy men of all sorts, who write charms, read incantations, enjoy alms and pilgrimages, and prescribe for ailments greatly to their own profit. For most complaints the prescription is uniform and simple, and merely consists of enveloping the patient in the skin of a newly-killed sheep until he perspires freely, which, combined with a strong purgative, dry bread and a good climate and constitution, answers as well as anything else.

But unlike other Pathâns, they are credited with some regard for honour, and, still more remarkable, with comparative truthfulness. Many of the Waziri customs are also peculiar to themselves. For adultery they kill the woman, but cut off the nose of the man, though in some cases the lady apparently escapes with the lesser punishment. Their women do not cover their faces, but live freely with the men. The bridegroom gives a dower to the bride's father, in other words buys his wife ; the cost of an eligible young lady ranging from Rs. 60 to Rs. 150 ; but this does not prevent her having fifty or sixty bridesmaids, who bring double that number of young men, and indulge in a regular flare-up, including a dance with a liberal drum-accompaniment. Contrary to the usual rule about the avenging of blood feuds, the Waziri greybeard of ancient times ruled that the actual murderer must be the only victim ; thus avoiding many of those ramified feuds and indiscriminate vengeance where a blood account-current is handed down for generations from father to son ; and it ultimately becomes almost impossible to strike a balance.　Again, the "make up money," or pecuniary commutation, has been fixed in the case of Waziri lives at exceptionally high rates.　The fixed price for a Waziri, for instance, is Rs. 1,300, half of which must be in cash and the other half in produce or commodities, including two girls at Rs. 100

Darwesh Khel Waziris.

each.　A woman can be killed for half price, or Rs. 650 and a *langi* or silk scarf of Rs. 50.　The cost of a limb which permanently incapacitates a man is compensated for by a payment of Rs. 500 ; and this is the cost of an eye.　The tariff for sword-wounds is apportioned much in the same way as cuts on a club billiard-cloth, and at very nearly the same rates—Rs. 12-8 for the first half-inch.   But it costs Rs. 250 to cut off a nose—by mistake of the Waziri Baron Cresswell presumably—Rs. 100 for an ear, and so on, down a scale it would be tedious to extend.

The moral to be pointed in connection with the Waziris is however, less their ethnological peculiarities, than the fact of the importance of so large, warlike, and independent a people on our immediate border, a people that cannot be left out of consideration when military interests are at stake.   It is notorious that, two or three years ago, the agents of the Amir were doing their utmost to gain over the Mahsuds to surrender their independence, permit posts to be built in their hills, and to pay even the most nominal tithes.   So far without success, and as matters now stand Waziristân is particularly open to British influence, which we could extend without in any way complicating our relations with Kâbul. An opportunity that would certainly cease if at any time Kâbul garrisons were posted in strong positions in the country; and without some active interference on our part, it is quite within the bounds of possibility that Kâbul persistence may establish such a position.

CHAPTER XII.

THE PRICE OF BLOOD.

Whether Ban-i-Afghân and Ban-i-Israil are identical, or whether Ars-areth, where the ten tribes carried into captivity ultimately found refuge, represents the modern Hazârah country, or no, there is no doubt that all the race, Afghân or Pathân, has, among other Jewish practices, customs, traditions, and laws, followed pretty closely to the old Levitical idea of a "life for a life, an eye for an eye, a tooth for a tooth, hand for hand, foot for foot." The rudest form of this principle of retaliatory justice is probably practised among the "Children of Joseph" in Yusafzai. There it is applied to all sorts of offences. If A steals B's property, B is at liberty to lay hands on similar property belonging to any member of A's clan. Any of the latter may be called upon to "pay forfeit," as they call it, for A's misconduct. If A outruns the constable, and gets into debt to B, the latter, by the same summary process, can recover from any of the debtor's clan. Should A kill B's ox, and the tribal council cannot arrange matters, B's remedy is to kill an ox of A's. Finally, if A kill B, the council must hand over the former to the heirs and assigns of the murdered man, to be dealt with. Not to so hand him over is to ensure a lasting blood-feud between the two families or clans, which may run on from generation to generation, and finally defy all attempts at a settlement.

It may happen that B's next of kin is away, perhaps soldiering in a British regiment. He will have to come up to his commanding Officer with a story of " urgent private affairs," take leave, go away home again, kill A or one of his clan : and, having thus " put his house in order," rejoin, proudly conscious of having done his duty to his country. The Yusafzais are particularly notorious for following the law literally, and avoiding compromise. The majority of them are pretty sure to have been mixed up in some affair of the kind.

In Swât there are some curious varieties of procedure. If B's property has been stolen, he can call upon A, or any one he suspects, from C to Z, to give him a *Sayad;* that is the suspect must produce a respectable person to swear that he is not guilty, which, if he succeeds in doing, B must accept that as sufficient evidence of innocence. Should the *Sayad* not be forthcoming to take the needful oath, A is guilty, and B can treat him accordingly. Another is even a more simple, and certainly ought to be an effective, method of binding disputants over to keep the peace. It is simply to expel both from the place; deprive them of all civil rights, wife, children, home and property, which in some cases are confiscated altogether, and leave them to the charity of other villages, until they can come to an accommodation or reconciliation. The rule is more particularly applicable to the village headmen, but in spite of it, these are the people almost constantly at feud with one another.

Revenge may, as Bacon says, be a kind of wild justice, and though this particular form of it was enjoined by Moses, it is not particularly profitable. If a man cause a blemish in his neighbour, it is perhaps equitable to do the same for him again ; but to go for the particular eye for eye, or tooth for tooth, besides being unprofitable, must on occasions have been highly inconvenient ; and if not to the early Israelite, it seems to have soon occurred to the practical-minded Pathân, to reduce the damages to a money value,

I

and assess all kinds of hurt, from murder downwards, in rupees. The idea of "blood-money" is familiar everywhere in Afghânistân, and, in one form or other, is common to all the Border Pathâns. Among the Western Afghâns, says Elphinstone, a murder can be compromised by giving twelve young women; six with dowries and six without. Ordinarily, among the common people, the dowry would be about sixty rupees each, partly payable in goods. For the loss of a hand, an ear or a nose, the tariff is six women; for breaking a tooth three women (surely an excessive charge, even against a dentist); for a wound above the forehead one; but for a hurt below the forehead, unless it take a year to heal, an apology would be held sufficient. Nearer our Border, the people prefer more cash and fewer young women, and the aggrieved may, if he or his relations happen to be very much married already, or he prefer it, stipulate for the whole in cash.

With the Barzai division of the Mohmands, the fine for murder is Rs. 1,200, the same as for the abduction of a married woman, two-thirds of which goes to the husband or the victim's heirs and one-third to the village council. If it is not paid, the offender is expatriated. Besides this, his relations have to pay Rs. 100 to free themselves of responsibility for the action of their relative, and to insure the council a feast. Widow abduction is only half as expensive. A gunshot wound is costly, Rs. 600, but to own a gun is a luxury naturally reserved for the well-to-do. To keep a sword, like the old-fashioned classification of the man who kept a gig, is "respectable," and to wound with it, costs a Mohmand Rs. 100, a dagger-stab is Rs. 50; and a plebeian blow with a stone is only Rs. 25.

The Mahsud Waziris on one occasion, by way of showing their anxiety to conclude a treaty of peace with us, while expressing their regret that they could not guarantee us against occasional thefts and raids and consequent unavoidable injury to individuals, specified that our Government should be at liberty on all occasions to indemnify itself by looting their *káfilas* of merchandise on a regular scale! Their scale laid down Rs. 600 for all items of blood-money, Rs. 200 for all arms, legs, or blows equal to the loss of a limb, and a sliding-scale for minor injuries; offering to give us hostages to see the arrangement fairly carried out. The Kuki Khels paid a fine of Rs. 3,000 for the murder of a British officer rather than produce the murderer. And when the Utman Khels killed our coolies on the Swât Canal works at Abazai, and the compensation was adjusted after Cavagnari and Battye had surprised their villages, they agreed in addition to a fine, to " blood-money " at the rate of Rs. 200 for each coolie killed, and Rs. 100 for each coolie wounded who recovered. " To eight coolies killed at Rs. 200, and twenty-two coolies damaged at Rs. 100," was the bill actually paid.

None of the tribes, however, can come near the Waziri for system in matters of this kind. He, or his forbears, long ago codified the " customary law," and his " Criminal Code " dates back 300 years. The provisions of it are, in their way, a study, and refer to (1) offences against the person ; (2) against property ; (3) by or relating to women ; with provisions for taking oaths, trial by ordeal, and measures for enforcing them. Murder is classified according to the weapon or means used. A bullet, a knife, a dagger, a blow from a stone, strangling or cutting the throat, are all on the same level. Death by sword-cut is considered more painful, and to so inflict it is more expensive. If the heirs of a murdered man thirst for revenge, they may kill the murderer and plunder his house ; though, if the first murder was by a bullet, and the avenger elect to kill the murderer by the sword, he will have to pay to his enemy's heirs Rs. 100 as compensation for the difference in the mode of slaughter. Where the original victim was a woman, the penalty would be to cut off the murderer's right foot or his nose. The pecuniary commutation would respectively be Rs. 1,200 in the one case, and Rs. 600 in the other. At least nominally, for it would probably be largely payable in produce or commodities, including women at Rs. 100 each, which seems to be considered a sort of fancy bazaar price; the ruling rate being ordinarily much lower.

After the expedition against the Kâbul Khel Waziris in 1860, a very characteristic agreement was drawn up between them and the British villagers of Thal. The details of the negotiations lasted three days, and both sides pledged their solemn concurrence on the Korân. The first clause specified that bygones should be bygones; the second, that all hostilities should cease; the third, that neither side should take the law into their own hands but refer all disputes through a British officer. The fourth laid down all the details for "make-up-money," as follows:—For killing a Pathân, Rs. 1,200; for killing an inferior man, Rs. 360; for laming a Pathân in hand or foot (for which giving a daughter was to count as a set-off of Rs 80), Rs. 500; for laming an inferior man, to give him a daughter and do penance at his door; for a Pathân thumb or forefinger, Rs. 60; any three other fingers, Rs. 60; for an inferior man's finger, a goat or a sheep which the *jirgah* or village council are to help him to eat. Restitution for robbery to be made by proof on solemn oath.

The procedure adopted in doubtful murder cases is simple in the extreme. The suspect may bring a hundred men of his clan to swear before the assembled village headmen, oaths on the Korân that they are satisfied of his innocence, or if inconvenient to bring so many, he can bring a few men, but they must each take more oaths. Or, as a last resource, he may take the whole hundred oaths himself in the case of a man (reduced to fifty only, if the case relates to a woman). If after this, the aggrieved clan kill him, they are themselves held to be guilty of murder. For bodily injury, the Waziri tariff runs from Rs. 600 for "half death," such as the loss of a limb, to Rs. 20 for a blemish between waist and feet. For a still slighter assault, the aggrieved party may, with the assistance of his friends, throw the aggressor down, and "menace him with threats—" disgrace him, in fact, before his village. But here again wounded honour can be satisfied, and the disgrace prevented, by payment of the modest sum of Rs. 3; a course which is said to be "generally preferred."

These are but samples of a code that provides and often provides ingeniously for most cases of violence and theft either of the man's goods or the woman's honour; and whatever may be the value of its precepts in the abstract, on the old principle that even bad laws are better than none at all, it may be said to have prevented many a feud, and probably much bloodshed, among the Waziris.

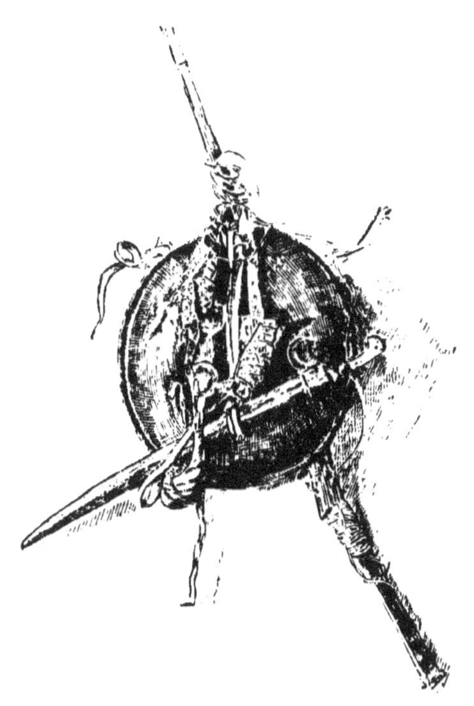

Knife, Shield, Jezail, and Belt

CHAPTER XIII.

THE DAWAR OR TOCHI VALLEY.

THE Dawar Valley has already been referred to as by no means the least important of the main highways into the heart of Afghânistân. It is considerably shorter, in some respects it offers more facilities, than the Gumal; and though, as a trade route, it is probably never likely to be of much importance, its value for military purposes, as affording direct communication with Ghazni, or effecting a flank movement on Kâbul, is even still greater. In the time of the Greek occupation and the early days of Hindu sovereignty, it must have been the scene of constant and direct communication between Western Afghânistân and India. The high mounds at the mouth of the passes, and the ancient remains scattered through the valley, mark the sites of what were once great and flourishing cities, while it is tolerably certain it was one of the routes most affected by Mahmud of Ghazni for his raids on India when not aimed directly at Peshawur. And in the ruins of Akra, among the scraps of Buddhist ornaments, Hindu idols, broken bricks and pottery, the hundreds of Ghaznavi coins, from the beginning to the end of the dynasty, which are laid bare after heavy rains, furnish a complete record of constant encampments.

Like so many others of the passes, the "tight places" are only at the Indian end; and it is perhaps no exaggeration to say, the whole route is better known from Ghazni than from Bannu, though the entrances are within a few miles from our outposts, and a morning's ride from cantonments. As with some other famous plans for action, there are from the Border three courses open, all perfectly practicable and of no great length— ways which only need the will to make them perfectly easy, but which, to judge by the holy horror the British Government has always seemed to entertain for them, might have all Dante's Purgatorio behind. The Tochi, just opposite the outpost of the same name, is the best known—a mere track, rough and stony but which is generally fairly level, and at most is only nine miles long; the Barân, somewhat to the north, much more rocky and more circuitous, involving a detour of about twenty miles, entering the valley near the village of Isohri; and a third by the Khasora Pass, about six miles south of the Tochi, which was used on the return of the Masaud expeditionary force in 1860—the easiest and best of the three, though the longest, a twenty-five mile march being needed before the valley is reached.

Once through this paltry range of almost uninhabited hills, the valley, or rather valleys,—for there are two, the Upper and Lower Dawar, separated by an unimportant *tangi* or waist,—open out into what may almost be called plains—rich, productive, and fairly well cultivated, irrigated by a considerable river, the Tochi, known in British territory as the Gambila, studded with more or less wealthy villages, walled and defended by flanking towers—the whole extending as far as Sherannia at the foot of the eastern slope of the Jadrân Hills, which form the head of the Upper Dawar Valley, and fix the limit of the trade that at present finds its way to India by this route. From Sherannia onwards are several routes not quite so plain, so well-known, or so open, but which recent information has shown offer no great difficulties Crossing the range, which is also the water-shed dividing the streams flowing to the Indus and the Helmand, the most direct

and the easiest passing by Urghûn, or Warghin as the Waziris
call it, and the Kotani Pass, leads to Sarâfza at the western foot
of the Jadrân range, and from thence by Shilgarh to Ghazni,
a country, which, as the result of the investigations carried on
by our native explorers shows, offers no obstacle to military
movements. Detailed information is still wanting. One of the
last of these explorers, a Sayud, was unluckily suspected and
imprisoned at Ghazni, from thence sent on to Kâbul, where his
survey books were taken from him, though he was eventually
allowed to return to India. But from information gathered in
this way and sketches taken during various expeditions, the
general features are pretty well known.

The Lower Valley, owing to the swampy nature of the ground,
is somewhat feverish, though not nearly so bad in that respect
as Bannu, but the Upper Valley is in every way desirable ; and
at the head of it are breezy, healthy highlands, more than
ordinarily fertile and with a splendid climate. A position might
be taken up there that would command some of the very best
parts of the Afghân border, and would, moreover, ensure a grip
on some of the best and sturdiest of the independent tribes. To
the south lie the highlands of Birmal, a tract of country only
lately prospected, much in the manner just referred to, where
rises the main stream of the Tochi, which flows northward through
it for forty or fifty miles, and then enters the Upper Dawar by
a sudden and sharp bend to the east, and flows on towards the
Indus. The course of the river, according to Major Holdich,
marks the line of a good road through the length of Birmal, and is
connected with its head by an easy pass across a low water-shed
with the Gumal system southwards. From the eastern slope of
what are shown on old maps as the Kohnok Hills, but are really
the southern continuation of the Jadrân Range, there rises also an
important affluent of the Gumal, called the Dua Gumal, a stream
not yet surveyed, but described as flowing through open valleys

till it joins the main Gumal to the south-west of Waziristân, and would doubtless afford an excellent second line of communication. The waters of the Tochi are sweet and good, and it may always be depended on for a plentiful supply. Along most of its course the bottom is hard and stony, and though liable to sudden rises it is never impassable even for footmen for more than a few hours. The Dawar Valley throughout is seldom narrower than one mile, and in many places, two or three miles wide : a great part of it well cultivated, a good deal of grain being grown ; and the villages are prosperous and possess considerable herds of cattle. Birmal is a more debatable land, some of the Powindahs grazing their cattle there in the summer, and the Waziris apparently holding it in winter. The former, dirty, wild, and unkempt, as they may be—do not look as if they came from a bad climate or a poor country.

There is probably no reason, save the persistence in a policy of non-interference with the tribes, why a force should not march in at the Tochi, travel round a great part of Waziristân, and out by the Gumal, without meeting with any serious difficulty; and one of the easiest routes to the Masaud country is admittedly from the Dawar Valley over the Râzmak Sir. West and south of the Jadrân Range is a wide undulating country, gradually flattening into broad level plains, with a few isolated hills, affording easy roads to Kandahâr, Khelât-i-Ghilzai, and Ghazni, from which last the road to Kâbul is well known.

Of the people who live along this highway, the very name Dawari is a byword of reproach. The Bannûchi, according to Edwardes, is an exceptionally degraded specimen—with all the vices of the Pathân rankly luxuriant, his virtues stunted; but the Dawari is universally described as somewhat more eminently vicious and additionally degraded. An object of supreme contempt to his warlike neighbours, the Waziris, he is even looked upon as a bad character by a Bannûchi. Worse probably could not be said of him. To call him dirty would be almost a compliment; his clothes, usually black cotton to start with, are worn till they would be considered malodorous by a Ghilzai. Rankness in this respect is with him a matter of pride, for it indicates he can afford to indulge largely in *ghee,* or clarified, but more or less rancid butter, which is in great demand, not only for food, but for anointing his head, his face, and his dress. He will carry, says Hyát Khán, a piece of bread saturated with it in his pocket or bound up in his clothes, as to him the sweetest scented sachet. His complexion naturally inclines to yellow. As a youth he will stain one eye black and one red; as a young buck have his beard plucked out to keep his face smooth, and wear flowers in his turban; as an older warrior, his idea is to shave one side of his face only, stain his eyebrows and eyelids red and blue and frighten his enemies by putting on a fierce expression. In old age his regularity at prayers is unimpeachable, but there is hardly any known narcotic with which he will not stupefy himself. He is essentially a non-fighting man, and an unenterprising man : he is ready for any robbery, or to back up any villainy, but he has not energy or pluck enough to venture out of his valley to attempt it; and even as a trader, he looks on the thirty miles to Bannu as an exceedingly far cry. He will tyrannise over the few Hindu settlers to a cruel degree—the Hindu has to give up a wife if she be good-looking, pay a tax on a son, and a ransom on a daughter's wedding; and though he manages withal to hold the purse strings, he will rather buy off, than cope with the Waziri marauder who harries him from time to time; and who has a proverb that one Waziri with one stick is equal to one hundred Dawaris. His unnatural licentiousness would have made him conspicuous in Sodom or Gomorrah, and it may fairly be doubted if the requisite number of righteous could be found in the valley to save the Dawar villages from the fate that fell on the cities of the plain.

From what wandering horde he originated is not clear. His history is ancient and obscure; but he has remained for centuries shut in by strong hardy neighbours, and has probably been as nasty for ages, and is only desirous to be let alone, to go on in his evil courses for ages to come. The fringe of warlike tribes by which the valley is surrounded has, however, really been its protection from annexation over and over again. It seems to have been included in the Mughal Empire during the time of Aurangzebe, whose son, Bahâdur Shâh, is said to have levied in person some heavy arrears from the wealthy inhabitants. The Durrâni lieutenants occasionally used their armies from Khost to extort revenue; and there are stories of a shadowy Sikh jurisdiction, but which really relate to mere forays. Though Dawar has at different times been nominally subject to the Kâbul authorities. practically it has been, and still is, perfectly independent. In 1855 the Government of India, as usual ready to disclaim any intention of moving over the Border, renounced any rights in favour of the Amir, Dost Muhammad, though neither he nor his successors were ever strong enough to enter into possession, and the sovereign rights of Kâbul remained just as imaginary as before. The people have several times expressed a wish to come under British rule, protesting against being handed over to any other power, and begging, if they must be subjects, to be subjects of the Queen. And though the proposal has always been refused, the Indian Government has dealt directly with them, and, when necessary, proceeded to expeditions or blockades without any reference whatever. Both have had to be resorted to on occasions either on account of raids and murders by Dawaris, or because they provided a rendezvous for others; and it is only some few years ago the valley was reported a hot-bed of disaffection and fanaticism. The Dawaris, however, may fairly plead it was not until they had asked and been refused aid against the Wazaris, that they made friends with the mammon of unrighteousness, and became notorious for harbouring rebels against us. Whether or no these Dawaris would make desirable subjects it is needless to consider; they would not make soldiers, though we could probably enlist their neighbours on both sides. The Jadrânis beyond them are a primitive, hospitable race, many of whom, excellent workmen but inveterate beggars, come into Bannu to work as navvies in the cold season, where they are nicknamed "hill-wolves," on account of the amount of earnings they usually carry back with them. They are said to be very well disposed, but their numbers are too insignificant to be taken into account.

The strategic value of a position among the well-watered and fertile highlands near the sources of the Tochi, and the possession of points like Sheranuia, Urghûn, and Sarâfza, that would practically command the highway from Ghazni to Bannu, cannot be doubted. If the Russians were at Bannu instead of ourselves, we should probably hear that a line of railway was in progress. When the line to Bannu is completed, and presumably this cannot be long left out of any sound scheme of frontier defence, a continuation up to the eastern slope of the Jadrân hills would be perfectly easy. Nor is there any apparent reason why these highlands should not be successfully crossed, certainly with less difficulty than the same range could be negotiated *viâ* the Gumal. These crossed, the reports of native surveyors show no special obstacles right on to Ghazni. From Ghazni to Bannu is considerably shorter than by any other route, and the principal argument against its adoption is, that traders do not use it. This, however, may be a good deal due to causes other than physical difficulties. It is quite off the Kâbul and Kandahâr lines of traffic, or for enterprising Border traders like the Powindahs. Its inhabitants are at the other extreme of the scale, not only the most degraded, but the most unenterprising.

The physical difficulties in the way of an occupation, are certainly the reverse of formidable. A mere cavalry reconnaissance proved sufficient to carry a scare that was almost a panic throughout the valley. The only expedition against the Dawaris, undertaken in 1872, was an affair of less than twenty-four hours. Early one morning some 1,500 of the Frontier Force fell in, occupied the heights covering the Tochi Pass, cleared and made the road through it passable for guns by breakfast time, marched through, occupied three or four of the leading villages, and burned their flanking towers by lunch, received the complete submission of the Dawaris, and were on their way back, if not to afternoon tea, at any rate were all outside the Tochi again for a late dinner.

It is at present perhaps unnecessary to annex the Dawar Valley, but that our surveyors, engineers, and soldiers should be perfectly free to come and go in it, might be reasonably insisted on. To permit so important a line of communication to remain a sealed book ; that within a short ride there should be passes a few miles long, with a great fertile valley behind them, affording free access almost to the centre of Afghánistán, but as much closed to us as the gate of Eden to the Peri, is an obvious absurdity. And to persist in maintaining a curtain immediately in front of our outposts, behind which no British officer is to be allowed to look ; to be dependent for our information regarding the country, its capabilities, its strategic positions, and its tribes, on native explorers in disguise, stealthily noting in rough sketches, and approximating distances regarding which precise information might at any time be of the greatest importance to us ; surveyors whose field books are liable to confiscation and their persons to imprisonment at the hands of our allies—is to persist in a policy that can only be described as fatuous. The Dawar Valley and the Jadrán Highlands should, at least, be as free to us as is Kashmir ; and we should be assured that Mahmud's highway to Ghazni, is fairly passable in case circumstances should ever compel us to go there ; for it is impossible to say how soon such a contingency may arise.

CHAPTER XIV.

As regards means of communication, though almost the worst provided, Bannu is, in many respects, one of the most important, one of the prettiest, and not the least interesting of our Frontier stations. Its position, its history, its scenery, and its fertility, "an emerald set in a country pre-eminently of rocks and stones," have all combined to make it a favourite subject with Frontier writers, from Edwardes downwards. Geologists talk of it as a great lake before the Aryan race had left its cradle. To the earlier immigrants, it was "*Dand*," "the Marsh," The Bannudzais, who dug drains and sowed corn, took to calling it Bannu, after their mother, the wife of Shitak, because, they said, it was fruitful, even as she was. And Edwardes, whose *Year on the Frontier* would alone have made it famous, and whose name has still stuck to the modern cantonment, has left a series of pictures of it, perfectly idyllic. "In spring," he says in one, "it is a vegetable emerald; and in winter its many-coloured harvests look as if Ceres had stumbled against the Great Salt-Range, and spilt half her cornu-copia in this favoured vale. As if to make the landscape perfect, a graceful variety of the sheesham-tree, whose boughs droop like the willow, is found here, and here alone; while along streams, and round the villages, the thick mulberry, festooned with the wild vine, throws a fragrant shade, beneath which well-fed Sayuds look exquisitely happy, sleeping midway through their beads. Roses, too, without which Englishmen have learnt from the East to think no scenery complete, abound in the upper parts at the close of spring. Most of the fruits of Kâbul are found wild, and culture would bring them to perfection; as it is, the limes, mulberries and melons are delicious. Altogether, nature has so smiled on Bannu, that the stranger thinks it a paradise: and when he turns to the people, wonders how such spirits of evil ever found admittance." Even settlement officers grow eloquent over its prettiness; and not only did Thorburn enliven a most interesting report with picturesque bits about yellow corn, green trees, murmuring waters, reapers, and pet lambs with tinkling bells in every field, haunts of peace and content, with a background of grey hills, weird rocks, gloomy glens, and snowy peaks in a blaze of glory—but he overflowed into a graphic volume, dealing more fully with the district and its people, their stories, songs, and proverbs.

Historically, it has been the scene of a succession of changes, exceptional even for a Border along which they have everywhere been numerous. The ruined mounds of Akra mark what was probably a flourishing city before ancient Greece became a power. Alexander is still a popular local hero, known as "Sikandar Badshâh." His Macedonian successors have left distinct records, both of Greek art, and of the permanence of Greek occupation. So have Græco-Bactrians, Indo-Scythians, and Buddhists. Hindus re-colonized it, and fill up a gap by traditions of the city of Sat Râm. The Brahmin kings of Northern India were a power there in the ninth century, and Sabaktigin seems to have followed and adopted their heraldic device of the lion rampant. Mahmud and two centuries of Ghaznavis passed and repassed, and from their camps on the banks of the Kurram and Gambila, raided on India till they were finally crushed by the Ghoris at Lahore in the twelfth

century. The valley was a highway for the armies of Timour at
the end of the fourteenth century, and was ravaged by Bâber at the
beginning of the sixteenth. Before Timour, it had been colonized by
small bodies of Afghâns; the Bannudzais that Bâber found there,
had already driven out the Mangals and the Hannis, and had a

A Border Fruit-seller.

comparatively long spell before they were gradually ousted by the
Niázais. Closely following the latter, came their still finer kinsmen,
the Marwats; a great host of splendid men, who drove the Niázais
eastward, settled down, and possessed the land which they called
Marwat, after their forefather. Their children hold it to this day,

and very fine cultivators they are. The last wave of colonists were the Waziris. For a while they were content to drive their flocks from their own bleak, dreary hills, pitch their black blanket tents in the luxuriant valley during the winter, and go back to their highlands again in the spring, but as flocks and herds increased, and as they looked on the fields and the harvests, the Waziri became, as Edwardes describes, possessed with the lust of land, and promptly proceeded to take it. While their Mahsud clansmen exercised their profession by taking toll from the Powindah, the Darwesh gradually took to acquiring fertile lands from the Bannuchi, and what is left to the latter is probably due to the advent of British law and British protection.

All these changes, however, are only a part of what has gone to make up the hybrid Bannuchi, a designation which has now come to include, not only all the so-called descendants of Shitak and his wife Masammat Bannu, but nearly all the Muhammadans, and even the Hindus, who have been long domiciled among them ; the *Jhuta* or "leavings" of all the adventurers who have at different times, and for various reasons, found their way to the irrigated tracts in the valley. These have, in Edwardes's words, "contributed, by intermarriage, slave dealing, and vice, to complete the mongrel character of the Bannuchi people. Every stature, from that of the weak Indian to that of the tall Durrâni; every complexion, from the ebony of Bengal to the rosy cheek of Kâbul ; every dress, from the linen garments of the South, to the heavy goat-skin of the eternal snows,—is to be seen promiscuously among them, reduced only to a harmonious whole by the neutral tint of universal dirt." Small in stature, sallow, fleshless, and wizened in appearance. " Shut up in close villages amongst heat, dirt, squalor, and stagnation ; hot beds of all that is enervating and demoralizing "; bigoted in the extreme, a mosque for every thirty-four houses, praying at all hours and in all places, blindly obedient to the direction of the lowest type of priests; " impudent impostors, who contribute

K

nothing to the common stock but inflammatory counsel, and a fanatical yell in the rear of the battle"; vicious in all manner of ways; "litigious, utterly regardless of truth; ready to take any advantage, however mean, over their enemy; without any manly feelings about them, always harping about 'honour;' '*izzat*,' though possessing none,"—they appear certainly well qualified for the epithet "degraded" that is applied to them by Edwardes, Reynell Taylor, Thorburn, and almost every one who has had anything to do with them. After this, it seems a small merit to credit them with being "excellent revenue-payers, quiet, inoffensive subjects," or to charge off most of their bad qualities to their prolificness and the climate in which they live.

Climatic influence, *plus* canal irrigation, may have had much to do with it, as some theorists persistently urge. Certainly the adjoining Marwats, with their sandy soil and dry air, are almost the reverse of what has been said of their immediate neighbours. Fine, tall, muscular, well-bred Pathâns, with ruddy complexions. Fair and handsome women, not ashamed of a rather mischievous face and a fairly good ankle. A people frank, open, and truthful, mainly agriculturists, with a profound contempt for the Bannuchi. The Waziri has previously been sketched; where he has settled within our border, he seems, in spite of climate, to have improved rather than deteriorated; he has lost none of his characteristic virtues, but has been somewhat weaned from his passion for plunder, and is rapidly learning the rudimentary lessons of civilization.

Interesting as may be the climatic, historic, or ethnographic characteristic condition of Bannu, it is still more so from its strategic position on the Border; one which on all hands is admitted to be of exceptional importance. To say this, is only to echo the opinion of those best informed military authorities who have had exceptional opportunities for judging, and who have given special attention to the subject. Whether we accept the view, that our true strategic position cannot stop short of the Kandahâr-Kâbul line; and recognise what is, perhaps of more importance, the desirability of bringing the border tribes behind this line into our own recruiting field, as soon as political circumstances permit; or whether, as one of the authorities referred to has put it, we propose to leave this factor of strength to become in the future the steel point of the enemy's lance, ready to be turned on to our most vulnerable point—the importance of Bannu remains undiminished. It is the centre on which converge, or whence diverge, several of the main roads between our frontier outposts —from Kohât and Thal, from Dera Ismail Khân, Tânk, and the Gumal. From it we could at any time most effectively control the Khost Valley, the Mangals, or the entire Waziri country. It would be the initial point for a road by the Dawar Valley to Ghazni, which, as already described, involves no special difficulties, and a distance less than 150 miles. When the railway to it is constructed, Bannu will become the natural base for the alternative route to Kâbul by the Kurrum, from which we could best outflank an enemy advancing by that route. To a great extent this has now been recognised, and under the present administration much has been done. Railway communication has been brought up to Khushalgarh on the one hand, and to opposite Dera Ismail Khân on the other. The frontier road, which in places was little better than a track, from both these points has now been converted into a first class military road, bridged and metalled throughout. The important streams, like the Kurrum and the Gambila—sources of constant danger and frequent loss of life—have now been crossed by bridges that, if necessary, will carry a broad-gauge railway. A survey for a new line of railway from the Sind-Sagar system, *vid* Mianwali and Mari, Kâlabagh and Isakhel, to Bannu itself, has been finished, and it is to be hoped that no plea of financial difficulty will be permitted to stand in the way of the early completion of a project so vitally important.

As a position for any large garrison, the present cantonment of Edwardesabad has been charged, and perhaps not without reason, with certain disadvantages as regards climate. The irrigated part of the valley is said to be as malarious and unhealthy as Peshawar formerly was, probably to a great extent for a very similar reason. The Bannuchi makes the same water serve for drinking, washing—whenever he does wash—and irrigating his field : only he frequently reverses the order, and lets the water flow over his highly manured fields first. A pure water supply, which could easily be obtained, would do much to remedy this; and there are excellent sites for sanitaria that might, and undoubtedly ought, to be made use of. The Ghabar Mountain, over 6,000 feet high, lies within the Batanni country, midway between the Kurrum outpost and Peyzu. It possesses many facilities for a sanitarium, and its occupation would bring advantages both to the tribes and ourselves. While going a little further afield, the Upper Dawar, the Jadrân highlands, or the mountains around Khost, would offer a climate equal to Kashmir.

One other matter in connection with our position on this part of the Border is too important to be overlooked. Whatever the merits of the Kurrum route, as an approach to Kâbul may be, the construction of a railway to Bannu will undoubtedly make it still more the point of departure from which operations might be most properly undertaken. Our furthest post west in the Kurram direction is Thal, 167 miles from Kâbul, and some sixty-six miles from Kohât, which is again thirty miles from a railway. From Bannu, following approximately the course of the Kurram River, to Thal, is about forty-two, or about ten miles more by the Gumati or Barganattu Passes, by either of which it can be turned. Here, again, this route is in the hands of the Waziris, a wedge of whose country is driven right into the middle of our territory, and for all practical purposes the road is closed to us. In fact, until lately, it was unmapped, and Major Holdich's assistant was only allowed to make a plane table survey of it in 1882 under the most stringent conditions—one of which was that he never slept on the far side of the Border. The railway completed, the construction of a thoroughly efficient road direct from Bannu to Thal, should be promptly insisted on, and the opening out of the Dawar Valley be at the same time taken in hand. There is no need to anticipate any special obstructions During the winter of 1878-79, the Thal-Bannu route was used by a detachment of our cavalry, the whole of the Jhind and Kapurthalla contingents marched by it, and up to the beginning of 1880 convoys were regularly sent under a *badraga*[1] escort. The Dawaris have, over and over again, asked to be brought under our protection; and so far from either route proving a source of trouble, nothing is wanting but a little firmness and tact to insure Waziri acquiescence in the case of both, once it is made clear to them that the British Government will insist, and they are keen enough to see they would have much to lose by obstruction, and everything to gain by assisting us.

[1] Safe conduct.

CHAPTER XV.

BORDER ECCLESIOLOGY.—A SHORT DISCOURSE ON THE PATHÁN CHURCH.

THE superstition of the Pathán is said to have no limits, but perhaps in this respect he does not, after all, differ very materially from the Christian of the Middle Ages, who notoriously "lived in an atmosphere charged with the supernatural." On the Border, miracles, charms, omens, are believed as a matter of course, just as the miracles of the Church, magic and witchcraft, spirit-rapping and table-turning, were—in some cases it might even be said still are—accepted by the average worshipper in the West. There is no necessity, therefore, to be too severe on the former in respect of his belief; the wonders accomplished during the *Jandah* festival at Peshawur by Pir Bâba in Buneyr, or Kuka Sahib in Khattak, are not more incredible than the stories about the fish thronging to hear St. Antony preach, the restoration of amputated limbs by the virgin of the palace at Saragossa, or the liquefaction of the blood of St. Januarius at Naples. In spite of much outcry about the spirit of the age, the progress of Rationalism is slow; prayers, alms, fasts, pilgrimages, reverence for saints, and respect for their modern representatives, are among the binding and fundamental duties of the Pathán—as of several other people much nearer home. All classes and both sexes resort to the "sacred shrine," interesting devotees confess their sins, talk of their "pure prophet," and "blessed religion," and yield as implicit obedience to their holy men, as, for instance, an Irish peasant does to his parish priest.

Wherever the demand for miracles is so considerable the supply is pretty certain to equal it. The Border Muhammadan has few or no relics, images, pictures, or crucifixes—in fact, hardly one of his sacred shrines boasts any building more imposing than a big heap of stones—and the collection of rags that resemble dilapidated scare-crows, is the only outward and visible sign of the offerings of the faithful. But a visit to some of the *ziârats* of the Border, equivalents to the Saint Cuthberts, Beckets, Nicholases, or Dunstans, will ensure a cure from fever, ophthalmia, rheumatism, and most of the ills to which mortal flesh is heir. Others will protect the believer from the evil eye; render his cattle prolific, or, on too frequent occasions, vouchsafe the desires of intriguing lovers. The earth from the grave of Akhund Darwaza at Peshawur, or of Akhund Musa near Jelâlâbâd, is a specific for burns or snake-bites; and lunatics can be restored to mental health by going to the last resting-place of Mian'Ali at Ali-Boghân. Women, who are not blessed with children, can obtain their wishes at quite a number of shrines; and the pious pilgrim, who cannot afford a journey to Mecca, can do himself almost as much good by paying a round of visits to holy places in his own locality, and feeing the local institutions.

He has his own primitive fathers, compared to whom Clement, Ignatius, or Polycarp are quite modern creations. The Pathân, like the Irishman, again, dates back to the early patriarchs, and apparently, the older they are, the longer their graves have become. Near Bâlâbâgh in Naugrahâ, the grave of the patriarch Lot, *Hazrat Lût*, is over 380 yards long. The *Ziârat* of *Mehtar Lam*, who corresponds to Lamech, the father of Noah, is in Laghmân; and the ark of Noah himself is said, after the deluge, to have rested on the Kund Mountain, the adjoining valley being called Dara-i-Nuh, the Vale of Noah, to this day.

The prophets *Ayub* (Seth), *Sis* (Job), and others, are nearly as famous, and of proportionate dimensions. Fifty feet is a moderate length for a prophet of this importance. Minor dignitaries who have fallen as martyrs (*Shâhid*) or warriors (*Ghâzi*) fighting against the infidel Hindus, or Kâfir British, are honoured in a similar way. *Nao-Gaja* "nine-yarders," is the term by which they are known in the Punjab. As their sanctity increases so does their reputed stature ; one celebrity, buried in Peshawur cantonment, kept on growing till his tomb bid fair to entirely obstruct the thoroughfare, and the district authorities had to put a wall round him. " Shrines of the mighty " they literally are, but not even the most austere Puritan could complain that anything had been wasted upon art or decoration. A long, low heap of stone or brick masonry, or even mud, suffices to cover the most famous. The reputation of the Border Saint does not depend upon either palaces or shrines made with hands, any more than his officiating priesthood does on canonicals.

Of modern ecclesiastical offices and dignitaries he has a goodly number with sufficiently long-sounding names ; and if a Pathân clergy list was to be published, the *Valor ecclesiasticus* might perhaps be broadly defined somewhat as follows :—

· Astânadârs, literally holy place-possessors, might stand for Lay Rectors with a traditionary devout reputation, or the descendants who, by virtue of the sanctity of an ancestor of pious memory, enjoy the present endowments or benefits of the *Astân*, *Ziârat*, or shrine. Theoretically the Saynd is the direct descendant of 'Ali the son-in-law of Muhammad ; practically he is a bishop or primate of the church, who would be usually addressed by the title of *Shâh*, " Your Grace," and to whom the Pathân would figuratively take off his hat.

Pirs would, however, stand almost at the top of the precedence

A Nao-Gaja near Peshawur.

list, for they would be saluted as *Bádsháh*, " Your Excellency."
" The congregation should rise when a Pir joins the assembly, and
remain standing till he is seated." He often has charge of a shrine,
and the Pathân Burke would show him as descended from a saint
of repute. Ecclesiastically he is as powerful as the Dean and
Chapter, having all sorts of exclusive hereditary rights and privileges, receiving a tithe of the fields and flocks. " His social
position is independent of his merits," and, says Bellew, " all
Pirs are comfortably off, if not rich."

A Miân might have the status of a Rural Dean, in that as a
prelate he is becoming more or less obsolete. The Miâns have
abandoned the world in order to devote themselves to teaching the
doctrines of Islâm, but they still hold positions of dignified ease,
luxurious benefices, the Barchesters of the Frontier. Some of
them possess special powers to combat pestilence and famine;
others are experts in discovering who are the sinners among
their neighbours, and in pointing them out with the finger of
scorn.

Sahibzâdas, the sons of holy men, occupy about the same
position in regard to Sayuds, Pirs, and Miâns, as Colonial Arch-
deacons do to Deans or Bishops, though all four classes are equally
place-possessors, often comfortable place-possessors.

It is not necessary that any of the foregoing should be on the
active list, but the Mullah is the ordinary hardworking parish
priest, who has taken holy orders, perhaps with the title of
Maulvi, the Muhammadan D.D.; has to attend to the services of
the mosque, teach the creed, and look after the schools. The
most numerous of all, he is the most important factor in ordinary
Pathân life, and his influence is immense. The residentiary Canon
or Precentor may be represented by the Imâm, whose business is to
intone the service and lead the congregation. The Fakir is a
mendicant friar, generally a Dominican or Black Friar. The
Shaikh, an elderly gentleman, who has relinquished worldly plea-

sures, or whom worldly pleasures have left stranded, and who has become a Lay Brother, or the disciple of a saint. And, last of all, comes the Talib-ul-ilm, or seeker after wisdom ; a curate with a taste for dining out; or it might be said, the reverse of an almoner. The latter dispenses alms and distributes doles ; the seeker-after-wisdom does just the contrary.

If the Border curate is the bottom of the scale, the nearest approach to the head of this church is probably an Akhund, literally a teacher, but the famous Akhund of Swât was, for almost half a century, practically the Border Pope—a character so famous as to deserve a subsequent discourse all to himself.

Nothing perhaps is such good evidence of the deference paid to a dignitary of the Pathân church, as the general security in which he lives. He is almost the only man whose life is sacred from the casual bullet or the hasty knife ; for whose blood the Pathân tariff does not provide a rate.

Not long ago, in the Peshawur district, a man went so very far to the bad, as to shoot a Mullah. It might have been an accident, or he mistook his man, or pure villany ; anyhow the Mullah died, and like many another outlaw, the murderer had to fly over the Border. First he tried Buneyr, but the news had preceded him, and he was refused shelter. He then tried the Swât valley with no better success, the country of the Akhund would have none of him. "You shot a Mullah," said the Mohmands, to whom he went next. "If it had been any ordinary tribesman, or even a Sahib, we would have stretched a point, but you must go." Even the Afridis, small reverence as they pay to spiritual advisers, looked askance, and would have nothing to say to a ruffian whose hands were dyed with the blood of a pious man. Wearied at length of being hunted from tribe to tribe, he bethought himself of repentance. "None of you will have me," he said, " then I will at any rate do something to make you. I can but be a martyr. I will go and kill a Sahib." So back he came to Peshawur cantonment, and walked down the Mall to look for a victim. Not finding one handy, he turned off and went for a rough rider sergeant, in difficulties with a troublesome horse, at whom he took deliberate aim. As luck would have it, the first bullet was stopped by a range finder the sergeant had on him, but before the latter could go for his assailant, the Pathân got another bullet through the sergeant's helmet, and made a bolt for it. A plucky native ran in, and the man was ultimately secured, tried by the commissioner the same evening, and under summary powers hanged the next morning. Perfectly satisfied, as he declared, with himself at having expiated his offence, and with only one request to make, which was granted—that his body might not be burnt. Some day perhaps they will put up a *Nao-Gaja* for him.

CHAPTER XVI.

By the Kurram valley to Kâbul has become almost as familiar
to the present decade of Englishmen in India, and has furnished
almost as good a text as the " Overland Route " did to the last.
Nearly ten years ago, in November 1878, our troops were in full
possession of it, scattering in all directions the followers of Amir
Sher 'Ali. Less than a year after, an avenging force under Sir
Frederick Roberts was pushing forward, by forced marches, past
the old Kurram Fort, up the "White Cow" ascent, across the
pine-clad Paiwar, among the glens of 'Ali Khel, through the defile
of the " Thousand Trees," and over the " Camel's Neck ; " caring
nothing for the snows of the Sufed Koh, deaf to the Jâji drums
and bagpipes, brushing aside the Mangals and Zaimukhts,
finding no pleasure nor delight in " Khushi,"[1] but anxious only to
get to Kâbul, and exact retribution for the dastardly murder of
the ill-fated Cavagnari and our embassy. In May 1879 Yakub
Khân had come into the British camp at Gandamak, and signed
a treaty by which, not only were the foreign relations of Afghânistân to be entirely subordinated to British influence, a British
Resident to be established in Kâbul, but our Frontier was to be
rectified by the inclusion within it of Peshin, Sibi, and Kurram,

---

[1] The abode of happiness.

and from the latter place there was to be a line of telegraph to Kâbul. By the middle of 1880 Yakub's complicity with the murder of our Resident had been established, he had been removed to India, and Amir Abdur Rahmân set up. The pendulum had swung again, the treaty had been abrogated, and October found General Watson announcing to the Turi *Maliks*[1] the withdrawal of our forces from Kurram.

The Miranzai, the western extremity of which valley now marks our border limit, and perhaps the pleasantest part of the Kohât district, has been arbitrarily divided into an Upper and a Lower, though the river which runs east down the latter is a feeder of the Kohat *toi*, or stream, and goes thence to the Indus, while the Ishkali, which runs west along the Upper, is a branch of the Kurram. Both Upper and Lower, equally with the Kurram, lie along the base of the great Sufed Koh range, the white peaks of which tower over everything else, a gigantic barrier between this and the still more famous " Khaiber " route to Kâbul. There is no very great dissimilarity between the characteristics of the Miranzai and the Kurram, except that, as in so many other cases, by far the best of the country lies across the Border. It is a land of mountains, small and great, of rocks, and of stones. The rivers that rush down the steep slopes are at one time dangerous torrents, at others yielding with difficulty a little water from the holes dug in their bed. With small and circumscribed, but well cultivated, valleys, where grain and fruit flourish abundantly, varied with " raviney " wastes, growing little beyond the dwarf palm which affords materials for one of the few staple industries the country possesses. These again are interspersed by grassy tracts, on which are pastured abnormally small cattle, and exceptionally fat-tailed sheep. Once past Thal, and the banks of the Kurram river reached, there is a marked change for the better. More or less all along are corn-fields and fruit-gardens, mulberry

[1] Head-men.

groves and fertile glades, passing up to ridges crested by oak and olive, yew tree and pines; the range behind again culminating in the snow-capped peak of Sita Râm, which rises over 15,000 feet high. Some parts of the valley have the reputation of being unhealthy, for the same reason as Bannu, but there are few more fertile spots along the Afghân border than the Kurram.

To pass from the place to the people. Though, according to Bellew, it is not improbable that the whole region comprising both sides of the Sufed Koh, and the districts at the base from Paiwar to the Indus, was, in the shadowy past, subject to one tribe, which he thinks corresponded to the Assarytæ of Herodotus—of which the Afridi is the modern representative, it is, in the present, certainly occupied by a great number of tribes and septs, Bangash, Turi Jâji, Zaimakt, Orakzai, Afridi, and many more, having perhaps a sort of distant family connection, but differing from one another widely and materially. Some of them are not even usually classed among Afghâns at all, and may probably have got not a little mixed with the swarms of Turks, who came in with the invasions of Subaktigin and Timur, or with the Scythic stock before that, though, for all practical purposes, no better term can be found for them, than Pathân.

Tradition has it, that the Bangash were of Arab origin, descended from Koresh, Muhammad's apostle to the Afghâns of Ghor, whilom living about Gurdez in Zurmat; but, pressed by the Ghilzais, emigrated eastward, sometime towards the end of the fourteenth century; or just subsequent to the invasion of Timur, settled in Kurram, and with the assistance of the Khattaks themselves doing a little invasion from the south, ousted the Orakzais and pressed them further up the slope. Local story further goes on to say that, to accomplish this, they fought a battle lasting three days and three nights, which only terminated by the appearance on the scene of the proverbial horseman in white, who declared that "the plain was for the Bangash, and the hills for the Orakzais," a legend still quoted in support of proprietary rights. By and by came the Turis, who, at first subordinate, gradually in their turn displaced the Bangash; and became, what they still remain, the dominant tribe. Originally the Bangash would seem to have been divided into two main branches, named *Gár* and *Sámil*, titles which Bellew, by a somewhat elaborate theory, traces back to the Buddhist and Magian influence upon Muhammadanism; the bitter enmity between the factions earning for them the title of "Bankash," or "root destroyer." Be this as it may, the distinction still remains, and is a notable factor in frontier politics, affecting not only the Bangash, but almost all the surrounding tribes, and is only rivalled by the still more rabid enmity existing between the Shiah and the Sunni forms of Muhammadanism. Some Sunnis by religion are *Sámil* in politics, some Shiahs are *Gár*, and sometimes both cases are reversed; so that, in addition to the usual cause for quarrels, the possibilities of ringing the changes in the matter of tribal feuds are innumerable, and complicated enough to enable even a Pathán to thoroughly enjoy himself.

The Kohát, Miranzai and southern part of the Kurram Valley are mainly Bangash; those towards Kohát mostly Sunnis; the bulk of the remainder Shiahs. The Westerns wear their beards long, with a few short Jewish ringlets on either side of the face, shaving the rest of the head: the Easterns clip them short; otherwise there is not much difference. Physically they are quite up to the average Patháns, though they are not generally credited with great fighting qualities. A few deal in salt, but they are eminently an agricultural rather than a pastoral people. Reported hospitable, many of them are undoubtedly treacherous and cruel, not specially disposed to wanton violence, but "much addicted to thieving." They are rather the victims of raids by their neighbours, than raiders themselves, and have generally behaved well from an administrative point of view. Their situation is such, they have had the sense to see that in this lay their best chance of security.

The Turis, the most powerful tribes of the Upper Kurram Valley, are generally credited with having migrated from their legitimate home on the banks of the Indus some three or four centuries ago, first as dependants or *hamsayahs* of the Bangash, then gradually setting up on their own account, and now it is the Bangash of the Valley who are *hamsayahs* of the Turis. Both they and the adjoining Jâgis differ considerably in appearance, dress, and customs, from most Pathân tribes. Edwardes calls them Hindkis, and speaks of the original emigrants as numbering only sixty families, but they must have rapidly increased and prospered, and could now turn out 5,000 to 6,000 fighting men. They are not very big nor very good-looking, and have somewhat of the look of the savage about them, but they are strong, hardy, and compact, and as essentially horsemen, as the Waziris, in spite of their well-known breed of horses, are essentially footmen. The Turi is a model moss-trooper. Profusely armed, he has probably a couple of brass-bound carbines at his back, two or three pistols in front, knives of many sizes and sorts in his waist-belt, and a sword by his side. His mount, often a small sorry jade, is necessarily wiry and active; for, in addition to the Turi and his armoury, it has to carry his entire wardrobe packed under the saddle, certain wallets containing food for man and beast, some spare shoes, nails, and a hammer, an iron peg, and a picket rope, all the requisites to enable this distinguished highwayman to carry on distant and daring raids, which is the Turi road to distinction. The local Dick Turpin is honoured with the title of *khhlak*, the Turi equivalent for the hero of the hour. The newly-born Turi is introduced to ordinary life by a number of shots fired over his head, to accustom him to the sound, and prevent him shrinking when his turn comes to be shot at. Nor does he usually have to wait long

L

for this, for he is at feud with pretty well all his neighbours, Waziris, Zaimukhts and Mangals, and most bitterly with the Jàgis; even a Bangash has to attach to himself a Turi *badraga* or safe conduct, an excellent word for a most ragged but faithful little ruffian, who protects him from all other Turis.

> "Malise! what ho!—the henchman came;
> Give our safe-conduct to the Græme."

And to violate a safe-conduct once given, whatever form it takes, is as exceptional on the Pàthan Border, as in the Scotch Highlands; no greater insult could be put on the Khân or the clan giving it. Plowden tells of a Turi Malik who gave his cap as a *badraga* to an Afridi *kâfila*, which was plundered, and fell himself in revenging it.

He is hospitable, this moss-trooper, even to allowing the women of the house to wait on strangers, and in a way he is religious. He divides mankind into straight and crooked men. The Shiahs —and all Turis are Shiahs—are straight, the rest crooked. To a stranger the question takes a masonic form; the Turi salute is a finger placed perpendicularly on the forehead for a straight man, and a contorted one for a crooked man. If the stranger is well advised, he will give the countersign with a perpendicular finger. When the Kohât district was first annexed, the Turis were inclined to give trouble, but the first and only expedition sent against them, in 1856, found them at once ready to submit. Their embassy made haste to explain "after compliments," how they had fallen in with evil counsellors, and acquired bad habits in regard to their neighbour's property, but, finding the British Government protected its subjects, bound themselves to good behaviour in regard to those subjects in future. And they seem to have loyally kept their bargain, acting heartily with us against the Kàbul Khels in 1859; when, besides doing a good deal of useful service for us, they, like Major

Dugald Dalgetty, having a knowledge of the use of war, failed not to make some small profit for themselves. Subsequently they resisted the Amir's demand for men and money in 1877, and took part with us against the Zaimukhts in 1879.

Westward of the Turis, again, and along the hills from the Paiwar to the Shutargardan,[1] are the Jâgis, who differ but little, except that they are Sunnis, a reason quite sufficient to account for the feuds between the two. Fine hardy mountaineers, though poor, and dirty withal, a condition hardly separable from their mode of life and the houses they occupy, or rather share with all their live-stock, and a great volume of the rankest smoke from the pine logs, with which they keep out the rigorous cold of winter on the upper parts of the slopes. There are other tribes of more or less importance on either side of the Kurram Valley, but before passing to any particulars of them, it should not be forgotten that the tribes just referred to were, a while ago, subjects of our own.

As noticed already, this was one of the clauses of the treaty of Gandamak, and when we evacuated the Turi country again in 1880, their independence was recognized. They were to have no connection with the Amir of Kâbul, but to be free to administer their own affairs, to keep up some sort of an armed force, to raise a little tax on their cultivated lands, and, in return for our recognition, were to take our advice. As might be expected, this arrangement soon fell through, and laid the foundation for some lively little quarrels amongst themselves, which lasted the greater part of 1882-83. While, as was almost equally certain, their neighbours took the opportunity of raiding them in force. Sometimes it was the Jâgis, sometimes the Zaimukhts, and when the Turis retaliated, the Amir of Kâbul, who had not forgotten his former unsuccessful attempts to coerce them, complained of their misbehaviour, and threatened the direst punishment. So that the result of our action has been to leave the Turis very much between the devil and the

---

[1] " Camel's neck."

deep sea. The moral is obvious. Here is a large tribe, affording excellent material for irregular cavalry, with all the elements for forming a prosperous colony, anxious to be our subjects, and to whose independence we are pledged, and who, if we do not bring into our Border again, are likely to have no choice but to fall under the authority of the Amir, or worse; and so, in all probability, be lost to us as fighting material for good.

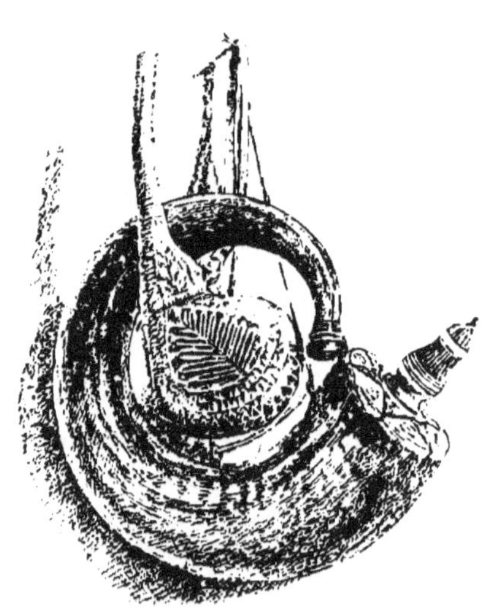

Leather and Horn Powder-flasks from the Kurram Valley.

CHAPTER XVII.

THE KHATTAKS.

Of all the frontier Pathâns there are perhaps few more favourable specimens than the Khattaks. Brave and industrious, warlike
and hospitable, they have lost none of the best qualities they
showed under a roll of famous tribal leaders, whose deeds have been
recorded in the only chronicle of the Khâns that has come down
to us. Ever since they became British subjects, their record has
been uniformly good—a striking instance of what excellent
citizens a strong Government can make out of what, at first sight,
might appear the most unpromising material.

A tribe whose importance can be judged from the fact that the
last census showed it as numbering some 118,000 in the Peshawur
and Kohât districts, of which a large proportion may be put down
as eminently "fighting men." A people whose country has been
described as the most specially desolate and unblessed on the
entire frontier, that of the Southern Khattaks the most so. Stony,
barren mountains, deep, abrupt valleys, with nothing much in the
way of water, but the brackish torrents that rush down them, with
a few forlorn straw huts that do duty for villages, whose farm-
steads are represented by an occasional patch of corn on the face
of a hill, or an insignificant green valley visible from some height.
They have no highways, save those made by us, whose village

roads are mere tracks, straggling over hills, and among the roughest ravines, or paths worn out of rocks, always difficult, and
occasionally dangerous. Their forests are a few clumps of wild olive,
or here and there a jungle patch. But their weird valleys are
varied by regions composed almost entirely of the most valuable
salt. At Bahádurkhel is a bed of bluish-gray salt estimated to
be over 1,000 feet thick and fifty miles long. In this valley the
roads are made of salt, the streams are brine, with snowy borders
of crystal, and where the blocks have only to be cut out, and
loaded on any beast that can be used as a pack animal.

It is not astonishing, therefore, that the Khattaks are rather
salt-carriers than agriculturists. Tall they are, of good stature and
strength, and if not handsome, not altogether bad looking, with
more of the appearance and manners of the people of Northern
India, and less like those of Afghánistán than most Patháns. Inveterate gossipers, whatever their occupations, great affecters of the
Hujrahs, or village clubs, enthusiastic dancers, noted pipers—the
pipes would astonish a Highlander, and the dances make a stir in
Drury Lane. They are a meat-eating, milk-drinking people, and
used to be a wine-drinking one. Their most famous leader wrote
an ode in praise of it: " The sun is a mere rushlight," declared
Khushhal Khán,—"compared to a well-filled goblet "—and they
make loaves, or rather cakes, excellent in quality, but about the
size of a waggon wheel. It is said—a shocking but not uncommon
charge,—they do not always speak the truth, but they are hospitable and festive, ready to kill the fatted calf, or rather the fat-tailed
sheep, for the Britisher who will go and take his chance of " pot-
luck." And even the salt carrier will produce a dark slab of
Pathán cake, possibly from under his pack-saddle, with an
invitation to the traveller to " stay and eat."

They have probably had more quarrels with their surrounding
world than most of their neighbours, which is saying a good deal.
There is hardly a neighbouring tribe or clan with whom at one

time the Khattak has not fought. With the Bangash on the north, for a while their allies in the Kohât district, they had the most severely contested battle; and again with the Niyazis of Isa Khel, and Mianwali on the south. On the west they had many a murderous combat with the Waziris, while the Marwats are their hereditary enemies. " Friendship is good," say the latter, " with any one but a Khattak—may the devil take a Khattak "; and both they and the Bannuchis have several most uncomplimentary proverbs against them. Three times have they warred against the Afridi, and for a century or so the Khattak was the bitterest enemy of all the Yusafzai tribes. The battles of the Peshawur Valley between Khattak and Yusafzai are like the historic quarrels between the Percys and the Douglases, they were fought out to the death. At Misri Banda, a sort of Pathân Otterburn, the Yusafzais lost a number of their chief maliks, or Khâns: the Khattaks their great leader Yahiya and many of his kindred. Sometimes it was the Khattaks who were beaten back to the foot of their own hills, sometimes they were in full cry after the flying Yusafzais across the plains of Peshawur. In those days every traveller was a fair victim; the freebooters who infested the roads are spoken of as either avoiding a party strong enough to resist, or watching till the party should be weak enough to attack.

Under the firm rule of our Government, all this has changed. The Khattaks have now neither war nor feud with tribe or clan, and if among themselves the remains of old wrongs still smoulder, they are carefully restrained, or confined to individual acts of vengeance. In the main, the Khattaks of the nineteenth century busy themselves with their own affairs, their salt carrying, trading and tilling; while the hot youth to a great extent take service in the British army, and are reported capital soldiers.

Their national dance has already been referred to as a special characteristic. Any assembly, or occasion for rejoicing, furnishes sufficient excuse. It is danced by a number of men with drawn

swords to the music of the *Surnai*, or flageolet, and drums, round a
huge blazing fire. First slow and measured movements to time,
the swords alternately waved on high or cutting imaginary
enemies; then gradually becoming quicker, the music more spirited
the dancers shouting their war-cry; finally they revolve like a
band of demons, their swords gleaming, their songs more exciting,

Khattak Horsemen in Chain Armour.

till the whole party is exhausted. One section of the tribe is held
in particular sanctity, the Kâka Khels, who are the descendants
of the great Khattak saint, Rahimkai, whose shrine is at Naushera,
a noteworthy place of pilgrimage and the scene of many miracles.
The reputation of the Kâka Khels extends far beyond that part
of the country, and is more or less of a talisman away in the
distant wilds of Afghânistân. Another only less noted section are

the Fakir Khels, the descendants of the elder brother of the noted Khushhal Khân the first, who retired from the world at the instigation of the saint. Curiously, the eldest son of the late Khân, Sir Khwâja Muhammad, has, in a similar way, become an ascetic.

Perhaps the most marked peculiarity of all, is the power of the hereditary Khâns, or tribal chiefs, who among the Khattaks, in contrast to the intensely radical feeling among Pathâns generally, always seem to have possessed exceptional influence, and to have been looked up to as the real leaders of the people. In many cases they exercised, and still continue to exercise, distinctly feudal rights. Of waste and uncultivated lands they claim ownership, take from cultivators a share of the produce or cash rents, and levy a percentage on the salt trade. They could call the tribes to arms to take the field; themselves naturally taking the lead, and for some time at least, all the Khattaks rallied under one leader. The result is, that the chronicle of the Khattak Khâns has a special interest of its own, and being in its way almost the only history of the doings of Pathân chiefs, told by one of themselves, is worthy of more than a passing notice.

There is rather a characteristic, though familiar, story as to the way the Khattaks came by their name. In the good old times when the tribe lived in the Shwâl Valley, west of Bannu, near the Ghul peak, now a summer retreat of the Waziris, four brothers came down from the hills for a hunting trip in the plains, where they fell in with four Pathân young women, from their dress evidently maidens. As the ladies came near, the eldest brother, Lukmân, suggested that it would be high sport to sieze one each for a wife. The brothers agreed, and proposed to draw lots for choice, but Lukmân, as senior, claimed the right of first choice, and unable to see their faces, selected the one most gaily dressed. When all were appropriated and examined, Lukmân's prize proved to be old, shrivelled, and "disappointing exceedingly."

"The youth was by her veiled face and fine apparel gulled.
He lifted her veil, and chanced on his grandam."

The three remaining ladies seem to have had their full share of good looks, and though pride compelled Lukmân to stick to his selection, the joke went against him. It was suggested that he had *Pa Khatta larye*—"got into the mud," which is the Pathân equivalent for "putting his foot in it," and ever after, the mud—*Khatta*—stuck to him, and all his belongings, for they were known as Khattaks. This Pathân 'elderly ugly daughter' whose name transpired to be Sabâka, "of a dark complexion and stout figure, but withal intelligent" had at least two sons by Lukmân, and each of the other damsels a numerous progeny ; though by the irony of fate, somehow they all came to be called Khattaks. At least, so says the "Khân of high renown," Khushhâl the Khattak, in his own notes, which his grandson embodied in the *Tarikh-i-Murâsa*, or "the bejewelled chronicle."

From the settlement in Shwâl, the tribe emigrated eastward to what is now the British district of Bannu, where they found two other kindred tribes, the Honai and the Mangalai, who about 1150 A.D. had taken possession of the valley, after it had been pretty well depopulated by a century and a half of ravages by Mahmud and his Ghaznavi successors. After a while, say about 1300 A.D., followed the closely related family of Shitaks, who driving off the Honais and Mangalais, settled down amicably with the Khattaks, and for some time shared the lands between two branches of the Kurram river, where is now the cantonment of Edwardesbad. Shortly the Khattaks found they needed more elbow-room, and extended themselves eastward again. Leaving the Bannu country to the Shitaks, who became the ancestors of the Bannuchis, or rather furnished the original stock for all the subsequent mongrel grafts, they spread themselves gradually and surely east and north. Up towards Junoghar, "the Virgin's peak," or Kafir Kot, "the infidel's stronghold," as tradition variously describes a mass of pre-eminent peaks, that in the distance might well be mistaken for the outline of some huge impregnable castle—up to the Teri valley, which is still the chief settlement of the western branch; over the whole south and east of what is now the Kohât district, uniting with the Bungash to drive the Orakzai up Tirah and the spurs of the Sufed Koh; and finally reducing the country as far as Nilâb, the "blue water" of the Indus near Attock. In the main the different branches of the Khattaks hold these lands still, and subsequently Malik Ako, the contemporary of the Mughal Akbar, extended them to the south-east part of the Peshawur district, where he founded Akora, the present capital of the division.

This Malik Ako, who "laid the foundations of Khattak fame," was perhaps the first recognised Khân of any consequence, and the founder of a line of chiefs, who in one way or other are among the most famous of the Border Pathâns. Ako seems to have been a shrewd, as well as valorous warrior. When Akbar returned from Kâbul, and founded the Fort of Attock, he found the road from Naushera to the Indus a terror to travellers, and in durbar appointed the Khattak chief, whose people were certainly not the least of the terrors, a sort of Warden of the Marches, offering him a title. But the Malik said, "No, lest my tribesmen be jealous; instead let me impose a transit duty on cattle." An "ear tax" he called it, to be shared by the tribe. The ear tax soon extended to ferry dues, a well tax, a house, a salt, and a land tax; finally to a royal grant of the country from Naushera to the Indus. He built a serai for travellers, and entertained liberally. "If he had aught in the morning, it was all expended by the evening;" but whether he kept the road clear of freebooters is not so certain. He undoubtedly cleared it of Hindu fakirs and their kind, for he showed Akbar two large earthen jars full of earrings, from the ears of the *jogis*[1] put to death for declining to become Muhammadans.

---

[1] An order of Hindu mendicant priests.

" I have made no other calculation of the numbers put to death," said he.

He and his successors, nominally at least, held their seigniories under the Delhi Emperor, and though each chief seems to have ruled a goodly number of years, they were in the end generally murdered by some relative. Ako, for instance, ruled for over half a century—1550 to 1600—but in spite of what a Khattak poet calls, " wielding the silvery blade," viz., spending his money to win men's hearts, he was eventually killed by his own clan. His son, Yáhiya, " of lofty stature and in due ratio brave," enjoyed about twenty years of power and of feuds, before he fell fighting the Yusafzais. His grandson Sháhbáz, a man of talents, " in bounty Hatim's peer," but undoubtedly cruel, was killed after twenty-one years of rule, in a foray with robbers, 1641.

Then came the most famous of all, Ako's great-grandson, Khushhál, who stands out among his fellows, distinguished as a warrior, a poet of some skill, a man of some education, who contributed to the history of his people, and who, as a chief, is still referred to as " the Khán of high renown." He served in the armies of Sháh Jehán, by whom he was honoured and rewarded. He repressed the Yusafzais and other tribes raiding the Peshawur Valley, and though he was subsequently seized and imprisoned for six years by Aurangzebe, that monarch had to let him out again, and send him back in state, as the only man who could restore and maintain order on the northern Border His spirit, however, was broken by his imprisonment, though some of his best and most spirited odes were composed during this period ; and shortly after his return, he retired from public affairs in favour of his sons and grandsons. He lived in his retirement for many years, and died in 1809 at the age of seventy-six, his dying request, that he might be buried where " the dust of the hoofs of the Mughal cavalry could not light upon his grave," his

last resting-place concealed, lest his enemies "might seek it out
and insult the ashes of him, at whose name, whilst in life, they
quailed; and by whose sword, and that of his clansmen, their
best troops had been scattered like chaff before the gale." Asraf
his son—one of some twenty-four, Raverty says fifty-seven—who
began to rule in 1659, the year after his father was seized by
Aurangzebe, continued till 1682, and eventually finished by dying
in a Mughal prison. Afzal, a grandson, was the ruling chief for
nearly sixty years—1682 to 1741; inherited all the literary
tastes of his grandfather, and was the author of a history of
the Khattaks from which this sketch is taken.

In his time, however, a split occurred. One son who did not
get on well with his father, established himself at Teri, which
from that time became an important place, and a separate
chieftainship. A small section had previously split up in Ako's
time and moved down to Shakardarra, where they established
themselves, and became known as the Sagri Khattaks. For a
while the Teri chief was subordinate to the elder branch, residing
at Akora, but when the Sikh invasions came into the Peshawur
Valley, the Akora overlordship was entirely broken up, only a
few petty Khâns surviving the wreck. The Teri Valley was
practically unaffected, and through a line of three or four distinguished Khâns, the chieftainship passed by regular descent
to the worthy representative of his race, who has just died,
Nawab Sir Khwâjah Muhammad Khân.

Born in 1824, Sir Khwâjah was always distinguished for his
steady loyalty to the British Government. During the second
Sikh War he rendered conspicuous assistance to our force at
the risk of having to fly for his life. Again his good services
were equally marked in 1857, and from first to last, during all
recent Afghan troubles. The head of a warlike and turbulent
race, he has—as Macgregor wrote—"though tried in a hundred
different ways, never faltered in his allegiance." In 1873 he

was made a Nawab and a K.C.S.I., and until a few months ago, he lived in undisturbed enjoyment of his well-earned dignity, a fine example of a gallant, courteous, hospitable, faithful Border Pathán chief, coming of a stock, in their way, hardly less distinguished than many a line of heroes chronicled in Western story.

CHAPTER XVIII.

PATHÁN HIGHLANDS AND HIGHLANDERS.

WHEN our Border policy is sufficiently advanced to insist on a road between two positions as important as Bannu and Thal, and we have so far tested the "kindly feeling" of the Waziris as to venture to look into the Dawar Valley, which, with some other items of communication and exploitation to be referred to anon, may fairly be described as necessary complements of any policy worth the name, a little further prospecting might with advantage be done in the adjoining valley of Khost. Shut in by a circle, rather than an amphitheatre of hills, it lies between Dawar and the Kurram, and is really open only where a branch of the latter, known as the Shamil River, makes its exit. This, by a branch road leading out of the one from Bannu to Thal, would be the natural approach, but it can be entered from the Upper Dawar Valley, past the village of Darpakhel, from the Kurram Valley, and, with still more difficulty, from the west. Though it was visited by several officers and some of our troops in 1879, not much more seems to be known about it than about the Dawar. Some forty miles long, not so broad, but quite as fertile as the Kurram, watered by three streams—branches of the Shamil—it is reported to afford plenty of timber, fuel, and pasturage; to produce very good rice, wheat, and tobacco, which the Khostwals trade into

Bannu ; and large quantities of asbestos. The climate is excellent, the people about as mongrel a lot as their kindred Bannuchis and Dawaris. They have no very large villages, but many small ones ; are numerous and well-to-do, paying no revenue to any one, save when the Kábul troops have been able to get so far and collect it by force : and to do this the Kábul forces have either to come by Ghazni and the Jadrán highlands, or the Mangal country.

The Jadráns have already been referred to as a tribe whose industry is proverbial and whose country is particularly blest. Hyát Khán describes it as consisting of "beautiful mountains, the rich green slopes watered by numerous torrents and shaded by dark firs, where fruit-trees of many sorts grow readily, and the air is fresh and invigorating"—just the place that Bannu would like to have for a sanitarium. Nevertheless, it does not produce enough for the needs of the tribe, which the same author estimates, but probably over-estimates, at 15,000 fighting men ; or possibly, like some other highlanders, they consider the noblest prospect is the high road to British territory, for they come in large numbers every year to seek employment. Not naturally quarrelsome, their position between the Mangals and the Ghilzais necessitates their being always ready to fight ; and not the least curious of their tribal customs, is one ruling that an unarmed Jadrán is liable to be fined an ox, to be eaten in full tribal assembly.

The Mangals—possibly hailing from Mangalai or North-West China, who muster pretty strong—probably 8,000 fighting men—on the southern side of the Kurram Valley, and hold a tower on the Paiwar—are not very well known, nor have we had many dealings with them ; but the little that is known is mainly to their discredit. Both they and the Zaimukhts made every use of their opportunities to harass the communications of the Kurram force under General Roberts, at times causing considerable anxiety. Their particular function seems to be theft, though they have no scruple about murder when a safe opportunity offers. Opposed to anything like organised attack, they would be insignificant in every way, while they can be easily coerced either from the Jadrán highlands or from the Upper Kurram.

The Zaimukhts, on the other hand, are stalwart highlanders; physically fine-looking, powerful men, comparing in this respect very favourably with the Turis adjoining. Sunis in creed and Sâmil in politics, there is no great love lost between them and either Turis or Bangash, but their relations with both are peaceful, compared to the quarrel between their own two chief sections. These number about 2,000 fighting men each; and afford a good instance of a tribal feud, which, beginning about the possession of a village commanding a small stream, has lasted for forty years— so bitterly that, to a great extent, it has prevented the development of what is naturally a fertile country. Roughly speaking, a triangle drawn between the towns of Hangu, along the Miranzai Valley to Thal, and thence by the Kurram to Ibrahimzai, with the Zawaghar hills for a base, would include the whole of the Zaimukht country. The hills along the base of the triangle, which separates them from the Orakzais, rises in places to a height exceeding 9,000 feet, and up among the higher glens in the centre is a collection of hamlets called Zawo, the chief stronghold of the tribe, by them considered impregnable; until, to punish them for their raids on our lines of communications already referred to, General Tytler went there in 1879, and occupied not only Zawo, but the ridge above, destroying the settlements of one section. The principal Zaimukht villages, often pleasantly situated among terraced fields, lie up among the precipitous and rocky spurs—the peaks and ridges that are thrown off this part of the Sufed Koh Range, are as a rule here somewhat barren of timber, save a few stunted oak and wild olive. In the glens and valleys water is plentiful, and but for the feuds of the people, the country would possess great possibilities for cultivation and development.

Before going on to the more powerful mountaineers who hold

the upper slopes of the range, the petty settlement of Chamkannies, dropped in amongst them, deserves a passing word of notice—a people described by Bellew as originating in a heretical sect of Persian Islamites, driven out of their own country by constant persecution on account of their peculiar religious ceremonies and immoral proceedings. One of the stories against them is not altogether without a savour of the " Love Feast " of more modern sects in England ; and consisted in putting out the lights at a stage of the religious performances, in which both sexes joined indiscriminately, and which was the signal for possible improprieties. The Persians called it *Chiragh-kush*,[1] and the Pathâns *Or-mur* ;[2] but the Chamkannies, however, have turned over a new leaf, and become orthodox Muhammadans.

Those settled in the western part of the Kurmâna Valley are sometimes associated with the Orakzais, albeit the " lamp extinguishers " are in every way a distinct race, little colonies of them occurring from the Peshawar Valley to Kâbul and down to Kanigoram in the Waziri country.

East of the Zaimukhts, and along the southern slopes of the Sufed Koh as far as the Kohât Pass Afridis, and between the Lower Miranzai on the south and the Bâra River watershed on the north, is the Orakzai country—sometimes spoken of as Tirah, though the name belongs properly to a more restricted area—the home of one of the most numerous, powerful, fanatical, and, in some respects, inaccessible of our immediate Border tribes, or rather group of tribes: for though usually referred to as one, it must be understood in an ethnographical and not a political sense. Their six main divisions are split up into many parties, are variously *Gâr* and *Sâmil* in politics; and their intertribal warfare, which has often furiously raged between the Tirah Sayuds and Sunnis, formed the subject of a special report to Government by Cavagnari. Some sections in a great measure are dependent on

<hr>

[1] " Lamp extinguisher."   [2] " Fire extinguisher."

British territory; others but slightly so; and reprisals are not easy. One, the Daulatzai, has committed many acts of hostility; and against the Bizoti and Rubia Khel clans special expeditions have been undertaken, while some of the most numerous have so far never given any serious trouble. Any relations with them as a body would hardly be possible, and probably nothing, unless it were lust of plunder or hatred of the infidel, would unite together the different elements that go to make up a fighting strength estimated at over 25,000 men. As a body, though not such fine men as the Afridis, they are robust, wiry-looking mountaineers; and though opinions differ as to their martial qualities, they admittedly shoot very straight. It is more than doubtful if by descent they are Pathâns; but if not better, they are probably not much worse than their neighbours in the Pathân qualities of deceit, avarice, and cruelty. Macgregor says " there is no doubt that, like other Pathâns, they would not shrink from any falsehood, however atrocious, to gain an end. Money could buy their services for the foulest deed; cruelty of the most revolting kind would mark their actions to a wounded or help-less foe, as much as cowardice would stamp them against deter-mined resistance." On the other hand it must not be forgotten that they have been embittered by centuries of bitter religious feuds and the influence of fanatical teachers; they have never had a Government of any decent sort, its place being supplied by superstition; and they do not understand our theory of tolerance or non-interference. They are certainly not worse than the Afridi —to whom these crimes are second nature, but who under a tight hand is transformed into a soldier ranking with the best in our native army. What we call "wonderful forbearance," to these people is a mere excuse for further misbehaviour, while prompt punishment has a magical effect in pulling up the worst conducted. What they would understand, and in time appreciate, would be a strong government; and once brought under this, we should transform a troublesome set of neighbours, torn by crushing feuds, into a prosperous people—another reserve of stalwart highlanders to draw upon.

Tirah, in its restricted sense, includes the main Bâra River Valley above Torabela; the Orakzai, or southern branch of the same river, above Hissar; the Khanki River Valley, above Sidurra, and the Kurmâna, above Khazina. When it is understood that

An Orakzai.

all these rise pretty near to one another, and the first two flow past Peshawur into the Kâbul River, the third into the Kohat *toi* [1] near Hangu, and the fourth into the Kurram near Ibrahimzai; that this comprises an area of about 700 square miles, with an altitude, for the most part, between 5,000 and 6000 feet,—its situation and advantages will be more easily realized. The first of these, including the valleys of Raigal and Maidân, is occupied

<hr>

[1] "Stream."

by Afridis; the other three, and the smaller ones that open into them, by Orakzais, many of whose tribes and clans vary their quarters every summer and winter, coming down with their flocks into the low hills, and often into British territory, during the latter season. All are more or less shut in by wild and precipitous hills, the crests often covered with magnificent oak and pine forests; especially is this the case on our immediate border. The Zawaghar and the Sammanoghar, which bound the Khanki Valley on the Miranzai side, rise over 9,000 and 7,000 feet respectively. The Muzzeoghar, which separates this from the Southern Bâra, is over 8000 feet and rises 5000 directly above the Khanki River below it. To say that they are difficult of access is to use a somewhat weak figure of speech. The Ublân Pass—a strong position six miles from Kohât, and the scene of one or two affairs against the Bizoti clan—is over 4000 feet high, while below, the Southern Bâra sweeps round the base of Mulloghar, a spur 7,000 feet high, almost directly opposite. A situation it would hardly be necessary to have three hundred Spartans to make a Thermopylæ of. There are two or three passes or paths further on, practicable for very little beyond laden oxen, but when crossed, the real difficulties of advance would only be beginning: for the main valleys are split up into a succession of rich, fertile basins; by bold, rugged spurs, which here and there form "waists," affording splendid natural defences and proportionately formidable obstacles to the passage of troops. On the opposite side the approaches are through the Afridi territory.

Higher up, these valleys broaden out and become extensive, almost open highlands; the Kurmârna Valley is estimated as a basin of nearly 200 square miles; frequently terraced into a succession of fields, and dotted with hamlets and towers. Well wooded, abundantly watered, producing in plenty apples, pears, grapes, and most fruits, a variety of vegetables and excellent timber. And if to a poorly-clothed Orakzai it seems cold in winter, the summer climate is described as delicious. Nevertheless, as far as the British Government is concerned, the valleys of Tirah might be as those in the kingdom of Amhara, from which Rasselas found it so difficult to escape, though we have more excuse for knowing something of the inside, than the Prince of Abyssinia had for surveying mankind "from China to Peru." Not so long ago the Quartermaster-General of India excused want of information, on the ground that "though the furthest point is not more than eighty miles from the cantonments of Peshawar or Kohât, though the inhabitants are constantly to be met with in our territory, its tribes form one of the largest sections of our frontier neighbours, and its politics one of the most important items of frontier business—nothing of any value has yet been recorded regarding it." This is perhaps not quite literal. Captain Tucker ventured into Lower Tirah in 1872, for which he was severely censured; a native, Agha Abbâs, has written an account of it; and one surveyor, disguised as a native, and associated with Pathân *Shikaris,*[1] reached points from which he could overlook it, and was able to map a part of Maidân. Another attempt to reach points from which the Bâra Valley could be overlooked failed, and though British officers have surveyed all round it, the inside is to them still a *terra incognita.* Definite information cannot therefore be said to have been yet advanced very far in the matter of these Highlands or Highlanders.

---

[1] Hunters.

CHAPTER XIX.

A PATHÁN SURPRISE.

IN "Piffer"[1] parlance "the tribes were out," and this in a frontier station always meant some additional excitement. Although the sentries had been doubled—no officer's verandah was without one or two, and patrol parties moved promiscuously about with buckshot cartridges handy—there was always the off chance of a wily Pathán getting a snap shot at any one going home from mess. The walls of Kohát Fort were the subject of constant attention on the part of certain tribesmen, who seemed to spend their evenings in long range practising at any exposed part, and must have remained with a perpetual bead drawn on the opposite embrasures, in the hopes of eventually catching an unwary passer by. Outside of the cantonment limits no road was safe without an escort, and travellers had to keep a pretty smart look-out when passing outlying hills. The trouble was mainly with the Orakzais, some of whose clans had taken to frequent raiding on the country adjoining their border. The adjacent villages were pretty constantly fired on, and although the raiders bolted as soon as they were attacked in turn, it was seldom before one or two of the villagers had been killed or wounded. Unprotected cattle were, as a matter

---

[1] A word compounded from the initial letters of the old Punjáb Irregular Frontier Force.

of course, promptly carried off into the hills. Becoming bolder the raiders had recently succeeded in surprising some police outposts; one or two policemen had been cut down, others carried off and detained. A small force sent out under the Deputy Commissioner's orders to retaliate, had, owing to some unfortunate misunderstanding, advanced too far into the hills, got involved in the steep ground among the Ublán spurs, and had to come back unsuccessfully, having lost one officer and some dozen men killed, besides many wounded. The most unsatisfactory feature of the whole business was that the leading offenders belonged to a most insignificant clan; though holding a position of such natural strength, successful operations against them must necessarily be on an extensive scale. In fact, the Bizotis fancied themselves absolutely secure, and traded upon the supposition. At the same time, to take out an army against a handful of professional cattle-lifters and thieves seemed a veritable breaking of a fly on the wheel. The Ublán Pass affair was too serious to be overlooked, and they were strictly blockaded, but this was a small punishment to a clan with no trade to lose, who sowed a rice crop in their lower valleys, and went away to Tirah till it ripened; who could run down from their summer hill station in twenty-four hours for a fight, and disperse to the four winds again in half that time. Their winter settlements, though really only an hour's ride from Kohát, were on the other side of a formidable range of hills, approached by a horse-shoe shaped pass, in which all the nails represented positions for riflemen, and the centre lowest point to be crossed, a lip 4,000 feet high. On this stood the Kotál or watch towers, from which the Bizotis could watch the doings of the garrison, pretty nearly as effectually as Kohát is supposed to do for the tribes generally. A decent look-out on this tower, with the assistance of a goodly supply of spies in the bazaar, kept the villages of their valley nearly as well informed of the garrison doings as the commandant himself. The rest of the Orakzais professed the part of good-natured friends; they were ready to ride with the hounds, but not to assist in catching the hare, and resisted all the efforts made to induce them to coerce the refractory Bizotis. An expedition requires much more than a good reason, it needs the sanction of Government to the probable expenditure of a lot of money, and the possible loss of many lives—it might easily cost a lot of lives—to rush the Ublán Kotál. Still it was evidently necessary to adopt some more active and potent measures than the blockade, and as it was already February, anything to be done must be done promptly. Delay would have meant indefinite postponement. The Deputy Commissioner and the commanding officer, therefore, determined to try, and cast about to frame a scheme to surprise the Bizotis; and so well did they keep the secret, that, until the whole train was laid, it was not suspected even by the garrison.

It was arranged that on a certain day a force should move out from Peshawar, a part towards the Aka Khel country, and so attract the attention of the tribes to possibilities in that direction; the remainder into the Kohát Pass, and create some little diversion there. At the same time the pass Afridis were brought into Kohát to discuss business, which they found necessitated their remaining a few days to settle; so that if suspicion was aroused, it was all in the direction of the Afridis and the pass. Finally the commanders of regiments in Kohát received confidential instructions, and one night, towards the end of February, they all came to dine at the garrison mess, and play a little quiet rubber after dinner. Just before midnight the officer commanding the artillery was directed to proceed to the fort and get the mountain battery ready for service; half an hour later the men were to be warned. At the same time two regiments of native infantry were paraded, and at one o'clock, a third—all without a single bugle sound. Meanwhile, a regiment of Punjáb cavalry had quietly formed a cordon round the town, and prevented any one entering or leaving it; and police pickets had taken up and stopped all the points by which a footman might enter the hills. At 1 A.M. the Deputy Commissioner and the commandant, with a boly of picked men, and certain chiefs of the friendly clans, followed by a mountain battery, two regiments of infantry and some dozen of mule loads of ammunition, made straight for the pass. According to the programme, the friendly chiefs were to be put forward to square the sentries while the police rushed in and seized them; but so little was anything suspected, and so confident the Bizotis of the strength of their position, that they had entirely neglected this precaution, and the watch had actually gone into Kohât for a spree. Quiet possession of the Kotâl was therefore taken, the troops brought up in the dark to the crest of the ridge, and by dawn had moved down on one of the principal Bizoti villages. The friendly chiefs, who had been let go a quarter of an hour ahead to warn the villagers against resistance, seemed to think it was but fair to do a turn for their own people, and were energetic in spreading the alarm, so that by the time the troops arrived at the first big village, the women and cattle were streaming out of one end, and the fighting men had opened fire at the other. It was, however, taken at a rush, the leaders of the offending faction being the first to fall. The surprise was complete, but to have attempted a further advance would have been to risk a heavy loss of life with no proportionate gain. The lesson had been sufficiently sharp and severe; a large number of cattle and live-stock captured, the whole of the village, with the exception of the mosque, was completely destroyed, and the Bizotis, who fought bravely enough, had lost pretty heavily in killed and wounded. The mountain guns were therefore brought into action, and under cover of their fire the force returned, and were in Kohât again within twelve hours, with the loss of three men killed.

Nothing probably could have more effectually disabused these troublesome neighbours of their fancied security against punishment; it was to them a genuine " Pathân surprise," and there is no doubt all the tribes round envied such a stroke of luck, and appreciated it more than if a big expedition had been successfully undertaken against them. The effect, at any rate, was equally great. By the end of March, their *jiryahs*[1] had come in and agreed to pay a fine of Rs. 1,200, to give nine of their principal headmen as hostages for future good behaviour, and had laid down their swords at the feet of the Deputy Commissioner, a young man whose name was Cavagnari. The tribes were quiet again.

[1] Tribal Councils.

CHAPTER XX.

KOHÂT AND THE FRONTIER FORCE.

A PICTURESQUE town among water-courses and wheat fields,
orchards and shallow pebbly streams, with ranges of blue hills
for a background. To the east the rugged mountains of the
equally rugged Jawâki Afridis. Rising steep up, almost close
behind the *Kotâl*, over which the pass leads through the Gallai
Afridi country to Peshawur, and the steeper Ublân pass to the
still more lofty peaks of Mulloghar. Westward the Orakzai hills
and the rich Miranzai Valley, seldom without a breeze to temper
the fierce heats of summer, at times so sharp and biting as to have
made the *hangu*, famous as the very coldest breeze along the Border.
More to the south rises Mir Khwaili covered with wild olive, and
the range round which the Toi river works through a fertile strip
of cultivation towards the Indus. The foreground dotted with
mulberry groves and gardens, or a group of walnuts and Indian
fig-trees, marks some more than usually famous shrine, like Haji
Bahâdur, to which the Border Pathân resorts when he wishes to
take an exceptionally sacred oath, one more binding than any
court could ever extract from him. Such is Kohât—an oasis in a
district, bare, barren, and stony more than most.

Alongside the town is the Fort, practically within rifle-shot of
the Border line, the exact range of spots where any careless member

of the garrison might for a moment expose himself, well known to the tribesmen, who have had opportunities for the most extended practice. Not far from this, the cantonments with two or three regiments of infantry, one of cavalry, one mountain and one garrison battery, a total force probably amounting to 3,500 men, belonging entirely to the Frontier force, the "Piffers" as they are called in the Punjâb. Trim little houses, with trim, but very little gardens, for there is not much scope for gardening where sentries have to patrol nightly, keeping a watchful eye on the flower pots, and anything as big as a gooseberry bush may afford shelter to a trans-border scoundrel, intent on plunder. A little church, an assembly room, convertible for either ball or theatricals, a library, racket-courts, tennis-courts, cricket-ground, polo and racecourse, also convertible. All within a ring fence, so that society can take its exercise, or its afternoon tea, enjoy its band or its last novel from Mudie's; cultivate Terpsichore or Melpomene, without going beyond the range of the mess; that garrison mess whose hospitable doors are open to every one duty or pleasure carries in its direction. It is not the fortune of every one to be a resident, but the veriest wayfarer is not permitted to be a stranger. No strangers are possible within the gates of the Kohât garrison. And Kohât is only a sample of every one manned by the Piffers, from Hoti-Mardân to Râjanpore. If hospitality is a reputed characteristic of the Border people, it is the first and most scrupulously observed regulation of the Border garrisons.

But the garrison will do more than entertain the traveller, they will furnish him with an escort, and surround him with the best of sentries. And in many parts he is liable to want both badly, for ruffians on the other side of the line allow no traditions of hospitality to interfere with business. They may not take his life—it is not profitable to kill a sahib—there is more fuss about the one English *Kâfir* than the ninety and nine self-righteous Pathâns; but they will not willingly leave any of his property that is movable, while as artists in negotiating this form of exchange, they are probably *facile princeps.* To steal the horses of the Commissioner, the camels from the camp of the Lieutenant-Governor under the noses of the guard—or the rifles out of the racks in the Peshawar barracks, is merely routine business, nearly as easy as driving off cattle from the villages, or abducting the trader's only son—the apple of some fat Hindu's eye, a wretch who prefers to pay up on a receipt of the first bit clipt from the boy's ear, to waiting for any of the remaining pieces. To take however, the revolver from under the colonel's pillow; to gut the district officer's tent of its entire contents, leaving for manners a square bit of carpet cut out neatly round his bed; or cut a hole in the tent of the sleeping police officer, and carry off his, and his wife's, only clothes, from among the drowsy constables, are forms of practical joking requiring a proficient hand. But to carry off an entire tent, pitched in the middle of the Kohât cantonment bristling as it does with sentries, who shoot at sight, was a master-stroke performed not so long ago.

The sentries of the force moreover are not as other sentries. Instead of conspicuously walking up and down, in heavy boots, with a glittering bayonet, a sort of friendly beacon for the Border thief to skirmish by, the Piffer sentries are probably lying *perdu* behind a wall, watching for a chance, or in small parties carefully stalking lively spots where a marauder might be flushed. They are pretty certain to be dead shots, their weapons not unlikely to be loaded with buckshot in place of bullets, and to act on the famous principle of a word and a blow; to challenge and shoot, but to shoot first. There may be no addition to the guard-room, but "two *budmashes* (scoundrels) were shot last night, and a third got away badly hit," is a not improbable morning report. If challenged in the dusk on the Border, it is always well to speak quick, and at one time the Peshawur tradition held it to be the safest thing to fall down flat, and then shout "friend." The average Piffer sentry is far more discerning than to shoot a sahib, but the guest may possibly get a tip, "not to let his servants stray too far about the place to-night, as a couple of patrol parties are starting at dark to cruise about in search of suspected raiders, thought likely to visit the lines." The raider for his part would "snipe" the sentry who came at all in his way, with a light heart, and so the latter takes the best means he can to get first shot.

What the sentry does to protect the unit, the Piffers as a body do for the Border, or a good part of it. With the exception of Peshawur and Quetta, they garrison India's most important outposts, are the advance guard of its army. In every sense they are a Border force, recruited almost entirely from Border people. Sikhs, Gurkhas, Punjâbi Muhammadans, Afghâns, a few Biloches, and a large proportion from the Pathân tribes on the other side of the line. The Queen's Own Corps of Guides, for instance, a splendid body of both infantry and cavalry, with permanent head-quarters at Hoti Mardân, in the Peshawur Valley, includes among its ranks picked trans-border men from all parts, familiar with most of the country and the passes, between the Indus and Kâbul. Tribes against whom we have, at one time or other, had to undertake expeditions, and with whose fellow clansmen we might at any time have a burst again.

In countries where patriotism is exalted as a primary virtue, the policy of enlisting men, whose duties might involve the carrying of fire and sword into their fatherland; who might have to march against their own kith and kin, or watch their own village being fired, would be doubted. The Pathân Piffer, if he has read Dr. Johnson, would probably agree in considering patriotism that declined this, "the last refuge of a scoundrel." Perhaps also he has an opinion in the matter of being "faithful to his salt," or a strong sense of military honour, but in the Frontier force, the policy has always been found to work admir-

ably. He will march anywhere, fight any one against whom
he is led, and it has been found, when he goes home again
he carries with him good feeling to the Government, whose power
and resources he has come to know, and exercises a good influence

A Distinguished Guides-man; killed trying to save Wygram Battye in Afghánistán.

in its favour among his own people. Over and over again these
men have actually marched against their own clansmen, and their
own homes. Not only against fathers and brothers but even
against the still more potent religious appeals from the local
Gházis. On one occasion in the Miranzai campaign a native

officer, whose father was on the hill to be attacked, urged his commanding officer to get blood spilt between the troops and the Ghâzis before nightfall, so as to stop any feeling of sympathy that might arise.

That before he enters our service, he may have raided our villages, stolen our horses, shot our sentries, or fought stubbornly against us, does not make him any the less valuable when he comes over to our side. Contrariwise, on the plan of setting a thief to catch a thief, or turning a poacher inside out to make a gamekeeper, a desperate foe sometimes makes a most useful Border soldier. Not only does the Piffer officer feel that joy in meeting a foeman worthy of his steel, he sees in him a possibly fine recruit. While the fight raged fiercest at 'Ali Musjid, a band of horsemen in the Amir's service came under the full fire of the Guides infantry, and suffered so heavily that they had to retreat. But there came back one Pathân, and shouted defiance while he took the fire of half a regiment. Somehow he was not hit, but he was promptly marked by the eye of the colonel, who took the first opportunity to enlist, and turn him into as good a Guide as the best. Mr. Rudyard Kipling makes a capital ballad out of another Guide recruit, whose father, a well-known Border outlaw, lifted the colonel's mare, but spared the life of the son, who pursued him to his lair, from whence the Borderer sent back his own son to be a trooper in the regiment, to swear on the bread and salt, to guard the boy with his life, and to harry the old man's hold if such should be the need.

One thing he does not give up, but brings with him to his regiment, keeps through his service, must have leave to look after, will resign promotion to gratify, and looks forward to retiring to thoroughly enjoy—and that is—his cherished feud. If he has not got one when he joins, he may inherit one, which may become just as binding, though it concerns people he has not seen for years, and hardly knew when he left home. In India, the white man

N

wants leave to get married, he is sick, he needs a change, or to avoid a bad station; very much less frequently, to go home and enjoy a fortune. The black man has lost his mother, or any more convenient relation, has a lawsuit, or a boil as per margin. For the Pathân soldier there is only one class of "urgent private affairs," but for this he must have leave. "Six months, O Father of the regiment," or, "three months at least." Then "O friend of Allah, for God's sake let me have six weeks, for my business is pressing and I cannot possibly manage it in less." Every one knows for what purpose he goes, it is the only reason where refusal of leave would justify desertion. He will do nothing rash within the Border, there will be nothing too rash for him as soon as he is on the other side, and if he does not come back, he has probably met with misfortune, in the shape of a too skilful enemy. There is an old story of a very bad blood-feud between two men, Mauladin Khân and Isa Khân, uncle and nephew, both in the same regiment, who could never be allowed leave at the same time. For years they campaigned together, both were equally ready to fight the enemies of the Queen, and behaved perfectly, but so bitter was the feud, if both were allowed to go home, only one, it was certain, would come back. After a while there came new officers, and both unfortunately did get leave. Isa Khân alone came back. He did not mention that before starting he had got three days off parade and walked from Bannu to Dera Ismail Khân and back, some 170 miles, to beg a flask of powder from his former officer, a crack shot; but he confided on his return, that he never should have been able to settle his affair, had it not been for Norman sahib's "straight shooting powder."

Among the low hills of the Kuki Khels, is a small tower which commands the surrounding country for some little distance. The residence of an ex-Guides-man, a man who would have rejoiced Ouida. Of great strength, keen eye and iron will; who had shared in the sharp fighting of 1857 against the mutineers; fought with

our troops, against the combined tribes at Ambeyla and the second
Black Mountain expedition; accompanied the Forsyth Mission to
Kashgâr; but finally cut his name to carry out a feud. The path
was open to him to high honour and distinction, but he stood out,
and to an inquiring officer, he said, "I never knew what real happiness was, until I had taken this tower, and could send a bullet
after my enemy whenever he ventured to show his face." Unless
that enemy is dead, the ex-Guides-man probably watches for him
still. From the regimental records of the Piffers could be extracted
volumes of such stories, records of the most gallant deeds performed
by the men whom the law as we understand it would have undoubtedly hanged for murder. We hold "one murder makes a
villain, millions a hero;" the Pathân is not casuist enough to see
the difference. For him it is not numbers, but fancied obligation,
that "sanctifies the crime." One more, quite modern instance,
which gives characteristically enough, murder from the Pathân
soldier's point of view, must suffice.

"Riding from Bannu," says the narrator, "just before reaching the
outpost in which was my camp for the day, I overtook a particularly good-looking, upstanding Pathân, from his smartness
and salute evidently a soldier, but with no uniform, and a
manner that looked an unmistakable grievance. A handsome,
almost a pleasant-faced man, who evidently seemed to have
something to say, so I asked him of his welfare, and in return
he told me his story. 'The other day,' he said, 'I was a Jemadar,
in the 1st Punjab Infantry, a regiment that to me was everything. I have served in it for fifteen years; I was with it all
through the Afghân campaign, and along all this frontier. There
has never been anything against me. I liked my officers, and
looked to be made Subadar. Recently some urgent family business'—he alluded to the family business in so delicate a way, it
might have related to the birth of a baby, instead of the death
of an enemy—'compelled me to take leave and go home to

Abazai. I got four months' leave, had the best of rifles, and made every arrangement, but the man I wanted had gone, and would not come back till he knew my leave was up. It was therefore impossible for me to return, and I did not send any letter to my adjutant, because I thought every day the man would come back. Well, sahib, I waited and waited, but he did not come for nearly three weeks. The very day he did,'—here his eye glistened just a little—'I managed to shoot him, and started back to my regiment next morning. And now, surely no one had ever such hard luck, they have cut my name and broken my service, because I was absent without leave. I am sorry about the leave, but it was not my fault that the man did not come to Abazai sooner. And, sahib, can you tell me where is the General just now? I am on my way to find him. He is a good man and a just. Knows the Pathân people, and is certain to see me righted as soon as he hears my case. * * * And here, sahib, are your tents. *Salâm-a-laikum.* May it be well with you.'"

Besides the garrisons of Abbotabad, Kohât, Bannu, Dera Ismail, Dera Ghâzi, Hoti Mardân, and Râjanpore, the first five of which are also the head-quarters of civil districts, and the last two, of civil sub-divisions, there is a line of small forts or outposts, which are also garrisoned by the Frontier Force, and the Frontier Militia. On the Hazâra, Peshawur, and Kohât borders, these are comparatively few, and held in considerable strength; along the Bannu and Derajât borders, they are smaller but more frequent, often ten or twelve miles apart, so as to command one or more passes; and the Piffers are associated with the militia, or the outposts are held entirely by the latter. In Border slang the militia-man is a "Catch-'em-alive-O," in appearance he is not very different from those wild moss-troopers already described. In practice he is a tribesman and a raider, employed to restrain his fellow tribesmen and raiders from pursuing their trade within our limits, only furnished with better weapons of which he is proud in proportion, though as his name implies, he is not to kill, but to catch the offender, and bring him in alive for the law to deal with. His inclination would of course naturally be to utilize his superior talents and weapons to prosecute little wars or feuds of his own, but this disposition has been sternly, and in the main successfully repressed, so far as our territory is concerned. He is not a soldier in that he is not trained as one, but he has a very intimate knowledge of the country and of the movements of his friends on the other side, with whom he manages to spend not a little of his time, and he furnishes capital material out of which soldiers could be made.

Excluding these, and the tribal levies, the Frontier Force is approximately some 15,000 strong[1] commanded by a brigadier general, up to a few years ago under the immediate orders of the Lieutenant-Governor of the Punjâb, but now directly under the Commander-in-Chief. Every regiment keeps up its own carriage, organizes its own transports and commissariat, and is ready to start for active service at a moment's notice. An emergency that necessitated a council of war in Kohât or similar garrison, would within a few hours see infantry, cavalry, and artillery marching out prepared for a campaign. There is probably no more mobile force possessed by any power, no soldier of whom that power might be more proud.

The progress of events that have necessarily to some extent modified the organization of the force, will probably entail some further changes in the not distant future. Though it still retains its distinctive character, it has by passing under the orders of the Commander-in-Chief, become essentially a part of the Indian army. With the extension of the Quetta position and a more or less general moving forward, it can hardly remain a local and also a Border force. Râjanpore and Dera

---

[1] The Frontier Force at present consists of four regiments of Punjâb Cavalry ; the Corps of Guides, Cavalry, Infantry, to which screw guns are to be added ; four Mountain Batteries ; one Garrison Battery ; four regiments of Sikh Infantry ; five regiments of Punjâb Infantry ; two Battalions of Gurkhas.

Gházi Khán are no longer Border stations, the outposts have moved a couple of hundred miles to the west of them. The Piffers have already as many men on detachment at Khur, Rakhni, Kingri, and Kot-Muhammad Khán, as remain at regimental head-quarters; while beyond again, in the Bori Valley and Peshin, are stations garrisoned by Bengal regiments. Higher up, Dera Ismail Khán may shortly find it necessary, to detach a part of its garrison to Apazai and the Zhob Valley; or that at Bannu find a way through the Tochi to the Jadrán Highlands.

It would, at the same time, be a misfortune if these changes in any way involved sacrificing the distinctive character of the force, because apart from its special value, it appears essentially the best organization, to which additional militia and tribal levies could be gradually attached. The day has entirely passed for considering it in any sense an irregular force, but there is no reason why to its splendid regiments should not be affiliated irregular ones of excellent militia. For the organization of special tribal levies, there can surely be found no agency more suitable than the men who have graduated as its officers, and acquired the most intimate acquaintance with the Border people. A moderate estimate places the fighting men of these tribes at 160,000 Pathâns, and 150,000 Biloches, for the Punjâb alone; without taking account of the Sind Border or Bilochistân proper; and whether as regulars, militia or levies, there is no doubt of the value of the material.

Whatever the precise figures may be, the field for recruiting is undoubtedly immense, the extension of the Frontier Force merely a question of policy and of funds; and should future changes develop either in this direction, or in change of location, it is certain to take a foremost place in any comprehensive scheme of Frontier defence. With equal safety, it may be predicted, that the Piffers may be looked to supply, in the future as in the past, leaders capable of directing the most important operations in connection with that defence.

CHAPTER XXI.

AFRIDIS AND THE KOHÂT PASS.

WHAT is true of the Orakzais and their country to a great extent applies to the adjoining Afridis, the next great group of tribes occupying the Sufed Koh Range, and our neighbours for upwards of ninety miles along the Border in the Kohât and Peshawur districts. A still finer race, they are equally numerous—certainly over, 26,000 fighting men—more than most others important, inasmuch as they hold possession of the Kohât and Khaiber Passes, and, for the purposes of defence, their positions are nearly inaccessible. Classed among the most lawless and savage of Pathâns, but, at the same time, the bravest, most open in manner, and most treacherous, the Afridi is perhaps the Pathân whose manliness and manner most strongly prejudice Englishmen in his favour. The frontier highlander of whom we hear oftenest, who is the hero of so many characteristic stories, and about whom it is very difficult to write, save in a series of contradictions, is in appearance a lithe muscular man, with a rather fair complexion, high nose and cheek bones, frequently associated with a not unhandsome face; a self-possessed, independent, and almost courteous manner; as Macgregor —himself a distinguished kinsman of Rob Roy, and no bad judge —describes him, "a fine, tall, athletic highlander, whose springy steps, even in traversing the dusty streets of Peshawur, at once denotes his mountain origin;" but, as the same authority continues, "a ruthless, cowardly robber—a cold-blooded treacherous murderer; brought up from his earliest childhood amid scenes of appalling treachery and merciless revenge, nothing has changed him; as he has lived—a shameless, cruel savage—so he dies. And it would seem that, notwithstanding his long intercourse with us, and the fact that large numbers have been and are in our service, and must have learnt in some way what faith, justice, and mercy mean, yet the Afridi is no better than in the days of his father." Both estimates are perhaps somewhat extreme. He is not so tall and fine as some of the Khattaks and Yusafzais; and in Peshawur he might almost pass for a righteous man. Hospitality is one of his virtues, and more than most things wins his heart. Stories are told of his sacrificing his life for his guest, and equally of his plots to take that guest's life so soon as the latter is outside his lands, or has passed beyond the shelter of his roof. Not a few of his feuds are about women, yet he is credited with small regard for the sanctity of marriage rights. "Frequent cases," writes Mackeson, "occur of an Afridi in good circumstances marrying first a good-looking girl, but as times get harder exchanging her for one of fewer personal attractions and so much cash." Nothing but blood can wash out an insinuation about his honour, but his "women are willingly offered to the embraces of those who can afford to pay for the indulgence."

Eminently a "professing" Muhammadan, and strict observer of the precepts of the Korán, he has really little religion of any sort, and has small reverence even for the Mullahs. "As to the Orakzais," says the Khattak poet Khushhál—

> They are altogether from orthodoxy astray.
> No call of Mu'azzin is to be heard in Tirah,
> And the Afridis, than those erring ones more heretical still,
> Neither say prayers over the dead, nor Mullahs have they,
> Nor alms, nor offerings, nor the fear of God in their hearts."

The confiding priests who ventured into Afridi land fared so badly it was never popular with the Muhammadan clergy, and is somewhat a dangerous place still. Among unfaithful Pathâns, the "faithlessness" of an Afridi is notorious. Nothing is perhaps so dear to a fanatical Pathân as a plentiful supply of *ziyârats*, or sacred shrines to martyrs and saints; a heap of stones raised over a *ghâzi* who has murdered an English *kâfir* will serve the Pathân purpose equally as well as a Westminster Abbey or a City Temple. But Afridi land is strangely deficient in this respect. At one time, according to Bellew, there was not such a thing as a *ziyârat* in the whole country; and he tells a good story of the way the Afridi managed to remedy this. Through very shame the tribes had been driven by their more orthodox neighbours to entice a zealous Mullah from Peshawur to come and minister to them. Once installed, the priest naturally wanted some place to set up his altar—his *Beth-el* [1]—dilating on the necessity for the establishment of *ziyârats*, and the advantages to be derived from the contributions and offerings pilgrims would bring who came to worship. This was enough for the Afridi, avaricious at any time, here was a fresh prospect of gain opened out. What was easier than to have a *ziyârat*; and who more suitable as a martyr for the faith than the venerable priest? So the Mullah was forthwith sacrificed, and the first *ziyârat* in Tirah was raised over his remains.

On another occasion a Mullah was caught copying the Korân. "You tell us these books come from God, and here you are making them yourself. It is not good for a Mullah to tell lies," so the indignant Afridis made another *ziyârat* for him.

As in morals and religion, their politics and pleasures are hardly less anomalous. The most democratic and disunited people among themselves, uncontrolled, and often uncontrollable even by their own chiefs, all the clans have uniformly joined in hostility to us whenever opportunity offered; still more so to everything connected with Kâbul, whose Amirs, instead of levying tribute, have

---

[1] "The place of God."

always had to pay toll. In punishing one contumacious tribe, an expedition has invariably had to consider the possibility of combined action by all, should retribution be pushed too far. Their extra-tribal feuds are almost as uncommon as their internal ones are innumerable. That is, the Afridis do not care to waste their energies in fighting with their neighbours, but reserve the luxury for home consumption. Among themselves, feuds occupy a great part of their lives, possibly for the same reason that an Irishman at a fair, or an English navvy on Saturday night, is not really happy until he has broken a head, or given or received a black eye : so a feud to an Afridi is the one pleasure that makes life tolerable. It has been described, as to him the salt of life. He does not need the plea of difference between Gâr and Sâmil, Sunni and Sayud. It may be about *Zan*, *Zar*, or *Zamin*,—woman, money, or land, or water,—but, like Sir Lucius O'Trigger, any excuse will serve to begin ; and, once begun, it is never spoiled by explanation, interrupted save by pressing business, nor terminated as long as any male representative remains on either side. Just as the Englishman, who, when he finds time hanging heavily, is credited with proposing to go and shoot something, the Afridi's one idea of sport is to shoot some one. Having no business in hand, he will take up his position, rifle in hand, and wait patiently behind a rock for hours, till he can put a bullet through a neighbour ; and the patience with which he will wait with a bead drawn on the spot that neighbour must pass, would, if it were not murderous, be almost meritorious. Not to mention the disputes between clans it is common to find one half a village, or one half a family, carrying on a skirmish with the other half, taking advantage of any shelter or any artifice ; keeping up a guerilla warfare until several casualties have occurred on either side, their ammunition is exhausted, harvest operations, or a marriage between the factions necessitates a truce. We call this "cold-blooded, treacherous murder"; the Afridis considers it superior to pigeon shooting or fox-hunting. The women, who are in every sense the real hewers of wood and drawers of water, are of course too much occupied—in the fields, no less than at the hearths—to take any prominent part in the quarrels; but they are deadly shots with stones, and can make excellent defence at a pinch, Whether, in addition to other objections, the Afridi looks upon us, with our judicial and criminal regulations, as likely to spoil sport; or whether, as is more probable, our frontier procedure is altogether too gentle and wanting in savour for him: in his own mountains he has certainly been uniformly hostile to us, and not slow to take advantage of opportunity to show it. The little we know about him or his country has been information gained at the point of the bayonet; and, again to quote Macgregor "though we have been intimately connected with the tribes for so many years, no Englishman has entered Afridi land as a friend," *Per contra*, he has uniformly shown himself most ready to enlist in our army. It is estimated that not less than 3,000 to 4,000 Afridis are now serving in our army or those of native chiefs; and, considering the short period of service, a very considerable proportion of their total fighting strength must have passed through the ranks. Moreover, the Afridi has gained a greater reputation for fidelity as a soldier than in any other way It is, it may be argued,—considering his normal relations with his own kith and kin,—not saying much that he should cheerfully fight with us against them: and he would no doubt be quite ready to help us to conquer his native country. But in many campaigns he has shown all the qualities of a good soldier—perhaps a little more ready to plunder than to fight, and maybe a trifle home-sick in the hot weather: but a very different man from the "savage" whose safe-conduct would hardly run in his own hills, and who has not got the honour possessed by a Waziri robber.

Antithesis applies not merely to the Afridis themselves, but in a measure to their country. Strong as are the natural positions they hold among the spurs and defiles of the Sufed Koh and the bare rugged inhospitable ranges of the Khaiber; difficult of approach the passes, which might have to be forced, and unanimous as the clans may be to defend them at the signal of a common danger, the people are so dependent on the plains, their position—secure though it may sound—is really their weakest point, and makes it easy to shut them up in their own hills. Peshawur, the great field for their plundering operations, is also the market for their produce and the source of supply for their many domestic wants. Exclusion from Peshawur is to many clans a severe form of punishment; and an effectual blockade that will cut them off from the outer world, would probably bring them to terms sooner than an expedition.

It is unnecessary to discuss the origin of the Afridis. Bellew identifies both the name and the position with one of the peoples referred to by Herodotus, and thinks they and their allies occupied a much greater extent of country than at present, but were pressed up into the hills in the general struggle for territory. They come admittedly of a mixed stock, and though what has just been said of them applies ethnologically to the whole, they are divided into several distinct communities. Broadly speaking, of the eight chief clans, or *Khels*, into which they are divided, six are usually spoken of as Khaiber Afridis. The Aka Khels have no connection with these, and are entirely south of the Bâra river, in the Peshawur Valley; while the Adam Khels, the most numerous of any clan are again distinct, inhabiting the hills between Peshawur and Kohát, the great wedge of country driven into our border almost up to the Indus, and across which lies the road between two important frontier cantonments.

This, the Kohát pass, has not of course either the military or political importance of the Khaiber, but it is of considerable strategic value. From Kohát to Peshawur by this pass, is thirty-seven miles, of which ten only are in independent country. By Khushalgarh, where the Indus is still unbridged, to Peshawur by railway, is 200 miles, by road suitable for marching with all arms, 150 miles. Two clans of the Adam Khels are the keepers of the pass, and however good may be the arrangements for keeping it open, there is no disputing the fact that the whole arrangements, in regard to a most important section of our main frontier line of communications is in the hands of a lawless and uncertain tribe, who have in the past, and may at any time in the future, give infinite trouble; who, if they could not absolutely close it against us, could occupy the attention of a large force, at a critical time, when it is possible such a force could be ill spared. Further, although we pay a considerable subsidy every year, we are even now not allowed to make a road, or to remove the boulders that obstruct the path. Here and there a cultivator runs a plough across, and a great rock that blocks the way at one point, is a standing joke. The Afridi chuckles and swaggers about the lakh of rupees the Government would give to have it moved. The whole history of our proceedings in regard to this pass is a striking instance of the unfortunate infirmity of purpose, that, under the guise of tender feeling for the proud spirit of independence, accepts any excuse for avoiding decisive measures. The pass might be compared to the "direful spring" of innumerable woes, not only to our frontier troops, but still more to the Afridis themselves—the cause of most of our complications with the Adam Khels. From the expedition in 1850 against the Gallais, to the occupation of the Jowáki country in 1877-78,—which alone was the cause of much more suffering to them than absolute annexation could have been—there is a long record of troubles arising out of it. Over and over again the question of a road, to be made practicable for wheeled traffic has been taken up only to be dropped again. In 1878, it formed one of the terms laid down by Lord Lytton at the commencement of operations, and could have been carried out while we occupied the country, but was put aside to avoid "breaking the spirit of the tribe;" who, by the way, had just requested their losses during the expedition should be taken into account, in adjusting the fine to be levied. At present the total amount paid in the shape of pass allowances to the Adam Khels and a few of the Orakzais amounts to some Rs. 12,000 a year; an insignificant sum, but perhaps a fair guarantee, in the absence of any better offer, for the good conduct of a poor clan. There were rumours of their intentions to close it during the last Afghân war, and again, in 1883, on the occasion of the enhancement of the salt tax, but these came to nothing; and it has never since been closed, except by ourselves to settle some local tribal dispute, or it has been impassable from bad weather. But, in spite of Afridi promises to do something to improve it, the whole length, through their lands remains in a state of nature. They will do nothing themselves nor permit us to divert the track out of the bed of the nullah, where for miles it is impossible for anything on wheels. Nor has any real attempt been made to coerce them. All negotiations attempted by the local officers have come to nought, because the tribesmen well know there is only weakness and vacillation at the back; while every failure only tends to make matters worse. The Afridis affect to believe that the Government cannot, or dare not interfere with them, and though they pocket the subsidy, will do nothing whatever for it.

It may be unhesitatingly admitted there is no inducement, from a financial point of view, for us to occupy any part of the Afridi country; but there are other considerations that seem to make it very undesirable to leave such a position, in the middle of our territory, almost on the banks of the Indus, and within striking distance of Peshawur and Kohât, unoccupied. There may perhaps be a difference of opinion as to the actual occupation of territory, but there is no doubt about the need for the road, and that we should be contented with the state of things on this part of our Border is certainly not a subject for congratulation.

CHAPTER XXII.

A LITTLE more than a mile to the left of the fort of Jamrûd, before entering the Khaiber, is an insignificant cluster of detached towers and buildings, known as the village of Jam, belonging to the Akakhel Afridis. Rûd is simply the Pashtu for river, and here the stony and generally dry bed of this one forms the Khaiber defile. The village is by the river; there is a tank with no water, but a pavilion in it, enjoying a sort of tradition, that Jamshid, the famous wine-bibbing Persian king, used to sit there—and during a reign of 700 years, which Firdausi credits him with, he certainly might have found plenty of time—for quaffing his cup of Zahar-i-khush, or the " bewitching poison." And there is a little streamlet that waters the village lands, from which the fort is permitted to take its share of a very scanty supply. Otherwise there is nothing noticeable about it. The surroundings are dreary in the extreme, and the bare rocks and stones look as if they could heat up to a temperature that would have made the *Inferno* seem chilly, and, if the people had anything worth fighting for, it might be a share in that stream, which indeed seems to be very much the opinion of the residents of Jam. If it had occurred to any member of the Viceroy's staff, dashing past on a recent visit, to stop and visit Jam, he would probably have had an Afridi guard of

Jezailchis told off to go with him, who would have scattered about·
ahead, and on either side, looking carefully behind walls and roun¹
corners, as though they expected to flush a brother lying *perdu*
with a rifle, and it behoved them to do their best in the interests
of sport. He would have been perfectly safe, however, for the
residents of Jam were just then at peace, and in any case would
have had no quarrel with him. But he might have carried back
some curious particulars regarding the domestic life of village communities thereabouts; and though they perhaps might not have
provided an exactly suitable commentary on Lord Dufferin's con-
gratulatory address to the chiefs, regarding the peace and prosperity prevailing on the frontier, they would have furnished him
with an excellent instance of a characteristic Afridi feud.

It began long ago—so long ago, no one could quite remember
how it was started, but all agreed it had lasted generations; and
somehow the water-course always came in. This, a little channel
about eighteen inches wide and half as deep, ran meandering all
through Jam, or rather through the three scattered hamlets that
constituted the village. Four or five hundred yards apart they might
be called north, south, and east divisions of Jam, and their chronic
condition be said to be that of open war on one another, varied by
an occasional truce to enable the ordinary business of life to be
carried on. About three years ago the northern had killed a man
of the southern division, and the eastern had killed a northerner
so that if south and east could only arrange a settlement matters
were fairly even. But then came the question of improving the
channel to supply the fort, and the division of the remaining
water upset everything again. All three divisions found it necessary to throw up earthworks, so as to approach the stream and
obtain water under cover. Amir Khân, a pensioned Subadâr of a
native regiment, and a man of light and leading in North Jam,
constructed a regular shelter trench—*sangar*—and swore he would
have the life of Khaista Khân, the chief person in South Jam, and

every morning sat down with his rifle and waited for a chance. He succeeded in shooting two Southerners, and after many days of patient waiting, he caught Khaista Khân in an unguarded moment and broke his thigh with a long shot. The latter now hobbles round on crutches, and, if the member of the staff understood Pushtu, Khaista would have been happy to explain the circumstances in detail, more especially what happened next. This was merely that Khaista's party, with the assistance of Akbar Khân, a prominent citizen of East Jam, went one dark night and dug a trench outflanking Amir Khân's,—who had unaccountably neglected to protect himself by a traverse,—and then waited for him. In the grey dawn Amir Khân took his pipe and his rifle, and sat down in his trench to watch for any Southerner rash enough to expose himself for an early drink. Hardly had he lit his pipe and adjusted the sights on his neighbour's wall, when—"ping, ping"—he was bowled over by a couple of Snider bullets, and, as Khaista Khân remarked, went where he could not take his rifle. After this triumph there was a lull; it was, moreover, necessary to commence the season's ploughing operations—and the Aka Khels are not the people to allow pleasure to interfere with business. A truce was declared for six months, which, at the time of His Excellency's Peshawur visit, had about two months to run; though preparations for the renewal of hostilities were by no means being overlooked. Amin Khân, the brother of the unlucky Subadâr, boasted of having two field-pieces of long range up in Tirah, which were to be brought down, and from the tower of North Jam to deal destruction to the perfidious Khaista; while the latter was reputed to have a "cannon of sorts" already in position in his court-yard: and all three divisions possess many excellent shots, not a few trained in British service, and have well loopholed walls.

This, however, may be said to be almost a family affair, and it must not be supposed that similar amenities are not extended to other villages. A few miles on the opposite side of the road from

Jamrúd Fort towards the Khaiber is a village of the Kuki Khel
Afridis, that might be called after its owner Rahimdil Khán, with
which Jam in general, and North Jam in particular, has established
a very pretty quarrel. The last phase of this began about a
woman. A Jam lady was robbed of her jewels by, it was reported,
a man of Rahimdil's village. Thereupon her friends took her
there, and said, your people have stolen our woman's jewels—you
must take her also, she is no use to us without them; and, in
spite of disclaimers, left her. The Rahimdil folk did not want her
either, so took her back next night and left her outside Jam. The
following night Jam returned the compliment, and so on—the unfortunate woman spending alternate nights outside each village, until
she was made away with by one side or the other. Now both professed extreme indignation, because, though to kill a few men may
be a desirable thing to do, it is almost discreditable to an Afridi to
kill a woman—a reflection on his character that justifies anything;
amply sufficient to justify a Jam man killing a Rahimdil one, and
a Rahimdil man doing the same for a Jam. Once fairly started, it
was evident a big thing might be made of it, big enough to induce
Rahimdil Khán[1] himself—a native officer of high rank, highly
honoured and twice decorated in in the British service, who had
been in London and Paris and seen much of the world—to take six
months leave and go down to the barren desolate hills of his native
village, and see that the whole thing was put on a proper footing.
He apparently still retained some of the salt of his youth, and, in
spite of all temptations to serve with other nations, considered there
was no place like home, an Afridi home, for a really good feud.

[1] The supression of Rahimdil's real name is the only departure from literal fact in
this account.

CHAPTER XXIII.

THE best known and most famous road from India to Kâbul—
the Khaiber—has been more than any intimately associated with
former invasions of India from Afghânistân. With expeditious,
past and present, Mughal or English, to that country—though to
our troops probably most associated with heat, cholera, fever, and
flies, and consequently more detested, by both British and Native,
than any other bit of trans-border country. Has for centuries been
a trade highway from the markets of Central Asia, Bukhâra, and
Kâbul, and still, in spite of Amirs and transit dues, sees strings of
camels starting almost daily for Khorasân, Persia, Turkistân, and
even Russia itself. Is the route about which engineers have
reported, specialists have written the most excellent confidential
memorandums, and a good many others, not specialists, are responsible for a great deal that is far from excellent—and it may
perhaps be considered too familiar to justify any lengthened notice.
More particularly as the specialists are always, in a strictly confidential way, already so much better informed : while to some of
the "others" nothing could probably be more distasteful than any
accurate information that does not fit in with their own particular
theory. Nevertheless, the notions on which certain of these
theories are built—especially for the home market—are probably

based on delusions as many and as startling as about most things Indian. Not merely among certain excursionists,—who barely realize the difference between Jamrud and Jagdalak ; whose idea of a scientific frontier is associated with a defensive line of bricks and mortar, like the Great Wall of China, and who, having rushed out to 'Ali Musjid or Lundi Khâna and failed to find it, return feeling qualified to expose one more Tory fraud—but even among those better informed, the students of large scale maps, but who still associate the " dreadful Khaiber " with the disasters of 1842 and many of our misfortunes ever since. Men to whom all the tribes for over 200 miles are Khaiberis; who are thoroughly satisfied that success is only to the nation, as to the man, who knows how to wait ; and whose doubts probably do not extend beyond the question of letting the Russian Army fill the Pass, and then stopping both ends, or—like Macaulay's Romans, who kept the bridge in the brave days of old—of taking up a position at the mouth, and disposing of them in detail as they come out.

It may, perhaps, be doubted if the advocates of this Fabian policy fully realize that there are three parallel routes between Kâbul and Peshawur perfectly practicable, and all protected on their southern flank by the Safed Koh Range : the first by the Khurd Kâbul Pass, the Tezin Valley, Pesh Bolak, and the Bazâr Valley ; the second by Butkhak, the Lataband Pass, Jagdalak, Gandamak, Jelâlâbâd, Dhaka, and the Khaiber, both debouching near Jamrud ; the third by the Lataband, Lughmân, Jelâlâbâd, Dhaka, the Shilmân Valley, and the Tartara Hill debouching by Shahgai—which latter can be varied again from the Shilmân Valley by crossing the Kâbul River at the Shamilo ferry and debouching by Fort Michni, and probably by other roads through the Mohmand Hills, which, though sufficiently steep and rugged, are by no means impassable. That when Nâdir Shâh found the Pass closed against him by Afridis and Shinwâris, the Orakzais led him by a road through Tirah. That it is quite possible to advance on Jelâlâbâd by the Kunar route from Chitrâl, instead of from Kâbul at all, while, there are several well-known ways of reaching Chitrâl, both from the north and south; and, moreover, there are at least a couple of routes from Badâkhshân, through Kâfiristân, by which it is possible to operate on the north flank. To assume, therefore, that, in the event of troubles arising, it will be safe to sit down at Peshawur, and "wait till the clouds roll by," can only be compared to the method of the ostrich, who imagines he is safe when he has hid his head in the sand. It would be obviously a mistake to be found waiting in the wrong place.

The route through the actual Khaiber defile has been compared to a passage between two combs placed with their teeth pointing inwards—the teeth, which correspond to the spurs of the ranges on either side, being prevented from quite meeting by two insignificant streams flowing, respectively, towards Kâbul and Peshawur, the shingly beds of which constitute the only possible road. Assuming the combs to be old and broken ones, the comparison will do very well; according as the teeth are sound and approach each other, is the width of the defile, the intervals between them representing the drainage from the hills north and south, while here and there a larger gap forms a small glen in which may be found a village, or a practicable road into the Afridi or Mullagori country. In other places these spurs are so steep and precipitous, as to be impracticable from the Pass on one side or the other, occasionally on both. Thus at Kadam, the real gate—some three miles from Jamrud—the hills begin to close in, and the Pass is only some 450 feet wide ; a little further and it narrows to 250 feet. Then a few teeth have been knocked out; but approaching the spring and mosque of 'Ali, —the "Lion of God,"—it has diminished to forty feet, with slaty perpendicular cliffs 1,300 feet high on either side, and a fort, called after the mosque below, stands on an isolated hill commanding the road. Another six or seven miles and the Lataheg Valley has opened to a mile and a half wide, only to close a little beyond, to less than ten feet between quite perpendicular walls of rock. Over the Landi Khâna Pass, called the *Kotal,*—probably the most difficult part of the road—it rises by a steep ascent between steep cliffs less than 150 feet apart, and down again till the valley of the Kâbul River is reached at Dhaka. Over thirty miles of comb that, in good hands, would be calculated to intercept most living things.

But the Khaiber defile is only one of the obstacles on this route. There are several more combs, though the teeth may be occasionally set further apart, that have between them a series of small plains—barren and stony ones generally, though even here there is more cultivation than might be supposed; and in halting places —named like Haft-Chahi, the "Seven Wells;" Hazarnao, the "Thousand Canals;" and many others named after springs and gardens—there is evidence that the people associate them with things pleasant. At Jelâlâbâd—ninety miles from Peshawur—the cross ranges of hills are, for a change, replaced by a well-watered fertile stretch of country, a score of miles long by a dozen wide, dotted with towers, villages, and trees; and where the Kâbul River—that has all along had to struggle through mere cracks —becomes a broad clear stream 100 yards wide. Thence the route lies through a thoroughly unattractive country again, over long stony ridges, across rocky river-beds, varied with an occasional fine valley like Fathâbad, or an oasis like Nimlah, to Gandamak, which, by way of comparison with what is beyond again, is a land flowing with milk and honey: for on by Jagdalak and the Lataband Pass or Tezin and the Khurd Kâbul, is a wild waste of bare hills, surrounded by still more lofty and forbidding mountains: the teeth become more closely set together; the road narrower; the stony ridges change to bleak heights from 7,000 to 8,000 feet high the river-beds, deep valleys, or narrow defiles, like the fatal Jagdalak, almost devoid of verdure, and into whose gloomy ravines the winter sun can hardly penetrate—these are the outworks that have to be negotiated before the gardens and orchards, the bazaars and forts of Kâbul, can be approached.

Any description of the Khaiber route—about 170 miles from our Peshawur frontier to Kâbul—naturally sounds formidable; and though it is admittedly difficult, too much should not be counted on this. The road was immensely improved by our Engineer officers during the operations in Afghânistân, and the feasibility of constructing a railway through to Kâbul was abundantly established. Such a line would not present the difficulties, or equal the cost of what has been accomplished in the direction of Kandahâr; and its importance is at least equally great. When it is taken into consideration what it cost us in the way of transport to keep the present line of communication intact, the 15,000 men that during the last war had to be detailed for the duty, the endless posts and forts and commissariat yards, and when it is fully realized what a foreign occupation of Kâbul would mean for India, the railway will probably be in a fair way to be accepted, as probably the most pressing of our present frontier requirements; and the question is of such vital importance as to demand some separate consideration. As an outer defence of the approach to India, there is no doubt that in the hands of scientific defenders the Khaiber could be made practically as unassailable as the Fortress of Gibraltar. But it is not in our hands, and until it is, its defence is by no means that simple business which is too often assumed.

Of the tribes who inhabit the country along this route—working back from Kâbul—the valleys and defiles about Tezin Jagdalak, and Gundamak, almost to Jelâlâbâd, are held by Ghilzais, the Bâbakar Khels, Jabbâr Khels, and others of the powerful Suliamân clan. Ever notorious highwaymen, they were specially distinguished for their unremitting attacks upon Sale's disorganized army and defenceless camp-followers during the retreat from Kâbul. They were the persistent opponents of Pollock's army of vengeance, the implacable foes of every invader; and yet, under good management, are undoubtedly capable of being converted into most useful allies. Jabbâr, the founder of the clan of that name,—a man of weight in his day, founder of many Ghilzai institutions,—lies buried in a miserably cold, bleak spot between Khurd-Kâbul and the Haft-Kotal, or "Seven Passes"— a place still the lurking-place of robbers and of wolves—a byeword of evil report even among Kâbulis. Opposite Jelâlâbâd, and up the northern slope of the Sufed Koh, a broad strip of country is held by the Khugiânis, a tribe closely related to the Jâgis and Turis on the other side of the range—the former at one time including both the latter, and, with a number of the Khostwâls, were not improbably originally Turks who came in with Chengiz and Timur, but by long separation formed into distinct tribes. The Khugiânis are estimated as mustering 5,000 families, the men manly and warlike, always a thorn in the side of the Governors of Jelâlâbâd, but engaged mainly as tillers and shepherds, and seldom leaving their home; their rugged slopes, though under snow for three months of the year, yielding abundance of excellent fruits in due season. Two sections of one clan are credited with a feud which began about the merest trifle when Jehangir reigned at Delhi, cost a thousand lives, and was only put an end to by both parties submitting to the Kâbul ruler, whose subjects they are still.

East of them, the whole northern slope of the Sufed Koh is known as Nangrahâ, a word which several authorities would trace back to Nangnahâr, "nine canals,"—a pear-shaped country between the crest of the ridge and the Kâbul road, with its base near Jelâlâbâd and its stalk at Lundi Kotal, occupied by the Shinwâris, a powerful tribe of some 10,000 or 12,000 fightingmen; and if among a people who, like Cacus, would have stolen the cattle from Hercules, there can be said to be any degree, their habits are possibly not quite as predatory as their neighbours. Nominally, they also profess to be tillers, and they cultivate a certain amount of rice and fruits, especially figs and almonds, and they export silk and wool, but their most congenial occupation was, and is, pillage. They attacked our forces at Pesh Bolak, in 1841; they carried off a good share of plunder after the disaster of 1842, for which they were subsequently punished by a force under Monteith; and during our later campaign in Afghânistân, they caused considerable annoyance along our line of communications, necessitating several punitive expeditions. They have little more regard for the property of the present Amir, unless it be sufficiently safe-guarded. Of the four chief clans, the worst are the Sangu Khels, short, thick-set men of a proverbially fierce and headlong courage, who have always enjoyed the most sinister reputation, and are said to be nearly as good with the stones of their native hills as with the bullets of more lethal weapons. At the other end, the Alisherzais, who inhabit the Loargai valley round about Lundi-Kotal, generally known as the Loargai Shin-wâris, are largely engaged in the carrying-trade between Peshawur and Kâbul, are exceedingly well-behaved and give no trouble whatever.

To the north, down the Kâbul River from Jellâlâbâd, including a strip of land along the right bank, the river itself, until it reaches our border, and the network of hills and valleys east of Lâlpura, are all within the lands of the various clans of Mohmands, a great and important tribe to be noticed anon. Occupying a little corner, between the Kâbul River and Jamrûd or near it, and between the Shilmân Valley on the west and our Border on the east, are the Mullagoris. Put down as original settlers from the Mohmands, whose vassals they still practically are, they are not now classed as either fish, flesh, or good red herring. Neither Mohmands, Afridis, nor Shinwâris will acknowledge them, and the latter say they are descended from an illegitimate child found in a graveyard, who grew up to know something, and originated the name. Besides being despised by the Shinwâris, they have a chronic feud with the Afridis, and were it not for a little backing from the Mohmands would soon get the worst of it. The whole tribe is excessively poor; nominally they sell ropes, mats, and sandals made out of the dwarf palm : but this mainly is an excuse for opportunities of robbing the Peshawur cantonments. Numerically they are utterly insignificant, barely mustering 400 fighting men; but their principal merit is in possessing the Târtâra Mountain, nearly 7,000 feet high, which represents a possible sanitarium for Peshawur of much value, and is strategically a position of importance, as it would command the approaches to the Khaiber, Târtâra, and Abkhâna routes; form a useful point for checking Lâlpura and the Shinwâris; and give a good hold on the Khuki Khel Afridis and the Mullagoris themselves, who ought in some way, best known to political officers, to be brought as soon as possible to see the advantage of selling mats to a cantonment established there.

Almost the whole of the Khaiber defile is in the hands of the half-dozen clans of Afridis already referred to, collectively spoken of as the Khaiber Afridis; the most influential being probably the Zakha Khels,—though the Kukis, Malikdin, and Qumba Khels are also powerful clans, composed of fine men, well armed, in many cases with English or Kabul-made rifles,—who have furnished us with many good soldiers. In our earlier Afghân campaigns, they fully maintained their ancient fame as bold and faithless robbers; but from the time the Punjâb was annexed, up to the second Afghân war their behaviour has always been, for Afridis, fairly good. They have never ceased from marauding excursions whenever opportunity offered, and though now and then minor expeditions have had to be undertaken against one clan or the other, we have never had against us any formidable tribal combination, or regular stand-up fight, as against Mohmands or Yusafzais—a circumstance doubtless partly due to the ultra-democratic nature of the Afridi constitution, and partly to so many of them being dependent on

Peshawur in winter. In 1878 some of the clans took sides with us, and others played into the hands of the Amir, necessitating a couple of expeditions into the Bazâr Valley, which is one of the alternative routes referred to, but where the clansmen are least dependent on Peshawur.

Under the treaty of Gandamak, the control of the Khaiber and Michni Passes, with all relations with the connected tribes, were

A Khaiber Pass Afridi.

retained by the British Government, and on the retirement of our troops arrangements were proposed; a complete *jirgah* of all the Khaiber tribes called at Peshawur, and in February, 1881, they affixed their seals to an agreement under which their independence was recognized, provided they maintained exclusive political relations with us. The tribes were to furnish a corps of *Jezailchis*[1]

---

[1] Irregular riflemen.

for the protection of the Pass, to be paid by our Government under whose political officers they would be. The tribes to abstain from all raids on British territory, and to undertake to be jointly responsible for maintaining order in the Khaiber in consideration of certain subsidies to be paid by Government, which, *per contra* was to take all tolls on caravans using the Pass. The subsidies are divided proportionately among the six Afridi clans, and a very small sum is also given to the Loargai Shinwáries. The whole, with some trifling allowance to head men, only amounts to between 80,000 and 90,000 rupees a year, and the tolls realized are fully three-fourths of this; so that, as far as it goes, the arrangement is an economical and an excellent one. There have been some trifling difficulties raised occasionally by the more turbulent spirits—a body of Zakha Khels attempting on one occasion to raid a caravan, but they were promptly stopped by the *Jezailchis* and several of their number shot down; and individual Border outlaws like the notorious Kamal Khán, have been guilty of local outrages but altogether the tribes have loyally kept to their bond. On fixed days an escort takes charge of travellers and caravans at Jamrúd, and hands them over to the Amir's representatives at Lundi Khána, receiving in return the charge of convoys for Peshawur; and the political officer, to whose tact not a little of the success is due, is able to report the Khaiber now as safe as the Grand Trunk Road.

Beyond Lundi Khána the traders may be secured against highway robbery; but there are complaints that even the Shinwáris and Ghilzais were less exacting than the Amir's dues, by which, and the high duties imposed by Russia on exports to Bukhára and Samrkand, the trade is much hampered—so much so, that it is said to be cheaper to send goods to Bombay and Moscow than by the Khaiber and the Hindu Kush. This may not be literally true, and it was even hoped that after Abdur Rahmán had established himself as a strong ruler, trade would revive; after the war of 1878–80 such, undoubtedly, was the case, but any expansion was summarily checked, and the trade has since been falling off. Between 1887 and 1889 the total exports and imports of the Western Border fell from an annual value of 121 lakhs of rupees to 95 lakhs, any increase due to the extension of railways in the Kandahâr direction being more than covered by the diminished trade through the Khaiber. Nor is this to be wondered at; from the Khaiber to Kâbul the Amir's dues are Rs. 21 per camel load of merchandise, with further dues at various points, if the journey is continued on to the Oxus. By the Ghazni route a camel load of piece-goods is mulct of Rs. 26 and one piece out of every forty. The Border trader may therefore say with Maréchal Villars—"Defend me from my friends, I can account for my enemies myself."

CHAPTER XXIV.

THE KÁBUL POSITION.

WITHOUT going deeply into vexed strategical questions, it is perhaps not too much to say that if ever an invasion of India is attempted from the north-west, one of the first objects of each contending army will be the possession of Kábul. The great triangle comprised in the Panjsher, Ghorband, and Paghmán Valleys, with the command of some of the most important passes over the Hindu Kush towards Turkistán and the Oxus, over the Koh-i-Bába to Bamian and Balkh, or by the Unai Pass to the Helmand and Girishk, forms probably the strongest natural position in the whole of Afghánistán. The city itself is the historical capital of the country, and there is a well-known proverb that he who holds Kábul holds Afghánistán. Similarly the Khaiber is equally the historic route for many of the most successful advances on India. Whatever, therefore, may be the fate of Kábul in the earlier phases of the great campaign of the future—

"When the big guns speak to the Khaiber peak,"

it will undoubtedly form, of all the cities now ruled by Abdur Rahmán, the most important factor for offence or defence : and it will carry with it a proportionately valuable prestige.

Its importance has, of course, long ago been fully recognised by

Russia, and for some time, at any rate since the Penjdeh affair, the deduction has been tolerably obvious, that, in the event of any movement against Afghânistân or India, Russia's objective is more likely to be Kâbul than Kandahâr. Assuming that Russia has already by railway extension linked her garrisons in the Caucasus and Central Asia proper, and can concentrate troops pretty well anywhere between Kizil-Arvat and Samrkand, and that a fairly good line will be completed to Sarakhs, the latter place is still upwards of 200 miles from Herât. Herât is again 370 miles from Kandahâr, itself distant 70 more from our outpost at Chaman, or 640 in all. The route along this line is through a country held by certain of the most warlike and independent of the Afghân tribes; it has but scanty supplies, and it lies open to flank attacks by way of Persia, Bilochistân, and Kâbul. Any force advancing by it must also count upon meeting a powerful army in an almost impregnable position at the end of it. On the other hand, from their base at Jam, near Samrkand, to Kilif on the Oxus, is 230 miles through the Bukhâra khanates, quasi-independent, but for the purposes of an advance practically Russian. From Kilif as a base, *viâ* Mazâr-i-Sharif and either Walishân or Bajgah, and the Unai Pass, to Kâbul is 460 miles, while Kâbul is only 170 miles from Peshawur and India. In this connection it must be noted that a survey for a line of railway from Samrkand to Kilif has been ordered, and that the rails are being also laid from Charjui to Kerki along the left bank of the Oxus. An advance in this direction would, consequently, be from excellent bases in the Oxus valley through a country with a fair capacity for food-supply, which could be largely supplemented from the fertile valleys of the Zerâfshân and Ferghâna. Transport could be drawn from Bukhâra, Khokand, and the trans-Oxus country generally; while, Mazâr-i-Sharif once cleared by a successful engagement, there would be no risk whatever of a flank attack—for a rapid movement upon Herât would naturally be coincident with the invasion of Afghán-Turkistán. The physical difficulties on the Kábul route would undoubtedly be greater than those on the Kandahár side ; but the distance from the Russian base would be much less, and the Afghán resistance to her arms, would have to be measured mainly by the assistance that could be given from India in good time.

It is undoubtedly true that the Kábul position could not be taken by any possible *coup de main*. Even with our admittedly imperfect system of intelligence regarding Russian movements on the Afghán border, no important advance in the direction of Kábul could be made without due notice reaching us in time to enable assistance to be sent to the Amir. A request for that assistance might, however, and probably would be, delayed ; and though the Afghán power of defence, combined with the enormous natural advantages offered by the Hindu Kush, would enable Abdur Rahmán to hold the northern passes for some time against any force Russia could hurriedly push forward, we should hardly be able to effectually assist him in maintaining his hold on Afghán-Turkistán and the Cis-Oxus territories unless the Khaiber communications had been very greatly improved.

But all this is supposing matters stand as they are. Should party faction, supineness, or more exhibitions of " masterly inactivity," result in a repetition of the many blunders of the past, and some fresh Penjdeh lead to a Russian occupation of Herát without a shot being fired by England in return, it is hard to say what new development might not succeed. Certainly the annexation of Balkh and Afghán-Turkistán would follow in the natural order of things. There is known to be a road, though at present a very indifferent one, along the valley of the Harirud to Daulatyár and Chehl Burj, which latter place is only 268 miles from Kábul. If this road were made practicable for all arms, and good communications established between Herát and Mazár-i-Sharif, the long-coveted frontier of the Hindu Kush would be practically realised. Russia would by that time have her railway extensions southward from the main line well advanced, and she would be within striking distance of Kábul. At this stage, though the need for an efficient system of railway communication between India and Kábul would have become more imperative, it would be somewhat late to set about its commencement. Whether we had then to go as allies of Afghánistán or the reverse, we should be compelled to go and to hold Kabul at all risks. Its possession would mean the influence of 50,000 fighting men for or against us. It would mean more, for the occupation of Kábul by the enemy would involve a loss of prestige that would affect us throughout India; we should have against us not merely the Afgháns—certain to ally themselves with the side that appeared successful—but the bulk of the fighting tribes between them and India, if not indeed many within our own border. Our power in that direction for offensive measures would be *nil:* we should only be able to act on the defensive, and to wait and see from which direction the next attack would be delivered.

To reverse the picture: the possibilities of the position for defence are exceptional. The resources of the country are naturally great; the valleys round Kábul are capable of furnishing a large amount of excellent supplies, and so is the Jellálábád district; and with a railway even to the latter place the whole of the best part of the northern Punjáb could be directly drawn upon for grass and fodder, men, material and supplies of every kind. It would in fact be much easier to maintain a couple of army corps, or 50,000 men in Kábul, than half the number in Kandahár. The importance of a line of railway through the Khaiber to Jellálábád and eventually onward to Kábul will hardly be disputed; how momentous its importance might become, is best realized by those who have most closely studied the position.

There is nothing either as regards the magnitude of the cost, or the engineering difficulties in construction, that need be considered as exceptionally formidable. There are at least two, if not three feasible routes through the hills to the west of Peshawur. (1) From Jamrud, to which point a railway was actually sanctioned and commenced, through the steep cliffs of the Khaiber proper, knocking out a few more of the rocky teeth here and there, and over or by partially tunnelling the Lundi *Kotal* or pass, to Lundi-Khána. (2) Peshawur, by the plains to Shahgai, through the Mullagori country by Murdadán, the saddle at Kambayla, and skirting the Tatára peak by Spol and the Jazeri pass; or from Yakubi following the Kábul river to the Shulmán valley, whence either alternative would work through the Loargi plain to Lundi Khána. The latter for part of the length would involve gradients of 1 in 50, and possibly occasional bits as steep as 1 in 33, with perhaps 3,000 to 4,000 yards of tunnelling, along a distance approximating forty miles from Peshawur. (3) A third, and possibly better alternative, turning the actual Khaiber pass altogether, would be from Fort Michni, our outpost north of Peshawur, following the Kábul river all the way to Dhaka. The distance in this case would approximate to forty-five miles or less, and the difference of levels between Michni and Dhaka is known to be little more than 300 feet. The river no doubt occasionally runs in very narrow deep ravines, in places not more than sixty or eighty feet wide; the sides are generally steep, occasional places rejoicing in perpendicular spurs that would have to be negotiated by more or less of cutting. By thus following the Kábul river the steep gradients needed to climb up and down the passes to the south would be avoided; on the other hand this route would be somewhat more liable to attack or interruptions by the Mohmands on the opposite bank, who are outside our present jurisdiction; while as already noticed, under the Gandamak treaty, the tribal arrangements of the Mullagori country and the Michni passes, are equally with the Khaiber, entirely in our hands, and the railway arrangements would involve no risk of political or tribal difficulties. So this, by no means the least in portant part of a railway to Kábul, could be at once begun quite independently of any existing treaty arrangements with the Amir.

From Lundi-Khána, or Dhaka, to Jellálábád, and for some distance beyond, there are no serious physical obstructions to prevent a railway from being rapidly constructed, with the single exception of a short bit between Barikáb and 'Ali-Bughán, which would require more careful aligning and more time to construct. Beyond Jellálábád the location of the line as far as Gandamak, would not be difficult. A formidable, but short cutting would be needed through the Daronta gorge, while a certain amount of rock cutting, though nothing insurmountable, by Katz-i-Aziz, would bring it up to the Adrak-Badrak *Kotal*, not very far from Jagdalak, or to within fifty miles of Kábul. A three days' march, with what might be made a second Chaman in the fertile Jellálábád valley as a base.

Further again, difficulties undoubtedly become more formidable, and it is a question if from Jelálábád, a better alignment would not be by the Lughmán Valley, and again, by the Kábul river. There is every reason to believe that a perfectly practicable route could be obtained in this direction, which in former times was used for the movement of formidable armies, and is now only avoided by trading caravans on account of the want of proper escort.

There is no reason why such a railway to Kábul should be exceptionally costly. For the greater part of its length the outlay would not exceed that on ordinary Indian or Russian frontier lines, and on even the most expensive lengths should not be nearly so great as similar ones on the Hurnai railway to Quetta. What difficulties there are, are mainly political. Would it be possible to obtain the Amir's consent, and having his support, to carry out the work without encountering the serious opposition of the tribesmen, is really the problem for solution.

Situated as Kábul is, the centre of trade with a great part of

Central Asia, the majority of the people, the *káfila* traders and the merchants at both ends of the Khaiber route, are fully alive to railway advantages. There can be no doubt of its importance to Indian traders, and to English trade with Central Asia *viâ* Afghánistân, now diminishing as fast as that of Russia is expanding. As far as the tribesmen are concerned, there is no reason why the benefits that have come home in so substantial a manner to the Bilochi, Marri, Kâkar, or Kandahári between Sibi and Chaman should not in a short time be equally appreciated by the Afridi, Shinwâri, or Ghilzai between Jamrud and the Koh-i-Damân. All are particularly fond of rupees, and would soon discover that it was better to earn these by some form of labour in connection with the railway than by risking their heads for insignificant loot from the Amir's *káfilas.* The Amir, though generally jealous to a degree of anything savouring of interference with his kingdom, is a shrewd man and not blind to his own interests, political or commercial. So far as his light goes, though his short-sighted policy in the matter of prohibitive customs duties—is even more than Russian competition—fast killing such trade with India as remains. A railway to Kâbul would be as much to his benefit as ours: it would immensely strengthen his position against any Russian encroachment and his hold on the tribes most difficult to manage. Last year,[1] while the troubles with Ishâk Khân were still unsettled, the suggestion that an Indian division should be sent to Jellálábád was the Amir's own: it is to India that he evidently looks for assistance against all his enemies. Although the motto of the Indian Government in dealing with him is necessarily *festina lente,* there is no reason why the strongest pressure should not be brought to bear upon him to lower his transit duties, and by affording more facilities for communication to develop a greatly extended trade. By failing to do this his own subjects are equal sufferers, while a railway would, in the form of greatly increased

---

[1] 1888.

trade, bring to his treasury not only considerable additional receipts, and enable him to develop many of the mechanical industries for which he has a taste; but in the event of certain by no means improbable contingencies, the successful defence of his Cis-Oxus provinces might to a great extent depend on his capital being linked in with the railway system of India. If he objects to intrusion into his territories he may be encouraged to make the line himself beyond the Khaiber, and be left to enjoy the pleasure of personal ownership when it is finished. It is quite possible that, with a little careful handling, he might be brought to recognise these advantages, or at any rate to accept them as a necessity of the situation. Meanwhile nothing should be permitted to delay the construction of the portion of the line either through, or turning the Khaiber, and in having ready a complete scheme for the remainder, which events might at any time compel us to carry out not merely without the Amir's consent, but in spite of his opposition.

CHAPTER XXV

THE PESHAWUR VALLEY OF THE PAST.

The Buddhist Prince Siddhârtha, from Yusafzai.

HOWEVER interesting the attempt might be, it is, for the present purpose, unnecessary to go back in any detail to the ancient history of the Peshawur Valley. A valley colonized by the first Aryan patriarchs, the Gandhâra of the early Hindu, the Pushkalavati of the Vishnu Purâna; that boasted a populous city in Alexander's day, and under his successors became the centre of an important Græco-Bactrian kingdom. That figures in San-

skrit, Chinese, Greek, and Arabic literature; was described by
Strabo, Ptolemy, and Arrian in the first and second centuries;
whose Buddhist Stupas were famous when the valley was visited
by Fa-Hian in the fifth, Sung-yun in the sixth, and Hwen-thsang
in the seventh; was the subject of long notices by the Arab
geographers, Masaudi, and Abu Rihan in the tenth and eleventh,
and by the Mughal Bârber in the sixteenth. Where the Chan-
drâvans, or Lunar race of tradition were succeeded—by how many
intermediate stages we do not know—by the people who held it
against Alexander, and whom he calls Asaceni; where, on the
rocks, the great Buddhist king Asoka cut his edicts over 2,000
years ago, in mystic characters, a puzzle to Hindu, Muhammadan, and Sikh, not altogether deciphered yet. And where
since then successive dynasties have flourished, through a series
of Brahmins like Pushpamitra, Graeco-Bactrians like Eucratides
or Menander, Scythians like Kadphises or Kanerki, Buddhists
again, and again Hindus, Muhammadans, Sikhs, down to the
present excellent one of the British Deputy Commissioners.

But to arrive at any clear idea of the relations of the tribes that
are now located in the valley, or that wonderful semicircle of hills
round it, some short notice of their past connection and how they
got there seems desirable. The first appearance upon the scene of
the Pathâns was towards the close of the seventh or beginning of
the eighth century, then described as forcing a Hindu Râjah of
Lahore to cede to them the Kohistân, or hills west of the Indus and
south of the Kâbul River, in which localities they may probably
represent a part of the original stock of Bangash, Orakzais, Afridis,
and Shinwâris already noticed. These, most likely aggressive
Afghâns from Ghor, joined with Gakkars from the Salt Range,
were to hold their lands conditionally on their guarding the
frontier. The Peshawur Valley and hills beyond were then
occupied with tribes affiliated with India. Those of Swât are
credited with sending a contingent to the assistance of the Chittore

Rajputs early in the ninth century; when Peshawur is bracketed with Lahore and Kangra under one Anunga, a chief of Delhi. But the invasions of the Ghaznavis, Subaktagin, and Mahmud, not merely proved a deathblow to the power of the Hindus in northern India; they changed the whole aspect of affairs in the valley. After the final defeat of Jaipal at Naushera in 1001, and Anung Pal at Peshawur in 1008, Mahmud dealt out summary punishment to the tribes who had in any way assisted the enemy—possibly Pathán, but probably in few cases Muhammadan—insisted on their wholesale conversion to the faith of Islám, and proceeded to harry the country generally. In his subsequent invasions he made Peshawur the place of arms for his army, which valley and surrounding hills consequently received his special attention in this respect. However civilized and populous it may have been before, his continuous invasions left it, as Bellew says, a deserted wilderness the haunt of the tiger and rhinoceros, only occasionally visited for the sake of pasture by the shepherd tribes accustomed to roam about the neighbouring countries. "By these it was gradually repeopled and cultivated in scattered spots, till, in time, other tribes of cultivators came in and settled over the plain, much as they are at the present time. The country, however, has never properly recovered its former condition of prosperity. Wretched mud hovels stand on the ruins of former towns and cities, the buildings of which are still in many places traceable by the remains of massive stone walls." Mahmud slipped his dogs of war in the eleventh century, and such was the effects of the "havoc" they created, that Bárber in the sixteenth recounts the pleasure taken by his followers in hunting the rhinoceros there.

One of the first of these tribes of the fresh settlers was the Dalazák, doubtful Patháns to start with, and who by intermarriage and adoption of many of the customs of the "unconverted," speedily lost any national characteristics they may have had. To

the Afghân of to-day they are little better than *Kâfirs*,[1] but while
Ghaznavi gave place to Ghor, and Ghor to Mughal, the Dalazâks
seem to have held possession of the entire Valley. Meanwhile two
important Pathân divisions—the Khakhai and Ghoria Khel, so
called from two brothers, whilom credited with settling at
Kandahâr—had increased and multiplied, and the former, accompanied by the Usmân Khel and Mudammadzai tribes belonging to
other divisions, sought fresh fields, and established themselves at
Kâbul. When Timour invaded India in 1397, the Khakhai had
acquired considerable importance, and became numerous enough
to divide into clans called Yusafzais, Gigiânis, and Turkilânis. At
Kâbul they waxed fat and kicked, and were even then notorious
for their turbulence and feuds, and for a preference for their
neighbour's cattle. First useful to Ulugh Beg, Timour's grandson,
to establish himself as ruler at Kâbul in 1470, he eventually found
them more than he could manage, so took the first opportunity to
entrap and slay some seventy of their head-men, sparing the
remainder on condition the whole tribe cleared out of Kâbul.
They did so, and moved on first to Bâsâul, Jelâlâbâd, then called
Adinapura, and Laghmân. Shortly after the Yusafzais, Muhammadzais, and Gigiânis advanced another stage, and came through
by the Târtâra route to the Peshawur plain, and begged from the
Dalazâks permission to occupy lands in the Doâba. Having thus
gained a footing, they commenced their old habits of cattle-lifting,
charging their Dalazâk neighbours with the same offence.
Breaches of faith soon brought about a war; a great battle was
fought on the Swât River, in which the Dalazâks were routed with
great slaughter and many fled across the Indus, leaving the
aggressors to divide the spoil. The Gigiânis took as their portion
the fertile, well-wooded Doâba—the " land of two waters "—
between the Kâbul and Swât Rivers; to the Muhammadzais, or
Muhamandzais, was assigned Hastnagar, " the country of the eight

---

[1] Infidels.

cities," a strip about thirteen miles wide, west of the Swât River; and to the Yusafzais, and their great offshoot the Mandanrs, the remainder of the country north of the Kábul River, an open plain or *maira* broken with ravines and studded with mounds that mark the habitations of bygone peoples. The Usmân Khels shortly after obtained a place in the hills about the Swât River; the Turkolânis remaining partly in Laghmân, and partly effecting a settlement in Bâjaur, ousting a chief who, like the ruler of Swât, called himself Sultân. The descendants of all five divisions may be said to retain pretty much the positions their forbears then appropriated in this summary way.

Not very long after, the Yusufzais extended their conquest to Swât. Advancing to the foot of the hills, they surprised the Swâtis by a ruse, and obtained possession of the lower valley. Towards the end of the fifteenth century they added Buneyr and Chamlah, and about the end of the sixteenth separated into two great divisions; the first known by the general name Yusafzai, and the second Mandanzai after Yusaf's nephew—the former finally locating themselves mainly in Dir, Swât, Buneyr, and the Upper Indus hills; the latter in the Yusafzai plain and the valleys between Buneyr and the Indus. Roughly speaking, and excepting one little corner, the whole country, both within and without the existing border, from the Swât River to the Indus, came into the possession of one tribe or other of the great Yusafzai family, and except among themselves, the name of the superior division still covers the whole. The aboriginal Swâtis, once a powerful nation, that Elphinstone thinks extended from the Jhelam to Jelâlâbâd, were forced eastwards over the Indus, where they took possession of the bit of country adjoining the Hazâra Valley, now occupied by their descendants. Those who remained were either reduced to servitude, or subsequently emigrated under the leadership of a famous saint, and the Swâti tribe have now no connection with the country or the inhabitants of the Swât Valley. The small corner above excepted, includes the southern slope of the Mâhâban Mountain in the south-east of the Peshawur Valley and a bit of Hazâra, and is the home of the Jaduns or Gaduns, a people quite distinct from the Yusafzais, who had a little, though somewhat doubtful, history to themselves.

By and by, the Ghoria Khels, comprising the divisions known as the Mohmands, Khalils, and Daudzais, followed their friends from Afghânistân, and took possession of Bâsâul, Jelâlâbad, and Laghmân; the Mohmands beginning to occupy the hills between Lâlpura and Peshawur, where they or their kinsmen are still. In 1504 Bârber acquired the sovereignty of Kâbul and Ghazni, and in the following year made an extensive frontier tour, coming by the Khaiber Pass to Peshawur, going along the whole Border, returning by the Sakhi Sarwar Pass and the Bori Valley to Ghazni. At this period the Pathân settlers are described as pretty well established in Laghmân, Kuner, Peshawur, Swât, and Bâjaur; though some of the original occupants still struggled for independence under their hereditary chiefs. During the next twenty-five years the Mughal Bârber undertook many forays—for most of them could not be called anything else—to punish the hill Pathâns, or to protect his own subjects, dispersing the men, carrying off the women and cattle; but, as a rule, the tribes were even then fully able to hold their own. Guided by the Dalazâks, he marched against Bâjaur, carried the fortress of the original Sultân by escalade, using the new matchlocks, "which greatly astonished the enemy"; the net result being to extend the power of the Tarklânis. Discretion, in the case of the "troublesome Yusafzais," suggested diplomacy; he forbore an invasion, but added a *Malik's*[1] daughter to his harem.

Both his sons—the restless Kamrân and the patient Hamâyun—figure in the history of the valley—the former as a fugitive with the Ghoria Khels at Pashut on the Kuner River; the latter as follow-

____
[1] Tribal chiefs.

ing him there, and hunting him from tribe to tribe, chastising those who sheltered him, but making no particular impression. In fact, no sooner had Hamâyun gone, than, about 1554, the three tribes of Ghoria Khel—the Daudzais, Khalils, and Mohmands—entered the plain of Peshawur, drove out the balance of the Dalazâks, and established themselves in their existing holdings—the Daudzais, from Michni eastwards between the Adizai branches of the Swât and the Budni stream, about as far as Akbarpura; the Khalils from Michni, southwards along the base of the Khaiber range to Peshawur and round east to Jalozai; and in the hills about Michni Fort, one clan of Mohmands established themselves, and another powerful colony across the Bâra River, among the intricate valleys and ravines of the extreme south-west corner right up to the Afridi Hills—a rich, well irrigated, and productive corner, but one that has probably become most famous in the criminal annals as a specially criminal district. The balance of the Dalazâks were finally driven across the Indus, and all that remains of the tribes now are one or two villages on the west, and a few more on the east in Hazâra.

The south-east of Peshawur, from Naushera to the Indus, by Attock round the Akora Hills to Kohât, and the whole south and east of the Kohât district, is held by the Khattaks, one of the finest tribes on our whole frontier, but located almost entirely within, rather than across, the Border. Their original home was probably the northern slopes of the Sulaimâns, and they also moved gradually eastward about the thirteenth century, by Bannu and Kohât, until, about the close of the fifteenth, they had divided the most of the latter with the Bangash; later again, about the middle of the sixteenth; they appeared in the Peshawur Valley—the plain from Khairabad to Naushera being granted to them by Akbar for services rendered by Malik Akor, at that time chief of the whole tribe. They made further progress under Akbar's immediate successors, have encroached from time to time somewhat on their

Mohmand, Khalil, and Mandanr neighbours, and under a less settled Government would probably soon extend still further into the valley. In the case of many of these tribes history not merely repeats itself, it becomes monotonous. The Khattaks, like the rest, increased, and have since divided into two divisions; the first making their head-quarters at Akora on the Kábul River, the other at Teri in south-west Kohát.

Excluding the Khattaks, the settlement of the Ghoria Khels may be said to have practically completed the location of the tribes that fringe the Peshawur border. Though there have been minor changes, modifications, and developments, no subsequent immigration seems to have taken place. And, though during the last three centuries they figure in history more frequently than those along other parts of our Border, their position relative to the ruling powers within it has not changed very much. Their subjugation was determined on by Akbar, but his control was at best never more than partial. He lost one famous general—Bir Bal—who was killed by the Yusafzais, and his force cut up. Even distinguished leaders like Todar Mal and Raja Mán Sing had to content themselves by taking up positions in the valley and keeping the tribes out of it. Under succeeding Mughals they were still more independent, and after some years of struggle, Aurangzebe is found agreeing to terms that were all in favour of the Patháns. The earlier Durránis brought them more under control, and, by inter-marriages, into occasional alliances; yet the hold of Kábul has since been less than nominal. With the beginning of this century came the Sikhs, who under Runjeet Sing reduced the valley to subjection, and the surrounding hills to obedience. Where previous rulers employed whips, the Sikhs substituted scorpions. They employed not merely the " only remedy " the Pathán understands,—force,—but their force was brutal. When a resisting village or tribe fell into their hands, their measures were as severe, and their cruelty as indiscriminate, as the Russians are credited with dealing out to the unfortunate Turkománs. There is probably no name more hated by the Pathân than Hari Sing, who lives in their memories as their most tyrannical oppressor, yet withal admired for his bravery and skill. His name is the bogie by which Pathân mothers frighten unruly children ; and old grey-beards are described as " loving to point out hills over which they were chased like sheep by the lion." But in spite of all the harrying, the fines, and the punishment, the tribes have maintained their own local institutions, their customs, their freedom, and their position in the hills ; and they have probably suffered far less from all the invasions put together, than from their own petty wars, and their own bitter and unceasing feuds.

The Great Renunciation—Buddhist Sculpture from Yusafzai

CHAPTER XXVI.

THE PESHAWUR PATHÂN OF THE PRESENT.

Peshawur Aftába and Chilmchi.

THERE are in many ways, wide differences between the various tribes and divisions of Border Pathâns, even at present, located round the Peshawur Valley, and it is perhaps dangerous to attempt generalizations that cannot apply to all. Still, however much they may differ in detail, there is a decided family likeness; and before passing to notice rival houses, it may be worth while to consider a few leading characteristics, common to all these Eastern Capulets and

Montagues. The manner in which the tribes established themselves round the valley has been examined; from the time they did so, in spite of the troubles that have swept over them, they cannot be said to have been subject to any man. For some centuries at least they have acknowledged no law outside the custom of their tribe, and in the rugged fastnesses of the frontier ranges, have led a wild, free, active, albeit lawless, life, and acquired a spirit of independence rare in India, and not common in any oriental country. The style of the tribesman is a little after the manner of Rob Roy. " My foot is on my native heath," and " Am I not a Pathân ? " Even when he leaves his native heath behind, he takes his manner with him. He will come down, a stalwart manly-looking ruffian, with frank and open manners, rather Jewish features, long hair plentifully oiled, under a high turban, with a loose tunic, blue for choice—the better to hide the dirt—worn very long—he wears his clothes very long in both senses—baggy drawers, a *lungi* or sash across his shoulders, grass sandals, a sheepskin coat with the hair inside, thickly populated, a long heavy knife, and a rifle, if he is allowed to carry either. He is certain to be filthy, and he may be ragged, but he will saunter into a Viceregal durbar as proud as Lucifer, and with an air of unconcern a diplomatist might envy. Not in the least like any other Indian subject, he is not always subordinate, even to his own chief. At best the chief is but an equal perhaps a delegate, for tribal purposes, with a little brief authority, but in no other respects superior to the humblest radical of them all. This inordinate pride is one of his marked characteristics, and the " Am I not a Pathân ? " embodies all he is most proud of. He will glory in robbery, is rather vain of a successfully conducted murder, will admit being avaricious, not deny being faithless, distrustful, envious, resentful, and vindictive; or he will boast perpetually of his descent, powers in arms, or independence; but the being a Pathân more than covers all the one and caps all the other.

To honour, in the Western sense, he does not attach much importance, but he has a code of his own which he strictly observes, and refers to proudly, under the name of *Nang-i-Pukhtána.* This code imposes upon him the necessity of recognizing the right of asylum, even in the case of his bitterest foe who comes as a suppliant; the necessity for revenge by retaliation, an eye for an eye, a tooth for a tooth, or a life for a life; and, almost the most obligatory of all, open-handed hospitality to all who may demand it. There are differences of opinion as to the genuineness of this hospitality. There is often not much to give, the little may be of a simple kind, and sometimes given to avoid the ridicule and scorn attaching to the suspicion of being considered a miser, a name of infinite scorn. But those who know the tribesman best, most readily credit him with the virtue of good fellowship, and of sociability among his own people. Festive gatherings are frequent, the men—for the women have their separate opportunities for bits of scandal—delight to meet at the shrine of a saint, or the village guest-house, make a noise and be happy; while a tribal Malik will entertain as recklessly as the old-fashioned Irish landlord, or the Bengal planter, and will get deeply into debt to do it. Nevertheless the over-zealous traveller would do well to bear in mind the Abbot's maxim—" *Who suppes with the Deville should have a long spoone.*"

Bracketed with hospitality, the Pathân puts courage as the first of virtues; the two have often to do duty for all the others. He is undoubtedly brave to rashness, sets no value upon life, either his own or any one else's. Trained from youth to feats of strength, endowed with wonderful powers of endurance, he commands the admiration of most Englishmen. There is a sort of charm about the better sort, that inclines many people to forget his treacherous nature, and even his " vice is sometimes by action dignified." Equally certain is it his courage is too often of a coarse and brutal kind. He will meet his enemy, and kill him or be killed, without flinching, but he prefers to shoot him from behind, or stab him while asleep, and will not meet him on equal terms, if it is possible to take him at a disadvantage. Moreover, though said to be born for war, he is notoriously impulsive, and best in attack. If that fails he is easily disheartened and difficult to bring up again. He will fight splendidly in his own hills, though a flank attack upsets him, and a suspicion of being cut off causes a precipitate retreat.

Peshawur Cooking Bowl and " Long Spoones."

He is predatory to the last degree. There is not much need to discriminate between tribes here, and it is no libel to say that pillage and theft are to many the business of life. The mother's prayer is that her son may grow up a successful thief; not perhaps so shocking as it seems, for it is only another form of petition for daily bread. Another story from the nursery, is of a child who stabbed his tutor, the latter being implored not to mind it, as it was the poor child's first attempt; a parable which suggests *Punch's* picture of the Sheffielder on his knees, the bull pup pinning his cheek, and the child encouraging his father to "bide it" if he can, as it would be the making of the pup. A successful use of the knife is part of a liberal Pathân education. "Give or I take," with a knife at the victim's throat, is a comparatively modest request. "Your money or your life" is the formula of the highwayman in the West; the Pathân will take the life first, and the plundered who is let off with the loss of his purse only, may consider himself extremely lucky.

His superstition is unlimited—the women worse than the men. The Mullahs, the Pirs, the disciples, the vagabond "seekers after wisdom," are to him all so many St. Peters, who hold the keys of heaven, and any jargon that sounds like an Arabic verse is infinitely more terrible than the whistle of an enemy's bullet; the "air drawn daggers" have for him more terrors than the assassin's knife. He has the firmest belief in miracles, charms, and omens; will never pass a shrine without stopping to salaam; can hardly say a sentence without an "Inshalla," or cut a throat without a prayer; but he will not allow the creed of the Prophet, or the ordinances of his religion to stand in the way of his business, his desires, or his passions. "At one moment a saint and the next a devil" is a common proverb about him. He is not a believer in woman's rights. As often as not he purchases his wife, or employs an agent to select her; but once acquired, she is so much property in which his honour is invested, and he becomes more suspicious of her than of anything else. To see her speak to a stranger man sets him alight, and is sufficient ground for mistrust; a chance gossip might probably cost her life, and be ample grounds for a feud against the man. Therefore, elopements are common, every young blood is bound to establish his reputation by an intrigue, and rumour credits the wives with exceptional willingness to risk having their throats cut.

There is no doubt the Pathán is extremely avaricious and grasping, and gold, the saint-seducing gold, weighs—as does it not elsewhere?—heavy in the scale against patriotism, honour, fidelity or friendship; but he has sometimes been condemned in what appear too sweeping terms; the whole being sampled by the worst. The worst is, however, undoubtedly very bad indeed. If he is to be tested by the standard of a Peshawur judge, or official who has mainly to do with the criminal classes, it would be almost impossible to paint his picture in colours dark enough. The story of "crime on the Peshawur Frontier" has been told in a recent work by a distinguished officer of wide experience. An appalling record of five years' experience as a Border Commissioner and Judge, Mr. Elsmie speaks of it as a greater mental strain than all the rest of a long Indian service together. "Crime," he says, "of the worst conceivable kind is a matter of almost daily occurrence; murder in all its phases, unblushing assassination in broad daylight, before a crowd of witnesses; the carefully planned secret murder of the sleeping victim at dead of night, murder by robbers, by rioters, by poisoners, by boys, and by women sword in hand. Blood always crying for blood, revenge looked on as a virtue, the heritage of retribution passed on as a solemn duty from father to son." Murder, as a business—and it is perhaps hardly more difficult to find men who, for a consideration, will carry it out, in any of the above forms, than to obtain a porter to carry a parcel. The Peshawur District is approximately about a thirty-second part of the Punjâb; but it accounts for about a third of the murders of the whole; the police report one in every 4,500 of the entire population, or in every 3,000 Pathâns as murdered annually. The necessity for revenging feuds, wrongs at the hands of the seducer, jealousies in regard to women and girls, and still more, of boys, the objects of unnatural lust, account for much of the bloodshed. "It would seem," says Mr. Elsmie, "that the spirit of murder is latent in the heart of nearly every man in the valley." There is almost a worse feature. Public opinion is mostly in favour of screening the murderer. The discovery of the offender is almost impossible, if the influential men do not wish it, and they seldom do, while wilfully false accusations against innocent persons, supported by fabricated evidence of the most astounding and circumstantial character, are often concocted to divert suspicion from the real criminals, or wreak vengeance upon old enemies. Justice is almost as much baffled by false accusations established in this way, as by the difficulties in bringing home real crime. In most villages it is almost impossible to do so with any certainty at all, and "it is but seldom the police have been able to bring offenders to justice." Special regulations have been found necessary, frontier officers invested with summary powers, and recently, tribal councils empowered to deal with some of their own crime, which, in a rough way, they are often capable of doing effectually.

It is unnecessary to refer further to the records of crime. Grant that it is equal or more degraded than the Newgate Calendar— so probably are the dark stories of other Oriental countries. Or that the city of Peshawur may rival Constantinople or Port Said; as startling chronicles come occasionally from the West, and few cities or peoples could afford to be judged by their police reports. It may also be urged that the position of the valley encourages a great immigration of lawless spirits, in addition to its own indigenous scoundrels. Outlaws who have made life too hot in their own country, and find British protection convenient, and where at the same time, temptation is offered to adventurous criminals of all kinds, in the form of a certain asylum when needed, with tribes all round who will have to give it, no matter how red-handed the seeker comes. It is, however, improbable that the average tribesman beyond the Border is any better or worse than his brothers or cousins within it, and it may fairly be hoped that both have, as a people, many more good points than they are likely to have developed by examination of the class that mainly come into our courts.

It is more true of this Border Pathán than of most men, that he lives in a state of war by nature. Life for him has no charms without it; his surroundings during all these centuries have made it a necessity of his existence; his hand has been literally against every man; he is seen at his best when raiding or plundering. Trained from his youth to add to the narrow resources of his bare hill sides, by the plunder of the more fertile valleys and plains, nothing will prevent him doing so, but the knowledge that his neighbours are too strong for him, or too much on the alert. Naturally he hates all government which introduces law and order, or binds him over to keep the peace with his neighbour. He looks upon such restrictions as an interference with his most sacred rights, the depriving him of legitimate pillage, and the best part of his revenues. For years the plains of Hastnagar and Yusafzai were the hunting grounds of bands from Swát, who chased the Hindu trader, and put him to ransom. Their mountain fastnesses the rendezvous for any one hostile to our Government. They are so still. For a long time the Mohmands are recorded as averaging twenty-five formidable raids a year, to try and force the British to buy off depredations, by paying blackmail. It was mainly suspicion and dislike to the Swát canal project that brought down the Utmán Khels one night, to knock the tents over the sleeping coolies, catch them like birds in a net, and hack them to pieces through the canvas. The recent construction of a border police tower on the high road to Kohát was a grievous wrong in the eyes of the Aka Khels, because it would stop their ancient right to highway robbery along that length, and they did their best to prevent it, by carrying off the masons. But just as the extension of civilization is closing the happy hunting grounds of the red man in the Wild West, so the enforcing of law and order up to the very edge of the Border hills, while it brings substantial benefit to the people within that border, has possibly made life harder for the tribes beyond it; has indirectly increased the Peshawur criminal list. Gradually being deprived of all opportunities of war, the Border Pathán, may, like Othello, complain that his occupation is gone! Whether he is likely to be, or is, satisfied with the altered condition of things, and whether it would not be worth while to find him some congenial occupation, is a problem well worthy of consideration.

CHAPTER XXVII.

FITZHARDY'S MURDERER—A DOMESTIC BORDERER.

PERHAPS it is as well to disarm suspicion, and, like Bottom, to start by disclaiming any attempt to affright the gentle reader. In spite of the title, nothing is going to happen to Fitzhardy; and his faithful Pathân henchman, known to all familiars as "the Murderer," would have waited behind any reader's chair as harmlessly, and almost as well, as a London footman; and, lion as he undoubtedly was, have roared you "as 'twere any nightingale." He had a salute for all his master's guests, inquired in the best Pashtu if they were well, strong and in good case; and, as they departed, commended them to be in God's care. Unfortunately he had come to the regiment originally with the brand of Cain upon him, a fine, tall, clean-limbed, well-set-up, tough old Yusafzai Pathân, from the Ranizai country up by the Swât River, with a straight nose, dark hair, and a complexion almost fair. His manner was frank enough, and he made no secret of his reason for enlisting. An unavoidable business engagement had compelled him to kill a couple of his countrymen, whose clansmen waited for him, and made return to his paternal hills impossible. He had, therefore, taken the Queen's rupee, and, with a heart as light as his name, Khushhal [1] Khán fell to soldiering in a native regiment.

[1] "The happy-conditioned."

As chance fell out, he became attached to Fitzhardy as orderly, and the two saw much service in different parts of the country, including an occasional brush with his own people along the Border, but he never developed any further sign of abnormal bloodthirstiness, save on one occasion when the old Adam came out. Like a good many other soldier officers, Fitz, as the regiment called him, did not suffer from a superfluity of dollars, and was occasionally despondent about ways and means; a circumstance that did not escape the notice of his faithful orderly, who one day asked if there was nothing the *Sahib* could think of by way of mending matters. Had the *Sahib* no expectations from his family, no one likely to give him any money? The *Sahib* could think of no one but an old aunt who might leave him her money when she died—a prospect, however, that seemed very distant. Khushhal looked carefully round to see that the coast was clear, shut all the doors, and, with a gleam in his eye, and his hand searching for a knife, whispered, "*Sahib*, I'll go home and kill her. They may perhaps catch and hang me, but any how you will be sure of the money." The offer was perfectly genuine, and the Murderer was greatly disappointed to find his officer had so little spirit of enterprise as to decline it.

By and by, finances improved. Fitz got a civil appointment and blossomed into a District officer—a reason quite sufficient to induce Khushhal to "cut his name" also, and join the new concern as general manager of Fitz's bungalow at Pindabâd, and every thing pertaining to it. A master stroke that marked a tide in Khushhal's affairs, and led him on to fortune and to fame. He took absolute possession of all domestic affairs, regulated Fitz's household, engaged his servants, managed his camp, and eventually did it so completely, that his fame passed into a proverb, as "Fitz's Murderer." To speak of the Murderer's Fitz, would perhaps have more accurately described their relationship. The great feature of the management was based on the very equitable law of contracts. The Murderer contracted for everything. He had a monthly contract for the supply of matches, for blacking, for lamp oil, for tooth picks. However, all was on a sliding scale. When Fitz was a captain, matches cost him eight annas a month; it was inconsistent with his dignity as major to use less than twelve annas a month, while the Murderer held no lieutenant-colonel could light his pipe effectually for less than one rupee a month. His ponies were fed and groomed by contract. His tents were carried in the same way. If he was not clothed, he was at least mended by contract; the Murderer tying up little holes in his stockings with bits of string on regular monthly terms. He was fed, and at times almost well fed, by contract; but the arrangements were conducted on the most thorough-going Pathân principles. Sometimes they ran rather long in the direction of tough salt beef; at others the supplies were on an almost extravagant scale, and Kushhal stood by urging master to try "just one more slice" of a particularly succulent joint. This chance, unduly neglected, the menu would revert to salt beef once more. The story of the Great Beef Contract was almost as famous in Pindabâd as Mark Twain's. A long course of salt beef in various disguises, through a series of deadly hot days, induced a remonstrance even from Fitz, and resulted in a day or two's respite and change to elderly chickens; but all too soon there followed more instalments of junk. Fitz had to explain that the flesh of the cow had become altogether hateful to him. "*Sahib* come here. Look at these casks!" said the Murderer, pointing to a corner of the verandah, "I have bought a whole cow, which has been salted, and which has to be eaten. What can I do?" Obviously there was nothing for Fitz but to work steadily through, hoping for better times when the contract was next revised.

Of course Fitz never married. That could not have been brought within the four corners of any contract. But the Murderer came in radiant one day, having bought a girl, a bargain, for twenty-five rupees. His matrimonial bliss, however, was of short duration. There was a row one day; a sound of great wailing. The small wife had been caught talking to the gardener, and was being corrected. Fortunately the flirtation was in British territory or . . . . he sold the little baggage next day, and made, as the old ruffian informed Fitz, sixteen rupees on the transaction.

Occasionally, it occurred to Fitz, that the grim Pathân heathen might like some leave, and the suggestion was put to him in various forms. But no, it was not convenient to go home, and Khushhal was not like some grumblers. He knew a good place when he had one, and was not going to desert so kind a master. Finally, Fitz went on furlough himself, and took long leave, having some sort of lingering idea, that perhaps this old man of the sea might be induced to visit his mountain home, where peradventure his friends might persuade him to stop. If there is persuasion in an Enfield bullet, or a Pathân knife, they probably would. Fitz had a two years' holiday with no salt beef, and submitted to buying his matches casually at the street corners; but eventually the time came round when he had to return. The first man to meet him when he landed, was Khushhal Khân. The staunch old Murderer had come to Bombay, and he had brought a *Nazar* [1] for the *Sahib*, because, he said, he had learnt in India, that it is never good to come empty handed into the presence of a superior. At Watson's Hotel he spread out the presents for Fitz; a second-hand Continental Bradshaw, which he thought the *Sahib* might find pleasant reading, and a thing like a fiddle-stick or plectrum, made out of the wood that grew on Adam Khân's grave, which as every Yusafzai knows, will enable any one to play perfectly on the fiddle, though he did not say Fitz's performance on the instrument was not perfect. The third gift was a remarkably mongrel pup, for the keep of which he proposed to enter into a contract at once; and the fourth was an old Letts's Diary, which he felt sure the *Sahib*

---

[1] The present with which it is Eastern etiquette to approach a superior.

would find useful to keep his accounts in. With these he wished
the *Sahib, Salam-a-laikum. Ma khware ye.* "May evil not come
nigh him."

They had many an adventure and many a contract after that,
Fitz and his old Murderer ; and the latter was perfectly deaf to all
suggestions that involved any break up of the arrangements. Fitz
once went so far as to offer to pension him. "*Sahib*," he said, "if
I had not left my regiment to take your service, I should now have
been *Subadar Major.* You know I *cannot* go back to Ranizai.
Why should I take pension while I can work on full pay and
allowances? You are a good master, *Sahib*, and I'll never leave
you. Never."

CHAPTER XXVIII.

BEFORE Max O'Rell undertook to educate them, our Gallic neighbours affected to suppose that John Bull bought and sold his womankind in the market of Smithfield. Just so most Border Pathâns purchase their wives. Not that the practice is universal; the Pathân sometimes spends his money on feasts, ornaments for the bride, and fees to "go-betweens," or there is an exchange of presents, a sort of Eastern marriage settlement, and entertainments to satisfy the guardians as to his position, and that the bride is not going to absolute poverty. Some, in fact, like the Shirânis on the Dera Ismail Khân border, go so far as to give a dowry; but in a great many cases, and with most tribes, wives are literally bought and sold, exactly as so many cattle; quotations varying according to the circumstances of the purchaser and the youth and beauty of the purchased.

In England, according to the same excellent French authority, elopements are common. "A young girl goes out one fine morning to post a letter, and on her return informs her parents she is married." In Scotland it is an easier business still. "It is sufficient for the young people to say, 'I take you for my wife; I accept you for my husband;' and the thing is done." The Pathân, on the other hand, though he takes care to make it very easy to get out of the toils of matrimony, has a process for getting into them elaborate enough to furnish matter for another volume by the gifted author of *Les Filles de John Bull.*

The most Arcadian are the Waziris. For instance, when the Waziri youth wants a wife he gets some respectable old clansman to consult the girl's parents. If to them the connection seems desirable, they reply, " Bring us the *hiri* "—about 60 or 100 rupees. The admirer then deputes his father with his friends, who, taking with them a sheep or two for a feast, repair to the girl's house and pay up the stipulated amount over the roast mutton, a trifling sum being returned as luck-penny. The couple are then held to be engaged, and whenever Corydon goes to visit his Phyllis, he takes with him the wherewithal for the savoury dishes, which possibly Phyllis dresses, and Thyrsis, Damon and company eat. He is then expected to put two or three rupees into the dish, and the father, in return, to make him a small present—a scarf, a pair of shoes, or a cheap ring. The custom, with a fine touch of humour, is called " Binding the ass." When the wedding day arrives, the bridegroom's friends, men and women, go to the bride's village, and provide a feast, to which all parties are invited. Towards evening, the bridegroom's party arrives ; and after a feigned attack on the village with sticks and stones, join in the rejoicings, which last all night. No sort of sleeping accommodation is thought of ; " the hearth, with oily brands of pine an abundant fire, blackening the door-posts with perpetual soot," and even in winter they reck no more of the cold than did the Shepherds of Virgil. Next morning the bride is carried off mounted on an ox or an ass, the bridegroom remaining behind for a day or two, to console her parents for their loss. After a fortnight's honeymoon she visits them, to take back the presents given by her family, which the bridegroom usually divides among his party. It is doubtful if the privileges of leap-year are understood in Waziri land, but occasionally the woman chooses, and she makes known her fancy by sending the village drummer to pin a handkerchief on the favoured one's cap with a hairpin. The drummer watches his opportunity and does this in a public place, when the swain has to marry the lady if he can pay her price to the father.

In Yusafzai, Cœlebs to a great extent employs a professional go-between to arrange his matrimonial affairs. The preliminary negotiations over, he and his confidential agent settle the matter of presents with papa, and quaff a cup of *eau sacré* together as a pledge of good faith. The engagement is then given out, and the hopeful Benedick may visit the family as often as he likes, taking presents each time for his *fiancée*, though he never sees her. That privilege does not indeed become his till the marriage ceremonies are over and the bride has been conducted to her new home by the "best-man" and his party, the bridesmaids being left to comfort the old people—an improvement on the Waziri arrangement. Even then Benedick has to entertain his guests for three days and two nights before he unveils his bride and sees her face for the first time. Such is the theory at any rate. Both look for wedding presents from their friends, on very much the same understanding as prevails about such matters in the West; only, not to return the compliment to friends under similar circumstances, would in Yusafzai probably lead to a serious feud. The bridegroom has to stand the "shot" on both sides, and the cost is sometimes heavy A cheap marriage with a maid would probably run to Rs. 100, an average one probably Rs. 250, while a rich Yusafzai might have to spend several thousands to marry himself respectably. A single regular one is, therefore, as much as most can afford, and quite apart from the adage about "two women together making cold weather," for which there is an excellent if slightly broad Pushtu equivalent. A Khân must be well off who can afford to run to the full Muhammadan limit of four.

In many parts of the country there is naturally much less restraint. Women who in towns or large gatherings would not venture out unless covered from head to foot in the *burka*, a sort of large white cotton blouse with a little network in front of the hood that covers the head, and a pair of large ungainly white cotton boots, or rather leg coverings, go about in their own camps and villages unveiled, and bare-legged, with no other restraint, than the general opinion that it is indecorous to be seen associating with men. Intercourse between the sexes is therefore much more free, and matches are made up by mutual attraction, and the pre-liminary negotiations are at the best of the most nominal kind. This however does not exempt the lover from paying some price to the girl's parents. To elope with a girl is by many clans considered an outrage equal to murder, and to be punished with the same mercilessness.

Among most Border Pathâns, or among the Afghân people generally, the ceremonies do not vary materially. Sometimes the bridegroom has to stand treat to the lady's family, sometimes to the tribal *Jirgah* or Council, sometimes to the village. The " hospitable Pathân " does not like to throw away a chance of dining out at any one else's expense ; but among the majority the transaction is essentially a business one, and in addition to all the feasting, a sum has to be paid down as purchase-money. Even tribes who look on all business as vulgar are not above trade in wives. The 60 rupees *hiri* of the Waziri is probably Rs. 100 with the adjoining Ghilzai. Rs. 30 to 100 is the quotation for Bannu ; it is about the same among the Khattaks, and rises on the Kohât border to Rs. 100 or 200; in Miranzai, brides are still more expensive, the tariff ranging from Rs. 200 to 500. Along the Kohât, and part of the Peshawur Border, the trade in women is notorious. A hard work-ing, useful Afridi wife can, according to Tucker, easily be procured for Rs. 150 to 200. One remarkable for beauty will run to a fancy price—Rs. 1,000, or even more. " The ordinary hill woman," he goes on to say, " has little in the way of good looks to recommend her On the other hand she works like a donkey, cuts grass and

Mahsud Waziri Women.

R

wood, carries water, is accustomed to poor living, and does twice as much as the more delicately nurtured woman of the valley."

Not only do the Trans-Border tribes sell their own relations, but the trade in wives brought from Swât, Bajaur, and other valleys —sometimes stolen, sometimes purchased—was, a few years ago, brought to the official notice of Government. On the Indian side the Border measures were taken to check it. The stolen women were taken from their purchasers and sent home again,—possibly to be made away with on their return by their dishonoured relatives. But the market is reputed still well-stocked with those sold, or for sale by their relatives, and the instances that come before the District Officer are many. To take one of Tucker's, a sketch of the life of a Trans-Border woman is more than enough to point a moral. Born a Ningrahâri on the slopes of the Safed Koh, her parents died when she was young, and her relatives sold her in marriage to a Zakha Khel Afridi, who was afterwards killed fighting against us in the Khaiber. Her father-in-law at once sold her with her little daughter to a Bazoti Orakzai for Rs. 100. He beat her so badly she ran away in a month or two, leaving her little daughter, and reached the Mani Khel country in Tirah, where she stopped three months, and was sold for Rs. 120 to a Bar Muhammad Khel Orakzai, residing in British territory, with whom she lived happily for three years, until the Bazoti found out where she was and came to claim her. The Bar Muhammad paid the claimant back his Rs. 100, and the case was settled—a fair sample of the possibilities fate may have in store for the "widowed wife and wedded maid" on the Border.

The effect of all this is, that though the woman may be well treated—and, of course, according to the standard she has been brought up to, she is more often than not well treated—she is mainly looked on as property. Maid, widow, or divorcee, she cannot marry without the consent of her male relations. The husband can divorce his wife without assigning any reason. The wife, even with the best of grounds, would have small chance of obtaining a divorce, were she rash enough to sue for it. Theoretically, the Pathán knife would flash to avenge even a look that threatened her with insult, though certainly not from the chivalrous feeling imagined by Burke. Actually, the purchased article is treated in the most casual manner. So long as the owner is satisfied, and she looks well enough, or works hard enough, he keeps her. If she fails to please, or falls out with the mother-in-law, or the sisters, cousins and aunts, or the times grow hard, he sells her with the other live-stock. That female dishonour can only be washed out in blood, is another theory; and adultery is supposed always to demand the blood of both the respondent and the co-respondent. Occasionally, indeed, the Pathán is young and ardent enough to prefer vengeance. Oftener he is sufficiently cautious to reflect that the market value of the erring one represents to him a considerable sum in rupees, and who so likely as the lover to make a liberal bid? So he foregoes the blood, and comes to terms with the co-respondent. So common is adultery with some tribes, the Southern Khattaks for instance that it is almost a rule for a woman to elope once. She is sold in the first instance to a selected husband, with whom she has to live till she meets the man she fancies, or who will run off with her. And so common is the subsequent money arrangement that the Pathán has invented a special and most expressive word for it— "sharmuna," which might be freely translated "blush-money." A son gets blush-money if his mother re-marries; a man seducing a widow or spinster, has, marriage or no marriage, to pay blush-money to her male next of kin; and a surprising number of husbands pocket their wrongs on the same terms. To draw on Tucker for one more specimen case—an atrocious one enough. An Afridi policeman was charged with adultery with a Trans-Border woman. Her relations killed her, and a claim for Rs. 300 blush-money lay against him. His relations, therefore, bought a poor Hindustâni woman for Rs. 40, took her to their village and pretended she was married to one of themselves and had gone away with one of the opposite party. They then killed her and set up a counter-claim for blush-money; the two claims being held to cancel each other.

This is perhaps an extreme instance of the treatment of women, but there is no doubt that the wife-selling, the theory that the sex generally are only fit for playthings or slaves, and certain other Pathân vices combine to place them in a position extremely low and degraded. At the same time it must not be forgotten that the worst cases are those which come most often to notice, and the average of Pathân wives are married in their own villages, live among their own people; and it may be hoped that the current of their domestic joys glides just as smoothly as in other parts of the world.

CHAPTER XXIX.

THE MOHMANDS.

By comparison it is pleasant to turn from the Pathán of the Peshawur Border to his surroundings. If his country is not altogether "divine," it is by no means without its charms. To leave the court and bazaar—the atmosphere of murder and evil reputation—and go up to the top of the Gor Khatri, the old caravanserai that tradition places on the side of Kanishka's great Vihara, where esoteric Buddhist monks instructed in the "Lesser Vehicle." The holy place of the Hindu *jogi*[1] converted into the residence of Afghán refugees, and from the top of which there is a view of the whole of that great picturesque amphitheatre, from the stony slopes of the Khattak range, by the banks and the marshes of the Kábul and Swât rivers, the glens of Yusafzai, to the black peaks of Hazâra, with the snows of the Hindu-Kush and the Sufed Koh for a background. And it is tempting to dwell longer on the beauty of the valley itself, with its luxuriant fields and innumerable water-courses; its villages and hamlets half hid among mulberries and pomegranates, poplars, and willows; its orchards and gardens—for there are roses at the Bâra as fine as by Bendemeer's stream. A scene which from this point of view, might almost as easily pass for the "haunts of ancient peace," as one of continuous feuds.

[1] Druid (?) or mendicant priest.

But the scenery of the Peshawur Valley has been so often painted in glowing terms by enthusiastic artists; the halt within the Border has here been already somewhat too long; and it is necessary to pass to the people beyond it.

Crossing the Doâba, to the bare stony irregular hills that rise almost abruptly from the plain on the north-west between the Kâbul and Swât Rivers, is the country of the independent Mohmands: a tribe both numerous and important, and the only one on our immediate border that professes even a nominal allegiance to the Afghân Amir. These low, bare hills, the last outworks of the Hindu-Kush, rise until they reach the higher ranges which separate the Mohmands from Bajaur and the Utmân Khels on the north, and the Kuner Valley, which forms the western boundary. The little bit of Mullagori country and the Khaiber route to Kâbul, as far as Jelâlâbâd, being the boundary on the south. The aspect of the country generally is on all hands admittedly dreary in the extreme, but the most rugged and unfruitful, and, at the same time, the least accessible hills are those on the south-east bordering the Peshawur Valley; the best parts the Bâizâi Hills on the west, down from Bajaur to the Kâbul River, and the rich alluvial land along its banks from Jelâlâbâd to Lâlpura. In one way or other, by transit dues or by irrigation, the river is the principal source of Mohmand wealth. The three largest valleys approached from our border,—the Shilmân, Gandâo,—"Fetid water valley,"—and Pandiâli, covered by the respective forts of Michni, Shabkadr, and Abzai,—are for most of the year little more than dry, stony water-courses, changing to raging torrents in the rains, with barren slopes leading from the beds of shingle to the rocky spurs which flank them. Some of the glens opening out north towards Bajaur, and south to Lâlpura, are better; but dry ravines, alternating with rows of sterile rocky hills and crags, are the most striking characteristics of the country. There is little vegetation beyond coarse grass, scrub wood, and dwarf palm. In the summer the heat is said to be very great, and the lowlands are not then particularly healthy. There are two or three roads that have been improved by us, like those from Shahgai by the Shilmân Valley to Dhaka, and from Michni, by the Shâmilo ferry to the Shilmân; but, with few exceptions, the country is without roads, the rudest tracks leading straight up the hills and down again. Roads and water are the two great wants. In the hot weather the latter is everywhere scarce; even that for drinking has often to be brought long distances, from springs whose supply is uncertain, or from small tanks made to store the rain; the laborious task of carrying falling to the women.

The resources of such a country, as may be supposed, are few. The crops are mainly dependent on the rains; and if these fail, more or less distress is certain. The villages are small and are poor, the extent of cultivation round them limited; a little grass, firewood, charcoal, and dwarf-palm mats, added to a few cattle and some honey from the Bâizâi Hills, is all the people have to offer in the way of exports. All the manufactures of civilization they have to purchase. They do a certain amount of business as carriers; the Kachi clan depending almost entirely on the carrying trade between Peshawur and Kâbul, and the Lâlpura and Michni chiefs realising a good deal in the way of dues on rafts and goods floated down the Kâbul River. "Guide money," levied on *kâfilas*[1] from Bajaur or Kuner to Peshawur, is another source of revenue; and one or two clans are credited with a scandalous trade in women stolen from Swât, Buneyr or Bajaur, and sold to the Afridis and Orakzais. But even in ordinary times there is a surplus population that is unable to find support, and which is steadily emigrating, whenever opportunity offers, to the Peshawur district. Many of these have taken up land on the Swât Canal; and numbers would only be too glad to follow their example. In bad times, it is quite intelligible that the unfortunate Mohmand, with

[1] Caravans.

the drought in his own country, and the prospect of loot in his neighbours, should occasionally become a desperate man.

In physique, though there are among them fine men, they are as a rule, inferior to many of the surrounding Pathâns; and though they have on occasions fought well against us, their courage is decidedly open to suspicion. They have plenty of pride and haughtiness, sufficient reputation for cruelty and treachery, and like other Pathâns, a good deal to say about their honour; the value of which may, perhaps, be best judged by the frontier proverb concerning them to the effect that " you have only to put a rupee in your eye, and you may look at any Mohmand, man or woman." They are on fairly good terms with their neighbours of Bajaur and Kuner, have usually avoided collisions with the Afridis, though between them and the Shinwâris a guerilla war has lasted for centuries; the belt of desert from Lundi Kotal to Pesh Bolak bearing witness to the destruction caused by raid and counter-raid. Private blood feuds are common, and the tariff for injuries runs somewhat low. In many other social and domestic customs they resemble the Yusafzais; but they have no *hujras*,—an institution which to the Pathân "Young-blood" corresponds to the English notion of a club,—the want of which, in a Pathân's opinion, is to stamp a tribe as little better than savages. They differ, moreover conspicuously in having a more aristocratic tribal constitution, in that they have hereditary chiefs or Khâns, drawn from the old families, who from ancient times have supplied leaders. The Khâns are appointed and are removable by the Amir of Kâbul: the most important being the Khân of Lâlpura in the east, and the Bâizâi Khân of Goshta in the west, who both enjoy *jagirs*[1] in Nangraha or the Jelâlâbâd district.

The whole tribe is divided into four principal divisions, of which the Bâizâi is by far the most numerous; but the Halimzai probably possesses the most influence, as they hold command of the im-

[1] Freeholds.

portant passes. The entire strength is put at 17,000 or 18,000 fighting men: but nothing like this number has been or probably ever could be brought into the field. So far, the tribesmen have never shown themselves very ready to enlist in our army, though there are a good many in the regiments of the Amir, and in the contingents of the local Khâns. Their relations with the British Government have never been altogether satisfactory. For many years after the Punjâb was annexed they gave more trouble than any other tribe. Up to 1864 their history is one of continuous conflict or raids, often on a formidable scale; and the murder of British officers who ventured too far from our outposts. There were expeditions against them in 1851-52 and 1854, and between 1855 and 1860 they were charged with no less than 125 outrages on the Peshawur district, the object plunder or murder; many being more or less serious. In 1863 the emissaries of the Akhund of Swât sent round the fiery cross, and brought 5,000 Mohmands into the field, but they were defeated with heavy loss. From that time, which corresponds with the lesson taught the tribes by the Ambeyla campaign, the record of Frontier Expeditions describes Mohmand history as a period of "*comparative*" peace; though they murdered Major Macdonald at Michni in 1873, attempted to murder Captain Anderson at Shabkadr, attacked our Survey party in 1879, and on three occasions between 1878 and 1880 were in conflict with our troops; the last time at Dhaka, where their force was nearly annihilated. Since the close of the last Afghân war the Shilmân Valley section, adjoining the Khaiber route, has been under exclusive political relations with us, and the tribe has been on better behaviour, though they threatened to give trouble in 1882; and there is little doubt that any future difficulty of ours, would be the Mohmand opportunity.

The branch of the family that settled in the south-west corner of the Peshawur Valley, when their progenitors finally ousted the Dalazâks, have now been so long separated from their country

cousins of the hills, they have practically lost all touch. They hold
very productive lands irrigated by the Bàra River; are reported
excellent farmers, superior in this respect to the adjoining Khalils,
who have also a share in the Bàra water; but the villages nearest the
Afridi hills have ever been proverbially troublesome; and recently
so far forgot their position within our border, they appealed to
arms, rather than to the Deputy Commissioner. Their quarrel
was with the Khalils, over that most fertile cause of disputes—
water,—which developed into something like a pitched battle;
eight being left dead on the field, and many more wounded. The
final settlement, however, naturally finished in the court of the
Divisional Judge, who sentenced one batch to be hanged, and a
larger one to transportation for life.

Besides the four main divisions of the hill Mohmands, there are
certain affiliated clans, of which two, mainly agricultural and
numerically insignificant,—the Dawezai and Utmânzai, located between Bajaur on the north and the Utmânkhel on the east,—may
be practically included among the Mohmands proper. The
Mullagoris on the south have already been noticed; but on the
west, the Safis—a tolerably numerous tribe—are a people entirely
distinct. They occupy the hills north of Jelâlâbâd, and some of
the valleys opening on to the Kuner River. Geographically the
Safis come between the Mohmands and the country of Kâfiristân
and probably, ethnographically and ethnologically, furnish a con-
necting link between two peoples otherwise almost diametrically
opposed. In appearance often florid, with light eyes and hair,
speaking a language only distantly related to the Pushtu of the
Mohmands, whose dialect has much in common with that spoken in
Kâbul, both they and the Dehgâns of the Lughmân Valley are
either directly descended from, or largely admixed with, the
Kâfirs, and are comparatively recent converts to Islâm. In
Bârber's time they were still called Kâfirs; in Nâdir's, Safis—a
name which Masson suggests they may have acquired by becoming

" pure," in comparison to the adjoining " impure " idolaters. Now, like many converts, they are fanatical Muhammadans; but they still retain many peculiar customs and vestiges of ancient arts. Their hills—which are little known, are reported as yielding lots of grapes, the chief products being wine, vinegar, and honey—for the Safis are great bee-keepers. The country, moreover, is the natural home of the Narcissus.

Politically, the position of this powerful Mohmand confederation in regard to our Border is another somewhat unsatisfactory feature. Their being nominal subjects of Afghánistán necessitates, at least in theory, a reference to that court for the redress of offences committed by the tribe ; while even if the Amir wished to exercise his authority, the tribesmen are almost entirely beyond his influence. He cannot even collect his revenue. For the last few years they are credited with " settling down to peaceful intercourse with us on the Peshawur border." '*Cras credemus, hodie nihil.*' If they should at any time become troublesome as regards our communications with Kâbul, we should, no doubt, be able to take such measures as would speedily bring them to their bearings ; but, as already pointed out with regard to other tribes, there are times and seasons when it would become eminently inconvenient to have to do this.

CHAPTER XXX.

TRIBAL JIRGAHS.

EACH Pathán clan is a separate democracy, but a democracy in which the interest of the individual comes first, the welfare of those neighbours who compose his sept or his *khail*, second; and save in the presence of a common danger, or some question where combination is absolutely necessary, the general community runs a bad third. He is content, as an old Miân Khel said, with civil discord, is content with war's alarms, is content with blood, but is not, and never will be content with a master. His science of government would seem to mean that every man be a law unto himself, with the maximum of personal, rather than civic, or national, liberty. The "greatest happiness" of the average Khân is to dispense his own justice; his proud privilege to redress his own wrongs, to wreak his own vengeance—on the original offender if this can be done conveniently, if not, on brothers, cousins, or uncles, the next of kin, or even the offender's tribe. The Pathán Mrs. Grundy looks to him to do this, and across the Border Mrs. Grundy is also a power in the state. Her notion of what is scandalous is the only respect in which she differs from her Western relative. And after all, on either side of the Border, or on either side of the globe, is it not very much the surrounding society that establishes the custom? "Revenge," according to Bacon, "is a kind of wild justice ;" and it is not so very many years ago that Elphinstone described duelling as "only a generous and well-regulated mode of revenge." A Pathân without a blood feud, or neglecting to avenge it, would be to show himself just as wanting in good Pukhtunwali *ton* as, in their respective countries, it would now be for a French editor or a German student not to fight duels, or for an Irish patriot to pay his rent.

Nevertheless, necessity has forced the Pathân, like the rest of the world, to recognize the need for some form of government, some system that shall enforce even the rudest customary law, some tribal organization to fall back on at a pinch. And his tribal *jirgah*, or council of elders, does all this for him and more. Composed of Khâns, Mullahs and headmen, it combines his House of Lords, bench of Bishops and Legislative Assembly ; it discharges the functions of all the divisions of the Queen's Bench, Probate and Divorce, the Board of Trade and the War Office. It is at once his Convocation and his county court. In fact, it performs for him most offices, from those of the Senate to those of the Vestry. Tribal customs affecting village society, the parish politics of Border Little Pedlingtons, of course, furnish a lot of business ; so do matters concerning debts, deeds, mortgages and sales. And curiously enough, among the most lawless, as perhaps among the most civilized, the law is much more severe on offences against property than against the person. The Border ruffian has the greatest respect for legal documents of the kind—the most scrupulous regard for the tenure of land being often associated with the greatest risk to its owner's life. Just, for example, as his more fortunate Western representative is privileged to kick his wife to the verge of death, or ill treat his children, at a far cheaper rate than he can snare a partridge, or steal a pair of boots.

While the legal business of the *jirgah* is far the heaviest on the civil side, it has also considerable criminal jurisdiction. Life, even for an Afridi or a Yusafzai, is not always beer and skittles ; the luxury of reprisals, and the pleasure of personally killing one's enemies, must perforce be occasionally carried out by deputy, or entrusted to a tribunal. Where blood feuds are so common and so bitter that though they may be allowed to slumber for years, still remain a sacred heritage to be eventually taken up and continued as long as possible, many a man, whose ancestors have been violent, may find himself with more legacies on his hands than he can hope to carry out. The constant anxiety and watchfulness entailed by a lot of feuds, is an inheritance calculated to make life a burden ; and, wearied out, the Pathán's only resource is to leave his country for service in India, or to get the most trouble-some of his quarrels patched up by a *jirgah*. That he should so often prefer expatriation is only further evidence of Mrs. Grundy's power.

In the face of common danger, or in defence of the common faith, the *jirgah* proportionately enlarges its base. Rival parties, rival clans, and occasionally widely separated rival tribes, patch up their disputes, and selections from the smaller councils become the representative *jirgah*. Among the Afridis, perhaps the most dis-united of all, the patching up is somewhat quaint. Each clansman takes a stone, and in turn placing it on his neighbour's, swears a solemn vow, that until the common cause be settled, and these stones removed, any feud between the parties shall be dormant— an oath generally religiously kept. The *jirgah* assembles on the bare ground, and having gone through its opening formula of prayer, to the effect that though events are with God, deliberation is still with man, settles the plan of the campaign, the number of men each branch of the tribe is to find, and the quota from each village, usually in proportion to its numerical strength. Each man takes the field with a sheep's skin full of flour and as much am-munition as he has been able to collect. And the period that these will last is very much the measure of the probable length of the campaign. Even the *jirgah* seems powerless for any extensive commissariat or transport arrangements. In matters of treaty, however, they show a much more decided power of holding together, and there is no more satisfactory instance than the Khaiber Pass agreement, made by the British Government with all the Afridi tribes concerned in 1881. On the Biloch border negotiations would naturally be with the tribal chief; but dealing with Pathâns, the *jirgahs* are the only bodies that Government can recognise, and though it is not always easy to be sure that the *jirgah* is really a representative one, the real leaders sometimes holding aloof and putting forward men of no importance or influence, agreements once entered into by a genuine tribal council are generally respected. With certain tribes, like the Buneyrwals, their word once given, offers probably a better security than many treaties with the more civilized nations.

Of late years the detective and judicial functions of the *jirgah* have been turned to account within our own Border, and in the Peshawur district now form part of the regular judicial system, the Deputy Commissioner being empowered to accept and award punishment on their decisions. Where our police would be utterly unable to fathom the dark mysteries of Border crime, and our executive fail to convict or punish perfectly well-known offenders, but against whom evidence is not forthcoming, the trial by *jirgah* —on the principle that no one makes so good a gamekeeper as an old poacher—has not unfrequently come in most happily. Crime has been detected, brought home, and punished, that could not have been satisfactorily dealt with in any other way.

Sometimes the process is peculiar. For it is only a Pathân mind that can take in the strange working of the Peshawur criminal; can follow up the reason, or trace the still more extraordinary course his vengeance, lust, or greed will take. And sometimes the finding of the *jirgah* would be calculated to astonish Her Majesty's judges. A recent instance of the latter is a fairly illustrative one. A man, notoriously of the worst character, was charged with the most brutal and aggravated murder. Every presumption, short of judicial proof, was against him, but no direct evidence being forthcoming—it is not always safe to give evidence against a ruffian of influence—the Deputy Commissioner, unable to convict, made him over to the tribal *jirgah* for trial. After due consideration, the *jirgah* to a man came forward and swore to the

"Sherdil," a Representative Khân from the Bajáwar Valley.

prisoner's complete innocence, but recommended his deportation across the Border. The Deputy Commissioner had no choice but to accept the finding, and the man was subsequently sent out of the district. The *jirgah* followed, and the day he set foot out of British territory, slew him themselves. Their train of reasoning was probably somewhat as follows. If we bring him in guilty, the most the Deputy Commissioner can give him on our finding will be some seven years' imprisonment. This would not meet the case, but once beyond British jurisdiction, the summary process adopted would be much more satisfactory. A procedure clearly not judicial, but a rude notion of justice quite sufficient to satisfy a Pathân *jirgah*.

CHAPTER XXXI.

THE CHILDREN OF JOSEPH.

With all his republicanism, the Pathán, Hibernian in many respects, is especially so in matters of lineage. Every petty Border tribe prides itself on its descent from some—possibly imaginary—ancestor in the distant past. To speak of themselves as " *Bani Israil*," the children of Israel, is common, and the grey-beards are fond of carrying history back to " Ibráhim, I'sák, and Yákúb." However far fetched the idea of the connection may be, there is, as discussed at length by Bellew, a savour of Israelitish custom, and an often remarkable similarity of name surviving, more especially among those to be now noticed. Amazites, Moabites, Hittites, or Amazai, Muhibwal, Hotiwal, will be found on Mount Morah, the hill Pehor, the plain of Galilee (Jálála) ; the valley of Sudhum ; observing the " passover," offering sin and thank-offerings, or driving off the scapegoat laden with the sins of the people. In venturing, therefore, upon a genealogical tree—always with the risk of dulness attending the recounting of a " lang pedigree "—no more historical value need be attached to it, than would be to the undoubted belief of the people themselves and such historians as they possess.

Joseph—not the hero of that somewhat doubtful adventure with *Zulikha*—but the grandson of that Khakhai, whose descendants, four centuries ago, drove the Dalazáks out of the Peshawur Valley, had at least one elder brother, named Omer, an exceedingly worthy man, who came to India, married a lady there, and died, leaving a disconsolate widow and one son, Mandanr. Joseph, as in duty bound, though much against the lady's inclination, married his brother's widow, and, either by her, or other wives, had five noted sons of his own, Uriah, 'Isa, Musa, Mali, and Ako. From whom, and Mandanr, are descended all the innumerable tribes of Yusafzai, distributed over the country, both within and without our Border from the Swât river to the Black Mountain, on the Hazâra side of the Indus. A tract, that conformably to Pathân custom, has been named after the tribes possessing it. Mandanr, according to the story, married a daughter of his stepfather, Joseph, by whom he had two sons, Usmân and Utmân, as well as some half dozen others by a slave girl called Razai. Three comparatively insignificant divisions, Alazai, Kamazai, and Akazai, are located beyond our Border, along the eastern slope of the Mahâbun Mountain, down to the right bank of the Indus. The Khudukhel section of the fourth, or Saddazais, occupies the western slope of the same mountain, between the Gaduns and the Chamla Valley: the whole of the much more numerous remainder dwelling in the south-east corner of the Peshawur district, and the south-west corner of Hazâra. Their clans would now include the town of Swâbi on the west, and Harripur on the east of the Indus.

The descendants of Usmân are still more numerous and important. Primarily they split into two divisions, the Kamalzai and the Amazai, and each again into two more. Originally—and the remark applies to the whole Yusafzai Border—each division included, under the direction of a famous priest named Shaikh Mali, in its share a portion of hill and a portion of more favoured plain, the residents having to exchange lands with each other at intervals, but by degrees the custom became obsolete, more especially since British occupation. If those in the plains have lost their possession in the hills, they have, with the protection of the British Government, stuck to the more fertile lands; and for the descendants of Usmân, who have become firmly established in the "Malik Mandanr," or Yusafzai plain, the result has been a better share of good fortune than has fallen to most of the children of Joseph. The Kamalzai have among their chief towns, Toru, Mardân and Hoti, and the Amazai, Rustam and Chargholai in the fertile but significantly named valley of Sodom. A branch of the Amazai have given their name to the north-eastern slopes of the Mahâbun Mountain beyond the Border; but though in social matters they still keep up their connection with their brethren in the plains, they are politically in alliance with the adjoining Buneyrs, and have a tribal chief of their own at Charorai. The half dozen sons of the slave girl have done no more than found a single division named after their common mother, Razai, and that one of secondary importance, established mainly about the villages of Ismaila and Shiwa, &c., between the Amazai and the Utmanzai.

More or less, though it is only in an Administration Report any one would venture to use the optimist sense, all these Mandanr clans within our Border have beaten their swords into ploughshares; or as Bellew describes it, "the cultivator who went to plough with a rifle over his shoulder and a sword at his side, or watched his crops with armed patrols day and night, now casts his seed into the ground far away from his village, and is troubled with no further anxiety." His children graze the cattle and play on mounds formerly used as pickets; while the old women of both sexes, "delight the youth untutored in the use of arms with thrilling recitations of the manly deeds of their fathers." It is true that the son of Joseph, with these advantages, is in many respects a fine fellow, a peaceful, well behaved, almost industrious Pathân, and where he has the further benefits of canal water and an easy settlement, is becoming rich and well to do. The alarm drum may no longer rouse him up to do battle for his hearth or his crops; but it is probably only a poetic imagination that credits him with so much pacific virtue. Although he roar you as gently as any sucking dove, Bottom is not quite so much translated as he looks.

Of Joseph's own sons, far the largest proportion of their posterity are entirely across the Border. "Uriah," who was called Bâdi, "the windy," on account of his villanous temper, fell out with his father's widow, and got cursed; the lady praying his progeny might never exceed thirteen souls, which tradition says they never did, the Badikhels dwelling in poverty till they became extinct. "'Isa" had twelve sons, of whom nine were killed in an affray with some cattle-lifting Mughals. From the other three are descended the Hassanzais, Akazais and Madakhels, settled on the spurs of the Mahâban and Dumah Mountains, on the right bank of the Indus, and, more extensively, in the Agror hills to the left of that river, where, with some others, they are now known as the Black Mountain tribes. In comparison with the other main Yusafzai divisions, they are small and unimportant, though for a long series of years they have caused more annoyance than many of our far more formidable frontier neighbours. The Hassanzais brought themselves into the front rank of frontier scoundrels, by the deliberate murder of two defenceless Customs officers, Messrs. Carn and Tapp, in 1851; an outrage that, like the recent Black Mountain one, took place within our Border. They are split up into some ten sub-divisions, aggregating altogether probably not 2,000 fighting men, the most troublesome of all the clans being the Khân Khels, a mere handful, but whose head is for the time being the practical leader of the whole of the 'Isazai. The Akazai division is not quite half as numerous as the Hassanzais, and has only taken to giving trouble to us within the last ten years, inspired not improbably in the first instance by the Khân of Agror.

As with so many other Yusafzai clans, not a little of the trouble is brought about by the fanatical colonies of religious adventurers, who, from early times, have been the cause of the most of the bloodshed and mischief in this direction, and who in the shape of the Pariari Sayuds, were again found associated with the two foregoing divisions in the outrage that cost us the lives of Major Battye and Captain Urmston. These Pariari Sayuds are an insignificant colony on the east face of the Black Mountain, north of Agror, and close to the fort of Trund, but their glen has always been a refuge for discontented settlers from all the surrounding tribes, both Pathân and Swâti, and they exercise considerable influence. There is no doubt that all these Black Mountain tribes, which, however much they may be spilt up among themselves, are identical in their ill-feeling against us, have, with the exception of the expeditions against the Hassanzais in 1868, and the recent one under General Mc Queen, enjoyed almost entire immunity from punishment; owing partly to their position being difficult of approach, and partly to their insignificance rendering them hardly worth the trouble of attacking. It might be said with equal certainty, that the most effectual method of dealing with them would be to summarily annex the whole Black Mountain and its tribes, right up to the Indus bank and open out a road along it from Derband, a route that on the published maps is still shown as a practically unknown country— an unfortunate bit of ignorance that cost General Galbraith's column the life of the gallant Major Beley.

But to continue the traditions of Joseph's family tree. "Moses" had one son, "Elias," from whom sprang the five important divisions called the Iliaszai. Four of which, the Salarzai, Gadaizai, Ashazai, and Nasozais, are located in Buneyr, and the Makhozais on the eastern slope of the Dosirra Mountain beyond "Mali" left four sons by two wives, of which two main divisions, the Daulatzais and the Nurazais, are also settled in Buneyr. A third, the Chagarzai, is partly in Buneyr and the northern slopes of the Duma Mountain, on the right of the Indus, and partly on the western slope of the Black Mountain. So that with this last exception, it may be said that the Buneyrwals and their adjoining allies, are the modern representatives of Joseph's sons Musa and Mali. There is probably no finer race on the whole north-west frontier, and in their way, they are the pick of the family. With almost all the good points, and several of the failings strongly developed, they are peculiarly representative Pathâns, not the least marked characteristic, being the way they have always stood aloof from us.

Of Ako, the last son of Joseph, the descendants have proved the most numerous of all. To begin with, he had by two wives half a dozen sons, each of whom subsequently founded several important divisions. The chief of which are (1) the Khwazozai, that with half a dozen sub-divisions, holds a good part of the right of the Swât Valley, the country north of it, as far as Dir, and the mountains that separate the latter from Chitrâl. One clan, the Malizai, under its chief Gazân Khân, holds Dir and the Panjkora valley right up to the border land of Kafiristân and Kashkâr. (2) The Bazidzai, or Baizai, whose seven clans extend from the Lundkhwâr Valley in British territory above Mardan, by the left bank of the Swât, the northern slope of the Dosirra Mountain, and the highlands of Ghorband, round to the valleys draining into the Indus, by the Kohistân that separates Yusafzai from Gilgit; and (3), the Ranizai, whose clans occupy the western end of the Swât Valley adjoining the Utmân Khels.

These are the sons of Joseph, according to the Akun Darwaiza, their most learned priest, historian, and saint; and such their approximate distribution along the Border at the present time. Other Pathân tribes are here and there settled within the limits of their country, and of course large numbers of Hindus, Hindkis, Gujars, Kashmiris and other tribes, that, taken together, considerably outnumber the Yusafzais. These have either descended from the original inhabitants, or immigrated, and throughout the country form perfectly distinct little societies of their own, retaining most of their religious rites and national characteristics undisturbed. The Hindus particularly flourish, and even among the most bigoted of the Muhammadan population, transact the bulk of the mercantile business. There are again other tribes, like the Gaduns, Jaduns or Yaduns, in the eastern corner, and the Utmân Khels on the west, who though, in the former case especially, not even remotely related to the Yusafzais, are in

A Border Gentleman, Rissaldar Muhammad Khân.

other ways associated with them, and can for many purposes be most conveniently considered together.

Bellew estimates the total Yusafzai population at close upon a quarter of a million, the larger half within our Border. Almost every man capable of bearing arms may be reckoned as a fighting man, and he puts the total strength at 30,000 without, and 43,000 within the Border, though of course the former are scattered over a vast extent of country. Eminently an agricultural, as opposed to a trading, people, living on the produce of their fields and flocks, they at the same time have always been famed for turbulence and reluctance to submit to any form of government. As shown above, though they are collectively bound to one another by a common descent, the various clans, or groups of clans, have formed distinct communities, governed by separate chiefs, with rival and opposing interests, which have developed continual feuds and jealousies. Of tribal combination, or regular government, they have none. Each son of Joseph that has been able, has set up for himself, exacts such revenue as he can from the mixed population, allows the cultivator to retain a third or fourth of the produce of his land, and recognises no master, or acknowledges no suzerain, unless it be a religious chief or Akhund. But in their relations with foreigners, individual feuds and jealousies would to a great extent be put aside, and it is not improbable that the entire community would act together against an invader.

CHAPTER XXXII.

THE southern half of the Yusafzai country, which is under British rule, is practically the only portion accessible to Europeans. Information regarding the larger portion of that across the Border north of the Hazárno and Mahában Mountains, is but uncertain and scanty. Probably the best obtainable on most points, is still that contained in the report by Dr. Bellew. Long residence in Mardán, and an exceptional knowledge of Pashtu, enabled him to command the best native sources ; and his vivid and entertaining account, of a most interesting country and people, has become the recognised standard work. Physically, among all our Border lands, it is one of the most difficult of approach, consisting of a confused mass of lofty mountains, divided by deep, though fertile valleys, that alternately stretch, almost continuously—till, far beyond the Yusafzai country, they converge in the great central mountain knot, expressively described as the " roof of the world," from whence spring so many famous Asiatic ranges. So that to move round, and to take it in rear, would be still more formidable than by direct assault.

This physical inaccessibility, and the hardly less unapproachable nature of its people, is all the more to be regretted, in that it is a country full of interest. Though not altogether a " Land of

Promise," yet many of its valleys are flowing with milk and honey. For "corn and wine and oil," read, corn and honey and *ghee*,[1] which are among its principal exports. Its hill tops are clothed with rich forests, giving place to a variety of excellent fruit-trees in its well watered valleys. Its climate is temperate even in summer, and its capabilities great. Many parts of it are known to be rich in ancient remains; the frequent ruins in Swât and Bajâwar indicate the former presence of Greek, Buddhist and Hindu, and innumerable inscribed tablets, in Greek and Pali—probably becoming fewer and less valuable every year—only await scientific investigation, to throw much light on the ancient history of this part of the world.

Although the people of various valleys may offer very striking differences—and in fact from their habit of mixing so little with the world outside their own circumscribed holdings, and constant intermarriage, the divergence between the clans is so great, they would hardly be credited as belonging to the same stock—there is a great natural similarity between the valleys themselves, and it will be unnecessary to do more than briefly notice one or two of those that occupy the most prominent position from the Border point of view. Of these the most important and extensive, the richest and most fertile, but most unhealthy, and perhaps most inaccessible, is the valley of Swât, or Suwât. The river from which the district takes its name, probably the Suastos of Arrian, debouches on British territory near the fort of Abazai, whence, up to the junction with the Panjkora—the ancient Garaois—it is a swift, deep torrent, rushing between precipitous banks; the surrounding hills impracticable for any except foot passengers, and not easy for them, being in the hands of the Utmân Khels. From the point of its meeting with the Panjkora, some seventy miles north-east, nearly to its source, is Swât proper. The main valley, intersected by ravines and glens draining the ranges on either side, is in places ten miles

---

[1] Clarified butter.

wide, in others the hills narrow to a few hundred yards apart, dividing it into natural sections, of which the principal are Ranizai, Swât Kuz or Lower Swât, and Bar or Upper Swât. Beyond, further north-east again, the country is known as the Kohistân of Swât, and is inhabited by an entirely different race, having more affinity with the people of Yasin, Gilgit, and Chitrâl, than with the Yusafzai. Ranges of lofty snow-clad mountains shut in Swât, which is approached only by a few negotiable passes. A formidable one, locally called the Larani, from what is probably the only feasible pass, separates it from the net work of valleys that make up the Panjkora; the Kohistân on the north-east rises from snow fields and extensive glaciers, to peaks of nearly 20,000 feet; on the south-east the Gorband and Ilum oppose a great barrier between it and the valleys draining to the Indus, while the Mora range lies between it and British territory. The passes that afford the best entrance are over this last named. The easiest and most used from the Peshawur district through the Ranizai country is the Malakand, a fairly accessible one. Not quite so easy is the Mora approached from the Baizai country, and a still more difficult one is by Shahkot.

Referring to the children of Joseph, it has already been said that, throughout Swât, the inhabitants belong to the great Akozai Division. Speaking generally, the Khwazozai sections are mainly on the north of the valley, the Ranizai occupy the west end, and the Baizai the left bank along a considerable length. The two latter have overflowed for some distance to the south of the Mora range, up to our Border by the Lundkhwâr valley, being there known as "Sâm" or lowlanders, in contradistinction to "Bar" or highlanders. But all the natural divisions of the Swât valley, down to each minor glen, are occupied by different clans, with as many factions as villages; and even in these often several factions, each, with its own quarrels and its own chief, not seldom at mortal feud with his neighbours.

The whole valley is highly cultivated, and densely populated, each glen or gorge has its village or hamlet, and the total population has been estimated at not far short of 100,000 souls. The fields are in terraces one above another, extensively irrigated by channels diverted from the river or the torrents flowing into it. The course of the river itself, working from side to side of the valley is marked by more numerous villages, groves of trees, and almost unbroken cultivation. The very burying grounds, usually especially sacred to Patháns, are regularly ploughed up, and the dead buried in the fallow lands; hardly a single yard of tillable ground is neglected. Wheat and most grains, sugarcane, lucerne, tobacco, lots of vegetables, are extensively grown, and Upper Swât yields excellent fruits. In the hot weather, when a great portion of the valley can be irrigated, the lands everywhere near the river are a sheet of luxuriant rice, the steamy exhalations from which no doubt contribute largely to the unhealthiness of the valley. Picturesque it is in the extreme; the upper reaches of the mountains are well clothed with forests of pine or deodar; below lies a beautiful velvet-like turf, and again stretches of cultivation, dotted with houses—wretched hovels enough, but artistically half hidden among rich clusters of plane or poplar; and bright clear streams everywhere rushing down to the brisk noisy Swât, dashing over its boulder-strewn bed, like a Scotch salmon river. All the same, the notorious insalubrity of the valley is a very serious drawback to all this beauty. Completely shut in by the high ranges referred to, the winter is much milder than in the plains; there is little frost, and still less wind; almost without a breeze, it is the very reverse of a Pathán highland, while the hot weather is more oppressive and continuous. The storms that burst over the hills produce little more than an atmosphere of hot steam, which, combined with the malaria from the rice cultivation, seems to bring on fevers which affect the entire inhabitants, who all look more or less unhealthy. The men especially are weak, thin, and feeble, hardly resembling

Pathâns in form or feature, and more like the Gujar of the Lower Punjâb The women, on the other hand, seem curiously much less affected, for they are described as stout, strong, and buxom, and though by no means good looking, retain far more of the Pathân appearance. They have, moreover, entirely reversed the position of the sexes prevailing in ordinary Pathân communities. Not only do they go unveiled, and enjoy more liberty, but rule the men to a greater extent than is known among Pathâns elsewhere. The men of the Swât valley are, in fact, credited with living to a great extent under petticoat influence.

Swât, however, is only one of a series, that, parallel or nearly so, drain into the same river. Five of the principal of these unite to form the group known as Panjkora—"the five torrents"—which is also the name of the stream, that, having absorbed the drainage of Bajâwar and Talash, joins the Swât, as already noticed. All are more or less narrow, hill-bound, valleys, with many glens and gorges defiling into them, the whole sloping steeply from the north-east to the south-west. The description of Swât answers generally for all; villages with strips of terraced cultivation, a range of hills rising behind, a stream flowing past in front, which, as the snow melts, is frequently impassable; the country equally fertile, but with a finer peasantry and much better climate, a colder winter and a healthy summer. A country suggestive of plenty, where 90 lbs of wheat can be bought for one rupee, a fat sheep for three, and a buffalo for fifteen; where animal fat, being plentiful, is largely turned into soap—a commodity so foreign to Pathâns—it stamps the people with a civilization of their own. And unique in another respect, it is reputed exceptionally safe and hospitable to all travellers and traders who are enterprising enough to get there. Enterprising they must needs be, for it is almost without roads—the best being mere tracks winding along precipitous slopes, skirting the river banks, with very occasional passes across the hills possible only for foot passengers or draft cattle, and at times, from floods in the valleys or snow on the mountains, altogether impracticable. Nevertheless, there is a caravan route through both Swât and Panjkora to Chitrâl and Turkestân, reputed a three months' journey.

The chief of the group is the Yusafzai *Ultima Thule*, right up under the base of the Laori range, the valley or valleys of Dir, also the name of the principal town and residence of the Khân, who is the recognised head of the Malizai Division, and whose authority extends from the Swât boundary up to the passes leading west into Kunâr and Bajâwar, which mark the furthest limits of the Yusafzai. The town of Dir, which boasts a respectable fortress, is one of the principal marts of the country, and is the centre of exchange for produce brought by the Chitrâlis from the north, and by the Yusafzai and Khattak carriers from the south.

Omitting minor valleys, like the Talash, which, along side the Swât, is said to be exceptionally rich in grain, and the still less known tributary ones, like Biraul, or Barawal, reputed to be equally rich in iron; a route from Maidân, the most southern of the series, leads altogether out of the limits of Yusafzai, into Bajâwar, that, by comparison, is almost open country; the valley being in places as much as fifteen miles wide and some forty in length. Here again are great natural advantages. It does a fair trade in grain, especially wheat, and affords excellent grazing ground for large herds of cattle, but is chiefly known in connection with the supply of iron, which is largely exported to Peshawur. The iron is obtained mainly from black sand washed down by the streams, and mixed with charcoal, is fused into a consistent mass, which sells in Peshawur from three to six rupees per *maund* or 80 lbs. Fine forests of oak and pine abound in the neighbouring hills, and the climate is said to be like that of Kâbul. It has lately been the subject of a great deal of unpleasant attention on the part of the Amir, who evidently persists in endeavouring to establish his authority there; though heretofore it has been a distinctly independent State, only paying tribute to Kâbul when forced to do so. The ruling people are the Turkolânis, numbering probably 10,000 to 15,000 fighting men, whose immigration has been noticed, and whose Chief rejoiced in the title of " Bâz " or Bâdshâh. The " Bâz " possesses almost absolute power to break or bind, is independent of the *jirgah* and enjoys a large revenue, derived from a tax levied on the Hindkis, and a land rent from the Rudbâris, a mongrel race the most numerous in the valley, who probably represent the remnant of the aborigines subduded by the Turkolânis. This absolute government is in marked contrast to the custom of Yusafzai, otherwise the people resemble one another in many ways.

West of these again is the Kunâr river and Kâfiristân, with which latter people Bajâwar is generally at war, carrying off Kâfirs as slaves whenever opportunity offers. While east, between Bajâwar and our Border, are the hills of the Utmân Khels, who occupy the strip between the Mohmands and the Yusafzai. From our actual Border, up to the Koh-i-Mohr mountain, is called the Larmân or Damân, and the larger number of the clans are located in a series of valleys which radiate from this mountain. Everywhere the country is difficult in the extreme, there are few roads passable for horsemen, and the only means of crossing the Swât, which here rushes between steep cliffs a deep swift torrent, are a few rope bridges. As a tribe, the Utmân Khels are comparatively unimportant, probably under 5,000 fighting men. They are neither powerful nor influential, their country more like that of the Mohmands, cultivation being very inconsiderable, and the people eking out a scanty livelihood as labourers in the Peshawur district. They are, however, quite a distinct people, unconnected with any surrounding Pathâns, either Mohmands, Bajâuris, or Yusafzais, and claim to be descended from the five sons of Utmân Bâba, who came in with one of Mahmud's expeditions, and settled in the Peshawur valley about 997 A.D. During the first years of

British occupation they did a great deal of raiding, sheltering outlaws, and mischief generally, and in 1852, were summarily punished by an expedition under Sir Colin Campbell. In 1876, when the Swât canal was being made, a gang of them came down and hacked to pieces a number of Pathân coolies, an outrage that remained unpunished till 1878, when certain of their villages were surprised by the "Guides" under Cavagnari, their ringleaders killed, and the fullest retribution exacted; since when the Utmân Khels have given no further trouble. They are a hardy set of mountain brigands, tall, stout, fair, sober, and hardworking—often naked from the waist up—a custom opposed to Pathân ideas— but not very civilized. They live in small groups of houses, rather than villages, stuck on the mountain sides, secure in their inaccessibility.

CHAPTER XXXIII.

To look at a Frontier map, even one of the famous India Office "large maps," and find Yusafzai printed across a big space between Káfiristán and Kashmir, does not convey much idea of that country, nor make clear that the Yusafzais of Swât are separated from their relations of Buneyr, and the valleys draining directly into the Indus, by so formidable a barrier. A range of mountains, seldom less than 20 miles wide, with peaks like the Ilum, over 9,000 feet, or the Dosirra, over 10,000 feet, though there are several passes more or less practicable. The family connection of the clans on both sides would probably bring them together in cases of emergency, but Buner and its neighbouring valleys may to all intents and purposes be considered a separate group, and the tribes, under the name of Buneyrwals.

Geographically, the position of the group is somewhat as follows. Commencing from opposite Torbela on the Indus, and from the boundary of our Border on the right bank, the Gadun country extends right up to the crest of the Mahában Mountain, or rather that cluster of peaks and ranges which, rising 7,000 feet from the Indus, extend back as a great spur of the Mora, or Ilum. A thoroughly classic ground; the "Great Forest" of the early Aryans; the "Sinai" of Sanskrit, where Arjuna wrestled with

God, and, like the Jewish Jacob, though defeated, still won his irresistable weapon, ground that if not identical with Alexander's Aornos, is probably not very distant; that was famous for its numerous monasteries (Mahâwana) when Hwen Thsang visited it in 630 A.D., and is studded with ruins to this day.

The Jaduns, or Gaduns, who now occupy the southern slope of this famous historical hill, are not Yusafzais at all, or even distantly connected with them. Their name is evidence of their Indian origin; but though not improbably the descendants of Râjputs, they have nevertheless thrown in their lot with their neighbours. Further to the west are the Khudu Khels, and immediately on the other side of the range is the Chamla Valley, the eastern end of which, adjoining the Indus, is known as the Amazai country. A spur of the Guru Mountain separates the Chamla Valley from the larger and more important one of Buner, or Buneyr, an irregular oval with the Barandu, a perennial stream running down the centre. Beyond, again, are three or four more narrow, deep, and winding valleys or gorges between as many ranges, with small tributaries to the Indus down the centre of each, of which the largest are the Puran, Chakesur, Kâna, and Ghorband—the latter called after the range at the head of it, and all exceedingly difficult of access.

The clans of the group collectively known as the Buneyrwals, numerous, and in some respects divergent, as they occasionally are, mostly, as already noticed, claim their descent from Joseph's sons, Musa and Mali. The Amazais and Khudu Khels are only distant connections, being descendants of Mandanr, though, for political purposes, all may be treated as more or less influenced by Buneyr. The characteristics of the climate of Swât would serve as a fairly accurate description of Buneyr, though the latter is rather more open, a trifle more healthy, and a thought less feverish in autumn. Perhaps equally fertile, it is richer in cattle, but poorer in grain, which to some extent is imported; while as regards the ranges that surround it, and the difficulties of communication with the outer world, the difference is only one of degree. In both cases, the direct approaches from British territory are the easiest. Among the best known is one from Ghazi Bala, at the head of the Lundkhwâr Valley, by Pali and Sherkhâna in Baizai, and Bâzdara—the "falcon country," a name suggestive of difficulties—into the Salarzai district of Buneyr. Another in more general use by merchants, is by Rustam in the Sudum Valley, and the Malandri Pass into the Nurazai district of Buneyr. A third, still better known, is the Ambeyla—the "Rhinoceros" pass, according to the old Persian—the scene of the long and hard fighting in 1863, by way of the Chamla Valley. Finally, on the east, having crossed the Indus, Buneyr can, with still more difficulty, be entered by the defile of the Barandu River.

The people themselves are infinitely superior to the enfeebled men of Swât; in fact, there are in many ways few finer specimens of Pathâns than the Buneyrwals. Simple and temperate, they are content with the plain wholesome food, the produce of their own cattle and lands; courteous and hospitable to all who claim shelter, treachery to a stranger seeking refuge among them, being considered the deepest reproach that could fall upon the clansmen, and such a case is almost unknown. Upright in their dealings, with enemies as well as with strangers, they have always been adverse to us, and though probably not anxious to begin the war, they were among our most determined enemies during the Ambeyla campaign. They seem to avoid, as far as possible, intercourse with our officers, but to discourage robbery and outrage within our limits. Among the list of their misdeeds, there are hardly any of raiding, and though they harbour many outlaws, are seldom found participating in the depredations committed. Patriotic they certainly are, and in their way, which is a pastoral and agricultural one, industrious, though they hold all trade in the very lowest estimation; anything that savours of the shop or of trading is anathema to a Buneyrwal.

Therefore they are poor, but, for poor Pathâns, have an exceptional regard for the law of *meum* and *tuum*. Their word, once given through the council of the tribe, may, according to Warburton, be depended on with almost certainty. Lastly, they are " distinguished for their ignorance," and ignorance being the " mother of devotion," they are deeply religious ; greatly under the influence of the most bigoted of Mullahs, Sayuds, Pirs, and the many varieties of the priestly class, which is probably the most powerful and prosperous section of the community ; while, if there is any section whose heritage ought to be one of woe, it is this : for it is from the priests most of the offences come, throughout the whole of Yusafzai.

From the late Yusafzai Pope and kingmaker, the venerable and venerated Akhund of Swât, who at one time in his career and before the tribes had learnt the lesson taught them by the Ambeyla campaign, encouraged a system of marauding on our frontier, and undoubtedly incited his followers to deeds of depredation and violence, and finally, allying himself with fanatics he abhorred, and stigmatised as " Wahâbis," brought all his priestly influence to bear against us in the severest Frontier struggle we ever had ; to the ill conditioned, evil intentioned, fanatics of Sittana and Malka, the remains of the organised bands of *Mujahidins*—the " warriors of the Faith " that Sayud Ahmad of Bareilly grafted on to the most turbulent and superstitious of the border races—the ill-feeling of adventurers, yclept saintly, has been at the bottom of most of the mischief in Yusafzai.

Such adventurers have often, for their own ends, beguiled the simple and credulous children of Joseph, have scattered distrust among the clans, fomented rebellion, and intrigued with Wahâbis and the disaffected Muhammadan population from one end of India to the other. From the days of the Mughal, to the present, colonies in the recesses of the mountains on the Peshawur and Hazâra border, calling themselves " nurseries of saints," but that are really "hot beds of fanatics," have provided veritable Caves of Adullam for all the malcontents on both sides of it. Among the Adullamites may occasionally be burning enthusiasts, who are too pious or too zealous to live quietly under a Government tolerating all creeds; but the larger number are either grossly ignorant or exceedingly crafty, and many are criminals of sorts, debtors, convicts, traitors, murderers, too guilty to find a refuge anywhere else.

The larger number of our complications with the tribes on this part of the Border have been due to the intrigues of these fanatics. The colony of Sittana was a chronic cause of disturbance from the Sikh times. They were to a great extent responsible for the misconduct of the Hassanzais in 1851, and an expedition became necessary against them in 1853. They tried to form a general coalition against us in 1857, and their constant outrages necessitated a second expedition in 1858, that drove them out of Sittana only to settle again in Malka on the northern slope of the Mahâban. Two years after they had regained their influence, and become worse than ever. "Disloyalty of all kinds flocked," as Hunter describes, "to the Apostles of Insurrection." Ultimately, in 1863, they forced upon us the Ambeyla campaign, where tribe after tribe was drawn in, until we had at one time nearly 60,000 of the Yusafzai clans and their allies in the field against us. There they learnt a severe lesson, but a lesson that also cost us much, both in money and men, some 900 of the latter being killed or wounded. The combination broken up, the tribes revenged themselves on the fanatics who had brought war into their valleys, more especially on the Hindustânis; but again in 1868 the priestly party were within a measurable distance of raising another tribal combination on the Black Mountain, which only prompt measures, undertaken at the most unfavourable season of the year, suppressed.

It would be tedious to trace their efforts at mischief since, but it is not too much to say that this class of men has, under the guise of religion, contributed more than anything else to keep alive the spirit of unrest, and continues to this day the most formidable element of danger on our Border, a danger that cannot be overlooked, though it is at times perhaps not sufficiently appreciated.

CHAPTER XXXIV.

A BORDER POPE.

Born during the closing years of the last century, at Jabrai, a shepherd's hamlet in Upper Swât, of poor and obscure parents, probably Gujars—though his disciples have since discovered a religious origin even for them—Abdul Gafur, like other famous Eastern heroes, passed his early boyhood tending his father's sheep. And, just like the good little boys and early saints of the story books, his childhood is credited with a precocious development of those gifts and graces said to find such certain divine acceptance. He would not drink the milk of the cattle that trespassed on unlawful grounds. The single buffalo that "for years" generously supplied him with this nurture, he always led to pasture with a string, instead of whacking it with a cudgel, after the manner of Gujar boys generally, and finally took to muzzling the goats when driving them out, lest they took a sly nibble at the neighbours' pasture. A custom, so far removed from the average Gujar notion of the fitness of things, must have ensured him summary and regular mortification at his parents' hands. It is, therefore, quite intelligible that, at eighteen years of age, he had discovered the world was a wicked one, and resolved to sever himself from it, and devote his talents to a religious life.

No Samuel came to anoint him. No distinguished order of a

powerful church was ready to welcome him as a convert, and make him into its champion. According to the custom of the country, he attached himself to a priest, and became a "seeker-after-wisdom." For some time, he wandered from *ziárat* to mosque, from Pir to Mullah, from Fakir to Saint, of whom not a few had a great reputation for sanctity, and having gone through a course of the four modes of religious devotion, he especially selected the *Nakshbandia*, a perfectly silent and motionless one, in which the devotee sits, his head bowed on his chest, and his eyes fixed on the ground. And, the better to ensure its undisturbed observance, he took up his abode at Beka, a bare, barren, lonely spot on the banks of the Indus, about ten miles above Attock. Here he built himself a camelthorn hut and, about the year the Western world was fighting the battle of Waterloo, settled down, a young man, hardly twenty years of age, to a life of the greatest austerity. For twelve years he remained shut off from the world, absorbed in study, meditation and worship; his food during this period of penance was the seed of a very inferior millet[1] growing wild in the rice-fields, moistened with water.

In after-years the water was replaced by buffalo's milk, but, till his death, at the age of eighty-three, his only food was of an equally simple kind, and his only dissipation, large quantities of strong tea, which he subsequently drank to keep him sufficiently awake to perform his religious exercises. The ascetic rigour of his life gradually brought people from far and near to solicit blessings or intercessory prayers. His fame dates from this period of marvellous self-restraint. It spread from the Indus to the Kurram, from the Kurram to Kâbul; the renown of "the Hermit of Beka" finally extending throughout Eastern Afghânistân, to distant parts of Persia.

Temptation, however, came to the hermit once too often, perhaps in the shape of secular ambition—or it might with equal fairness

---

[1] A mere weed, *Panicum frumentaceum*.

be said, in the shape of patriotism—for in 1827 he got mixed up between his neighbour the Khân of Hund, and the famous Wahâbi, Sayud Ahmad of Barcilly. The former, who had just joined his forces with the Sayud, proved traitor and betrayed the latter's plans to Runjeet Singh, being in his turn betrayed and slain. To Abdul Gafur, the result meant abandoning his retreat and flight; a serious blow to his prestige, that cost him years of wandering, unknown and uncared for, to make good. It was not till he established himself in British Yusafzai, and had added miracles to devotion, that his notoriety as a "Man of God" made him again a centre of attraction, and earned him the titles of "Saint" and Akhund.

On at least two subsequent occasions the spirit of the patriot and the "warrior for the faith," proved too much for the asceticism of the saint. In 1835, when the Afghâns were at war with the Sikhs, and the Pathâns were rallying against their natural and hereditary enemies, he accepted an invitation from the Kâbul Amir, Dost Muhammad Khân, and joined the latter with a pious following, numerically considerable. But, ill-trained and worse armed, such a contingent could at best have been of little use against the disciplined Sikh army. The mere approach of Maharajah Runjeet Singh was sufficient to drive the Amir precipitately through the Khaibar, and scatter the rabble "champions of the faith" in all directions. The "warriors," "martyrs," and "seekers after wisdom" were noisy, but had small stomach to try conclusions with the Sikhs; and the Akhund had no choice, but to seek safety in Buneyr, and return to his life of unrest once more.

Again during the general tribal excitement that preceded the Ambeyla campaign in 1863, he was drawn into preaching a crescentade against us; for a while throwing in his lot even with the Wahâbi fanatics, whose tenets he had spent so much of his life in opposing. At this time he was close upon seventy years of age.

For the previous twenty he had mainly held himself aloof from the affairs of this world, preached peace, and counselled the tribes to avoid quarrrels with the British Government. In 1847, he had used his best influence to prevent the people of Swât from assisting the rebellious Bazai villages punished by our troops. In 1849, he endeavoured to persuade the Palli people to discharge their gangs of highwaymen, and refrain from raiding. When the fugitive mutineers of the 55th Native Infantry, flying from Nicholson, entered Swât, he summarily deported them across the Indus, where they were cut up almost to a man; and all through the troublous times of 1857, his attitude was one of friendly support to our Government, which assuming the lowest motive, does credit to his sagacity and foresight. On one or two occasions he took measures to repress the colonies of Hindustâni fanatics whom he stigmatized as *kâfirs*, and several theories have been put forward as to the reasons which actuated him in so entirely changing his front. There is really no need to go far for a reason; the pressure brought to bear upon him was practically irresistible. The Buneyr and other tribal chiefs and people, the mullahs and the priestly classes, who for the moment had put aside their sectarian disputes, and even the women made passionate appeals to him to take up their cause. This, combined with the fear of seeing his influence, then immense, pass to some more sympathetic and compliant leader, furnish motive enough, for an action that after all was again more patriotic than personal.

He accepted defeat handsomely. The expedition over, he resumed his former attitude, and for the concluding years of his life seems to have tried to restrain the wild spirits of the Border, resisted all the requests from Kâbul to make cause with the Amir against us, and remained firm in his attitude of friendship, nominal and diplomatic, if not sincere, towards our Government, till his death in January 1877. Among his last acts, he condemned the Jawâki raiders who appealed to him, as thieves and rascals for plundering their co-religionists in Kohât, and excommunicated the authors of the Swât Canal outrage at Abazai.

A few years after his defeat by the Sikhs, his wanderings were more or less brought to a close by a grant of land at Saidu in Swât, which the Yusafzais gave him for his own and his disciples' support, and which he ever after made his home. There he lived surrounded by numerous disciples, visited by crowds of devotees who looked upon him as practising all the saintly virtues, and performing the most astounding miracles. Credited at once with the possession of the purse of Fortunatus, the lamp of Aladdin, the Nepenthe of the Egyptian physician, and the Elixir Vitæ for all mortal ills, hundreds of visitors were daily fed and clothed, their multitudinous desires all gratified, the distracted in mind and body soothed, and the sick cured of their ailments. No matter how numerous the pilgrims who waited at his threshold, funds were never wanting to supply their necessities, though in outward appearance he remained as poor as the humblest, took no taxes or tithes, and steadily refused all offerings brought to him. It was no more necessary for him than for Elijah to take thought for the morrow. His simple wants were easily supplied, and every morning, on rising from his prayers, a sum of money, sufficient for the day's needs, was found under the praying carpet. Whether the ravens or the disciples were the custodians of the saintly treasure chest is an immaterial detail.

The fame of the Hermit of Beka was almost obscurity, compared to the influence of the Akhund of Swât. His ascendency over the Muhammadans of the Border and Eastern Afghânistân, was as great as that of Loyola in Rome, or Luther in Saxony; his edicts regarding religious customs and secular observances were as unquestioned as the Papal Bulls in Spain. When the chiefs of Swât recognized the possibility of British military operations extending to their valley, and the necessity for federation, it was to the Akhund they turned to select them a king. His selection was a Sayud of Sittana, who for some years carried on an organized Government, under the patronage of the Border Pope. Putting aside the incredulous stories about him as priest, his life seems to have been one of devotion, humility, abstinence, and charity; the doctrines he taught were as tolerant and liberal, as those of his Wahâbi opponents were intolerant and puritanical. Judged by the standard applied to other religious leaders, he used his influence, according to his lights, for good, supporting peace and morality, discouraging feuds, restraining the people from raiding and offences against their neighbours, and enforcing the precepts of Muhammadan law as far as ineradicable Pathân custom would permit him.

Celibacy he by no means regarded as the highest form of virtue, for he married a Yusafzai woman of the Akozai clan, by whom he had two sons and one daughter. The eldest of the former, Abdul Mannân, the Mian Gul, after his father's death, became involved in a struggle for supremacy in Swât with the Khân of Dir; and in 1883, aided by the Chief of Bajaur, and the virtue of his father's name, established himself for a brief while; when death cut short his chances of any wide-spread power, either spiritual or temporal. The younger son, Abdul Haq, still lives, an ascetic and a hermit, after the fashion of his father, but entirely without his father's influence, and outside his valley almost unknown. The Border Pontificate can be no more hereditary than plenary inspiration or apostolic succession; and no Border Pontiff has yet arisen who can successfully fill the chair of his eminence Abdul Gafur, the Akhund of Swât.

CHAPTER XXXV.

APOSTLES OF INSURRECTION.

CONSIDERING the Pathân's eminently material form of faith, his confidence in saints and shrines, prophets and priests, prayers and pilgrimages, it is not a little curious that religious reformers directly opposed to all this should from time to time have obtained such influence on the Border.   It can hardly be put down to the virtue of toleration; for there are few more bitter feuds than have arisen between Sunni and Shiah Muhammadans, or Gâr and Sâmil politicians.   There is certainly less difference between the orthodox believers in the Four Companions, and those who are the followers of 'Ali, than between the ritualistic Pathân and the puritanical Wahâbi, the latter very often a despised Hindustâni to boot.   Yet in spite of the long record of mischief, and the troubles which this mischief has led to, colonies of these and other religious adventurers of all sorts have been sheltered, and, so long as they refrained from interfering with Pathân custom, have been protected, and even cherished.   The complications due to their intrigues were as notorious three centuries ago as at present; but, except in the matter of trouble to us, the fanatics of Palosi and Maidan are as distinct from the surrounding clans as ever, and probably as little loved.   To the tribesmen they have been as much an influence for evil, as Mephistopheles to Faust; perhaps for a somewhat similar reason, for they have held out a temptation to the Border Pathân that is most dear, the hope of robbery and plunder. It may be said, moreover, that all the dangerous heresies that have afflicted the posterity of Kais, have been drawn from Hindustân, and after they have taken root in a soil especially devoted to their rapid development, the produce has been returned with interest—in a crop of fanatical thorns in the side of the dominant power for the time being, whether Mughal, Sikh or English.

In the middle of the sixteenth century quite a bumper crop arose out of an apostle who called himself Pir Rokhan the " saint of en-lightenment," or Pir Tarik the " saint of darkness," as he was more properly termed by the opposition. Bazid Answari, to give him his full designation, was the son of a learned, devout and orthodox Mullah in the Masaud Waziri capital of Kaniguram, where by the way a colony of intriguing Sayuds still flourishes. Brought up within the strict pale of the church, his early youth is said to have been " edifying; " but he went away, travelled, fell into evil company, consorted with *Jogis* and others, who taught the Mullah's son too much. He learnt a little philosophy from the Sufis, adopted a good deal of the Hindu dogmas regarding trans-migration of souls ; grafted on this some startling theories of his own, and went home to promulgate heresies enough to turn his father's beard grey. In fact the Mullah's feelings were so out-raged, that he prepared to close the argument—and Bazid's career —with the usual knife. The latter came to the common conclusion there was no chance for a prophet in his own country, and so left it ; and, after a life of adventure established himself on the Peshawur Border, adding to religious heresy, the preaching of sedition against the State. He put aside the Korân, the shrines, the miracles, or any set form of religion, and taught that divine manifestations were made in the persons of holy men, particularly in his own. The only way to heaven was through the intercession of the Pir Kâmil, " the perfect saint." He had also inspiration or genius enough to see, that in order to succeed he must adapt his

creed to the wild Border people; and he made his religious discipline proportionately lax and accommodating. All men who did
not recognize his sect were considered as dead, and their goods
were the property of the survivors, to be seized when or where the
self-created heirs might find opportunity. This, joined to the
further inducement of libertinism in the matter of women, and a
sort of social communism in the matter of property, at any rate of
other people's property, offered a form of Church Government that
obviously commended itself greatly to the Afridis, Orakzais, and
lawless clans of the Peshawur Valley. Eventually, though Bazid
was strongly opposed by the Yusafzais and the even more famous
champion of orthodoxy, Akhun Darwaiza, he was accepted at his
own value by a large number of the tribesmen, was able to raise
considerable forces, and enter upon an irregular warfare with the
Mughal ruler. He and his following became to Akbar, what the
Wahábis were to the Sikhs, and the Hindustani fanatics to the
British Government. They systematically plundered the high
road from Peshawur to Kábul, until communications were almost
entirely cut off, in spite of operations undertaken against them by
Mán Singh and others of Akbar's leading generals.

Finally the "perfect saint" was surprised in a night attack, and
died not long after at Hastnagar; but five sons followed their
father's steps and with their bands infested the Border, until they
were gradually hunted down, and burned, drowned, or beheaded, which
was the Mughal notion of a punitive expedition. The memory of
two is perpetuated by a pair of most dangerous rocks, Kamaliya
and Jalaliya, opposite the Attock ferry on the Indus. These rocks
were so christened by Akbar, for being as troublesome and
dangerous to his boats, as the two most notorious sons of Pir
Tárik had been to his troops. Gradually the heresy died out, but a
grandson named Ihdád, flourished in Tirah at the head of a band
of religious burglars and sanctified highwaymen for many years,
harrying his neighbours with exceptional cruelty and success.

No sects made a stronger point of condemning sepulchral honours to holy men, prostration before shrines, encouragement to their keepers, and the kind of religious exercises which Pathâns most affect, than the Wahâbis, or Muhammadan Unitarians; and yet no more formidable apostle of insurrection ever appeared on the North-West Frontier in India, than Sayud Ahmad of Bareilly. The colonies which he planted still exist, and the strength of their fanaticism has just been made evident during the Black Mountain campaign by the two hundred who came on to certain death at Kot Kai. The career of this particular man is well known in connection with the State trial of his supporters in India, and has been sketched in powerful lines by Hunter in his *Indian Musalmans*. A horse-soldier under a Pindari freebooter, a student of Arabic under the learned doctors of Delhi, a passionate pilgrim to Mecca, a zealous reformer of the faith of Islâm, proclaiming his divine commission to extirpate the infidel world from the Sikhs to the Chinese, his really great success was among the mountains of the Yusafzai. The tribes cared little for his reforms: when it came to the point they would have none of them. They massacred his retinue, and very nearly made an end of "the just prophet, the defender of the faith" himself, when he essayed to reform their marriage customs. They preferred to go on selling their women, and keeping their miracles; but they responded with enthusiasm when he proclaimed a holy war against the rich Sikh towns of the Punjâb. The chance of plundering the Hindus was a delight not to be missed. Those who fell, had the apostle's assurance of heaven as martyrs for the faith; and, better still, those who returned would be laden with booty.

The *Jehad*[1] against the infidel Sikhs began in 1826. To raiding, the apostle's followers added burning and murder, and for a while carried all before them. In 1830 they reached their culminating point by capturing Peshawur. The Sikhs retaliated by expeditions

---

[1] Holy war.

that were exterminative rather than punitive. The villagers turned out and hunted back the fugitives into the mountains, destroying them like wild beasts. The history of the time is a record of the bitterest hatred. The traditions tell of massacre without mercy. Hunter quotes one instance in which the very land tenure, was a tenure by blood, certain village lands being held by the Hindu borderers on payment to the Sikh grantees of an annual hundred heads of the Hassan Khel. The decline of Sayud Ahmad's fame as an apostle came after his ill-advised effort to reform the Pathân marriage customs, which was really an attempt to provide wives for his own Hindustânis. Something like the Sicilian Vespers were repeated, the fiery cross was passed round the hills as the signal for the massacre of his agents, and in one hour,—the hour of evening prayer—they were murdered by the tribesmen almost to a man. In 1831 he was finally disposed of by the Sikh army under Sher Sing. He was slain and his followers for the time being almost exterminated. Out of some 1,600, not more than 300 are said to have left the field alive. The Sikhs made apostolic succession almost impossible.

Nevertheless the colonies re-established by Sayud Ahmad's lieutenants, and recruited by the disaffected from India, and outlaws or individual Border ruffians, were left as a legacy to the British Government—perhaps one of the most troublesome legacies we took over with the Punjâb. Against the colonies at Sittana among the Utmanzais, at Malka on the slopes of the Mahâbun, at Zazkata in Buneyr, among the Black Mountain tribes on both sides of the Indus, there stands a long record of campaigns, a great expenditure of men and money, due mainly to their agency. Where they have not openly undertaken hostile operations against us, they have proved to be at the bottom of most of the tribal complications. Their nominal object a crescentade against English, Hindu or infidel Kâfirs of any sort, they seem never to lose an opportunity of inspiring ill-feeling, and to be always ready to join hands with any lawless Khân, or clan, that can be persuaded into taking the initiative. The colonies of Palosi and Maidân were founded after the Akhund of Swât used his influence to move them out of Buneyr; and from the Black Mountain Expedition of 1868 to the one of 1888 they have steadily practised their apostolic vocation of preaching sedition among the tribes, who have at length brought on themselves a just retribution for following their advice. Even of late years, though so much may not have been heard of them, they are known to have been active enough for mischief. During the last Buneyr difficulties in 1885 they were ready to join the Buneyrwals; and their missionaries were canvassing supporters in India for funds in anticipation of a disturbance. In the same year their leader, an old Maulvie of Maidân, had the effrontery to demand a contribution of 5,000 rupees from the Deputy Commissioner of Hazâra, and to threaten reprisals if it was not paid. The more closely the events which led up to the recent Black Mountain expedition are investigated, the larger the share of intrigue that seems to be traced home to Palosi and kindred colonies like the Parari Sayads. It was from among the latter that a proclaimed outlaw found the partisans who fired on our villages in 1884, raided on Bagrian, shot down peaceable villagers in 1888, and kidnapped others continuously till 1889. And it was from Palosi that another better known proclaimed outlaw, Hâshim 'Ali Khân, whose name has figured conspicuously in the frontier disturbances of late, originally drew the most dangerous section of his followers.

Whether the severe lesson which the tribesmen have had at the hands of General Sir John MacQueen, will induce them to once for all turn out these disturbers of the peace, remains to be seen, but it is probable nothing would contribute more to the establishment of a permanent peace than a convention for the summary extradition of all the insurrectionary apostles in future.

CHAPTER XXXVI.

BORDER ROMANCE—A PATHÂN ROMEO AND JULIET.

ALTHOUGH in a sense the Border Benedick includes a wife or
two among the properties with which he has to set himself up,
and to pay for at the ruling market rates; and though the position
of Pathân womenkind may too often be somewhat inferior to that
of the remaining live-stock—hewers of wood, and drawers of
water, rather harder worked than the ordinary household donkeys
—it must not be supposed that their menkind are by any means
impervious to the arrows of the blind god, or that in Border
hamlets, courts, camps, and groves, the warriors or saints, are not
ruled by exactly the same little word so potent everywhere else.
The character of the most ruffianly and murderous tribesman has at
times quite another side. For the most part, a love for the song
and the dance is a common characteristic. The famous Khattak
dance is an institution familiar to even the most casual visitors.
The huge blazing camp fire, the flashing swords, the circle of per-
formers going round with weird movements, and dancing to the
music of a wild chaunt. The Khattak pipes are as thrilling on
the Punjâb Border as the slogan to any Highlander, only rather
more piercing. Festive gatherings are more or less common all
along it, and wherever they have not been prohibited by the
Mullahs, music and dancing make up the best part of the amuse-

ment for both sexes. The performer on the flageolet (*surna*), the drum, and the guitar (*rabáb*), never fails to find a sympathetic audience, more especially if he adds a chaunt recounting the daring deeds of a warrior clansman, or trolls forth a love song, more or less anacreontic. The *mirasi*, or improvisatore, occasionally adds a little acting and burlesque, and if he varies this with a not uncommon spice of impropriety, fairly brings down the house.

To be able to play the guitar—for the *rabáb* has wire strings played with the hand or a short bow, and is more like a guitar than a fiddle—is no more discredit to a Pathân than it was to a Crusader, and the former will occasionally set himself down by the road, substitute the *rabáb* for the rifle, and do his best to vie with the *mirasi* in playing; accompanying himself by singing some favourite Pathân ballad in a very loud, but not by any means inharmonious voice. Similarly a gang of Pathân workmen will draw up together after a long day's tramp, and possibly a short meal, and troll out a wild chorus half the night.

Like the rest of the world, the Pathân has also his romance, in fact far more of it than most of his neighbours in Hindustân. Elphinstone doubts if there are any people in the East, except the Afghân and Pathân, that know anything of the sentiment of love, according to the Western idea of that passion. There are many Border courtships that are not done according to regulation, and much love-making managed without a go-between. An enterprising Khân does not always wait till the arrangements about the *hiri*, or marriage dowry are made up. If he does not mind fighting, he can get a sweetheart without her parents' consent, by stealing a lock of her hair, snatching off her veil, or mantilla, or the still simpler expedient of eloping with her. Nor is the Yusafzai always so dull as to observe the etiquette laid down for him of waiting till the marriage ceremonies are over before seeing his bride. He steals under cover of night to her house, and has a secret understanding with mamma, who contrives to leave the couple alone together and square papa, by whom the visit would be considered a deadly affront if he officially knew it. And these little kisses under the rose, "sports of the betrothed," as they are termed in Pushtu, no doubt compensate for any little delay in the remaining negotiations.

But besides the abduction and elopements, either with maid or matron, and the other dangers which so many Pathâns are ready to encounter in the cause of love—and in this Elphinstone's comparisons with the West seem very appropriate—there are lots of instances of what might be romantic attachments: where young couples fall in love, exchange pledges, have stern parents demanding solid assurance in the shape of land and beeves, and who have to separate, the one to work, and the other to wait, just for all the world like similar Western stories.

Their ballads, songs, and tales, moreover, mainly tell of love and war, occasionally in a very dramatic way. There is no Border Shakespeare, but the most popular of all the Border poems or tales might have been based on the story of Romeo and Juliet. Famous, more especially throughout the whole Yusafzai-country— it tells in good manly Pushtu the touching story of the loves of Adam Khân and Durkhâni—is perhaps the most representative specimen of Border folklore, and gives a particularly graphic account of one of the most pleasing phases of Border life.

The story, which has been noticed by many writers, from Elphinstone downwards, and translated from both Persian and Pushtu versions, but most completely by the late Major Plowden from the Pushtu edition compiled at Peshawur by Mulvi Ahmad of Tangi, goes back to the days when the Yusufzais of Swât used to leave their mountain fastnesses and come down at the end of every summer to the plains in the Peshawur Valley. Before the famous Shaikh Malli had divided out the hill and plain country among the different tribes; when bows and arrows were still the common weapons, and Bârber had not yet introduced them to matchlocks;

the Mithakhel sept of the Abakhel clan had then their summer home at Barikot on the banks of the Swât river, and among them Adam Khân, the son of Hasu Khân, was the most distinguished of the clansmen for his good looks, his grace and his prowess. Renowned as a hardy sportsman and a skilful musician—and none could equal his skill in playing the *rabâb* (the Pathân guitar)—the Romeo of the story was recognized as the chief of an admiring circle of friends. Durkhâni, the Juliet, was a daughter of Tâus Khân, a wealthy chief of the Khasi Khel sept of the same clan, and lived at Ghalagân, a village close by. She was no less famous as the most charming and accomplished of her sex. "Everywhere was the fame of her beauty, her amiability, and her talents noised abroad. Nowhere at that time was there her equal."

The first scene of the lovers' meeting is variously described as by the snow-fed waters of Swât, or by the spring at Bâzdarra— "The Hawk's Eyrie"—to which Durkhâni resorted for water when the clans descended to the plains for the winter, a huge isolated rock being riven in twain to enable them to meet. A still more favourite trysting-place was a blacksmith's shop on the road to the Malakand Pass, where Adam took his horse to be shod, and Durkhâni her spindle to be mended. "Their eyes met, and from that moment they loved." Similar easily devised pretexts sufficed for many meetings, and a tree is still pointed out, grown from the peg to which Adam used to tether his horse.

But between the Mithakhels and the Khasikhels was a long standing feud. An ancient quarrel, as bitter as any in Verona, and Durkhâni was by her parents betrothed to "Paris"—in the shape of Payâwai, a powerful chief of the Babuzai, a third sept of the clan. The mutual passion of the lovers remained a secret, and Durkhâni observed a life of such privacy, that even at festival times, when social restraint is a good deal relaxed, no one could get a view of her face. With difficulty she is persuaded to go to her cousin Basaki's wedding, though a long promised bridesmaid, and only goes on the condition that she may remain closely veiled in her mantilla, if such a word may be used as a translation for a garment which covers not merely the face but the figure. Vowed to keep herself secluded from the view of either man or woman, she sets out accompanied by her duenna, who throughout might be the counterpart of Juliet's nurse, for she never loses an opportunity of pouring into her

Pathân Woman in a "*Burka*" or Mantilla.

mistress's willing ear the praises of her lover. The cousins "gladden their hearts by recalling the events of their childhood," but none can succeed in obtaining a glimpse of the fair one's face. Bards vie with one another in making verses in her honour, verses of "such sweetness as to make e'en the sad smile and the happy weep." "They sang quatrains and roundelays till they were quite exhausted, but in vain. Durkhâni unveiled not her face."

Anon comes Adam, with two of his henchmen, who commence a serenade outside the courtyard, the verses of which in some of the metrical versions make up a large part of the poem. Durkhâni, touched by the strains, inquires from the duenna as to the singer. "A green parroquet is he," says she—the parroquet being held a type of manly beauty, as the nightingale is of song—"apparelled in right proper garments, and his two friends are his wings. If thou desirest to see him, this is thy time. Soon will he fly away, and then thou wilt grieve, for his name is Adam Khân." One of the "wings" extols her raven tresses, the other "her dainty arms, that, like polished blade, have cut in twain Adam's heart;" while he sings of the beauty of her face, laments in most touching notes his unhappy case, and speaks of seeking exile in some distant land. Durkhâni, recognizing the voice, her resolution no longer avails against the pleadings of her heart, and despite the duenna's cautions, she, "inflamed with the wine of love," flings the veil from her face, and, rushing out of the chamber to meet her lover, falls fainting to the ground.

> "Modesty and shame, nay, wisdom her forsook :
> Forgotten are by her the precepts of the book."[1]

Her kinsfolk upbraid her for this most unseemly conduct, accuse her of being bewitched, and proceed to fumigate her with wild rue, to avert from her the evil eye. "Good aunt," she replies, "have done, I am not bewitched, and since I have by the flame of love been burnt, scorch me not again with fire. If you would cure me, send me forth with Adam, that I may fly with him." The secret is out; from that time their love is a matter of notoriety.

Then, in the version as compiled by Maulvi Ahmad, comes what may not inappropriately be compared with the balcony scene. Durkhâni and her party have gone home to their winter quarters in Lower Bâzdarra, the lovers contriving to meet again *en route* at

---

[1] Viz., The Korân.

their favourite springs.   To Tàus Khan's house, with much caution,
comes at dusk the Yusafzia Romeo, with Mercutio and Benvolio
(Miru and Balo), and by the aid of a ladder made of a cradle,
scale her courtyard.   Balo holds Adam's horse *Majnun*," the love
bewitched;" Miru keeps watch; the usual troublesome boy Peter
(Bucha) is silenced by a gift of some silver, and under the close
curtain of civil night, some very dramatic love-passages take place.
Parting is such sweet sorrow, Durkhâni will not let her lover go,
though "she reflects that if day dawns, and her father becomes
aware of Adam's presence, he may say naught to her, but he will
kill him, and her heart will break."

> "The walls are high and hard to climb,
> And the place death, considering who thou art,
> If any of my kinsmen find thee here,"

are lines that might almost have been stolen by the Pushtu bard.

Now comes the soft breeze of the morning—"Nasim-i-Sahâr."
The nurse is uneasy, " the cocks begin to crow," but it is Adam that
urges, " methinks it still is night, the birds have crowed too soon."
They are still exchanging vows, when " the village priest chaunts
the call to prayers," and Miru has to interfere, and the nurse, abus-
ing the rashness and imprudence of Adam, to contrive a pretext to
remove the watchman.

Adam's love-lorn condition becomes obvious to everybody.   " He
is madly in love with Durkhâni," says his father.   " What makes
my dear brother look so sad ? " remarks his little sister.   Durkhâni
declares her heart is broken; Payâwai, the betrothed, who is away
hunting, hears enough to bring him back hastily, and, filled with
jealousy, he insists on hurrying on the marriage feast.

Durkhâni is forced to consent, but quoth she to him, " So in a
dream have I learnt that in seven days time I must die, but if
peradventure I survive, then I will be here for thee."   Payâwai
consents to so much grace, and thereon is called in the Friar

Lawrence, Pir Salih, the trusted confidant and preceptor, who with the nurse arranges a plot to carry off the lady by force on the day fixed for her wedding with Payâwai. Adam, moreover, goes to a tribal chief, Mir Bâmi, and in approved Pathân form [1] throws himself upon him, a suppliant for assistance, which is given in the shape of three hundred armed men, and a promise of shelter. These, and one hundred of his own, Adam arranges as his supports, while Miru and he, at a given signal catch up Durkhâni and the duenna in the approved Lochinvar manner, are off at speed and in Mir Bâmi's house before Payâwai's forces are fairly aware of what has happened.

Events in the tragedy now proceed apace. Mir Bâmi is heavily bribed by Payâwai to give up Durkhâni—an act of treachery, from a Pathân point of view, of unpardonable baseness. So much so, that Mir Bâmi's son, Gujar Khân, the friend of Adam, attacks his, own father, and resolutely pursues him until he encompasses his death. Death alone was not even sufficient to wipe out the dishonour of betraying a refugee: the whole of the perfidious chief's clan were afterwards seized with leprosy, and gradually died out, nothing of it surviving but the disgrace, which has caused the very name of Mir, or Pir, Bâmi to become a synonym for an exceptionally treacherous man—a Border Judas.

Gujar Khân unites his forces with Adam, but both are drawn into an ambuscade by Payâwai, and though the latter is beaten off, the Balo is killed, and Adam badly wounded. Durkhâni, meanwhile, spends her days and nights in tears waiting succour from Adam: her only solace the tending of two flowers in the garden, one named after herself, the other after her lover. On the day of the ambuscade the flower named after Adam appears to droop and languish from sympathy, and while she is watching it, Payâwai enters with his drawn sword, wet, as he boasts, with the heart's blood of Adam.

---

[1] Claims the *nanawatai* (something akin to the Hindu Dharma) which no Pathân can refuse.

The trial is fatal. "Overwhelmed with grief and sorrow, Durkhâni sinks senseless to the ground," and dies, "her hands and apron filled with flowers." The news is carried to Adam in his village, where his wounds have been bound up, and his kinsfolk are trying to induce him to find consolation in the charms of a beautiful young maiden, named Gulneza, "the flower-loving one." The flower-loving one is not altogether coy, "but he will none of her." "Were all the fairest damsels in the world assembled together, they could not equal a single finger nail of Durkhâni," he says; and when he hears of her fate, he starts up, his wounds burst out again, and he gradually sinks from weakness, calling on his mistress's name.

Another version kills Adam first, and makes Durkhâni first learn of his fate from the trusty Miru, whom she recognizes disguised as a wandering minstrel, playing his master's guitar, and hearing the news, gradually pines away; even Payâwai at last repenting for having caused the death of two such true lovers.

There are other variations and other endings, but all agree that the pair were separately buried at their respective encampments, by the Kâbul river near Naushera, and afterwards found by a man whose scarf or *lungi* was lost in the grave, and who, searching for it, found both lovers together in one. Twice, owing to the bitter feud between the clans, were the bodies again separately buried, but twice was love again triumphant, and both are found united in one grave. Finally, the clansmen, persuaded by the holy priest, gave in to such persistence, and agreed to bury their feud in the same grave that formed the last resting-place of Adam Khân and Durkhâni, of whom it may as truly be said as of their prototypes,

> "A pair of star-crossed lovers,
> Whose misadventured piteous overthrow
> Do with their deaths bury their parents' strife."

Near Mardân are two hillocks, Tâ-us-Derai, and Hasu-Derai, where the rival houses established their camps, and where tradition says these love-passages tragically ended. Not far away from Naushera, at Zira Maina on the banks of the Kâbul river, is the grave of the lovers, from which sprang up two acacia trees with intertwining branches, and from these the youth who makes himself a bow (*nakhun*) for his guitar (*rabâb*) is certain, like Adam, of becoming an excellent musician, but also, like him, of risking death in the bloom of his youth.

And in a hamlet almost adjoining Toru, near Mardân, is the grave of Pir Salih, the good friar of the Babuzais, whose shrine is still almost as famous as the memory of Adam Khân is dear to the pride of every Yusafzai.

A Pathân Romeo—Khwâjah Muhammad, the Khân of Hoti.

CHAPTER XXXVII.

Pathân Poetry.

Somewhere between the rich and occasionally extravagantly voluptuous Persian and the simple verse of the ancient Arab may probably be placed the poetry of the Pathâns, in fact of Afghâns generally. Like the former it is tinged to some extent with the mystic doctrine of the Sufis; poetry abounding in harmonious numbers and richness of fancy, but that suggests merely pleasure to the profane while professing to chaunt the fervour of love divine: that deals in metaphor often of the most extravagant kind: enthusiasm that takes the form of religious allegory scarcely distinguishable from very earthly depravity—just as the *khirkah* or dervish's cloak of rags, thickly-wadded and lined with silk, a form of spiritual penance, hardly conceals exceedingly carnal joys. For the more far-fetched a sort of slang dictionary would be needed; by zephyrs are to be understood outbursts of grace; by wine is meant devotion; the tavern is an oratory, its keeper a spiritual guide; inebriation, religious abstraction. The warmest description of beauty denotes the perfection of the Deity: curls and tresses are the attributes of glory; the lips inscrutable mysteries of his essence; kisses and embraces the transports of devout piety. But in the main the love that tunes the reed of the Pathân has undoubtedly a great deal of the human in it; while, as might be expected from a warlike race of hardy mountaineers, with few wants and little chance of obtaining more than the bare necessaries of life, their similes are more simple, and there is a breath of patriotism and freedom pervading the whole.

If some of the writers were men who devoted themselves to lives of penance and religious abstraction, others again were warriors who wielded the sword still better than the pen, whose sentiments were naturally chivalrous, whose devotion to the fair sex was great, and whose odes were distinctly less Sufistic than erotic. Such at any rate are the songs that commend themselves to popular favour on the Border. The average Pathân accepts the *'Amal-i-jismani* or " corporeal worship," without troubling himself to discover the *'Amal-i-ruhani* or " spiritual adoration," if even the poet ever intended his writings to bear any such transcendental meaning.

For Europeans this national poetry was practically discovered by Raverty, and considerable selections from the best-known writers translated by him and subsequently by Plowden as text-books. Among these writers, perhaps the most popular are the two Mohmand Mullahs,' Abd-ur-Rahmân and 'Abd-ul-Hamid, the Shaikh S'adi of the Pathâns who both flourished on the northern Peshawur Border about the beginning of the last century. Besides effusions of a religious character the former wrote a number of love odes, and two volumes of the latter bear the suggestive titles of *Love's Fascination* and a *Collection of Pearls and Corals.* Almost equally popular, and still better known, was the warrior-poet Khushhâl Khân the Khattak, the ancestor of the famous old Khan Sir Khwâjah Muhammad, chief of the Teri, or Southern Khattaks, who has been already referred to ; for besides poetry and history he wrote on many subjects, and translated Bidpâi's excellent fables from the Persian. Poetry, no less than the profession of arms, seems to have run in the family. His eldest son Ashraf, under the name of Hijrai, " the exile," before he was betrayed into the hands of Aurangzebe, and 'Abd-ul-Qadir, another son—who with ten brothers and several children were slain in one day by an intriguing nephew, and buried in one grave—both inherited their father's tastes, as did a grandson, Kazim Khân, better known under his *nom de plume* of Shaida, " the lovelorn." Among a still earlier series was Mirza Khan *Ansari*, " the assistant of the Prophet," a descendant of the notorious " apostle of light," though he is sometimes claimed by the Yusafzais, who two and a half centuries ago lived and wrote in Tirah, where among the wild highlanders of the Mian Khel, his descendants still flourish. The Yusafzais, the Bangash, the Durrâni Afghâns, even the Afridis, similarly claim bards of more or less note, of whose efforts fragments have been preserved in one form or other.

Beauty, the theme on which the poets of all nations from Anacreon to Moore, or Firdausi to Tasso, are so eloquent, is to a Pathân a subject equally popular in Pushtu. Be it East or West, the ruling theme various very little ; and though the Oriental standard of loveliness or the imagery of the Eastern may occasionally vary somewhat from those of the Occident, the Pushtu, like the Persian, is full of touches of nature with which the western world is at once made kin. Is the western lover sighing like a furnace, with a woeful ballad to his mistress' eyebrow ? 'Abd-ul-Qadir declares : " Her glance 'tis a flame, her eyes are like firebrands that lovers' hearts kindle. She hath lighted the lamp of her beauty ; and her adorer's hearts, like the moths, are oblations therein. Her eyes are lotuses, the pupils black bees, but their gaze is as free as the gazelle's. Her eyebrows are bows, her eyelashes the arrows, and to destroy her lover she raiseth them."

" Each of the eyelashes of the beloved," says 'Abd-ur-Rahmân, " pierceth me like the two-edged sword of 'Ali. . . . Her countenance is hidden by her curls, as the water of immortality is itself concealed in darkness."

> " From thy curls, thy ruby lips, and thy face
> Proceed the night, the sunset's glow, the dawn of day.
> Is it the teeth in thy sweet mouth that shine so lustrously ?
> Or are those glittering dewdrops in the rosebud ?"

Romeo is made to speak of stealing immortal blessing from Juliet's lips, but says a Khattak bard—

> "No one is capable of explaining their sweetness,
> The ambrosial nectar of Paradise is indigenous to her lips."

*   *   *   *   *   *   *

> "A single moment lip to lip with the belov'd
> And honey, milk, and conserves are alike forgot."

Conserves may not sound highly romantic, but perhaps is as much so as the modern slang has coined the expression "real jam." In a long ode of a different style Rahmán writes—

> "The face of one's mistress, the sun, the moon, all three are the same;
> Her figure, the cypress, and the fir, all three are the same;
> Honey, sugar, her lips, all three are the same;
> A garden, a paradise, her dwelling, all three are the same;
> Of my true love bereft, fire, or the bare earth, to me are the same."

And again—

> "This is the Adored one—that is the rival.
> This is the rose—that is the thorn.
>
> This is the beloved—that is the duenna.[1]
> This the treasure—that is the snake.
>
> This is wisdom—that is love.
> This is anguish—that the consoler.
>
> This is separation—that is conjunction.
> This is autumn—that the fresh spring.
>
> This is devotion—that is sinfulness.
> This is refulgence, but that is fire.
>
> This is Rahmán—that is the Adored.
> This is the sick—that is the physician."

The following, though hearty, perhaps hardly sounds so complimentary :—

> "When I look on thy face, I am amazed at Allah's grace,
> That He hath preserved thee safe from its ruddy glow."

------

[1] See the description of a duenna in Chap. XXXVI.

Beauty, says Pope, draws us by a single hair : Rahmân desires "no greater liberty than this, that I by the chain of my mistress' locks be bound," and some of the ideas in the following are distinctly novel as well as poetic :—

> "How many, Joseph-like,[1] my love would from that pretty pit extract
> If for her dimpled chin she let her tresses down as rope.
> Could they but view her rosy lips the jewellers, I ween,
> For Yaman sapphires would abandon further search.
> Should my love in her beauty visit the grove,
> The rose of the garden all claim to its beauty would waive.
> Think not that even in Doomsday's dire confusion,
> Kamgar[2] will let go his grasp on her skirts."

"He jests at scars that never felt a wound," is, for a country of hills, not inaptly paraphrased by Rahman :—

> "If thou fallest from the precipice of love thou wilt loose thy teeth,
> Oh thou who gnashest them at me by way of admonition."

Some of the verses by Khushhâl Khân and the Khattaks are suggestive of Moore :—

> "Where thou reclineth, the place a parterre of flowers becometh.
> When in the mead thou roamest, the heart of the tulip is scarred.
> When the sable locks about thy fair face zephyr dishevoleth,
> The fragrance of musk and amber is everywhere diffused.
> Since in thy tresses my heart is lost, show me thy face,
> For in night's gloom, with lighted lamp, do we not seek lost treasures ?"

> "My graceful mistress' beauteous form revealed :
> In every limb is kindled passion's flame.
> And when I view her languishing soft eyes,
> With wine of joy my goblet brimmeth o'er."

> "Stung by the serpents[3] of thy locks, the man recovers never.
> Fruitless to visit tombs and shrines, useless all magic arts.
> But pain and anguish and all grief hath fled :
> I have to-day within my grasp the cup of joy.

---

[1] The famous Eastern hero whose brothers " pitted him."
[2] The name of the author, which is generally introduced in the last line of the ode.
[3] Serpents are in the East guardians of treasure.

The nectar of thy lips has Kawsur[1] put to shame,
The stream of life in Paradise, the spring of Mecca's shrine."

* * * * * * *

"The lucky man who once his foot within her threshold plants,
He will the gates and walls of Paradise forget.
The prospect of heaven to come, is bliss to monk and priest,
But in meeting thee, Khushhâl hath gained Paradise at once."

Sometimes the lady is coy, and Ashraf Khân complains:—

"Her promised kiss she ever makes a draft to pay to-morrow:
How with such promise can I my heart refresh?"

Khushhâl Khân, whom Raverty credits with fifty-seven sons, was evidently susceptible where the Afridi ladies were concerned:—

"Fair and pretty are the Adam Khel Afridi maids,
With large eyes, long drooping lashes, and arched eyebrows.
Honey lips, rosy cheeks, and moonlike faces theirs.
Small mouths like rosebuds, teeth regular and white.
Round heads, covered with dark curls, of amber redolent.
Their bodies soft and sleek, smooth and glossy like an egg.
Their feet diminutive, heels round, and hips prominent.
Thin-stomached, broad-chested, and small-waisted.
In stature straight as *alif*[2]-and complexion fair.
Though like the falcons, I have wandered o'er the hills,
Many plump partridges have I my quarry made."

Thorns are, however, not unfrequently associated with the rose, and, quoth Rahmân:—

"Until a hundred thorns have pierced his heart.
How shall the Nightingale unto the rose gain pass?"[3]

And 'Abd-ul-Hamid puts a similar idea rather neatly:—

"As the rose, the more it is concealed, the more its perfume increaseth,
So the anguish of love from endurance becometh overpowering."

---

[1] The river of Paradise, from which all the others have their source.

[2] The first letter of the Arabic alphabet.

[3] The attachment of the nightingale for his "sultana, the rose" is a constant Eastern idea—
"The maid for whom his melody,
His thousand songs are heard on high."—*Byron's Giaour.*

That in the good old days the Khattaks cheered themselves with the wine-cup is well known, and Khushhâl sings its praises in several odes :—

> " From out the clear azure flask,
>   O cup-bearer, bring thou unto me
>   A full goblet of that potent wine,
>   The remedy for grief, the consoler in woe.
>   Tell me not of the riches of this world ;
>   They cannot compare with one cup of wine.
>
> *   *   *   *   *
>
>   From the cup-bearer then take thou the glass,
>   For therein is much gladness and joy."

The odes of this writer cover a wider field and offer more variety than most of the other Pathân bards. He is equally eloquent in the praises of " Spring that has made the country a garden of flowers," whose breezes " have cheered the clansmen even more than the wine," the time " when the maidens place nosegays in their bosoms and the youths in their turbans." Still more does he delight in describing how those youths " have again made their bright swords rosy with their enemy's gore, even as the tulip—the heart's seared flower—blossoms in summer ; " how they have " dyed red the Valley of the Khaiber, and poured forth the tumult of war from Karrupah to Bajâwah." " There is no deliverance in anything," he says, " save the sword." He glories in the deeds of his ancestors, " who had both the sword and the beard, both courage and courtesy, whose companions were men of spirit who sported with their lives, who in all their dealings were true and went to their graves dyed with blood. Such heroes were they all." For him there is no spot like home : it is " of all others *the* spot," and he thanks Allah that his forbears selected it, " with its dark mountain ranges and the blue waters of the Indus." " Who shall tell how beautiful it is in the spring after the rain," what " heart-ravishing sport for falcon, hawk, and hound

in the woods of Kálah-páni ? Do not its hills shoot straight up to
the sky and the climbing them soon diminish our corpulence ?"

Inscription round the lip of a Peshawur Wine-bowl.

Saqia bar khez o dar deh'jam rá
Khak bar sar kun gham-i-ayam rá
Sághar-i-mai bar kafum nah ta-z-sar
Bar kasham yen dalq-i-arzaq faru rá.

Get up, O Saki (wine-cup bearer), and give (me) the cup ;
Never mind for the cares of the world.
(Literally, throw dust on the head of the days of grief)
Hand me the wine flask in order
That I may remove the blue heavens from my head,
(Viz. That there may be nothing between me and God.)

Are not "its youths healthy and stout, active and agile, merry-
eyed, white and red, and tall in stature withal ?" "The waters
of the Kábul river and the Bárah stream, are they not sweeter and

more delicious than sherbet in the mouth ?" They are his Pharpar and Abner, and it is of them he thinks when an exile in the power of the Mughal, compelled to drink "the waters of Hind, more vile than its horrid climate :—"

> "Gentle breeze of the morn, if thou Khairábád pass,
> Should thy course be by Indus bank, by the Khattak Akora,
> Convey thou my greetings and greetings, again and again,
> Of my love and regard carry many and many expressions.
> Cry out to the father of rivers[1] with sonorous voice :
> But unto the little Landai[2] mildly whisper, and say
> Perhaps I once more may drink a cup of thy waters."

It is satisfactory to know that the gallant warrior-poet lived to get back and quaff many a cup of his favourite stream, and write many a song that still lives in the memory of the Border clansmen.

    [1] The Indus.   [2] The Kâbul river.

CHAPTER XXXVIII.

THE BLACK MOUNTAIN.

THE little strip of rugged mountain lying east of the Indus, and occupying the south-west corner formed by that river and the British district of Hazâra, is the last bit of country that need be referred to in connection with any, even the most unworthy, of the Yusafzai tribes. It has been recently invested with a specially melancholy interest by the wanton murder of Major Battye and Captain Urmston, and the punitive expedition that followed the outrage. Otherwise, neither its extent nor its population would warrant its being ranked as of any exceptional importance. The tribes are not numerous, nor particularly warlike, and most of them are miserably poor, but they, and the nests of fanatical hornets they shelter, have for long proved capable of inflicting an altogether disproportionate amount of annoyance. And just as in the interests of good cultivation it occasionally becomes necessary to smoke out or blow up the garden pests, it becomes, in the interests of good Government, occasionally needful to adopt measures that shall effectually prevent our villages from being burned, our villagers kidnapped, their cattle raided, and our officers from being murdered by pests of another sort.

A long narrow granite ridge, rounded rather than sharp, 25 to 30 miles long, having more of the characteristics of Murree or

Thandiâna than Simla or Dalhousie, but an average height of 8,000 feet, with peaks at intervals rising to 10,000 feet; many large precipitous and rocky spurs projecting from the sides in all directions, in the narrow glens between which lie the tribal villages. Along these spurs, which at the top occasionally widen out into plateaus, affording room for the assembly of a considerable force, are the routes by which the mountain can be easiest ascended, or the villages commanded, and it was by these that our troops advanced in 1852, 1868, and 1889, when the very highest peaks were occupied. The lower slopes are covered with berbery and acacia, replaced by forests of the Himalayan silver fir (*Abies webbiana*) further up, whose dark and gloomy shade has earned for the mountain the title by which it is known to both Europeans and natives. Shade that, all the same, is varied with the light green of the oak, sycamore, and horse-chestnut, and by frequent open glades rejoicing in short rich grass. The whole, as a rule, well watered; springs are numerous along the s'opes, and some of the streams flowing into the Indus attain a considerable size. A great deal of hill-side is of course rocky and stony, but many places in the season are fairly covered with Indian corn, a little wheat, barley, mustard and inferior grains, and quantities of fodder. A climate that in spring, summer, and autumn is excellent, but that in winter has occasionally snow enough to stop communication over the crest. All this, and more, is the Black Mountain, with possibilities for a far better sanitarium than Murree, and with very much about it, saving always "the spirit of man," that may be fairly described as "divine."

Certainly the dwellers on its slopes could not be brought under any such classification, though it need not be assumed they are all equally delinquents; and in some cases they might plead that their misdeeds have been the result of bad company—"villainous company." The tribes on the western face are the Hassanzais and Akazais, descendants of Isa, and the Chagarzais, descendants of

Mali; all Yusafzais. The Akazais are the weakest, but probably the best fighting men, and, with the Khân Khel section of the Hassanzais, have during recent years been by far the most troublesome. The Chagarzais are the most numerous, though less born to war than to trade and agriculture, their chief wealth being their cattle. Once they marched up the hill to the Crag-picket against us at Ambeyla, where their reception caused them to march down, and straight home again. The Hassanzais were the murderers of Messrs. Carne and Tapp, and all three tribes probably share with the Sayuds and their hangers-on the responsibility for the murder of Messrs. Battye and Urmston; but none are credited with the manly and many fine qualities of their kindred on the west or Trans-Indus. On all other sides they are surrounded by tribes, who, except as neighbours, are widely removed from them in almost every way, who do not even belong to the same race. On the south is Tanâwal, the wildest bit of Hazâra, the appanage of our feudatory the chief of Amb, whose people, Tanaolis, are not Pathâns at all. In the adjoining sub-division of Agror, which is under the direct management of another feudatory Khân, the inhabitants are mainly Swâtis and Gujars. In Tikari, Nandihar, Deshi, the three valleys which next lie in succession on the east and, with the still larger one of Allâi, come between the Black Mountain and the Hazâra district, the people are all Swâtis. Not, as their name might seem to imply, connected with the Swât Valley, but, as already noticed in connection with the general tribal distribution of the Peshawur Valley, the remains of a once powerful and widely-distributed race, driven by the Dilazâks from the plain country into the hills, and subsequently hunted by the Yusafzais out of Swât and Buneyr—mainly eastward into Hazâra, and a few westward into Kâfiristân. In the valleys where they now predominate, the term covers an exceedingly heterogeneous people—a little dash of Greek on an ancient Aryan stock, with a liberal mixture of Hindu and Turk, Pathân and Gujar. Though they would in many cases now describe themselves Pathán, the latter would probably have to strain his vocabulary to find an expression sufficiently contemptuous to describe the Swátis. They have little in common with the former save his vices rankly luxuriant, and the bigotry of Sunni Muhammadans. Inferior in physique, and without his courage, their instincts are nevertheless said to run naturally towards murder and avarice; and they are described by pretty well everybody all round as cowardly, deceptive, cruel, grasping, lazy. "Replacing the bold frank manner of the Pathán by the hang-dog look of the whipped cur." The Oswald Wycliffes, preferring a whole skin, but ready to commit any crime or to get any Bertram Risinghams who may be bold enough ruffians to do it for them. It is at the same time always dangerous to generalize in too sweeping a way regarding tribes by no means well known, and spread over so large an area, and the condemnation may be too sweeping. So far as we know them, in and adjoining Hazára, or have met them in expeditions, they would not, save in the matter of treachery and deceit, be formidable as enemies. It is improbable, with their own internal quarrels and feuds with the adjoining Patháns, that they would combine against us, unless it were to protect themselves from retaliation; and it would only be necessary to take up a strong and permanent position on the Black Mountain to ensure the submission of all the surrounding Swátis.

Colonies of Sayuds, and others of the baneful order, occupy several of the glens on the mountain itself. In two on the eastern slope, extending from the highest peak, the Muchai, down to the Deshi fort of Trund, are the Pariari Sayuds. On the western face, among the Hussanzais, are the Sayuds of Tilli; one or two more are scattered through the Chagarzai country, and a rather formid-able religious body, the Akhund Khels, holds the glens and spurs on the extreme north-west corner down to the river Indus. Numerically all are insignificant, but they could calculate on receiving more or less assistance from kindred colonies across the river. This was to some extent the case during the last expedition, and, had the operations not been prompt, and the force employed overwhelming, these colonies would probably have become centres to which the disaffected from the adjacent tribes, both Pathân and Swâti, would naturally gravitate.

All told, it is doubtful if the fighting-men on the Black Mountain, including all the Pathâns and the religious colonies, amount to more than 6,000 or 7,000 men, of which probably not half are armed with matchlocks, the rest having nothing better than swords, or spears. The Chagarzais might calculate on an extra 1,000 or 2,000 from the Trans-Indus sections of their tribe; and the adjoining Swâtis, Allaiwâis, Nandiharis, Tikariwâls, Deshiwâls, and Thakotis could possibly contribute 13,000 or 14,000 still more indifferently armed, but the extent to which they would be drawn in would necessarily be dependent on the policy declared.

The recent expedition under General Sir John McQueen was directed mainly against the Akazais, Hassanzais, Pariari-Sayuds and the Hindustâni Fanatics of Palosi. Undertaken, on a large scale, with a force vastly superior to anything the ill-armed and insignificant tribesmen were likely to be able to bring into the field—it was short, sharp, and in its way decisive enough. There was one advance, by a band of fanatics, brave to rashness, a handful of " warriors of the faith " charging regiments of breechloaders which cost us the life of the gallant Major Beley, and resulted in the practical extermination of what, had they been Englishmen, we should have termed a Forlorn Hope. After this there was nothing but a flying enemy, hiding behind rocks and trees, or skulking for a chance at parties advancing—possibly to burn his homesteads. As a lesson it may be hoped it was successful, but to judge from a standard of high policy, or of permanent results, it may fairly be doubted if it was worth the valuable lives and large outlay of money spent upon it. The offending tribes were severely punished, a considerable number of the fanatics were literally wiped out, a certain amount of crops or stores of grain destroyed or taken, perhaps not always belonging to the people actually concerned in the raids and outrages, and certain of the most notorious ringleaders were captured and their villages burnt. The troops marched up to the tops of the highest peaks, and encamped in the most difficult valleys, amply showing that the fancied inaccessible strongholds offered no security against our shells and our soldiers, and the seditious colonies had full opportunity of learning that their preachers and teachers of insurrection—scattering in all directions from the sacred training grounds of Maidân, were of no more value than their traditionary leather cannon. There was nothing for the tribesmen left but to come in and tender a submission, and promise to pay any fine inflicted, while their friends and neighbours fired upon our retiring rear guard, hurrying back to keep time to the necessities of a State despatch that should fit in with the opening of Parliament.

It is doubtful if the expedition stayed long enough to enable the mistakes in our maps to be corrected, or the notorious want of topographical information in the Intelligence Branch to be sufficiently supplemented, while it is certain a hurried withdrawal of our troops was liable to be misjudged and to leave any disaffected tribes more ready for future mischief than ever.

A more reasonable solution of the difficulty would surely have been to have given out from the first that our patience with the disorderly tribes was exhausted, and, seeing that during a long course of years they had shown it to be impossible to trust them as neighbours, we had decided once for all to move our Border line up to the Indus, and to bring the whole under regular Government as subjects. The Indus forms a natural boundary along the North and West, although the information regarding its course, or the facilities for running any road along its banks had, up to the date of the expedition, not been sufficient to enable it to be shown on any map.[1] From Derband the road is passable for horsemen for some distance; beyond Kotkai, in the Hassanzai country it is more difficult, as our troops found to their cost, while further up, spurs run straight down so steep that even mules cannot pass. A flying visit of a few hours was made by one detachment of troops to Thakot, but the long strip of Chagarzai country was not entered at all, and the opportunity for an examination lost. Regarding the country above Thakot we are still absolutely without information, till Major Biddulph takes up the parable of the upper Indus in his work on the Hindu Kush.

Looking at such maps as are available it would seem that the Allai Valley would make an excellent boundary to the North; it is conterminous with British territory in Hazâra, though separated by a range 11,000 to 12,000 feet high. This crossed, there is a long, rich, well-cultivated valley, some 12 miles wide, straight to the Indus, the Sirhan stream, which runs down its centre, joining the river opposite Barkot; while a vast range, upwards of 15,000 feet high, separates it from Kohistân on the North.

This, or any boundary that would have included the whole of the Black Mountain, would have insured a final settlement of a troublesome question at the smallest cost. The opposition would not have been greater than to our temporary occupation, while it would have brought with it the most permanently beneficial results; would have had an excellent effect on the whole of the Yuzafzai tribes; provided a splendid sanitarium for cantoning troops, well supplied with fuel and water, and afforded a magnificient strategic position, having the most formidable natural defence along its front, and which an easily constructed railway through the Hazâra Valley, would link in with all our communications behind. A few years of good government moreover

---

[1] That a river, within twenty miles of our outposts, should have to be indicated on the best maps by approximate dots, and which dots, on at least one important occasion, were found to have some miles of error, requires no further comment.

Kikâri Sayuds from the Black Mountain.

would go far to see a set of people now but little removed from savages, converted into a community as well-behaved and as prosperous as their neighbours in Hazâra; and might well have been hailed as the inauguration of a Border policy on thoroughly sound principles,

CHAPTER XXXIX.

A BIT OF "YAGHESTÁN."

MORE is probably known about many of the remote regions of
Central Asia than concerning the countries adjacent to the river
Indus within a short range of our own Border. This, of course, is
in a great measure due to the exceptionally inaccessible nature of
the higher Indus Valley; the immense mass of lofty mountains
through which the river forces its way; the deep valleys, often
approached by openings affording little more than a path alongside
some torrent, rushing between overhanging rocks, dangerous to any
but a skilled cragsman; with no roads, save the merest tracks; no
bridges beyond those of plaited birch twigs, swaying with every
gust of wind; and with no communications at all for many months
of the year. Not a little, also, to the character of the fanatical
and lawless tribes who inhabit the reaches immediately adjoining
us, and who bar the way to traders and travellers alike. But
among these mountains, and in these valleys, often very extensive
and of great fertility, are communities, numerous and prosperous,
that for many generations have remained little changed or influenced by the events passing around them, and have maintained
their own customs, their own dialects, and, to a great extent,
widely differing peculiarities of race and of creed.

The limits of the Black Mountain practically mark the limits of the Pathân to the left of the Indus, though on the right he extends much further up; and in the lateral valleys above Buneyr are more or less pure-blooded Yusafzais, who maintain their connections with Swât. Then come tribes with a good deal of mixed Pathân blood in their veins, and of Pushtu in their speech, often known as "Neemchas," or half breeds. Further, again, all trace of Afghân blood disappears, or is to be found only in scattered colonies. For a long distance, however, the creed is nominally Muhammadan, beginning with the fierce fanaticism of Palosa—the "Kila Mujahidin," a colony of "warriors of the faith," supported entirely by contributions from their sympathizers in Hindustân, who, until they were dispersed by the recent Black Mountain expedition, devoted their time to drill, giving the words of command in Arabic, firing salutes with cannon made of leather, and blustering about the destruction of the infidel power of the British,—but getting gradually diluted, till, among isolated spots in Kohistân, are found Muhammadans who shave their heads, worship rude sculptures of the horse, and are ignorant of a single word of the Korân.

In the comparatively small but fertile valleys of Tikari, Nandihar, and Deshi, the bulk of the people are Swâtis, Muhammadans by creed, classing themselves as Pathân, ethnologically more nearly connected with the people in the adjoining glens. The same is the case in Allâi, a larger and still finer valley, drained by one stream to the Indus, though about a fourth of this is possessed by Sayud or other religious fraternities. All are plentifully irrigated, and grow considerable quantities of rice and Indian corn. The eastern end of Allâi is described as possessing a succession of grass and forest-covered mountain slopes, dotted with fields of wheat and barley, and prosperous villages. The whole valley is perhaps capable of furnishing 7,000 fighting men, and the three former are credited with about 8,000, recognizing as leaders the Khâns of Trand and Batgram. On the opposite side of the river are the

Ghorband and Kânra Valleys, the latter being almost entirely a
Sayud colony, A range rising 15,000 feet separates Allâi from
Kohistân, "the land of mountains," which interposes a thousand
square miles of snowy peaks and rocky wastes between Khâgân, or
the upper part of Hazâra, and the Indus; and extends again on
the west of that river right away to Dir and Chitral. Among
Afghâns the name is often used to describe the whole country
westward to Kâbul, or districts inhabited by other races they have
only partly displaced; just as Yaghestân, "the rebellious or
independent country," is the general term for all the little hill
republics, who acknowledge no suzerain or at any rate pay no
attention to him. The main features of the Cis-Indus Kohistân
are two valleys running east and west from Hazâra to the Indus,
the Nila Naddi, and the Chicharga, separated from each other by
a range that, by way of variety, has an elevation of nearly 17,000
feet. The two streams fall into the Indus near Jalkot and Palas
respectively, and incidentally, it may be noted, a good road would
be possible down either to the Indus from Hazâra by opening out
one of the passes from Khâgân, or from Bhogarmang. At present
the country is destitute of roads as we understand roads, and in
winter the access is only by river, crossing and recrossing at
intervals. Of trade there is some in timber but little of anything
else, though Puttun on the Indus is reputed a large and flourishing
place, with much fertile land, a population almost redundant, and
may perhaps claim to be the capital of Kohistân, if such a collection
of mountains can be said to possess a capital.

By the people themselves the country is often called Shinkari,
"the land of the Shins," Muhammadans, but not Pathâns—
probably the remains of a number of cognate tribes of Indian
origin, forced by Moslem invaders to become Muhammadans.
They are reported powerful, well built, clean-limbed, dark-com-
plexioned, quick-eyed, sharp-featured people, brave but quiet,
given to hospitality, nowhere particularly zealous for the faith of

Islâm, and in many valleys retaining many Hindu customs, and still preferring their own particular idols. Some of the dialects, of which Biddulph, in an account full of interest, describes several, are founded on Sanskrit, with a pretty general admixture of Pushtu They, along with tribes to the north and north-west, have, by certain authorities, been dragged in to help to build up the theory of the Dards and Dardistân; a title which, so far as they are concerned, is altogether misleading. There are a few people on the Indus, near Koli and Palus locally called Dards, but they are only an insignificant tribe among a great variety of distinct races, speaking different dialects, frequently different languages, and called by the most diverse names. And unless the word Dard is to stand for any people of probable Aryan extraction, it is quite inapplicable. In language, dress, habit, and probably race, these Indus Valley communities have most in common with the peoples of Gilgit, of Astor in Kashmir, or of Ladâk, as described by Cunningham.

Chilâs, another thousand square miles of still more mountainous country, on its southern side for some little distance conterminous with Hazâra, comes in between Kohistân, the Indus, and Kashmir. The Kashmir Maharajah is, in a sort of way acknowledged as suzerain by certain of the little communities, some of whom pay him a small annual tribute of goats or of gold dust, and one sends three hostages, or residents, changed every year, to Kashmir. The officials of that State do not, however, interfere, or even visit Chilâs, and any attempt of the Maharajah to exercise his authority would probably be resisted. Many are so difficult of access either from the river, Kashmir, Gilgit or Yassin, that a very little resistance would suffice to keep off a considerable force, and a former Sikh expedition sent from Kashmir against the Chilâs valley met with a disastrous defeat. The highest peaks in this literally " land of the mountain" rise in the case of Nanga Parbat, " the naked mountain," to over 16,700 feet. A magnificent peak, but a mere hill compared to Gilgit opposite, which within a small area boasts of twenty peaks from 20,000 to 24,000, and eight from 24,000 to 27,000 feet high. The balance of Chilâs however is to a great extent snow and rock, over 11,000 feet, succeeded by pine forests, down to 5,000 feet, and on the slopes below, in some half-dozen principal valleys, a crop of grass and wild vegetables—rhubarb, carrots, onions, &c.—that afford grazing for considerable herds of cattle, with occasional fields towards the Indus, more especially in the valleys round the village of Chilâs; but the general aspect or the country is like the old Sanskrit description of Parbat—bare and poorly wooded. Practically it is rainless, a single fall in the year being a good average, though there is a fair amount of irrigation from the mountain streams.

The people are more recent converts to Islâm than the Kohistânis; some of their glens seem rather a favourite resort of Mullahs from Swât, and are consequently zealous and bigoted much beyond any of their neighbours. Others again have religious systems of their own, and in one case the tutelary deity is a rudely sculptured horse named the Taibans horse. They, or many of them, are Sunis, and any Shiahs who fell into their hands would be put to death without the alternative of slavery. They are not so absolutely cut off from communications as we are accustomed to think. There are roads from the upper Swât into the extensive Kandia valley; from Yassin to the Sazin and Tangir Valleys, both fertile and extensive, extending down to the Indus; and the road from Khâgân in Hazâra, by the Babusar Pass, is put at a seven days' journey to the Indus, and from the Kishen-Ganga Valley in Kashmir, by the Shoto Pass, as a five days' journey. The road, moreover, which under the present Resident, the Kashmir state has taken in hand, from the north of the Wular Lake near Srinagar, by the Rajdiangân Pass into the Skardo route, and from that again by the Kanuri Pass into the Astor Valley, and by Bunji on the Indus to Gilgit, some 170 miles, which is to be

made a good military road, will do a good deal to open out better
communications. At present the roads are only practicable for
footmen, and are closed in winter, while it is doubtful if Chilás
can be reached by way of the Indus at all; and it is, therefore,
not astonishing to find that this difficulty of access has contributed
to keep the little communities almost as isolated as so many
different nations. The distinctive character of this bit of Yaghestân is, in fact, the number of what are practically independent
States, republics in miniature. Mr. Drew describes one called
Thalich, which is probably well in the running, as the very
smallest existing, consisting of only eleven houses. The system
of government in these Liliputian commonwealths is, nevertheless,
advanced enough to suit the most gifted faddist. Each village,
according to Biddulph, elects its own representative or "Jushteros,"
according as the candidates are deemed brave, eloquent, and
liberal, and enjoys Home Rule, irrespective of its neighbours.
It has its own parliament, called "Sigas," which is quite
public, all who please joining in the discussion, the "Jushteros" encouraging outsiders to give their advice, which,
having heard, they seldom take. There is, moreover, already a
system of Federation, a single Jushtero being deputed from each
village parliament to the federal Sigas, which is also open to the
public. The public, having relieved its mind, a loud whistle is
given, after which only "Jushteros" are allowed to talk or to vote.
The Sigas does not deal with criminal offences; these are usually
left to the church, tempered by ancient custom. Murder is rare,
but is regarded as a personal matter for the nearest relative to
settle, though blood feuds are not permitted to stand over long.
Slavery is a recognized institution in most of the republics. A
still more singular custom exists in many valleys, and it is said to
be among the most ancient of the institutions. The sexes are
kept strictly apart all summer, from May till September. In the
spring, the young man has to take his flocks to the mountain, and

must wait till winter before he can permit "his fancy to lightly turn to thoughts of love." The old women are specially charged with the responsibility of seeing the rule observed, and any attempt to evade it is punished by fine.

Neither Kohistân nor Chilâs has ever given trouble to us as neighbours, nor are they likely to do so, unless dangerous fanatical colonies take root, or find shelter among them. The Allâiwals and sometimes Hazâra Gujars, have had occasional disputes with the Kohistânis, arising out of trespass into the Chor glen, a bit of good pasture in the south-east corner of Kohistân that lies temptingly near; and more recently with the Khaka Khel wood merchants for timber sent down the river; but the Kohistân *jirgah* has shown a willingness to settle all such matters with our officers. Both trade with us, mainly the produce of their flocks and herds, a little gold dust, and timber cut and floated down to Attock.

Any estimate of the fighting strength of communities like these would be obviously of the most uncertain kind and of small value. It is possible they might combine against a common foe, but to us any such combination could hardly be formidable, and their weapons are of the most primitive description. Their real strength is in their natural position, which we are not likely to want to interfere with. Their weakness, the fact that to a great extent they are a decadent race, liable to be either driven out or absorbed by more vigorous races like the Pathân, whose settlements will increase, and whose greater energy will ensure his gaining ground; while the little republics, with their "Jushteros" and village parliaments, are doomed to go downhill.

But from here again,—from Hazâra and the Indus, the Kohistân, or "land of mountains" which forms the western frontier of Kashmir, to the Kohistân, north of Kâbul, lies a series of lofty peaks and secluded valleys, occupied by communities, whose future is every year becoming of greater importance to India and its frontier defence. To the north of Chilâs, and the valleys already referred to

of Buneyr, Swât, Dir, Bajâwar, and Kunâr, are a series of still less
familiar states—Nager, Hunza, Gilgit, Yasin, Chitral, and others.
And, further west, the unexplored and almost unknown country
of Kafiristân. No mere congeries of robber tribes, but settled
and extensive agricultural communities, with rulers who in many
cases boast a long unbroken descent. Peoples of the most varying
types. Traces of Hindu, Mongol, and Tartar alternating with
Pathân, Aryan, and conjectural Greek ; or, according to a recent
Russian authority on the look out for natural subjects for the
Czar, "incontestably Slav." Of creeds, that include the worship
of rock-cut figures of Buddha, customs of the most orthodox
Brahmins, with others like the Shins, that hold everything
connected with the cow as the most hopelessly unclean—secluded
valleys where still lingers the influence of Zoroaster and the fire
altars, or again vary between the primitive Aryan to the worship
of the Lingum, the tree, or incantation pure and simple ; over
all of which an easy-going Muhammadanism seems gradually
spreading itself, which the Pirs and the fervid Mulahs from Swât
and Buneyr are doing their best to extend. Tribes and castes differing in almost every characteristic from anything, not only on
our more immediate Border, but from India generally ; speaking
languages and dialects often not understood out of their particular
valley, of which Biddulph gives glossaries of ten, and which require
a skilled philologist to classify ; societies given to drinking wine
and making merry, who lay down cellars of clarified butter, and
do not consider it is ripe till it has acquired the deep red of a
century's keeping ; with whom dancing is for both sexes the
national amusement and polo the national game ; who still practise
the ordeal of fire, and are so free from ordinary jealousy that custom
requires a man given to hospitality to place his wife at his guest's
disposal. Countries and peoples of the greatest possible
ethnological as well as political interest, of whom fragments
have been sketched in accounts by Messrs. Shaw, Drew, Leitner

and Biddulph, but which remain to a great extent to be still described.

Northward of the whole again, the Hindu Kush forms the great watershed between the Indus and the Oxus, the passes over which are probably sufficiently difficult to deter any large army venturing there. But the more we learn about them the easier it appears to be for a small force to effect a passage in many places, and, having crossed, to rendezvous in some central valley, such as Chitrâl, the seat of the ruler of Kashkâr, as it is sometimes called, which is sufficiently large and fertile, and thence work southwards towards Gilgit or Jelâlâbâd. The mischief would be almost equally great if the intruders stayed there, and extended their influence to Kâbul or Kashmir or over the fanatical tribesmen along our Pathân border, a contingency it is obviously necessary to take measures to prevent.

For the same reason it is undesirable these countries should fall in any way under the control of Afghânistân. A dozen independent and rival states between Kashmir and Kâbul is at any rate more or less of a safeguard against treachery in either. Amir Abdur Rahman is known of late years to have been casting a covetous eye in this direction. Their internal quarrels, which in Kâfiristân are unceasing, not merely with their Muhammadan neighbours, but among various sections of the people, he has readily seized upon as an excuse for interference, and there is no doubt this has been supplemented by still more active intrigues. His expedition against Kâfiristân and Bajaur was stopped not so much by the sturdy resistance of the Bajauris, as by the Shinwari rebellion nearer home, and his promises to return at a more convenient season have caused a certain amount of uneasiness, for the Amir's convenient season is oft-times a bitter one.

It would be well therefore in the first place to let it be clearly understood that these communities are to be considered entirely outside the limit of Afghân influence; and in the next to take more active measures to ensure that British influence shall be established instead. To some extent this has been begun already by the Lockhart mission to Chitrâl, and by the establishment of a resident in Gilgit. It will be assisted by the opening of the Kashmir Gilgit road, and would be materially increased by the construction of the railway to Dhaka which would enable regiments to move at a short notice in Jelâlâbâd. The states are as a rule ready to welcome English officers, Kâfiristân more especially so—a country whose tendencies and sympathy have more in common with the Aryan stock than any single community along our entire north-western border.

If the Yaghestân states can retain their independence, well and good, if not British influence must be paramount, and the sooner direct measures are taken to accomplish this the better.

Pathân Fiddle (*rabâl*) and Knife (*chhura*).

CHAPTER XL.

THE HAZÂRA VALLEY.

WHAT Shakespeare makes Bolingbroke say of English feasts, would apply to any account of the Border that should finish with Hazâra, "the daintiest last, to make the end most sweet." And along the whole frontier, from Karâchi to Kashmir, there is nothing that, for the grandeur of its mountains, its plentiful streams, picturesque scenery, and charming variety, can touch the Hazâra Valley; and probably few can boast a more interesting diversity of people, more thriving villages, or where prosperity more obviously marks the security of British rule. A long tongue of territory, of thoroughly alpine character, with a ring fence of lofty mountains that separate it from the rich valleys of Kashmir, and the vast waste of rocky and snowy peaks that go to make up Kohistân; between the impetuous Jhelum with its feeders, and the more solemn and severe Indus. To the north are the distant snow-clad ranges of Chilâs, with the mighty Nanga Parbat as a central figure. To the east the high rounded Khâgân peaks, affording excellent grazing almost to their tops, and whose sides, where not clothed with grass, are covered with forests. A vista of mountains, that from the perpetual snow of "Moses's seat," run south by a series of lovely hills and charming little stations, known as the Gullies, to Murree. Westward: beautiful wooded peaks, glens, and ranges, hardly less lofty, and not less attractive, separate it from the independent Swâti valleys that drain into the Indus, while the Black Mountain rises beyond the luxuriant glades of Agror. Cultivation covers every bit of level ground, from the prolific fields of Harripur and Pakhli, to the narrow strips industriously terraced out of the hill sides in the most distant glens; and everywhere, that cultivation is plentifully irrigated. Water, the one thing the Border so much wants, and the absence of which deprives so much of our mountain fringe of half its beauty, is here in every form. The deep blue silent lakes of Khâgân, the raging forces of the Indus and the Jhelum, the almost fiercer torrents of the narrow little Kunhâr, the minor tributary streams that run in all directions, and channels from which carry the water to every field, turn all the mills to grind the corn, husk the rice, or clean the cotton, and are what the Swâtis call the "female slaves" of the cultivator.

A wealth of wood and water, luxuriant grass and innumerable flowers, specked with thriving villages and prosperous homesteads: witness that, in Hazâra at any rate, the Empire is peace; while in the centre of the valley the practical embodiment of that Empire is marked by the station and cantonment of Abbottabâd. The most favoured of the Border stations, Abbottabâd seems to combine the views and the climate of the hills, with the freedom of the plains. Where English green lanes run through gardens filled with a profusion of tropical and temperate fruits and vegetables; where a wealth of superb English roses and English shrubs, flourish side by side with the most beautiful varieties of the cedar and the pine, the chestnut and the chenar. And where it may also be said—not in order to round off a sentence in an idyllic fashion, but as matter of history—English civilization and English administration have brought to a number of by no means the best types of Border races, a freedom from strife, and an amount of prosperity they could never have developed any other way. The district was taken over by the British, as a too turbulent bit of country for its Sikh Governor's taste, in exchange for a strip of territory on the southern frontier of Jammu, in 1847, and in 1848, almost for the first time in its history, was reported as " perfectly tranquil."   The story of its prosperity and development since then, is written at length in the official records of the district, the Settlement Report of Major Wace, and the statistics of the Gazetteer ; but still more obviously, over the whole face of the country itself.   Twenty years of British rule saw the population increased fifty per cent., doubled the area of cultivation, more than doubled the value of the cattle and agricultural produce.   Thirty years practically doubled the revenue, even with light assessments ; increased the imports six-fold ; and raised to important branches of trade, many commodities that in former times had no value at all.   The day labourer, who of yore received his food or one anna a day, now earns not less than two in the villages, and four in the towns.   The weaver who wove seven sheets for a rupee, and a fancy turban for fourteen annas, now gets a rupee for four sheets, and two rupees for the turban ; and the printer who dyes it, eight annas instead of four.   According to the statistical story, the labourer all round gets much more in the way of hire ; he eats, drinks, and is merry, though even he has to pay something more for it.   The whole stands as a striking example of what difference a good and strong Government has made, and might make elsewhere, for any bit of the Border.

Nor can it be said that the result is due to the superiority of the people ; rather it is in spite of what in many respects are points in their disfavour, for, compared to other parts of the Border, the contrast in regard to them is markedly unfavourable.   Notwithstanding their former character for turbulence and rebellion, they have neither the energy nor manly qualities of the Pathán or the Biloch, and though they are litigious enough, " the flinty and steel couch of war," is by no means the average Hazára's idea of repose, nor does he yearn for honour and glory.   He is quite willing to leave that to the Afridi or Yusafzai. His valley seems to have been the corner to which the less warlike races were gradually driven, and he is the modern representative of those races. Originally the valley was occupied by a mixed people of Indian or Aryan origin. When the inferior Pathân Dilazâks got pushed out of the Peshawur Valley, in the fifteenth and sixteenth centuries, they fled across the Indus to Hazâra. The Tanâolis followed suit in the seventeenth. Then the Jaduns, from the slopes of Mahâban, came and took possession of a strip for themselves. The Karlâgh Turks, who came with Timur, if not with Chengiz Khan, annexed a bit of the Pakhl plain. The Sayuds under Jalâl Bâba did the same in Khâgân, the Tarins lower down, and finally the Yusafzais crossed the Indus, pushed everybody back a bit, and took up the Black Mountain. When the variety that went to make up the original stock is considered, it must be admitted the population is likely to be a little mixed. Broadly, the present distribution is somewhat as follows North of Manserah the Swâtis hold pretty well the whole, about one-third of the district; descendants from tribes of Indian origin, like Gujars, Ghakkars, Dunds, and Karâls, with the admixture iust referred to, the south and south-east; Jaduns in the Dor Valley in the centre; Tanâolis west in the semi-independent appanage of Amb; Swâtis and Gujars again in Agror and up to the Yusafzai of the Black Mountain, with Sayud families scattered through the whole.

The unsatisfactory nature of the Swâti has already been commented on. His deceit is a proverb. The story of his agricultural partnership with the devil, a legend, with many counterparts in many countries. How under the first contract, when the Swâti was to have all that grew above, and the devil all that grew below, the ground, he sowed Indian corn ; and when at harvest time his partner complained of his share, the Swâti, protesting his desire to play fair, agreed to reverse the bargain. This arranged, the next season he sowed carrots, and got the better of his Satanic majesty again, who forthwith agreed to dissolve partnership. The Tanâoli is reported to have once been warlike, but it cannot be said of him now; in respect of bad faith and other ill doings, he is on a level with the Swâti. The saying that "a Tanâoli's word is naught" sums up the opinion held about him. The Jadun, whatever his origin, has clearly deteriorated since he crossed the Indus, and is now far inferior to his Mahâban relative. The Dunds and the Kurâls—both Hindu perverts to Islam—are credited with being faithless, crafty, and cowardly. Treachery among themselves discovered their plot to attack Murree in 1857, and they are now suspected of a taint of Wahâbism. Far the best of the bunch are the Gujars and Gakkhars. Industrious cultivators, skilful husbandmen, with good physique, fair to middling as soldiers, and peaceful, though not very courageous, citizens, although but for our rule they would probably barely hold their own.

In creed all are essentially Mussalmans—Hindus of all sorts, muster little more than five per cent.—but none are fanatical Muhammadans. The average physique is decidedly below the average of the Peshawur Valley, not to speak of the finer specimens of the Pathân highlanders. The Dunds and Kurâls are small; the Jadus and Tanâolis not very robust; the Swâtis of Agror are feeble and enervated, though very fine men are found among the Swâtis of Khagân; and lots of the inhabitants of the valley have pleasing, if not almost, classic features. The women are regarded much in the same light as among Pathâns generally; so much valuable property, but as drudges rather than wives, especially among the Swâtis though both they and the Utmânzai women have their share of good looks, and many of the Gujar race are decidedly pretty. The local proverb describes them as "the Swâti's toil, the Jadun's mill, the Dilazâk's whore, the Turk's trance, and the Turin's Home Rule"; and is curious as a summary of the tribal habits. The Swâti's wife is indicated as a field drudge; the Jadun's lady goes too often to the mill, and stays all night while the grain is grinding, with fatal results to her virtue; the Dilazâks brought with them many ladies of too easy virtue; the tendency of the Turk is to laziness and indulgence; and the Turin is greatly under petticoat influence.

Any outline of the social habits and tribal customs of so

Dress of the Banâwi Fakirs, Hazâra.

diversely constituted a community would occupy an altogether disproportionate amount of space. They agree in the one peculiarity of being fairly submissive subjects. Anything like open violence is rare; the bullet and knife of the assassin are more generally replaced by the weapons of fraud or intrigue; and the bulk of the people seem to have a greater inclination towards patient toil, than for letting their neighbours' blood. All the same, that most beautiful of mountain glens—the Agror Valley, is a perfect hot-bed of intrigue, and always contains the elements of possible trouble. The Khán was removed under surveillance to Lahore in 1868, but subsequently restored to his authority, and for a time all went well. There is, however, unfortunately reason to suppose that the recent Agror intrigues with the Black Mountain tribes have been at the bottom of many of our troubles in that direction; and it is a matter always requiring to be carefully guarded against.

INDEX.

INDEX.

U.

U'blân Pass, Kohât district, 165 ; surprise of, 167
U'rmân Pass from the Gumal, 94
U'smân Khels, original division of Pathâns, 217
U'steranas, Pathân tribe, 90
U'tmân Khel Pathâns, on the Swât River, 267 ; the sons of U'tmân Bâba, 278

V.

Vahoa Pass, Dera Ismail district, 77
Vidore Pass, Dera Ghâzi district, 49

W.

Wahâbis, 289
Warden of the Marches, instituted by Akbar, 155
Waziri Pathâns, main divisions of, 105
    Darwesh Khels, 100
        Utmanzais—Ahmadzais
    Mahsuds, 107
        Bahlolzais — Alizais — Shaman Khels
        Kâbul Khels, 106
        Lalais, 106
Waziris, description of, 108 ; courtship, 238 ; criminal code of, 115 ; inveterate robbers, 105 ; marriage ceremonies of, 238 ; peculiar customs of, 109

Waziristân, country of, 103
Wives, Pathân, 237 ; Waziri, 235 ; price of, 240
Women, Afridi, 187 ; buxom, of Swât, 270 ; frequent elopement of, 243 ; life of trans-Border, 242 ; in Hazâra, 334 ; Shirâni, 237 ; trade in, 242, 247

Y.

Yaghestân, the independent country, 320
Yâhiya, a Khattak Khân, 156
Yasin, State of, 327
Yusafzai, character of main valleys, 266 country rich in ancient remains, 267 ; retaliatory justice in, 112
Yusafzais, children of Joseph, grandsons of Khakhai, 258 ; gradual advance of, 218 ; extend to Swât, 218 ; distribution of tribes, 259 ; numbers of, 264 ; relations to foreigners, 265 ; matrimonial negotiations in, 239 ; Bellew, best authority on, 266

Z.

Zaimukht Pathâns, 161
Zamâri Pathâns, 91
Zangi Pass, Dera Ghâzi district, 48
Zawaghar Range, 165
Zhob Valley, 92

Yusafzai Pathâns, chief divisions of—

Yusaf	Mandanr, stepson, clans of, 259, 260	U'smân	Kamalzai, 259, 260
			Amazai, 259 ... Rustam / Chargholai
		Utmân	Alazai, 259
			Kamazai, 259
			Akazai, 259
			Saddazai—(Khudukhels, 259)
		Razai, 260	
		Uriah (Bâdi) the Badikhels, 261	
		Isazai, 261	Hassanzai, 261, 312 (Khân Khels)
			Akazai, 261, 312
			Madakhels
		Musa ... Hiaszai, 262	Salarzai / Gadaizai / Ashazai / Nasozai } Buneyrwals
			Makhozai
		Mali, 262	Daulatzai / Nurazai / Chagarzai, 312 } ..... Buneyrwals
		Akozai, 263	Khwazozai, 268 (Malizai) / Baizai, 268 / Ranizai, 268

www.ingramcontent.com/pod-product-compliance
Lightning Source LLC
Chambersburg PA
CBHW021730110726
47902CB00005B/1412